The Pull

The Demons Within, Volume 1

Len M. Ruth

Published by Ruthless Press, 2023.

THE PULL

First edition: May 4, 2022.

Second edition: August 15, 2023.

Copyright © 2023 Len M. Ruth

Paperback

ISBN: 979-8-9876574-6-1

Written by Len M. Ruth.

Edited by Em Davis

Cover by Ambient Studios, www.ambientpixeldesign.com[1]

Urn drawing by Jill Kovalchik, @chapinstreetstudios[2]

Seal of Solomon by Fuzzypeg[3]

---

1.   http://www.ambientpixeldesign.com/

2.   https://chapinstreetstudios.com/

3.   https://commons.wikimedia.org/wiki/
     File:Goetia_seal_of_solomon.svg?uselang=en#Licensing

Also by Len M. Ruth

Smiling Flu
Rachael's Apocalypse Diary
Rachael's Apocalypse Diary Vol. 2
The Unrecovered

The Demons Within
The Pull

Watch for more at https://lenmruth.com/.

For Em

Don't miss out!

Be the first to read new releases and take advantage of exclusive book giveaways. Sign up for Len M. Ruth's monthly Free Book Newsletter at lenmruth.com [4] There's no charge and no obligation.

---

4. https://lenmruth.com/

Warning!

IN ORDER TO CONTAIN the demon in this book, the Seal of Solomon adorns both front and back cover. This is no decoration, but a covenant and signal given to Solomon by God to contain evil. Ignore this caution at your peril. The demon is cunning, as you will see.

Affix no stickers or other adornments that obscure the seal on front or back cover. Obscuring the seal is like leaving the door to hell open, and the porch light off. You will not know the demon is loose until the rivers run with blood.

Sunday, September 3, 2023
Len M. Ruth

Chapter 1

Casey

Trull, Connecticut 2020CE

Casey's trembling hands shoved the too-long cuff of his borrowed shirt up the matching gray sport coat's sleeve. The outfit was so far from his normal jeans and T-shirt that he felt like an emaciated monkey waiting for the organ grinder to emerge from the three-story house, turn the crank, and get him to dance. While he waited, he shook his shoulders, rolled his head, and jogged in place, trying and failing to relieve the tension and keep warm.

"You can do this, Casey. You can totally do this. You just turn on the charm, be your old self, and appeal to her sense of...." What?

The door opened. Allison stepped out in her peach scrubs, turned without seeing him, and put her key in the lock. Her long angular body made only the vaguest impression through the baggy uniform, but Casey knew what the fabric hid, and it bolstered his resolve.

"Allison, hey!" he trotted toward her in a way that he hoped would come off as jaunty and confident but suspected looked pathetic.

"Casey...." She pulled her key from the deadbolt and stood on the stoop, hand on her hip. Three steps above, she towered over him.

He put his hands in his pockets, trying to look casual. Buck up, buddy. You can do this. "Hey, Allison...."

"You said that. What do you want? I've got to get to work."

"Well, I just happened to be passing by—"

"On your way, where? There's nothing but houses all the way up the hill. The only reason you'd be in this neighborhood is to see me. So my guess is that you've been standing out here since two when I usually leave." She checked her watch. "So a good twenty minutes. You can't do that, Casey—"

"Allison, please. I've changed. I've got my shit together—"

"Where? On Kelly's couch?"

"Well, I—"

"You got a job?"

"The thing about that is—"

"I loved you. But I'm not going to watch as you destroy yourself in slow motion."

"I'm off the sauce, stone-cold sober." It was true, in a way. But he'd been careful not to specify how long.

"Let me see your hands."

"Allison..."

"Hands."

Casey sighed and drew his hands from his pockets, trying to hold them steady with limited success.

"Uh, huh. Off the sauce? Since when? Breakfast? Look at you. You're wearing your brother's clothes, but they're hanging off of you."

"We're diff—"

"He's your *identical* twin, which means either Kelly put on fifty pounds since I saw him at the market last weekend, or you're malnourished. Your skin is sallow, bordering on yellow, and you've got the DTs. I'd say you've got maybe a year unless you *actually* get it together. Otherwise, when you check in to the hospital for liver failure, you've got as much chance of getting on the transplant list as you do of getting back on my dance card."

"Dance card? What are we, in a Joan Crawford movie or something?"

"Well, it sure as shit isn't the John Hughes movie you think it is. Go back to Kelly's, eat a sandwich, and check yourself into rehab."

"Allison..."

"No." She closed her eyes for a moment and pushed the air in front of her. "No. Don't fucking come at me with that cutesy tone, and the puppy-dog eyes, and the dimples... goddamn it." She sobbed. "Just go."

The sob meant it was working. God rest you and thank you for the dimples, mom. "Allison, wait—"

"No," she said again, this time with steel in her voice. "Even if you got a job, and a house, and a car, and a fucking clue, it would still be over. You hurt me too many times for me to even *think* about getting back on the merry-go-round with you. Now get out of here. I mean it."

"I love you...." The words hung in the air for a moment before they flamed out and crashed to the ground like the Hindenburg.

"If you ever come back here again like this, I'm calling the cops and filing a restraining order." She stared down at him with a frozen-hard winter scowl.

"Okay," he said, turned, and walked back down the hill.

Just around the corner on Bridge Street, Casey stopped into the package store and, using the fiver he'd found in the coat, bought a bottle of Wild Irish Rose and a nip of rotgut whiskey.

The clerk never met Casey's eye but commented on his hands, saying, "Wait till you get off the property."

Casey did. But as soon as he hit the sidewalk, the nip went down his throat, and the empty went into the gutter. The wine cap followed close behind. He wouldn't need that. The baggy sport coat offered scant protection from the icy autumn wind. Casey pulled it tight around him and held it there, the buttons useless because of his diminished size. He staggered down the street, clutching the edge of his jacket like a deranged Napoleon, periodically upending the bottle into his mouth.

As he crossed under the rusted green beams of the aptly named Bridge Street Bridge, the wind redoubled its efforts to get into his bones, whipping down the Nipwìmâw River. He should have known this would never work. It wasn't his fault. He didn't have the money to go to detox. He didn't have the money to buy clothes that fit, or a car. And because the hospital fired him for drinking on the job, he couldn't get another one. No one wants a boozy patient advocate. Doesn't exactly exude trust.

He only drank vodka at work because it blended with the astringent smell of the hospital. Apparently not well enough. But he was never drunk. Just, you know, a sip every now and then to take the edge off. It was a bullshit termination. He should get a lawyer, back to the money thing. He chugged the rest of the bottle and tossed it into the river.

As he watched the bottle somersault toward the black water, he saw his parents' car, an old black Chrysler, tumbling into the black ice-choked water. Taking a step back, Casey inspected the railing. Fifteen years later, his eyes could still detect the repairs where old railing met new. Strange that he hadn't thought about it in so long. Whenever Casey crossed this spot, his eyes always landed on the old mill. Its broken, arch-topped windows stared at him from the far bank. He could feel the building pulling at him, bricks and mortar calling him to give up, come in, and settle into darkness. He would, too, but he was out of booze, and that situation couldn't stand. Casey wanted enough alcohol so that *he* couldn't stand. He couldn't go back to Kelly's. Kelly threw him out. Maybe Martha...

The duck boots his brother gave him squelched through the slush that intermittently clogged the bridge's gum-spotted sidewalk. He turned right at the end of the bridge, away from the mill, but even at his back, Casey felt the Boiler House's insistent tug.

Martha's cart was in its accustomed spot, half a block up from Marv's Diner, parked between two dumpsters. He tapped on the cardboard 'wall' propped behind it.

"Over here, Casey," Martha called from up the alley. She waved from Marv's stoop. "Come on."

Casey hurried toward her.

"Look who it is, Marv," Martha gestured with a sweep of her arm, the loose sleeve of her ubiquitous, filthy pink bathrobe wagged in the wind. The legion of lines on her face formed a sunken toothless smile. "Don't you look dashing? Why if I was twenty years younger—"

"Twenty?" Casey asked.

"Don't be fresh." Her smile disappeared. She sipped from a foam cup, heedless of the imperfect seal against her lips or the dribbles it left on the patch of sweatshirt not covered by the robe. As she tipped the cup back, a few drops landed on the spot where her stained outer layer of slacks met her mismatched tennis shoes.

Marv's mountainous girth stood in the doorway. Soft brown eyes gazed out above a fat, stubbled face. "Casey?"

"Hi, Marv. I was wondering if you had anything to spare? Some day-olds, maybe?" Casey looked down. He couldn't look Marv in the eye while he begged. The shame welled up inside him like a living thing, breathing through his mouth, seeing through his eyes.

"Yeah, of course, hang on. You want a coffee too?"

Casey hadn't asked for the coffee because he was almost sure Marv would offer. "Yes, please."

"I'll be right back." The door closed.

"I knew you'd be back," Martha said it without judgment or a trace of 'I-told-you-so,' in her voice. "I kept your things. From the looks of you, you'll need them."

He gazed at the slice of gray sky between the buildings. Weather coming in. The wind stirred the trash into a frenzy and brought with it the smell of rancid grease. He shivered. "Thank you, Martha."

"Here," Marv said, drawing back the door. He handed Casey a Styrofoam cup of steaming liquid and pressed a folded brown paper bag into his hand.

"Do you want me to call the shelter for you? See if there's a bed?" Marv asked.

"No, thanks." He didn't want to be around people.

"All right, but get indoors; there's a Nor'easter comin'."

"I will."

Casey turned away. The door banged shut, and the deadbolt clicked into place.

"Come on. I'll take you to your things." Martha turned and started tottering back toward Bridge Street.

"Where'd you hide my stuff?"

"Where no one would take it." She offered no further explanation.

A pit formed in Casey's stomach. There was only one place he could think of that you could hide a shopping cart full of stuff safely. Someplace where no one went. That abandoned building reeled in a kite string attached to something inside him, something he couldn't name. That old mill wasn't a piece of architecture, but a living thing he orbited. He, Kelly, Allison, and Martha all lived, worked, and, well, panhandled, within a mile of the place, and always had.

They walked in silence, the weight of the air growing heavier in their lungs as they approached. The mill sat at an angle to the building in front of it, the old box factory. The two buildings formed a V-shaped courtyard, in the center of which stood the smokestack, towering into the gray sky.

Martha advanced into the gathering dusk and waved with a flourish at his shopping cart parked behind the smokestack. "Just like you left it."

"God bless you, Martha."

"Every day, I wake up. At my age, that's a pretty big blessing."

"How old are you, anyway?"

"Casey! I'm surprised at you. A gentleman doesn't ask. Old enough to be your mother, anyway. How old are you? Huh?"

"Thirty."

"Pup." She grinned.

Casey pushed the cart out of the dimness behind the smokestack and out into the twilight at the widest part of the V between the buildings. Inside the cart, black garbage bags kept the weather off of his things and, near the top, the coat Father Murray gave him. He pulled it out and slipped his arms through the sleeves.

"Well, I'm headed down't the shelter. Come with me, Casey."

"I want to be alone."

"Boy, get inside. Come with me. When my son picks me up in the morning, we'll go out for breakfast."

This is where Casey knew Martha, and reality parted ways. As far as anyone knew, there was no son. But each day, Martha insisted he was coming for her tomorrow.

"Tell you what, Martha. If he comes, I'll meet you for breakfast at Marv's."

"Don't patronize me, Casey. How will you know when we'll be there?"

"I—"

"Come to the shelter. Marv said it's going to be a nasty night out here."

"I'll meet you there later," Casey said, hoping she wouldn't realize there wouldn't be any beds left later.

"Make sure you do, Casey. Make sure you do. I'll worry."

"Well, don't."

"You're an ornery drunk." Martha shook her head.

"Good night. Thanks for keeping my stuff safe."

"You're welcome." And with that, she tottered off the way she'd come.

Casey dug into the crinkling plastic bags, taking a quick inventory and hoping against hope that he remembered right and that Martha hadn't gone through his things. Blankets, a few clothes, a bag of snipes, and... Eureka! An almost full bottle of Wild Irish Rose!

The nice thing about this new coat Father Murphy gave him was that the pockets fit a bottle of wine perfectly. As he stuffed the bottle in, Casey wondered if that was in the advertising. "Check out our latest line of coats for the discerning wino. With a herringbone pattern that hides the filth from sleeping under bridge abutments and hip pockets that hold a bottle of fortified wine without the neck sticking out, these coats are what all the well-dressed vagrants will wear this fall...." He reached out to get something else from the cart, but his hand had other ideas and came to rest once again on the wine. Casey sighed. He wrapped his hand around the bottle's glass neck as if he could choke off the thought—He couldn't, and instead unscrewed the cap, wound up to toss it, but decided he'd need to cap the bottle to get into the mill. Tipping the bottle up, he let the bitter liquid pour down his throat, bypassing his taste buds altogether. The wine imparted its color to the darkening sky as Casey looked through the upended bottle, turning it the color of blood. He tipped the bottle down and leaned heavily on the shopping cart, gasping for breath after the long pull. Then he capped the bottle and put it back in his pocket.

At last, with a bag of day-old donuts and another of snipes, clutched in one fist, Casey pried the rotten, green-painted plywood away from the window to the Boiler House. It cracked and came away from the weathered brick easily, allowing him to squeeze his upper body in between.

Inside, the mill was dark and quiet. Although the two-story arched windows on the river-facing side of the mill weren't covered, the light from the stormy twilight sky didn't filter in. The sound of the wind moaning through the empty sockets didn't quite mask the muffled choking and fluttering of pigeons in the rafters. While he waited for his eyes to adjust to the darkness, a chill stole over him. It wrapped its icy fingers around him and squeezed. He shivered. Maybe he'd try the shelter after all. He didn't relish the idea of sleeping on a carpet of shit from a thousand pigeons.

He couldn't explain why he wanted to shelter there tonight, *had* to shelter there tonight, at least not in a rational way.

The Pull

This wasn't the first time he'd felt it. Throughout his life, he'd look over at the mill's cracked brick façade as he crossed the bridge and feel a beckoning. He used to see it from his apartment on Riverside Ave. Some nights he stood, whiskey in hand, his eyes traveling down the smokestack's spire to the gnarled trees that grew from the shattered roof, down to the large arched windows. Windows that stared back at him. Now, with both his brother Kelly and his love, Allison, gone from his life forever, Casey surrendered to the sinister and inexplicable draw the abandoned mill held for him.

The shadowy hulks of old coal bins rose from the gloom. Broken pipes hung askew from the ceiling, where there was a ceiling. Some forgotten cataclysm had shattered a hole in the second floor and the roof. The scant light of the hole revealed silhouetted shapes of roosting pigeons in the rafters. The gnarled fingers of tree roots growing from the decaying roof reached down, twisting and grasping at the coming night.

The corner closest to Casey had a ceiling and a roof above it still. No pigeon droppings on the floor, only big flakes of lead paint and trash. He nodded to himself. It would do. The macabre surroundings echoed the despair and shame inside him. He squeezed back out from behind the plywood and slurped an extra-long pull on the bottle in a futile attempt to put that demon, shame, to sleep. He tossed a couple of ratty blankets, the bag of donuts, and the bag of snipes into the building and squeezed after them, tumbling into a pile of trash below the window.

Casey made a little nest out of refuse in the corner, rough bricks at his back. He laid a blanket over the trash, forming a kind of throne. The wind moaned through the windows' dead eyes, stirring the pigeons whose feathers came floating down out of the darkness. The black waters of the Nipwìmâw thirty feet below the windows weren't visible, but Casey heard the rushing water and smelled its putrescence.

He drank from the bottle, half-gone already, and rummaged for the bag of snipes—cigarette butts he'd spent the day picking from the gutter. The smell of one hundred dirty lungs assaulted him as he opened the bag. Casey tore open a dozen cigarette butts with alcohol-steady hands and scooted the tobacco into a little pile on a piece of filthy cardboard. Then he pulled out the rolling papers he'd bought along with the wine. He rolled a 'snipe smoke.' The cigarette tasted like despair.

As he smoked, he looked down the length of the building. It was as long as a football field, but Casey could only see about half of it in the darkness. Just before the gloom closed in completely, the great bulbous shape of a boiler stuck out of the rotten floor like a capsized ship going down bow first.

The Pull

Again. He had the urge to get up and climb into the old coal-fired furnace, but his warm blankets and the icy air of the coming night rooted him to the spot.

The wind kicked up another notch, blowing tiny red sparks of light from the end of his cigarette. They danced for a moment on the wind, then winked out, lost forever among the trash. The leaves from the trees growing on the roof made a shushing sound in the wind. One by one, they let go of their branches and died. Their corpses fluttered in through the hole in the roof. As they fell, they too were lost in the gloom.

Casey took another long pull from the bottle and shivered. The smack of wind-driven rain on brick grew loud in his ears. The echoes of water drops falling from the roof and dashing themselves on the floor joined the chorus. Casey's breath steamed and disappeared. The mill grew darker.

His father was reading to him and Kelly from a battered taped-together book of Greek Folktales. The twins snuggled down in their bed, maybe ten years old. The old man stank of whiskey and cigarettes, but that didn't usually bother the twins. His father's animated storytelling, though a little less coherent, made the story more enjoyable. The story was about a demon that came out of an urn and possessed a king. The king killed all the people of the city because they were wicked.

"What did the king look like?" Casey asked.

His father laughed a twisted, evil laugh. A clay jar appeared with purple glowing glyphs. His father opened it, smoke poured from the jar into his father's nose, and his eyes filled with blood. Then Casey's father raised an ax over his head.

Casey jerked up from a doze, heart pounding. The echoes of his scream faded into the dark mill. His crotch felt wet; he'd pissed himself.

The storm's violence diminished while he slept; now, Casey could make out holes in the clouds through the windows across the way. The wine bottle sat squeezed between his wet thighs under the blanket. He finished it and dropped it at his side. His fingers shook with cold as he pulled out the bag of snipes. He spilled as much tobacco as he used to roll the cigarette, but the warm smoke felt good in his lungs. The clouds opened up, and a single shaft of moonlight penetrated the hole in the roof, casting its pale light on the boiler in the middle of the room. Casey could see the door in front, open and big enough for a man to crawl through. The thick rusty smell of blood filled Casey's nostrils. The shaft of moonlight faded. Thunder crashed into the night. Beyond the door, somewhere deep inside the boiler, something glowed purple.

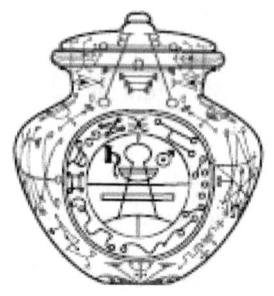

Chapter 2

Hili

Sumer 2988BCE

Hili struggled through the rising floodwater of the Euphrates River, heart pounding with fear and effort. Her younger brother, Nigmah, splashed through the thigh-deep current beside her. Hili faltered, foot stuck on some obstacle unseen under the muddy water. Nigmah, a man in body, but at seventeen, still a boy in mind, reached out and pulled her free. They were two in a crowd of hundreds fleeing the drowning city of Umashk. Baskets, boards, straw, and a thousand other kinds of flotsam bumped into Hili as she hurried for the safety of the cliffs. Thunder split the world into a thousand pieces. Fat drops of cold rain pelted her face. Behind the thick black clouds, the sun set on Umashk for the last time.

Cries of terror rose out of the gathering dusk. Blood scent filled Hili's nose. The brown water churned red around her. She couldn't see the source of the shrieks through the crowds, floating debris, and descending darkness. The choice before her was no choice at all; advance into the unknown nightmare ahead, or drown in the flood.

Dismembered corpses floated past. A severed hand caught in her tunic for a moment before bobbing downstream. Men, women, children all mixed together. The screaming stopped.

A man holding a clay pot shouted in commanding tones as he waded through the gore. Just for a moment, glyphs glowed purple on the side of the jar.

Things struck Hili, unseen in the fast-moving murk. Hard things, and soft, battered her legs.

A cart pushed sideways through the current tipped over. The man with the urn yelled and jerked his body away, trying to free himself. The cart pinned a leg under the water. Still, he clung to the urn.

Hili waded upstream, leaning hard into the current to reach him.

Nigmah splashed away toward the safety of the cliffs, so close now.

"Nigmah!"

"What are you doing?" he shouted.

Hili pointed. "He's stuck!"

"We'll all drown if we stop!" Nigmah waved an arm toward the cliffs, splashing water into his scruffy, black beard. "Come on; we're almost there."

"He's trapped. We need your ax!" Hili returned her attention to the pot man. She had to help him. *Needed* to help him. Something pulled inside her like an invisible rope, drawing her toward the urn. No, she told herself, to the man. What use had she for some old pot? "Let go," she called. "It's not worth your life."

"Yes, it is." The man didn't spare her so much as a look, just kept trying to jerk his limb free of the cart.

Hili sloshed to his side, the flood up to her waist now. The force of it churned whitewater on the upstream side of the cart. She pushed on the rough wooden side, trying to topple it toward the middle of the river.

"Let go of that jar and help me, fool!" she shouted.

Nigmah came up beside her.

"Use your ax."

"Underwater?" The river swallowed Nigmah's hand as he touched the weapon tucked into his belt. "I'd cut his leg off."

"Do it." The man's brown face paled visibly in the growing darkness. "Do it."

"No," Hili said. "Push with me."

With a grunt, her brother leaned a shoulder into the cart.

It was no use. The cart wouldn't budge. Something struck Hili's leg. Her knee buckled. The flood swallowed her for a moment. Foul water in her mouth. Rushing in her ears. A hand grasped her tunic and hauled her up.

Nigmah released his hold on her clothes. "We have to leave him."

"Take it," the stuck man said, his eyes glowing the same purple as the glyphs that appeared on the urn's surface. Their violet glow stained the water.

Nigmah reached out.

"NO! Not him!" The man did his best to pull the vessel from Nigmah's reach. He looked into Hili's eyes with purple-ringed pupils. "You must take it."

"Idiot." Nigmah waded closer and yanked the urn out of the trapped man's hands.

He clawed at the air.

"PUSH!" Hili hadn't given up. She turned to her brother. "Drop that and push!"

"Give it back!"

He waded away, ignoring both Hili and the doomed man.

One more hard shove at the cart. Nothing.

"Forget me." The man clamped his pruned hands around her wrist. "Get it away from him!"

"You'll die."

"Get that away from him, or many more will die. Go!"

"Why?"

"GO!" Those strange eyes blazed violet fire.

She went, saying nothing else to the man. As much as the man's words pushed her toward the mysterious jar, so too did the thing pull her. She did not need to look for her brother.

The Pull

It told her which way to go.

As she moved, the current grew weaker. The water shallower. She emerged from the muddy river at a run.

Nigmah straddled the pot in the mud at the base of the cliffs, working the top back and forth to break the seal. The skin of the vessel came alive again in livid purple glyphs.

"Nigmah—" A wave of fear coursed through Hili. Her stomach churned. Still, the urn drew her closer.

The lid came free with a pop.

An enormous peel of thunder hammered Hili's ears. The rain came in torrents, lashing at her.

Greasy white smoke, like wet leaves on fire, drifted from the vessel and poured up Nigmah's nose. He shook himself and stood. Thunder smashed down on the world, multiplying among the rocky heights and rolling back. Blood scented air filled Hili's nose, thick, rusty, and sickening.

Her brother stared at her, his face a mask of malice, eyes filled with blood. Then he drew the ax at his side as if seeing it for the first time. He ran the blade across his thumbnail. His mouth twisted into a thin-lipped sneer.

She tensed. "Nigmah?"

The ax inched up.

"You must pick it up." Hili knew that voice. The stuck man. She didn't dare look away from her brother.

"Woman!" the man shouted behind her. "Pick up the pot and live!"

Hili reached, obeying the vessel's call as much as the man's words. Her fingertip brushed its smooth clay surface. And then urn and lid were in her hands as if they'd jumped there.

A clap of deafening thunder shook Hili. Foreign, sinister energy tingled through her body.

The pot owner crawled up beside her, dragging a ruined leg that left streamers of blood in the mire.

Nigmah raised his ax.

The man struggled to his knees. "Yes. Finally. Release me."

Nigmah swung.

Hili closed her eyes. Metal cracked bone. Thick hot rain sprayed her, running down her face, working its way between her lips. She gagged on the coppery taste.

When she opened her eyes, the man's headless body fell into the mud.

Nigmah's eyes swept over her without seeing. Then he ran and scrambled up the cliff.

Hili rose and chased after her brother, clawing and scraping her way up the rocky ledge behind him. Acting on their own, her feet ran faster than they'd ever run before. Clutching the pot, she ran along the cliff's edge toward the other survivors. She lept impossible crevices and scaled steep hills with inhuman speed, each stride the length of a tall man.

The storm raged. Water slashed through the dusk, dousing Hili. To the East, a blood moon rose through an unnatural hole in the clouds. A cry on the wind, like the scream of a night bird, filled her with dread. As she drew closer, she realized it wasn't one cry, but many, rising and falling away to create one terrible sound. Shapes in the sand resolved out of the darkness, hacked and bloody bodies. The screaming grew louder. Ahead, metal glinted in the ghastly red moonlight.

Nigmah, his back to her, swung his ax high and brought it down in a mighty arc, slicing through both a screaming mother and the child who clung to her robes.

"Nigmah!"

No response. The ax slashed again.

A scream cut short.

Hili's feet stopped as she came up behind the visage of her brother. The pot crackled with energy. Words formed in her mind. Just as her legs had done, her mouth moved on its own.

"Beast, exile, harken!" Her voice boomed with the power of the gods.

The Nigmah-demon, face spattered with gore, raised its ax.

"Hold!" she shouted.

It froze, ax overhead.

"Return to your prison. Diminish, and await destruction at the hands of the least. By pride, shalt thou be undone, by shame, vanquished. Enter the vessel." Hili pointed the open end of the pot at her brother.

"The end of all men is delayed, but not the end of this one," the demon said, then drew the ax across its throat.

"No!"

Blood spurted from the wound. In mid-air, it turned to smoke and entered the pot. The Nigmah-demon remained upright, smiling, showing his teeth, as spurt after spurt of blood turned to mist and was consumed by the vessel's clay mouth.

Hili wanted to rush to her brother and staunch the bleeding, but the force making her speak held her to the spot.

Nigmah's smile faded. He crumpled to the dust. Blood from his corpse fell up and coated the lid in a ring. Hili pushed the top into place.

The blood formed a seal.

The rain stopped.

The wind died.

You are warden and protector now. The words rang so loud in her head that Hili wanted to clasp her hands to her ears, but she could not drop the pot. *Guard this vessel. Neither try to destroy it, nor open it.*

Hili's power ebbed and faded away; her mouth and body were hers to control again. "Why me? Surely, Nigmah..." her brother's name caught in her throat. "... would do... would have done... better."

There was no answer.

Hili rushed to her brother's body. "Nigmah..." she dared not look at the ruin below his chin. Instead, she swept a lock of hair from his forehead. Her tears dropped on his face, mixing with the last drops of rain.

When her tears stopped and her knees ached from kneeling in the sand next to his lifeless form, she stood alone on the bluff with only the thunder of the floodwaters in her ears. All around her, blood soaked into the sand.

A single beam of moonlight burned a red hole in the clouds and fell on the pot.

"You killed my brother!" Hili screamed. She stepped to the cliff's edge and threw the urn into the raging river.

Chapter 3

Kelly

Trull, Connecticut 2020CE

When the first fat drops of rain spattered the window of Kelly's loft, he gave up on the article he was writing. The order, cleanliness, and refinement of his home usually consoled him as he paced, but not tonight. The reproduction Persian rug had no comfort to give, and the cold, polished wood floor only made him think about how cold his brother must be. The overstuffed leather sofa poked the place inside him that knew Casey was out there under a bridge on hard concrete.

Back at his desk again but unable to concentrate, Kelly minimized the piece he hoped to sell to the Trull Chronicle and checked the weather. A Nor'easter tonight; rain changing to snow. The hesitant sprinkle grew bolder and tapped insistently on his windowpane like a finger of guilt. Water dashed against the buildings and pounded against the pavement, running in rivulets down the trash-choked gutters. The more he thought about it, the worse his mind made Casey's plight.

Two weeks ago, he'd agreed to let his brother stay with him to get his life together on the condition that his twin take the first available bed at Trull General's rehab unit. It went well at first; Casey showered and dressed in Kelly's hand-me-down clothes. He disappeared every day, on the pretext of looking for a job, but toward the end of the first week, he came home boozy, belligerent, and stinking of cheap wine. Kelly took deep breaths, counted to ten, then hid the good scotch in the trunk of the car.

Then came a call from Allison about Casey prowling her apartment parking lot and the bank's email locking out his online access for too many failed login attempts. Kelly walked in the door, found his brother at the computer, and said, "Get the fuck out, you drunken piece of shit."

Now, staring into the storm, he regretted his words. Had Kelly truly done all he could for his brother? Or were the clothes and the use of his couch just concessions to guilt passed down from his sainted mother? Head fakes toward doing the right thing.

The rational part of Kelly's mind knew it wasn't his fault. He knew Casey would fuck up in some other way. He would have just left on his own, eventually. But Casey needed help, and Kelly had it to give.

That last was Mother talking. Reaching out from her icy grave in the bitter twilight. *Don't you worry about your brother. I'm sure he'll be fine. You stay in your nice, warm loft. Isn't it nice you have more than one man could ever need, and your brother has nothing?* Nice. Even in death, the version of his mother that lived in Kelly's head still had a gift for guilty hyperbole.

A fleeting glimmer in the corner of his eye, accompanied by an insistent tug in his gut, snapped Kelly's head around.

Nothing there. Just his cello standing sentinel in the corner. It wasn't the first of these episodes. Far from it, in fact. They'd started when he moved into the loft. And though he had no evidence to support it, he suspected they'd increased in frequency since he started playing the cello again after a long hiatus.

The only visceral evidence anything had happened outside of Kelly's overactive imagination was an icy chill that stole across the room. The cold returned Kelly's thoughts to his brother.

Sighing, Kelly closed the laptop and gathered himself to go out. He wasn't rich or even well off. Still, the author of a successful detective novel and sometime newspaper contributor ought to present himself in a certain dignified way—slacks, not jeans, homburg hats, never a ball cap. As a result, he went out into the storm, looking like he was in his own detective novel. The exception to his vanity—a pair of L.L. Bean duck boots with rubber bottoms and a leather top. No sense ruining a good pair of shoes.

The trench coat fluttered out behind him as he squeaked down the stairs. Kelly stepped around wrappers and cigarette butts for fear of tracking them into the car. He pulled a leather BMW fob out of his pocket, then stuck its only key into an '88 Corolla, jiggling it until the lock turned. The old car was simply too battered and rusty for anyone to steal, and too cheap and reliable to part with. The engine burped to life, but it took a few minutes before the defroster cleared away enough fog for Kelly to feel comfortable pulling away from the curb. Now the real bitch, where to look?

The aged brick buildings and cracked, bumpy streets rose in cones of bitter, orange-tinted streetlight, then fell away behind the Toyota, revealing nothing. Even the most downtrodden vagrants had found a place to ride out the storm by now. Kelly could check the bars, but that was just wishful thinking, and he knew it. Casey didn't have money for bars, and even if he did, finding a bar in Greater Trull that would let him walk in unmolested, much less serve the notorious 'Casey,' would be quite a trick.

The best places to look were package stores, and there were only half a dozen within staggering distance.

On his first three tries, Kelly went in, asked the clerks if they had seen Casey, and after a "who?" from the clerk, he said, "Casey, you know, looks like me but..." scruffy was the word he used. At the fourth store, the clerk finished for him.

"... like you, but a bum. Yeah, I seen him." The craggy-faced clerk pinched his nose and waved a hand in front of it. "Couldn't wait to get him out of the store."

"Did he say where he was going?"

The clerk frowned. "Yeah, said he was staying at the Ritz, invited me over for a nightcap."

"I—"

"Of course, he didn't tell me where he was fucking going, but I followed him to make sure he didn't steal anything on the way out."

"Which way was he headed?"

"Toward the bridge."

"Do you know what time that was?"

"Six-oh-seven."

"Thanks, I—"

"I have no fucking idea what time it was. What do I look like, a crumoligist?"

Kelly was pretty sure the man meant chronologist, and he wasn't sure there was any such thing, but let it pass. He hurried out to the car before the clerk could annoy him further. As he dropped the Toyota into gear, he scanned Bridge Street, then drove slowly among a chorus of blaring horns and shouted curses. He hardly noticed. Every shadowed doorway held the promise of Casey hunched against the cold.

Nothing.

Kelly's tongue touched the corner of his lip as he piloted the old Toyota across the Bridge Street Bridge's metal grating, pulling on the wheel as if the old machine were a B-17 going down over Nazi Germany. The old machine rattled, swerved, and threatened to jump the roadway, smashing into the rail just as his parents' did fifteen years ago.

No time for that old sorrow. Kelly had a whole new sorrow to obsess over.

The abandoned mill buildings on the left were a possibility. They were the last ones in the city waiting for renovation. Something indefinable pulled Kelly toward them. As if a heart surgeon left a long thread on the last stitch and tied the other end to the mills. He tried to tell himself it was the bond twins shared—that he could *feel* Casey's presence. But the truth was that the buildings themselves tugged on that hidden attachment. He wanted to go in, to explore, to *be* there.

It wasn't the first time either. Kelly's odd fascination with the Boiler House and Power House inspired him to write more than one newspaper article about the place, speculating on why they were still abandoned. Tonight,

The Pull

was different. Infinitely different. The draw of the old buildings was as inexplicable as it was inescapable. The closer he drew, the more strident the call.

He turned left into the empty dirt lot at the end of the bridge. Kelly suppressed a shiver as he sat in his car with the headlights casting their pale, jaundiced glow on the chipped green plywood covering the entrance.

The stories he'd written about the place scrolled through Kelly's mind. They built both mills in the 1890s to provide a steady source of waterpower from the Nipwìmâw. They were built on backfill, where the river met the canal that wound through the city. In its day, the Power House was home to two giant steam engines that ran a series of driveshafts to the other mills in the complex. The Boiler House behind it, as the name implied, housed three giant boilers, furnaces that supplied steam to the Power House. Other mills got second lives as box factories, apartments, warehouses, and so on, but there was no further use for such specialized structures. As a result, they stood empty for nearly one hundred years, too difficult to tear down and too expensive to convert to high-dollar lofts or shops.

Kelly got out of the still-running car and stood at the door in the glare of its headlights.

The wind picked up.

Thunder cracked.

Something about the thunder bothered Kelly, but he couldn't place it. Then, just for a moment, he smelled smoke... and blood.

The rain came harder.

Shaking himself, he focused on the job at hand, prying at the plywood coverings on the door and windows. They were screwed down tight.

A gust of howling wind whipped the homburg out into the darkness over the river. The lapels of his trench coat flapped in the violent gale.

He got back in the car and wiped the water from his face. The back of his skull tingled. Kelly wasn't a superstitious man. He didn't believe in ghosts, UFOs, ESP, or any of that other tinfoil hat shit. Still, he should go in there. Casey was in there.

It was ridiculous, of course. He *knew* it was ridiculous. But going home without doing everything he could was out of the question. Again, the specter of his mother's Irish-Catholic guilt piped up. *Go on, just drive away, turn your back on your only brother. Go home to the nice comfy loft you threw him out of. He's out there because of you, but don't let that stop you. I'm sure he'll be fine out here in the cold and storm, alone, in the dark.*

"Oh, shut up." He got out of the car again, ran up to the building, and pounded on the plywood. "Casey! Come on! I'm sorry! Come get warm!"

Chapter 4

Casey

The tumult slashed at Casey, sending sideways rain through shattered pupil window sockets. But in the space between Casey's eyes and the boiler, nothing moved. Violet light escaping the furnace's door pulsed in rhythm with his pumping blood. The rain renewed its attack, pouring through every jagged hole and striking with such violence that the inside of the Boiler House shook with its ferocity. Yet through the maelstrom, a shaft of moonlight remained fixed on the boiler.

The cold deepened.

Shadows slunk across the night as if seeking out deeper darkness.

"Hello?"

Only the storm answered. Wind burst through empty windows, moaning as it came. Biting rain followed with it, gnashing into rotten wood.

The purple glow faded, then went out.

Casey needed a snipe. But bleary drunken-eyes and shaking too-numb fingers spilled the rancid tobacco. He put the makings away, trying three times before finding his oversized pocket.

Cold, greasy air pressed in on him. The stench of decay threatened to rot the inside of his nose. The night and the storm, the urine soaking his pants, the water dripping from the collapsing roof, and his very soul froze.

"Fire," Casey wheezed. "Sh-should... be okay?" Casey's vision swam in wine. "Place is brick... not gonna burn...."

He staggered around in the trash on the floor and found a bit of sheet metal to serve as a firepan. In a few minutes, Casey had a pile of trash and some bits of broken floorboards stacked to the side. Three matches fizzled under the ministrations of his numb, drunk fingers before he got one to light.

He kept the fire small so a cop crossing the bridge couldn't see through the window holes. He rubbed his hands together over the flames until the pins and needles came. "Fuckin' hurts." But he held them in place to toast like misshapen sausages. When they were warm enough, Casey rolled another snipe, the foul-smelling task dulled by alcohol, produced a cigarette that more resembled a paintbrush.

The fire warmed both body and spirit. Casey sang softly to himself, "D-daaaaaany boy," he puffed and blew the words into the night in a white cloud. "Dah-hannnny boy," he slurred, "the pipes, the pi—"

The words echoed off the old brick walls and came back twisted, as if a chorus of diseased children, mouths misshapen from some unknown horror, hid in the shadows, mocking him.

"Hello?"

Again, the word came back wrong. "*Hello?*"

Somewhere in the dark, glass skittered across a wood floor. Casey strained his eyes into the dark.

"Who's there?"

The sounds of the storm faded away. The pigeons above fluttered and made those damn choking sounds as if they wanted to tell him something. If they had his answer, some malevolent power stuffed it back down their oil-slick throats.

On the other side of the fire, shadows writhed independent of the flickering blaze, black on black, as if the night itself were alive. The wind groaned through the windows. A crack of thunder splintered the silence.

Casey knew thunderstorms come only in the summer. He'd read that some Native American tribes referred to winter as 'the season when thunder sleeps,' but tonight, it was up and moving around on its own.

A patch of moonlight held the boiler; the eye of a hurricane made as much from foreboding and woe as from wind and rain.

Casey went to take a pull on the wine between his legs and found it empty. Two bottles of fortified wine in just a few hours.

"Shouldvvve made it lassst." Casey dropped the bottle.

The moonlight vanished, leaving the mill in darkness except for Casey's little fire. The storm ramped up again, howling, raging, and gnashing its wet, windblown teeth at the mill. The fire flickered like a dancing savage, shaking its flaming spears of light at Casey. The onslaught of wind light and noise pushed Casey into the corner. He pulled the blanket tighter, a flimsy psychological barrier.

"Everythingzzz cool. It'zzz juzzzt the storm," he whispered, careful to avoid the unnatural echoes.

"Casey, come on!" Purple light from the boiler's mouth glowed in time with Kelly's voice.

Casey rose, fell, and rose again, then staggered toward the old furnace.

"I'm sorry. Come out of the cold. Come get warm,"

"Kelly!" He opened the boiler door wider and peered into the warm darkness. "You in there?" Maybe Kelly had a little fire going inside.

Casey couldn't see what made the purple glow. Couldn't see his brother. He got on all fours, scooting into a short brickwork tube that emptied inside the furnace. Rough brick scraped at his knees through his pants. The stink of old coal and blood assaulted Casey's nose.

Another scooch forward toward the purple light.

"Casey, come on; come out of the cold!"

All wrong. Kelly's voice wasn't coming from inside the boiler. Casey tried to turn around, but there was no room. He started backing out. Thunder blasted through the night, rebounding inside the boiler like a drum.

The door banged shut.

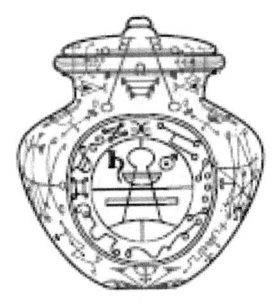

Chapter 5

Hili

The pot floated away in the angry floodwater until it disappeared in the darkness. Above Hili, a blood moon rose over the body-strewn bluff. It stood alone in the sky, as Hili stood alone. The storm and the urn vanished together—something inside her hardened, like mud-brick in the desert. The sorrow, Nigmah's grinning mouth, the sickening gore must all be pushed aside. A night's work needed doing here; she could not leave the bodies like this. There was no way to inter the dead in the rocky ground and no wood for a fire. She didn't want to leave her brother like that... leave any of them like that.

Her stomach heaved as if she were floating in the water with the demonic vessel. She *must* follow.

The Pull

The only thing Hili could think to do was arrange the dead face up so their spirits could join the gods, eyes open for the journey to the afterlife. The tears came, silent and unwelcome, as she rolled the corpses over. One dozen, then two. Hili pried their eyes open even as she did her best to avert her own from the carnage. Allowing herself just one more moment of sorrow, she kissed Nigmah's brow and walked south, following the river. Following the pot.

When she could walk no more, Hili laid down in a sandy hollow high in the cliffs and slept. The sound of rushing water woke her well after sunrise. Hunger gnawed at her insides, squeezing pain, urgent, awful. Her tongue stuck to the roof of her desert mouth. The gurgling flood below teased her thirst, but she dared not drink from its murky bounty. She sat up on her elbows and stared.

The urn stood at her feet, the glyphs on its sides glowing and pulsing with violet light.

The surrounding sand wasn't wet, so the flood hadn't risen and deposited it. There were no footprints in the sand but her own from the night before.

Determined to be rid of it, she found a smaller hollow in the sandstone nearby where a boulder had dislodged and fallen from the cliff face. Hili stuffed the vessel in. Even as she bricked it up with loose stones, the words from the bluff repeated in her mind. 'You are warden and protector now. Guard this vessel. Neither try to destroy it, nor open it.'

Job done, Hili continued walking south along the river.

The sun hammered down. Mouth and stomach aching, she staggered toward... nothing. There was nowhere to go. The events of last night, the killing, the urn, her brother's evil death....

Hili sat down in the sand. Delirious visions wavered before her. Slaughter in a forest. A ragged man climbing into a tilted metal beast. Fire. Men hanging in long rows from crossed wooden beams, the ocean lapping below. These things... they were what the demon who possessed Nigmah had done and would do. All this she saw as if the pot were part of her, and she a part of it.

Hili felt the urn in her mind. Her eyes sought it out... and... it was there, sitting in the dirt before her as if she'd never walled it away in the cliff.

New strength bourn of fear and hatred propelled her to her feet.

She ran.

Tripping, falling, and running again, she cast bleary eyes about for water. Then, finally, dropped to the ground and did not get up.

Footsteps.

A peddler stood over her, a small hand-pulled cart behind him.

"I thought you were dead," he said.

Hili struggled to sit and asked for water.

The peddler handed her a skin.

She drank.

"Water is precious now more than ever," he said. "The river water is foul and sandy from the flood. My water is clean and pure. I know where the secret springs and water holes are in this part of the desert. Are you hungry also?"

She nodded. Her stomach was now only a withered prune in her aching belly.

"What have you to trade?"

"I have nothing."

"What about your jar? What's in it?"

She sat bolt upright and followed his gaze. The pot loomed again at her feet. Hili couldn't believe it. She tried to think if, in her delirium, she'd gone back and taken it, but no. Perhaps the peddler followed and dug it out. But if he had, why would he ask?

"I can't trade it." As much as she wanted to be rid of the accursed thing, she knew she could not. The pot would not let her. It would follow her. She knew it. Felt it.

"What about a little of what's inside?" he asked. "Whatever it is, surely you can spare some."

"I can't."

He stepped over to the pot. "What's to stop me from just taking what I want? Here you are, starving, dying of thirst, exhausted by the look of you. I don't think you could stop me." His eyes returned to the pot as if it pulled him too.

As soon as he touched the vessel, she was in him. His fingers on the cold clay were her fingers. When Hili blinked her eyes, they were his eyes. She moved her arm, but it was his arm.

Her body sat in the sand staring at nothing; no pupil, all white.

They let go.

She was herself again, back in her own body.

The peddler shook his head and grasped the glowing urn a second time.

And for a second time, Hili was behind his eyes. Understanding dawned, aided perhaps by the urn's magic. As long as a stranger touched the pot, she controlled the stranger's actions.

The moment their fingers left the pot, Hili came back to herself.

The peddler recoiled, staring at the urn in wide-eyed terror. Then, without a word, he turned and ran north the way he'd come.

You are warden and protector now. Guard this vessel. Neither try to destroy it, nor open it.

She went through his things, stuffing his food, water, and money into a small sack.

Then Hili grabbed the fey jar and sprinted inland toward the green belt of trees on the Zagros Mountains. She struggled in the dusk, picking her haphazard way through the rocky desert wastes. Spiny plants reached out, catching her tattered, filthy cloak, tearing it. The silence of the desert day gave way to the scattered calls of birds and animals in the dusk as they emerged from their heat-induced torpor. The cries held notes of warning. Warnings that resonated inside.

As the darkness closed in, she felt the weight of the urn in her arms. The previously feather-light vessel dragged at her muscles, pulling her down, demanding she stop. Gritty tan sandstone gave way to jagged gray rock, creased with cracks, crevices, and caves. She paused in one of the latter, taking shelter from the evening breeze, which grew stronger and cooler the higher she climbed.

Nestled in her little alcove, she took stock of the stores pilfered from the peddler, eating half of the hard bread he carried, and drinking a great measure of the water from the skin. Momentarily sated, she closed her eyes and tried not to think about her situation: alone, directionless, accursed. The world receded.

She woke shivering. In the dimness, she eased herself from the ledge and set about gathering fallen branches from the nearby scrub pines and tossing them into the mouth of the cave. Then, satisfied there was enough fuel for the night, she kindled a small fire with the peddler's makings. The flames warmed her cold-numb hands. Hili scooted closer.

"Hili." the voice, strange but with a familiar timbre, came from deep in the cave.

"Who's there?" She flattened herself to the wall and gazed into the darkness. She trembled now from fear rather than cold.

"Show yourself!" Her eyes darted to the pile of sticks, seeking one that might make a weapon.

"I'm made of shadow. Why do you not step out of your skin and show *yourself*?"

"What do you want?" She reached for a bough with a jagged end.

"I'm here to aid you."

"Out of my skin?"

"No. That was a jest. I grow bored."

The voice, so familiar yet not, as if someone were trying to disguise their — "Nigmah?"

"Greetings from the afterlife, Hili."

"Nigmah." Hili sobbed. "Please let me see you."

A shadow parted from the rest of the obscurity outside the firelight's reach. Nigmah's countenance, completely black so that no feature showed, came forward and squatted across from her, arms on knees. Just a hole in the night. "I wish I could feel the fire's warmth. This shadow self is so cold."

"How come you to be here?"

"I do not know. The gods, I suppose."

"And why? What are—"

"I come with a message."

"What message? From whom?"

"The ones who made the vessel."

Chapter 6

Kelly

Kelly called into the night again. "Casey! Come on! Come out of the cold!"

The old mill stood impervious. Rain pelted the green plywood door. It dashed against the weathered brick and ran down in rivulets made the color of urine by the Toyota's dim headlamps. Kelly put his ear to the rough wood, straining to hear Casey's response above the pelting rain, howling wind, and bursts of thunder.

Nothing.

Back in the car, he sat for some minutes while the water on his trench coat drained into the cracked vinyl seats.

The Pull

He couldn't leave. Couldn't shake the feeling that his brother was in there. More than that, the feeling that *he* should be in there. And then the smells of fire and copper, in the middle of a deluge. Kelly couldn't make the connection.

Before he went home, Kelly decided to try the back side on State Street, though the place gave him the willies. He'd looked in while writing about the mills for the paper.

The whine of sirens grew out of the sounds of the storm, like a rotten seed blossoming into earsplitting wails.

The fire trucks weren't visible, but the flashing reflections turned the bricks on the buildings across the way the color of brimstone. Kelly smacked the shifter in reverse and turned out of the parking lot, swerving crazily onto Bridge Street for a moment before careening around the corner onto State. The stench of rotting, burning, half-forgotten wood poured in through the vents. Half a block down, a police car blocked the road. Its red and blue lights blazed on and off. Beyond that, firetrucks filled the road.

Kelly stopped the car at a crazy angle, jumped out, and ran.

"You can't go down there!" The cop was just getting out of his car.

"I think my brother is in there!" Kelly huffed as he passed.

A big man in a fire department jacket intercepted Kelly. "Hey! Where do you think you're going?" The man put a hand on Kelly's chest.

"I think my brother's in there."

"You think?" The older man's eyes bored into him under thick gray brows turned alternately red and blue from the police lights.

"Yeah."

"But you don't *know*?" the man asked in a tone both skeptical and belligerent.

"Please," Kelly tried to move around him. Blocked. The man moved fast for someone Kelly figured was sixty-five at least.

"What makes you think your brother is in there?"

"He's in there."

"You saw him?"

"No."

"He told you he was going there?"

"Please!" Kelly tried again to get around the man, and again, a meaty hand pushed back.

"I'm not going to have these guys risk their lives inside that building unless you tell me how you know he's in there."

"I'll go myself."

"No. You won't. Officer!" He called over Kelly's shoulder.

"He's in there, I know it. I can... I can feel it."

The Pull

"You can feel it? So you're a psychic?" The man's tone changed from skepticism to outright mockery.

"Mister... Please?"

"I'm *Lieutenant* Pontes. We've already been inside. There's no one there. If you want us to risk our lives doing a detailed search, you have to give me a good reason. A real reason."

Kelly deflated. "He's there."

"What if these guys go in, because they will, you know, and one of them dies, but it turns out you had the wrong 'feeling?'" Pontes made quotes with his hands. "How will that be? Will you attend the funeral? Set up a college fund for the kids? Visit the widow?"

That took the fight out of Kelly. The spray that blew from the hoses froze in the wind and peppered Kelly's face like cold sand. He stared at the diminishing flames gouting from the upper windows. "Casey...."

"Is he a vagrant, Mister...."

"Papas." Kelly sighed. "Yes, he is." God dammit.

"They don't usually come here," the Lieutenant said, relaxing a bit.

Kelly dropped his eyes from the burning building to Pontes. A thin crust of ice coated the brim of the Lieutenant's uniform cap, the nub of an icicle hung from one corner. "Who doesn't come here?"

"Vagrants, teenagers, anybody." The Lieutenant studied Kelly for a moment, then said, "Notice anything about the outside of the building? About the windows that still have boards over them?"

Kelly couldn't guess what the man was getting at. He shrugged.

"No graffiti. I guess it's too creepy even for the bu—vagrants. Like I said, no one comes here."

"Someone did." Kelly pointed to the charred, twisted shopping cart pushed up against the side of the building. Melted plastic hung from it like shreds of blackened skin. "Someone started the fire."

"We don't know the cause yet, and as I said, we found no one. Go home, Mister Papas."

"I need to know."

"You won't until I conduct my investigation and release my findings."

"My brother—"

"—wasn't in there. No one was."

Kelly looked up at the old mill again. No flames were visible in the upper windows now where the firefighters had yanked the boards away. Instead, clouds of steam billowed into the glare of the red flashing lights. A piece of hell come to earth.

"Officer!" Pontes called again, looking over Kelly's shoulder and waving the cop over. He scowled at Kelly.

Kelly scowled back. He barely registered the tug on his arm. He allowed himself to be led away, looking over his shoulder until the Boiler House was out of sight.

He was dimly aware of going home, stripping off his coat, lying down on the sofa, and falling into a fitful sleep.

His father was reading to him and Casey from a battered, taped-together book of Greek Folktales. They were snuggled down in their bed. The sour stink of whiskey and cigarettes carried from their father's mouth, across the top of the dilapidated book, and into the boys' faces. The story was about a demon that came out of an urn and took over the body of a king. The king killed all the people of the city because they were wicked.

"What did the king look like?" Casey asked.

Their father laughed, rising out of his chair and growing so tall that his hair brushed the ceiling. A clay jar with purple glowing glyphs appeared at his feet. His father opened it; smoke poured from the jar into their father's nose. His eyes filled with blood. Then their father raised an ax over his head.

Kelly came awake with a start and looked around the room. A diaphanous silhouette stood in the doorway. The pale incorporeal human outline evaporated before Kelly could comprehend its nature. For some moments, he cast his eyes toward the space where... something had been. He couldn't remember. Then he fell back asleep.

Casey burned; his body engulfed in flames.

Kelly reached out to him, but the closer he got, the further away Casey was.

"Help me! Don't leave me here!" The flesh melted from Casey's face. He screamed until his mouth was a flaming ruin.

Kelly sat up, hands reaching out from the dream. Sweat ran from his temples. He fumbled for his coat in the pale dawn that filtered in through the windows and made his way back to the Boiler House.

The firetrucks were gone, along with last night's storm. Kelly ducked under the line of police tape sagging between two lampposts. Ice from the firehoses covered the ground in a gray-brown muddy sheet. A fire department sedan sat at the end of the street, twenty yards from a shopping cart, now twisted and misshapen from the heat. The windows of the Boiler House, covered in green plywood just the day before, were now empty smoke-blackened sockets that stared out above ashy icicle eyelashes.

As Kelly approached, Lieutenant Pontes got out of the car. He placed his heavy rubber boots carefully on the ice and gripped the car door as he stood. "Mister Papas, right?" Pontes asked. He half walked, half skated over to Kelly.

"Yes," Kelly said and approached Pontes, slipping and sliding like a hog on ice.

"You can't be back here, Mister Papas."

"Press," Kelly said, reaching for his credentials.

"I don't care. It's not safe, and it's a crime scene until I say it's not."

"Have you been in—"

"As I told you last night, Mister Papas. There was no one inside."

"But have you been in since the fire?"

"Look, Mister Papas, I'm not unsympathetic here; I've got a wayward brother too...." He trailed off, looking at Kelly.

Kelly wasn't sure what the older man saw in his face. He hoped it was determination. Whatever it was, it had the desired effect.

Pontes sighed and pinched the bridge of his nose. "Follow me and watch your step."

Kelly fell in behind Pontes, skate-walking over to the window by the shopping cart. Inside, the building was nothing but blackened debris and charred floorboards, except for the corner closest to them and the hulk of an old boiler at the center of the room sinking through the floor at an angle, back end first, its round black iron sides festooned with icicles.

"The fire started there," Pontes pointed to a spot near the unburnt corner. "Given the shopping cart and the metal at the point of origin, it was probably a vagrant trying to keep warm. From there, the fire spread directly toward the old boiler."

"And there's nothing in the boiler? No one?" There had to be. The shopping cart was burned. A vagrant's shopping cart.

"Why would there be?" Pontes turned to Kelly, eyebrow raised.

"Maybe whoever it was went in there to escape," Kelly said, but the words sounded weak even to him. He hadn't planned on saying that, at least not aloud. There was something about that old furnace.

The Pull

As if the feeling, so strong last night, now somewhat diminished, came not from the mill but from the old black furnace itself.

"That makes no sense," Pontes said, turning again and pointing to the unburnt corner. "Whoever built the fire had a clear path to this window. The fire spread away from the person who may have been sitting in this corner. The fire got out of control, and they bolted. Simple."

"You didn't answer my question, Lieutenant Pontes."

"What question?"

"Whether there was anything—" Kelly swallowed down a lump in his throat, "—any remains in the boiler?"

"You never asked. You *stated* that there wasn't."

Kelly sighed. "Lieutenant Pontes, did you find anything in the boiler?"

"No." Pontes looked away.

Something about how Pontes avoided his gaze... and in the tone of the "no" bothered Kelly. He squinted into the gloom and noticed the floor around the boiler was burned away. It would be tough to access the boiler door, with nowhere to stand. "Did you even *look* in the boiler, Lieutenant?"

"There's no one in there."

"You didn't, did you?"

"We're done here. You can read the rest when I release my findings."

"But Lieutenant—"

"I said we're done." Pontes turned away from the mill, extending an arm between Kelly and the window. "Come on."

"What if someone's in there?"

"No one's in there."

Kelly walked gingerly across the ice. He reached the sidewalk and turned back. Pontes stared after him from the seat of his sedan.

As Kelly approached his car, an old homeless woman in a pink bathrobe stared at him, gape-mouthed from behind a shopping cart.

"Can I help you?"

"Casey?" she lisped the question toothlessly.

"I'm Kelly. You know my brother?"

"So. You'd be Kelly. Threw him out, did you now?"

Kelly stepped closer to her. "What did he tell you? When did you see him?"

"Yesterday," she said. "Right there." She pointed at the Boiler House, "Pigeon Palace."

Chapter 7

Casey

Casey screamed as he rammed his foot into the door of the boiler. He couldn't get much force behind it, stinking drunk on his hands and knees. As he paused for breath and made ready for another good kick at the door, crunching like breaking bones came from the bowels of the boiler. Then, the silence was as complete as the darkness. Another kick. And another.

The door didn't budge. Perhaps there was another way out on the other side. He crawled forward and fell face-first.

Something that crunched like half-burned charcoal briquettes broke his fall. There, in the middle of the coal, a cluster of irregular shapes glowed with an eerie purple light. Shadows writhed; misshapen men, nameless beasts with needle-like teeth, clawed at one another, trying to douse the purple light, testing the strength of the violet magic. Despair, violence, and evil made real.

Casey clawed at the boiler's cold black hide, scrabbling madly for an escape. Riveted seams of iron tore at his fingertips, hard and impervious. Electric malevolence coursed through him, radiating out from the horrid metal. Casey drew back. The only way out—the way he'd come in. He stopped his frantic search and turned toward the source of the light—those odd luminous shapes.

The Pull

He crawled to the pieces of glowing purple; the coal crumbling under him and turning to noxious black dust as he went.

A clap of thunder shook his bones and reverberated in the steel belly of the beast.

Casey's skin tingled at the touch of the strange, smooth shard. Two glyphs, a thick palm-sized spiral, the other a helix in a diamond, luminesced on its surface. The tingle turned violent.

Pain tunneled up his nerves.

Casey dropped the thing.

Twisted voices in a strange language pounded in his ears. Casey clapped his hands to his head. It made no difference. The voices came from inside him. Though he didn't understand the words, the tone was clear. The malformed hissed tones turned his stomach. His skin crawled but had nowhere to go.

From behind him, there came a crunching like a jackboot on a pile of bones.

He spun around.

A head rose from the floor. Maggots wriggled free of its shrunken, leathery skin and fell in the dim violet light. The coal cracked and parted as the rest of the desiccated body emerged, sheathed in a rotten suit that hung from its mummified bones in tatters.

Smoke rose from the purple shards. The Skeleton Man drew it in through a mouth devoid of flesh. It grinned at him, its leathern lips splitting open and flaking off.

Casey froze, glancing from the rising thing to the tunnel. His teeth knocked together, and the sound echoed off the tomb's steel skin.

Icy dread clawed its way up his spine and squeezed his heart. "P-please... l-let me out."

The thing raised its arm, bones showing through a tattered suit coat sleeve.

"Just hallucinations. T-too drunk, too cold," he whispered. "Not real."

Eardrum-fracturing thunder filled the iron sarcophagus again.

The coals erupted into a white-hot inferno.

Casey screamed. His body ignited.

"You're gonna burn!" The dead man shouted.

Inside the firestorm, Casey's throat filled with blood.

The air in the boiler itself caught fire. Flames engulfed Casey. His tongue burned. His lips and hair ignited. Clothes became ragged torch wrappings, sizzling and branding his skin. The pain, searing and unbelievable, crescendoed as his shoes melted into the soles of his feet. Flesh burned away from the bones of his face. Every nerve, every fiber, every cell in his body shrieked in agony. His nose burned away, exposing his brain to the flames.

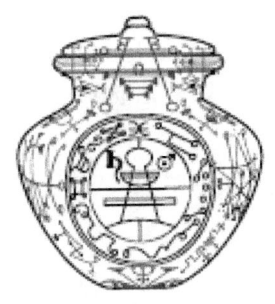

Chapter 8

Hili

Hili sat by the small fire in her mountain cave, waiting for Nigmah's shadow self to speak.

When he didn't, she asked, "What is the gods' message?"

"The gods placed a blood demon in this vessel. Six times the vessel shall be opened, and the demon set loose. And six times, another destined to stop the carnage shall speak its true name. When the demon's name is spoken, it shall return to the pot."

"And you were one of the six, then?"

"No. That's why I'm a shadow. And I will remain shadow until the demon is destroyed."

Hili threw her hands up. "How can I destroy the demon? I don't understand all this. Where have you been?"

"Neither do I. I was with you in the flood. Then I was nowhere. Then I was here by myself. And now you are with me. I have no memory of the spaces in between."

"Then how do you know all those things you just said?"

"I don't know them; they come to me from the gods."

"Then ask them how I get rid of this urn?"

"It's too late for that, Hili. You are its protector. You are the guardian for all time."

"Then, if I touched the pot, and I'm the guardian for all time, what happened to the last guardian? How was he killed in the flood?"

Nigmah shrugged. "He wasn't the guardian; he was the deliverer. You are the guardian."

"Why me?"

"The gods didn't tell me."

She clenched her fists in her lap.

"Beware, for the creature in this vessel is vengeful. It will try to destroy the six bloodlines destined to put the demon back in the pot. Each of the six carries one of the demon's six true names in their very blood. If the demon destroys that bloodline, humanity is lost, for the demon cannot be destroyed without its six true names."

"Help me understand. The demon will possess six people as you were?"

"Yes." Nigmah waved a black hand through the meager flames of Hili's fire experimentally. Then held the hand in front of his face and shrugged.

Hili huffed at him in irritation. He should be paying attention to her, not figuring out if his shadow hand burned in the fire. "And there are six more people who have the demon's true names?"

"That's right." He held his hand in the fire like meat on a spit.

"Nigmah!"

"What?" he turned his face toward her.

Hili couldn't make out Nigmah's expression. Shadows have no features. "So, each of the six who are destined to put the demon back carry one of its six true names? How will I know who they are? Or which people the demon is destined to possess?"

"You will know. Now, let me show you the glyphs. This one is the glyph of possession." He pointed a shadow finger at a symbol with a swirling border. "When a foreign hand touches the pot, you, the guardian, can possess that person for a time, make them go away, or serve the vessel's needs." Nigmah moved his finger to the next glyph. "This one allows you to slip through time."

"When will I be free of it?" Hili asked. She was awed by the pot's power and magic, but she wanted none of it.

"I told you. You are the guardian in life and death. When the six names are recited, the demon will be destroyed. Only then will you and I be free. Be careful, the urn can't be destroyed except by your hand, and if that happens, the demon will wreak havoc until the six names are spoken."

Hili felt the weight of eternity settle on her. Almost too much to bear. And despite Nigmah's words, she still didn't understand.

"What about that?" Hili pointed to writing that ringed the base of the pot. She understood the writing, but not the random combinations.

"Their meaning will be clear at the right time."

"So I'm to traverse eternity with this horrible thing, knowing nothing?" Hili grabbed a stone and raised it over her head. "Then I say curse the gods! Curse this thing!".

"Hili, no!" Nigmah tried to grab the rock, but his gossamer hand went right through hers. "You'll loose the demon forever. Humanity will die!"

Hili started to bring the rock down. Time slowed to a stop.

"I'm sorry, Hili," Nigmah said, then his shadow entered her body, consuming her.

FLOWING WATER CARRIED Hili back into the world. A skeletal body lay in a rocky cave. The corpse wore her tattered robe and clutched the pot.

Hands took the pot from her corpse. Hands belonging to the eyes out of which she looked—just like with the peddler. Yet this time, she found she could not let go of the pot and go back into herself. Herself... was dead.

"Nigmah?" she called.

No sound answered back from the stone tomb.

She did not rage, or despair, or weep for the life cut short. Everyone she knew died either in the flood or by her brother's hand. What life could there be after that? How long had her bones lain there? No one to pray, to grieve, to celebrate.

Had Nigmah killed her because she tried to destroy the pot? She didn't like to think she'd died at the hand of her brother like those others by the river.

"Nigmah?"

"I am shadow, Hili." The words came in a whispered echo on the evening breeze. "So I will remain until the demon is destroyed. Then we shall be reunited in the afterlife. Do not attempt to destroy the pot again."

So, Nigmah was right. She was the vessel's guardian, even in death. She searched for Nigmah's shadow, but there was only the stranger in whom she resided.

"Take the vessel to the temple at Umer," Nigmah's whisper came on the wind.

She wanted to shout, rage, and refuse the evil object, but even as these thoughts raced across her mind, her body picked up the urn and marched down the mountain toward Umer.

AFTER DAYS MARCHING through the desert wastes, the vast mud-brick maze of Umer appeared on the banks of the Euphrates. At its center, the temple tower made a stone spike in the sky, pointing to the gods. It squatted on a massive ziggurat base large enough to house the entire city inside it. The stairs were visible for miles.

On the ziggurat steps, she stood in the way of a descending priest.

"Stand aside—" the priest's mouth stopped moving.

The glyphs on the pot glowed.

She held it out to him, and when he touched it, she found herself behind his eyes, looking back at the hapless man who'd found her in the mountains.

"Where... how did I...." The man looked around, confused.

"Go," she said. "You have done well. The gods are pleased." With those words, she turned and ascended the steps into the temple.

"Hide it inside," Nigmah whispered in the faint breeze.

"Why?" she asked. "Tell me. No more riddles."

"Obey the gods," Nigmah whispered back, "so we can be set free someday."

Obeying wasn't in Hili's nature. Obeying her annoying little brother for eternity was nearly intolerable. She wanted to set the urn down on the steps and run.

"You must, for both of us," Nigmah whispered.

"Curse you and the pot."

Nigmah said nothing more.

What was there to do now but comply?

Though this temple was similar to the one in Umashk, she had never been past the worship room. So Hili searched, opening doors as she went. The other priests asked questions, surprised at the intrusion on their sleep, studies, or meals. Hili remained mute and kept looking until she found a room deep in the bowels of the temple. She hid the pot under a dusty skin among a great many other urns, vessels, and tablets on the shelves. The priest she inhabited let go of the vessel, and Hili faded away.

Chapter 9

Kelly

Pale winter light filtered through the window, illuminating the useless telephone. Calls to the homeless shelter, the hospital, and the police station yielded nothing. Yet, in that deep place where Kelly caged his despair, he knew they would. That indescribable sense, the same sense that drew him toward the Boiler House...

The Pull

...told him Casey was gone. Told him Casey was in that boiler. Past tense. Passed on.

After talking to the homeless woman and finding out that she'd returned Casey's cart to him right outside the Boiler House, which she'd inexplicably called Pigeon Palace, it was a near certainty that Casey perished in the old mill.

The only thing to do now—write about it. Kelly pounded the keyboard as a blacksmith might pound a chunk of hot steel on an anvil. His fingers battered the keys, forging molten words into sentences, sentences into paragraphs, honing and quenching the story, pausing only to check the facts. Lieutenant Pontes's preliminary report, posted on the fire department website's public information page, revealed nothing new. Then, his fury momentarily sated, Kelly sent the Boiler House story to his editor.

Half an hour later, his editor called.

"Hello, Mister Shields."

"Papas, I can't run this. There's no evidence anyone was in, or is in, that boiler."

"But Vic—" Kelly started, forgetting himself.

"Don't Vic me. This is supposition, and you know it."

Kelly sighed, "then just cut that graph."

"Even if I cut that paragraph, I still can't run it."

"Why not?"

It was Victor Shields's turn to sigh. "Do you know who owns this paper?"

"Of course, Tyre holdings."

"Right. And do you know who owns that mill?"

"MillCom Real Estate. I've done several pieces on the renovation of these old mills into lofts and condos."

"You live in one, correct?"

"Yes."

"And do you know who owns MillCom Real Estate?"

"No."

"Tyre Holdings. So if you want to continue placing stories with this paper, and have a place to live, don't write speculative and macabre stories about Tyre Holdings and their properties unless you have it cold. A story like the one you just submitted could make it difficult to sell condos in that building when they renovate, and more to the point, get us both in a lot of trouble."

"First," Kelly said, ire rising into his throat, "that's straight-up censorship. Second, *if* they renovate, every other mill in their portfolio, hell, in the city, has been renovated already. All the other mills in that complex were turned into housing ten years ago, and that piece of prime river real estate sits there crumbling.

You'd think they'd start with that one. Doesn't it seem strange to you?"

"Kelly, do yourself a favor, forget all this and send me the fucking dog show story. It was supposed to be in my inbox this morning."

"But why—"

"Don't know, don't care. Dog show. Now." The call ended.

"My whole damn career is a dog and pony show," Kelly muttered. He sat down to shit out the dog show story.

As his fingers pounded out the piece about poofy Pomeranians, his mind turned on the questions surrounding the Boiler House. It made no sense that a place like the Boiler House, both downtown and on the river with an excellent view, hadn't been developed first. He didn't like that the fire inspector made no mention of the boiler in his report. It was still unclear to Kelly whether anyone had even checked inside the thing. He didn't like the cold prickly feeling that Casey was there. Something else bothered him too, something about the fire inspector's report. He wasn't sure what it was.

The afternoon found him nosing around near the end of State Street. The wan winter sun melted some of the ice the firehoses left behind. It ran snake-like down the street in a twisting slurry of trash and ash. People came and went from the condos in front of the Boiler House. Kelly glanced around surreptitiously, then ducked under the police tape, subtle as a hammer, the hem of his trench coat dipping in the black ooze. While Kelly was concerned about being observed trespassing on a crime scene, he was more concerned that someone from MillCom Real Estate would come along and board up the windows again before he had a chance to check things out for himself. He looked over his shoulder.

A woman stood on the stoop of the condo building, looking at him.

"Shit." He turned and headed back to his car. Best to wait until night.

Kelly decided to get a cup of coffee at Marv's Diner; see if Marv had seen Casey. When they were boys, Kelly and Casey used to wait by the back door in the afternoon when Marv ditched the unsold donuts. So it was a good place for the down and out to pick up a few free calories.

The old Toyota knew the way. Kelly piloted it absently while trying to dig out the mental splinter of the fire inspector's report. Something was just *wrong* about it, apart from the omission of the boiler.

The diner was a downtown staple, built in the '40s right before manufacturing left the city for warmer and cheaper climbs. Its classic squat sausage shape and neon signs struck a vibrant contrast to the brick and stone buildings surrounding it. Kelly walked in under the stamped tin ceiling, stepped to the chipped Formica counter, and sat on a red vinyl stool patched with almost matching red tape.

Hazel, Marv's rotund wife, came around the corner from the kitchen in her classic '60s waitress uniform, complete with horn-rimmed glasses on a mother-of-pearl string. She flashed a gray denture smile. "Why Kelly Papas, I haven't seen you in a dog's age. You haven't been getting your coffee at that awful Starbucks down the street, have you?"

Kelly returned the smile. "I wouldn't dream of it, Hazel. You look great! Did you do something new with your hair?"

"Oh, go on. It's in a bun, for goodness' sake, just like always." Though she waved away the compliment, she blushed anyway. "Coffee?"

"Yes, please."

"You were always the well-mannered one." She smiled.

What remained unspoken was that his twin wasn't well-mannered. Hazel's offhanded comment struck Kelly's heart and brought his business at the diner to his tongue. "Have you seen him?"

Coffee poured, she looked up at Kelly. Her smile faded. "Who?"

"Casey."

"No, not for a while."

"Would you ask Marv?"

"Of course, Hon, be right back."

Kelly gazed at the diner's denizens. It was full of a mix of yuppies from Trull's scant financial district and the blue-collar workers who maintained it. Here and there, white heads perched around the booths like Q-Tips, some clean and white, others a dirty gray. These were the real purveyors of news — the retired gossips on fixed incomes who lingered over cheap lunches.

Marv came around the partition from the kitchen, wiping a greasy hand on the bespattered apron that struggled to contain his girth. "Kelly," he grinned, sticking the cleanish hand over the counter, "Hazel tells me you're asking after Casey."

"Yeah," Kelly rose and shook the offered hand. "I'm worried about him."

"Me too," Marv said. "Saw him yesterday. Gave him some day-olds and a coffee."

Kelly perked up. "When was that?"

"Dunno exactly. Wasn't full dark yet. Make it... four-thirty?"

"How'd he look?"

"I'm not going to lie to you; he looked about as bad as I've ever seen him. I asked if he wanted me to call the shelter, see if I could get him a bed. He just said he had a place to go, then he left. That's it."

"Okay." Kelly lowered his head.

"I'm sure he's fine. He said he had a place to go...." Marv trailed off.

"Yeah, okay."

"All right. Good to see you. I've got to get back to the grill."

"Okay. Let me know if you see him."

"Will do. Make sure Hazel has your number." He headed for the kitchen.

"Say, Marv?"

Marv stopped. "Yes?"

"The firefighters from the station up the street come in here sometimes, don't they?"

"Now and again. Why?"

"You know an inspector named Pontes?"

"Enough to say hello. Why don't you come on back? I've got burgers to flip."

Kelly grabbed his coffee and followed.

Hazel clucked her tongue. "Health code, Marv."

"Oh, dry up," Marv mumbled, but a smile peeked out from his stubble.

"You hear about that fire at the old mill last night?" Kelly asked as Marv took up his spatula.

"Yup," Marv punctuated the statement by flipping a burger with a slap and patter of grease. "Wish that damned place had burned to the ground, all the trouble it's caused over the years."

Chapter 10

Casey

Blood filled Casey's mind, cascading through his muddled thoughts. *You're drunk. You're dreaming.* But he didn't *feel* drunk. Dead then? That made no sense, either. Dead men don't dream. The blood poured into the body of another, taking Casey's consciousness with it.

As he came further out of the mind fog, he found himself walking across the Bridge Street Bridge, yet, he *wasn't* himself. He wasn't even sure he was *alive* in the strictest sense. And he *wasn't* telling his legs to move.

He tried to stop—and couldn't. He only stumbled. He was a passenger in someone else's body. He tried to yell—and couldn't. The mouth only made a dull, muffled sound. He tried to scratch his nose—and couldn't. The arm flailed awkwardly in front of him.

What the fuck? He yelled, but the mouth of the body remained mute. *What the fuck! What the fucking fuck! Calm down, Casey. We'll figure this out.* Casey tried to settle his mind and work the problem logically. First point of business: where was he? And more to the point, *who* was he?

The body around Casey featured downy hair rubbing inside denim, and a penis confined in cotton. Probably an adolescent male. Just ahead of him, two teen boys strode along the sidewalk of the Bridge Street Bridge, headed toward downtown Trull. They were dressed in the uniform of their tribe: denim jackets with hoodies underneath; one blue hood, one black, drooped down their backs. Their jeans disappeared into the ubiquitous unlaced tan work boots. One had short black hair, the other blond, with awkward feathery wings that flapped as he walked.

"Hey Freddie," the brown-haired kid turned his freckled face, "you like walking back there with the girls?"

"Shut up, Dukie." Casey's body said, then glanced over its shoulder. Behind him, two girls walked side by side, both pretty, one tall and thin, the other short and curvy.

"What are you looking at, Freddie?" the short one asked, face and voice full of derision.

"Just checking to see if you chickened out," his body said in a cracking, pubescent voice.

"Surprised *you're* still here, Freddie."

A stirring in his body's groin. Yup, definitely a teen boy. So, he was Freddie.

"We're gonna see if Freddie's got the balls to be a real Duke." The blond boy turned back and grinned with teeth too big for his head. "Real Dukes gotta get into Pigeon Palace by themselves."

Casey's body turned toward the view coming and going between the bridge's girders, the Boiler House. And...

The Pull

No! Oh Jesus, no! I can't go in there. I can't go back in there. Suddenly he was on fire again, burning up in another's head. The body, Freddie's body, stumbled.

"Ha-ha," the blond jeered, "Freddie's afraid."

"No, I tripped."

"Chicken shit," the brown-haired boy said without looking back.

"Fuck you, Paddy," Freddie said.

"Dukie," Paddy corrected. "I'm a Dukie. If you want to be a Duke, you got to get it right, dipshit."

So, a gang then? The Dukes? Casey grew up across the bridge in Farbank, but he'd never heard of The Dukes. Finally, it dawned on him that the cars passing on the bridge were wrong. They were mostly big '70s land yachts, but many were almost new. There, a shiny new Mustang GLX with blackout trim. Casey owned one briefly before he wrapped it around a telephone pole. The car on the bridge had no plate. New. That made it what? '81? '82? Add that to the list of 'What the fucks.'

Panic set in again. *What the fucking fuck is going on?*

Freddie's mouth remained mute.

Casey bent all of his will toward stopping the boy's feet from crossing the bridge. He detected the boy's pace slowing a bit. The girls following caught up. The tall girl put her arm in his. Once their elbows linked and Freddie was cocooned in the dense cloud of the girl's perfume, Casey's efforts to stop the boy were fruitless.

Is it even possible for me to stop this boy? Should I?

The kids crossed the bridge and turned the corner onto State Street. The condos and lofts that should be there, weren't. Instead, rat droppings lined their stoops like rancid chocolate sprinkles among empty bottles wrapped in brown paper bags. Boards covered the windows. State Street itself was cracked and broken like the buildings that leaned over it. They walked down the centerline, becoming more boisterous as they approached the dead end and the turn to the hidden Boiler House. In front of Casey, the boys hoisted their hoods over their heads against the first drops of rain. Freddie did the same.

Here was the hidden courtyard where Casey left his shopping cart some thirty-five years in the future, except to him, it was last night. Even in this time, the Boiler House was boarded up. The towering smokestack sat in the center of the V-shaped yard, impervious. A rusted fire escape clung to the building opposite the Boiler House, leaning to one side as if to pull away and strike out on its own. Two stories up, a rickety-looking iron walkway spanned the two mills. In its center, a locked gate blocked access to the Boiler House. Beyond that, a window socket looked down from some six feet above.

"All right, Freddy," the blond boy grinned at him with a smile that would sour milk, "you first."

Freddie stepped forward. Casey concentrated on holding the boy's feet to the spot.

"C'mon, Fraidy Freddy," the short girl sneered, and shoved him forward.

Whatever grip Casey held on the boy broke. The fire escape rattled under Freddie's boots, then sagged under the weight of the others climbing up behind him. The filthy yard dwindled in the iron slats between Freddie's toes as he ascended the rusty stairs. At the top of the second flight, he turned onto the rickety bridge. It swayed as he shuffled forward. He came to the gate in the middle, chained and padlocked, and looked back.

"Climb up on the railing and swing around it, dipshit," Paddy, the brown-haired one, jeered.

Casey didn't even try to influence the boy's movements here. In his estimation, the boy would plummet to his death with his lack of control. He wondered if the fall would be better or worse than what waited inside for the boy.

Freddie's foot slipped on the rain-slick metal as he climbed the railing. His body teetered over the void. His fingers clamped the gate harder. And after a sphincter-tightening moment, his boot found traction on the railing beyond the gate.

Casey felt the heaving of the boy's chest and the quick pulse in the squeezing fingers.

Freddie swung around and dropped onto the bridge beyond.

Paddy went next, swinging around the gate with the ease of a monkey. The boys on either side assisted the girls. The tall one protested she could do it herself, and the smaller one grinned madly as the blond boy put his hands on her ass to help her around. The blond boy was the last to go. He let out a 'yahoo!' as he swung around the gate, grasping it with one hand and extending the other to the sky.

The last obstacle, the window above, was the crux move. Freddie mounted the railing once again and reached for the stone sill. Once atop the railing, he needed to hoist himself through the window, now at his chest. His sweaty fingers found scant purchase on the wet stone. Freddie clawed and scraped the ends of his fingers until he reached the far side of the sill and hoisted himself in.

White paint peeled off the brick walls in chunks. The mixed scents of mold, decay, and ammonia-laced pigeon shit assaulted his nose. The birds chuffed in the girders high overhead. Outside, the rain came harder. Through a great hole in the mill roof, the saplings bowed and bent in the wind. Layers of trash and pigeon dung obscured what floor remained. He took a few steps, testing it. The pigeons in the rafters made those same choking noises. Casey quailed.

In his terror, Casey couldn't muster the strength to stop the boy from walking to the edge of the ruined floor and looking down. Below, the cursed boiler sank into the floor like a fat black turd. The boy gazed up at the hole in the roof. "Like it dropped from the sky...." Freddie whispered.

No kid, if it came from anywhere, it was the other direction.

"Check this out, Dukies," the blond boy said, pulling a crumpled pack of Marlboros from his pocket.

Oh, a cigarette. Thank Christ. Now, if only one of these little shits has a bottle.

The boy opened the pack and produced half a cigarette, twisted on one end. "I stole half a joint from my mom's ashtray." He grinned, raising his trophy aloft like an Olympian holding the coveted torch.

The kids gathered around in silent anticipation. Water dripped from the shattered roof of the mill, sending echoes chasing each other into the shadows.

The blond boy lit the marijuana cigarette, inhaled deeply, and held it.

"Don't bogart, Dave!" Paddy said, grabbing for the joint.

Dave coughed as he exhaled a plume of pungent white smoke. "Fuck yeah!"

The burning dope passed from hand to hand and mouth to mouth. Each kid inhaled, then nearly choked on the sweet-tasting herb.

Freddie inhaled deeply, then coughed until red splotches appeared on the edge of his vision.

Casey felt the sensations of smoke, coughing, and choking in the boy's body and wondered if he'd get stoned, too. He was a passenger, but he influenced the boy a little on the bridge and again at the foot of the fire escape. He didn't understand the connection they shared. He tried to access Freddie's thoughts and memories, sending out tendrils of energy. Nothing.

After the joint went around a couple of times, the blond boy, Dave, popped the lit butt on his tongue and swallowed it. "Fuck yeah!" he said again, grinning. "Come on, Hannah," he said, taking the short girl's hand and leading her away to the corner in the shadows. Paddy followed them.

Freddie and the tall girl were left standing by the window. Her expression showed tightly drawn features when she turned to look at him. Resignation.

Pigeons punctuated the silence, cooing in the rafters, ruffling their feathers.

"This place is pretty cool, huh, Tammy?"

"Yeah," she said, in a tone that suggested it wasn't cool at all.

Harsh wind moaned low through the empty windows facing the river and echoed off the bricks. The gathering storm dimmed the gray light inside the mill. Freddie reached out a hand.

Tammy took it.

"Are you stoned?" he asked.

"A little."

"Me too."

Silence.

C'mon kid.

Freddie leaned in and kissed Tammy, lips together.

She recoiled in surprise, then smiled. "You're supposed to open your mouth, Freddie."

"I know. I just didn't know if you...."

Jesus. This is the dorkiest kid in Farbank. Casey didn't mind hitchhiking on this part.

"Like this." She leaned in and explored his tongue with her own.

Casey considered trying to raise the boy's hands to Tammy's breasts. Hey, if he was going to sit through these awkward explorations of teenage hormones, he might as well get a thrill. Did that make him a pervert? A pedophile? Self-loathing slithered from under the rock of Casey's consciousness like a venomous snake and flicked the forked tongue of shame at him. He did his best to ignore the sensations of Freddie's body and concentrate on the problem. But, he was a prisoner, a passenger, a participant in a *Twilight t Zone* episode, and he couldn't figure out the plot.

Freddie's hands touched the girl's hips through her jeans.

"Yeah," Tammy said, pulling her mouth away, "put your arms around me."

Freddie did, and kissed her again.

"I touched her pussy! I touched her pussy!" Dave danced across the trash-strewn floor, holding up a finger.

Freddie and Tammy pulled apart, the spell broken.

"Dave, you're an asshole!" Hannah's voice rang out. She stood, parka tied around her waist, hiding her sex, struggling to get her pants from her knees to their rightful place.

"Enough of this shit," Paddy barked from his solitary spot along the wall. "It's time for the main event!"

"Just go along," Tammy whispered. "It'll be okay."

"Yeah," Dave said, "Time for Freddie to become a Duke."

"You said getting in here made me a Duke," Freddie protested.

"You think just going up some rickety fire escape makes you a Duke? You got to show some balls. BALLS! Come on!" Dave led the kids to an iron spiral staircase in the corner that lay on its side in Casey's time. "You first, Freddie."

Freddie's stomach roiled like a basket full of snakes. The trash-strewn floor below yawned and spun away below him.

"You scared?" Paddy jeered.

"Fuck you, Paddy," Freddie said.

Dave put a hand on Freddie's chest. "You don't talk to a Duke that way unless you *are* a Duke. Got it?"

"I got it." The stairs rattled and clanked with each step Freddie took. Flakes of decayed metal fell in his hair as the others started down behind him. Each time he came around, his view swung to the boiler.

Casey squirmed in the boy's skull. *Fuck no, kid. If they're going to do what I think they're going to do, you need to get the fuck out of here.* Casey leaned all his will into stopping the boy at the foot of the stairs. Whether or not it was his will, Casey couldn't tell, but the boy stood rooted to the spot until Dave came down behind him and shoved him forward.

The gray skies cast pale light through the windows by the river, and the hole in the roof threw a spotlight on the boiler door. Rain plinked off its iron surface like bullets striking a dreadnaught and lent the hateful thing a malevolent shine.

"The Boiler test," Dave grinned. "You go in a boy; you come out a Duke."

Noooooo! Again, Casey poured all his concentration into making the boy turn aside.

"What's-a-matter, Fraidy Freddie?" Paddy sneered. "I thought you wanted to be a Duke!"

"Fraidy, Freddie!" Hannah laughed.

They stood in a rough semicircle around the rusted boiler door.

"Come on," Dave said, grabbing him and pushing him forward. Then Dave leaned in close. "I can't go easy on you because you're my brother," he whispered. "You gotta do this. Don't worry." He pushed Freddie toward the boiler door.

No, fucking NO! Jesus, no!

"You want to be a Duke, don't you?" Dave said, releasing Freddie and opening the furnace door. It groaned on decrepit hinges, nearly drowning out Dave's words.

Freddie inched forward.

Casey tried to stop him, swirling his consciousness around the boy's feet and thinking about great slabs of immovable stone, but he couldn't overcome the push of peer pressure and...

The Pull

Slowly, Freddie climbed into the dark maw.

NO, NO, NO! By all that is holy NO!

Familiar sensations reached Casey. Rough cement crawlway under the boy's fingers. The stink of burnt decay burrowed into his nose. The same things Casey felt just before he died.

Ahead, complete darkness, as if the pale light of day itself were afraid to enter.

"A minute from now, you'll be a Duke," Dave whispered.

The clank of the closing door reverberated in the blackness.

Maybe nothing will happen. The others must have gone through this ritual and come out fine, right? Right, kid? Can you hear me?

Freddie crawled forward. An uneven brick bit into Freddie's hand.

That uneven brick bit Casey in a much deeper place. That uneven brick was the same one that cut Casey right before he died. He tried to launch the kid toward the door—and failed.

Freddie put his feet down. They crunched on old coal.

The muted voices of the other kids filtered through the cold steel as they made ghost noises outside. "Woooo!"

Someone banged their fists on the boiler's skin.

It's almost over, Freddie. Get back in the crawlway. Casey tried to push the boy's body back the way he came.

Instead, the boy squatted down on his haunches and chuckled.

The fucking kid is laughing now? Laughing! Unbelievable. There was no glowing light. No strange noises. No sign of the boiler's former evil. Just pure darkness and the silly voices of the kids outside.

Come on, kid, quit fucking around. Get out of here! Casey pushed himself inside Freddie's body, trying to get the boy moving. Nothing.

The boiler door groaned open.

Freddie, despite Casey's frantic efforts, didn't move. Didn't make a sound.

"Freddie?" Dave's voice echoed inside the iron sarcophagus.

"Freddie!"

Silence.

Come on, kid!

A thought cut through Casey's terror: The floor of the boiler... outside, the boiler sat on a steep angle. Inside, the crawlway and firebox were flat. That wasn't right. It should be crooked inside, too. It couldn't be built that way; otherwise, if the boiler was sitting level when you shoveled coal in, it would fall back on top of you.

"Okay, fine. Dukie, come on out; you're a Duke now, Freddie."

Silence.

"Stop fucking around, Freddie."

"I didn't think he had the balls," Paddy's voice drifted in. "Go see what the fuck he's—"

"You go see," Dave snapped.

"He's your brother."

"Fuck," Dave said.

Someone climbed into the crawlway. Cloth scraped on brick.

Freddie jumped up. "BOO!"

Dave screamed.

"Haha, motherfucker! I got you!" Freddie shouted.

"N-n-no, Freddie..."

"Oh fuck you, Dave, I got you, and you know it."

Dave scooted backward and launched himself out of the boiler.

Freddie burst out in a fresh round of laughter and started for the opening.

"Oh fuck, Freddie, come on," Dave wailed from the hatchway, his face pale as if he'd never seen the sun, never been to a picnic, never sat on the beach on a summer day. There were no beaches. No summer days. Just dank mills, tumbledown houses, and...

Casey went cold. It was happening now. Awful energy prickled and rippled around him, as if the boy's presence caused the boiler's gorge to rise.

Freddie turned suddenly. A shadow moved across a glowing purple spot on the floor.

"FREDDIE, COME ON!" Dave shouted.

The boiler door slammed shut.

The sound bounced back and forth in the iron belly of the boiler like a series of hammer blows.

Fuck!

"David!" Freddie hollered.

The purple spot on the floor grew brighter.

A shadowy figure coalesced in the eerie violet glow.

"Freddie!" Dave's muffled voice drifted in amid shrieks and pounding outside the boiler.

Flames erupted from the jagged purple shards on the floor and spread out like blood on blacktop. As they licked higher, the Skeleton Man appeared inside them. "You're gonna burn!" it screeched.

Oh, God, why?

"H-Hail Mary, full of...." Freddie broke off as the thing in the flames rose. "Der Ungeisthasse!"

Freddie reached for the opening.

"You're gonna burn among the fiery stones!" the skeleton screamed behind him.

"No!" Casey made Freddie's mouth move. His panic forced the boy's lips and tongue into action.

"BURN!"

A firestorm erupted from the Skeleton Man, engulfing the boiler.

"GET OUT!" Casey made the boy shriek.

Inside the fiery holocaust, Freddie leaped for the tunnel. Pain devoured every pore. Flaming fingers scratching themselves bloody on hot brick.

"GET OU—" No more air.

Freddie's hair and clothes became a torch.

"Burn, Burn, Burn!" The voice was like a thousand rats devouring a corpse, gnashing and slurping as it spoke.

The flesh of Freddie's face burned away, exposing his moist young skull to the stabbing flames. Freddie's silent, airless screams stopped as his tongue ignited and his lungs combusted.

Casey endured every white-hot neuron of agony, just as Freddie did.

The bubbling rubber of Freddie's boot soles seared the flesh of tender feet and boiled the bones.

Chapter 11

Hili

The blackness ebbed. Hili's thoughts liquified, pouring into the body of another. A cloud of dust floated in the air around the discarded, moth-eaten skin she'd used to cover the pot in the temple—centuries ago? She knew much time had passed, but didn't know how she knew.

A priest dressed in unfamiliar robes ran into the room, sandals flapping. "Hurry! Gutians have entered the city!"

Run, Nigmah's voice echoed in her mind, just a whisper of its former self.

Hili didn't need to hear her brother's voice in her ear to know she must grab the pot and run. So she took up the vessel and followed the other temple denizens through the maze of corridors and into sunlit chaos.

Gutian barbarians ran through the streets, heavily muscled, naked to the waist, and bearing wicked axes. Hili knew them well, for even in her time, the Gutians were feared among the people of Sumer. At the bottom of the ziggurat steps, Nigmah's voice came again to her mind. *Go west.*

Hili turned east against the flow of the fleeing Sumerians. Perhaps she was tied to the pot forever, but that didn't mean she couldn't fight the gods' will. The will of the pot. Even as she hurried against the crowd. Hili felt

The Pull

urging her in the other direction. As if some invisible rope dragged her very soul backward.

A man with dirty robes and a long black beard blocked her path.

Hili ran right into him.

"Give me the pot, priest."

"Never," Hili spat in an unfamiliar male voice.

"I could kill you for it." The man drew a dagger from his robes. Behind him, a Gutian clad only in a filthy skin that covered his loins ran toward them, bearing a bloody ax.

Hili gave no sign, and as the man in front of her raised his knife, the Gutian plunged an ax into his back. The knife dropped. The man's eyes bulged. He screamed as he fell at Hili's feet.

The axmen put a foot on the man's back and pulled his weapon free. The blade dripped gore onto the Gutian's chest as he readied it for another swing.

She turned to run.

The ax split her skull.

A clap of thunder burst from the sky and thrust its terrible sound down on the chaos ahead of the first drops of rain. When the sound rolled away, Hili inhabited the body of the Gutian. Inhabited, but had no control.

He's not meant to have it, Nigmah whispered, *just as I wasn't. You must stop him. You must honor the will of the vessel.*

As the warrior worked the lid loose, Hili tried to stop him. But the Gutian's body paid no heed. And when the lip came free, another crack of thunder poured Hili out of the possessed man's body. She looked up from the ground at the Gutian looming over her, smoke from inside the vessel filling his nose, just as it had done with Nigmah.

And Hili, Like Nigmah before her, became shadow.

But not her shadow. Instead, she moved as the Gutian did, mimicking his every motion.

The roiling clouds above the Gutian arced with blue lightning. Thunder followed with it, exploding with ground-shaking violence.

Spattered blood dripped from the Gutian warrior's long scraggly beard and dropped to the ground. Hili could feel it hit amongst the rain, imbuing a sense of power in her.

When the smoke stopped flowing from the pot, the Gutian rose, twirled his ax easily in one hand, and ran.

Hili floated on the ground next to him, his footfalls hammering in her ears.

The Gutian ran up to an old woman carrying a basket. He swung his ax sideways. Her head flopped forward, hanging only by a flap of skin on her neck. Blood sprayed as she fell. Hili felt the soft, warm pats among the cold raindrops as the old woman's essence hit the dirt in her shadow. The gore soaked into Hili, making her feel alive, not just some gossamer thing, as if the blood were bringing her back to the world of the living. The idea that such gruesome tragedy could aid her filled Hili with revulsion.

The possessed Gutian ran forward again. He swung his ax in wide arcs, gleefully cutting down all in his path.

Hili passed over their rain and blood-sodden bodies. She felt a thrum of energy. Her shadow self grew less gossamer.

The streets were nearly empty now. Fires raged through the bundled reed buildings on the outskirts of the city. Ash rained down like fetid snow.

A woman, shielding her infant's face with a scarf, hurried smoke-blind toward the advancing demon-filled Gutian.

He raised his ax.

His shadow, and so Hili, fell across the baby. And through force of will, Hili entered the child. "HARKEN DEMON!" she shouted.

The possessed Gutian stopped.

She dare not pause to wonder or have the gods stop her. But gods or no gods, she would not let the demon kill this child. The power of the vessel lent depth and authority to the baby's high voice. And just as they had on that long-ago bluff facing Nigmah, the words came to her mind. "That which is not yet named. Return to your prison. Diminish, and await destruction at the hands of the least. By pride, shalt thou be undone, by shame vanquished. Enter the vessel."

"Until next time, warden." The possessed Gutian smiled. Then, as he had with Nigmah, the demon drew his ax across his throat. The blood sprayed and turned to smoke in the air. It drifted to the rim of the pot, which appeared miraculously in the dust, and formed a seal. The lid levitated into place behind the last of the vapors.

The woman stood frozen, staring at her infant in horror. Hili didn't know if she could make the woman heed her baby's words, but she had to try. "Take the pot. Run!"

The woman, her face a mask of horror, reached out.

Instantly, Hili was in the woman. She bent down, awkwardly tucked the pot into the crook of her arm, and ran. This time she did flee west, heeding the vessel's will. That she was responsible for the deaths the demon inflicted sickened her.

The heat of the burning city grew intense. Hili feared for the baby, so she leaned down and, with her teeth, pulled the swaddling up over the infant's nose and mouth to protect the child. The alley crossed one more main street, then through a row of burning houses, and finally to the riverbank. The roaring fires sucked in the rapid slap of Hili's sandals on the street. She emerged from the alley's mouth and ran into another Gutian warrior. And before the surprised soldier could react, Hili thrust the pot at him.

As soon as the Gutian touched the pot, Hili was inside him.

The woman, whole again after Hili's intrusion, screamed and turned to run.

"Wait!" Hili called in a voice that thundered above the firestorm. "I have been sent by the gods to save you." It wasn't exactly true, but it wasn't exactly a lie. The woman stopped, but the terror in her eyes remained. Hili tucked the ax into her belt. She thought about throwing it aside, but decided she might need it. "We must go through the fire ahead," she said.

The infant screamed.

Hili looked at the fire and then at the baby. The woman spoke to her, but Hili had no time to listen. Instead, she unfastened the skin that covered her loins and draped it, outside-in, over the child. "Protect your face," Hili said, grabbing the woman's shoulders.

The woman stared.

"Go!" Hili propelled her forward. As they approached the mouth of the inferno, she broke into a run. Flames reached out from the reed houses and licked at her naked flesh. The acrid scent of burning hair filled her nose. Hili couldn't tell if the woman was behind her in the roar of the blaze, but she couldn't risk a look back. She slit her stinging eyes against the heat and said a prayer.

She didn't slow as she burst from the burning city onto the riverbank. Still running, she dove into the water and then looked for woman and child.

The woman, clothes smoldering, ran holding the Gutian's skirt over her child. She plunged into the water, then threw the skirt aside and rubbed cool river water on the child's face. The infant's screams subsided to whimpers.

"Can you swim?"

The woman regarded Hili with wide, terrified eyes and shook her head.

"Get on my back."

The woman stood frozen, babe in arms.

"The Gutians will kill you!"

"You *are* a Gutian."

"I saved you." Hili was responsible for loosing the demon. How many had just been cut down because of her? Hili had no tally. But she could do this one thing. Gods or no gods. She could deliver this woman and her child from death at Gutian hands.

Finally, the woman wrapped her legs around Hili's waist, and with the baby between them, clasped one arm loosely around Hili's neck.

Hili couldn't swim holding the urn. She could use it to float, but not to steer them out of the swift current. She let the pot go, watching with misgivings as it bobbed downstream. The pot always came back. Always. No matter how many times she'd tried to get rid of it.

The current grew stronger as Hili waded out into the river. When it reached her shoulders, she said. "Hold on."

Though the woman was slight of frame, and the baby was not much bigger than a loaf of bread, Hili struggled mightily to keep their heads above the rushing water. Bodies bumped into them, then floated away. Some badly burned, others still oozing blood from gaping ax wounds. Her strokes grew faster, then frantic, as the current swept them downstream.

The woman's prayers rushed past Hili's ear and across the waters.

The smooth strokes of Hili's arms turned to desperate flailing. At last, just as Hili thought she'd doomed the three of them to drowning, her toes squished into the silty river bottom. Gasping and lunging forward, Hili found tenuous purchase in the shifting sands underfoot, and she stood, shrugging off the weight of woman and child. The body of a man, face burned black, bumped into Hili's elbow. She pushed it away.

The rain stopped, and the clouds overhead dispersed as quickly as they had gathered.

"How is the child?" Hili asked. "Not burned or drowned?"

The woman shook her head as she splashed alongside, cradling the sopping infant. The setting sun glinted off of mixed tears and river water on her cheeks. "I still don't understand why—"

"It is a gift from the gods," Hili cut her off, not wanting to explain what she barely understood herself. She led them to a stand of tamarisk and found a hollow to hide in.

A splash of purple caught Hili's eye among the reeds. The Vessel.

The Pull

Hili sloshed over and picked up the urn.

Take it to the temple at Tyre, to the west, Nigmah commanded in her mind.

"What are we to do now?" the woman called after her.

For three weeks, Hili followed the tracks of other fleeing Sumerians from water hole to water hole, across the great desert, and eventually to Tyre. There she gave the pot to the priests at the temple and went into the black.

Chapter 12

Kelly

Kelly inhaled the thick, heady scent of cooking meat and frying potatoes. It was almost enough to bring his appetite back, despite his desperation for some news of his brother. "Pontes did the investigation on last night's fire. He was acting funny about it."

"Not surprised," Marv said, flipping another burger.

"Why?"

"Not his first investigation there, or his second."

"What were the others?"

"Well, the one that makes tongues wag around here is that business in the eighties with the Gottschalk boy. Let's see... must have been eighty-two or eighty-three."

"What can you tell me about it?"

"They never found him."

"What do you mean, they never found him?"

Flip. Splat. "Well, I don't remember exactly. I don't think anyone ever found out what happened 'cept the kids that were there."

The pale daylight gave up on downtown Trull as Kelly got into the Toyota. The trouble with these short hops downtown was that the car never warmed up. Kelly's breath steamed in the streetlight and cast smoky shadows on the cracked vinyl

86

dashboard. He put the key in the ignition. A presence behind him. He inched the key out of the ignition and held the ring in his palm with the key between his knuckles, sticking out wickedly.

He swung in a wild, awkward arc.

At nothing. There was no one behind him. Nothing in the dark backseat, but that wasn't where the feeling came from. Now that he was over his fright, he could feel it, a familiar presence.

The Pull

Kelly started the car and dropped it into gear. The old Toyota's defrosters could barely keep up as he exhaled onto the windshield. The streets were as empty as a churchyard after sundown. Kelly parked along State Street. The engine sputtered to a stop and ticked as it cooled, giving its heat to the night, getting nothing in return.

After a minute of fumbling, Kelly pulled a flashlight from the glove box and flicked it on to check the batteries. A good strong beam. He stuck it in the pocket of his trench coat and set off.

Kelly set a quick pace. The only sounds were his rapid breathing and the splatting footfalls of his duck boots on the cracked sidewalk. The streetlights imparted a sickly violet glow to Kelly's steamy exhalations as he ducked under the police tape and turned the corner into the icy moonscape outside the Boiler House.

Thick shadows filled the jagged V between the buildings. They came to an impenetrable point at the edge of the rounded smokestack. It jutted from the ground and thrust itself at the sky as if the only way to escape that corner of hell was to climb. Kelly slipped on the ice and almost cracked his head on the splintered brick window frame as he climbed inside the mill. The reek of wet fire enveloped him. He flicked on the flashlight and aimed its yellow beam at the corner where Pontes said the vagrant had his fire.

The first thing that struck Kelly odd was that the corner didn't burn. The fire was right there, but it spread only in the boiler's direction. He prodded the filthy blankets with the corner of his duck boot. His toe made contact with something hard and hollow. He threw the blanket aside with a gloved hand. Underneath lay an empty bottle of Wild Irish Rose.

"Casey," he sobbed. "I knew it. Where'd you go?" He swept the flashlight around in that corner. It landed on a muddy footprint in the only spot on the floor not covered by trash. It was a perfect match, not just in size, but in the pattern as well. It was the print of a duck boot. His duck boot, the old pair he gave Casey. Had to be.

He turned and followed the trail of fire with his flashlight to where the floor disappeared outside the old boiler. "Maybe, maybe the tails of that old coat caught on fire, and you didn't notice. You walked to the boiler spreading the fire, and then? Went inside to escape? Makes no sense." The pigeons above in the rafters cooed their agreement.

Testing each step before placing his full weight, Kelly followed the fire's trail toward the boiler. The wind moaned through the empty window sockets facing the river, doubling and tripling as it echoed off the fire-blackened bricks. Clouds of ash rose in the beam of Kelly's flashlight as he advanced. He stopped and coughed into the crook of his elbow. His flashlight beam caught something on the wall.

Pontes might be right about there being no graffiti outside the mill, but he was dead wrong about the inside. Kelly hadn't noticed it before, but there was graffiti inside the Boiler House. Spray painted on the brick, in dripping red letters, read the words: 'Zeek knew 287.' What the fuck did that mean? He moved his light around the walls, finding other graffiti: 'A horrible end' was scrawled in white between the river-facing windows with a childish cartoon penis under it. Under that, in red again, 'death of,' the 'of' was scratched out, and someone wrote 'to' underneath, 'the uncircumcised.' Higher up on the other side were the following numbers, 28234567. "Strangest fucking graffiti I've ever seen, except the cartoon dick," Kelly muttered and continued stepping carefully to where the floor disappeared in front of the boiler.

The boards creaked ominously as he put another foot forward. He retracted it and stood ten feet from the face of the boiler. He dared go no further. A gust of wind blasted in through the windows, producing the moaning sound again. In the beam of Kelly's flashlight, the boiler door creaked open with a grudging metal-on-metal squeal.

"GET OUT!" Casey's voice came from inside the door. Indistinct, as if coming from a great distance, terror and despair came through more clearly than the words.

Kelly stood frozen between diving for the boiler to look for his brother and bolting in abject terror.

"GET OU—" The voice came again and cut off suddenly.

The wind blew the groaning door open still wider.

Kelly ran, flashlight swinging crazily in hand. He lept at the window and scraped his knee as he jumped. He landed on the sheet of ice outside and went down hard, cracking his head.

Nauseous and dizzy, but no less terrified, Kelly scrambled to his feet. A figure in a hooded sweatshirt detached itself from the shadows of the adjacent building and started walking away.

"HEY!" Kelly called. His voice came out weak over a thick tongue. The fall knocked the tar out of him. He gathered himself and followed, slipping and shuffling over the ice. "HEY, WAIT!" he called again in a stronger voice.

The figure turned, its face obscured in the shadow of its hood, then disappeared around the corner.

By the time Kelly staggered off the ice and onto State Street, there was no sign of the man, if man it was. He ran for the scant safety of the Toyota, and after fumbling the keys in trembling hands, finally sat in the driver's seat, hyperventilating a film of frost onto the windshield. When he finally got himself under control, the outside world was completely obscured.

He calmed down, waiting for the Toyota's defrosters to cut through the icy terror he'd tattooed on the windshield. At home, he kicked off his duck boots even as he kicked himself mentally for getting spooked and running. It was Casey's voice. He knew it. He knew it as if he'd said it himself. Had he? Said it himself? His thoughts were foggy and suspect. He reached up and rubbed the egg on the back of his head.

Kelly grabbed a bag of frozen peas from the freezer, held it to the back of his head, and read the fire inspector's report again. No mention of a footprint. Shouldn't the report include that? In his mind's eye, Kelly tried to picture the scene the night of the fire. There was a storm wind coming through the windows just like tonight, blowing the boiler door open, blowing it open. That's what bothered him about the fire and the report. If the fire spread on the wind, it should have blown into the corner where Casey was sitting, not away from it, leaving it untouched.

He called the number listed for Pontes on the report.

The Lieutenant answered on the first ring. "Pontes."

"Lieutenant, this is Kelly Papas."

"Mister Papas. I released my initial report. It should be posted. It's late, so if—"

"I read it. I have some questions."

"I'm not answering questions from the press."

"You can answer them off the record, or I can raise them in a story," Kelly bluffed.

Pontes sighed. "What?"

"If it was a Nor'easter, with the wind coming off the river through the windows—"

"I'm not a goddamn meteorologist," Pontes interrupted.

"Why didn't the whole leeward side of the building burn? The wind should have driven the flames right into that corner."

"It didn't come directly through the windows. The building isn't facing directly northeast. Is that all?"

It was a bullshit answer, and Kelly knew it, but clearly he wasn't going to get a better one on this call. "No. There was also a footprint in that corner. Why wasn't that mentioned in the report?"

"Are you admitting you've been trespassing on a crime scene?"

"I have my sources."

"Willing to go to jail for them?"

"Always."

"Whoever made that print most likely set the fire. I'm not making that detail public. This is just a preliminary report, part of an ongoing investigation. What's included and redacted from the initial report are at my sole discretion. Now I have to go—"

"That is my brother's footprint."

"How do you know?"

"My identical twin brother's footprint."

"Because they're the same size as yours? Do you know how many people in greater Trull have the same shoe size?"

"Because it's the same shoe. My old ones. I gave them to him."

"That's very interesting, Mister Papas. You've just admitted that you have the same size and style of shoe as my arson suspect and that you trespassed on the crime scene. Arsonists often return to the scene of their crimes. They also like to stay to watch the show, usually sneaking away and returning in the guise of a bystander. Just. Like. You."

"Now wait, Lieutenant Pontes—"

"Don't worry. I have a feeling we'll be seeing each other very soon. Goodnight, Mister Papas."

The line went dead.

Kelly paced back and forth talking to himself, partly to break the oppressive silence in his loft after Pontes hung up, and partly to trick himself into forgetting it was because he had no one to talk to. "Okay, setting aside the footprint, the shopping cart, and the Wild Irish Rose, there's still a chance Casey isn't in there, that he fled, like Pontes said. But Pontes is acting funny. If I can't get into the boiler to look for Casey, maybe I can get into Pontes. Find out about the Gottschalk kid, and any other fires Pontes investigated in that building. Time to dig."

The first digging Kelly always did was with a white plastic scoop in a bag of coffee grounds. He thought of what Marv said:

One (scoop into the filter) Pontes was there. Two, Pontes was a young fireman. Three, not his first investigation there. Four, they never found the boy. Four scoops ought to be enough at this hour. Kelly flicked the machine on and opened his laptop as the coffee gurgled.

He logged into the Chronicle's archives, searching for Pontes. Not much came up: a mention, along with a group of others who made captain in '88, a similar article when he made lieutenant and became an investigator in '92. There were a half-dozen articles about suspicious fires where Pontes was mentioned as the investigator, but it was all garden variety stuff.

Kelly stretched, got up, and poured himself a coffee. He'd forgotten about it, and it already had a slightly burnt taste. Burnt...

He sat down and searched for mill fires. There were a few, but not, he noticed, in any buildings owned by MillCom Real Estate. Kelly changed tactics again. He ran a series of searches for Freddie Gottschalk, mill deaths, and firefighter deaths. He turned up dribs and drabs, but nothing related. He sipped his coffee, staring at the screen.

"Kelly," he said at last, "You're an idiot." And his reflection nodded in the now blank computer screen. "Shields said the paper didn't run stories casting MillCom in a bad light, and that's exactly where you're looking for them, where they aren't." Initially, he'd thought Shields was just chickenshit, but now he was starting to think it was some long-standing secret policy within the paper. It seemed unlikely that such a policy would stand for decades from editor to editor. But such stories might have been purged when the archives were digitized a few years ago.

He tried a few searches on Lexus Nexus and hit on an article from the Ware Patriot, a small but respectable rag from the next town.

The Ware Patriot, October 6, 1983.

A McCormick Middle School student is missing and four others injured in a fire that broke out in an abandoned mill in Downtown Trull last night. Fire officials said the blaze seriously damaged the old Boiler House building, which sits on the Nipwìmâw river just off Bridge Street.

Missing is Friederike "Freddie" Gottschalk, 13, of Trull's Farbank neighborhood. Firefighters contained and doused the blaze and continued to search for the boy throughout the night. The names of the injured youths are being withheld due to their age and the ongoing investigation into the fire's origin.

Two firefighters were also hurt. "Everyone did their best to locate the boy (Gottschalk) and put their lives on the line to find him," said Fire Chief Clarence Knapp. "I'm very proud of our team."

The fire broke out at approximately six PM and was reported by officer Charles Hadley, who spotted the flames as he crossed the Bridge Street Bridge in his patrol car. The cause of the fire is "of suspicious origin," the State Fire Marshal's Office said. No other details are available at this time.

The injured firemen, Floyd Pontes and Michael McKay, were treated for minor burns and smoke inhalation at Trull General Hospital. Both were released early this morning.

Associated Press.

Kelly sat back in his chair, rubbed the back of his neck, and read the article again. Two fires, same mill. Pontes responded to both in one capacity or another. The article raised more questions than it answered. How did the fire start? Was the boy ever found? How was Pontes injured exactly?

He desperately wanted to call Pontes and ask these questions. But given the man's previous responses to Kelly's inquiries, he didn't think he'd get anywhere. Best to keep digging. Marv hinted that there might be a third Pontes-involved fire at the same mill. Kelly settled in to find it. But mostly, what he found was either a rehash of the AP story or more of the same puff pieces on the redevelopment of the mills in Trull.

At midnight, Kelly pushed himself away from the keyboard and stretched. All his lines of inquiry were at dead ends. The Ware Patriot didn't have its archives digitized prior to 1980, so if Kelly wanted to keep looking, he'd have to find a different source. The fire marshal's office required a records request form and 5-10 days to comply. Too long.

Kelly went to sleep debating whether he'd really heard Casey's voice in the boiler and seen the hooded man running away, or if it was all a product of the knock to the head he'd received on the ice. Had it been the man in the hooded sweatshirt's voice? Was it Casey in the sweatshirt? Why did he run away? He hugged a pillow close to him, wishing it was a boyfriend he could bounce things like this off of. He held up his phone in the darkness, scrolling through his gay social media app, looking for 'the one,' and not finding him.

He woke sometime later, phone still in hand. The faintest impression of a creak on the old floorboards rang away into nothing. A pearlescent afterimage of a white dress hung in the doorway for less than the beat of a heart. A chill stole over Kelly.

He shook it off, plugged in his phone, and pulled the covers tighter around him.

THE COLD MORNING LIGHT filtered through the bespattered windshield of the Toyota as Kelly canvassed Farbank and downtown, looking for Casey in every tattered doorway, back ally, and bus stop bench. He saw no sign of his brother.

He dialed Pontes. The call went straight to voicemail. So he drove to the municipal building, a repugnant piece of modernist trash looming over downtown like an Orwellian wet dream. Its long, thin windows peeked out from between thick vertical cement dividers. It sat on squat cement legs, between which you had to venture to get to the front door, or in Kelly's mind, its revolving sphincter. He avoided this by using the parking structure at the back, another tasteless cement monstrosity blighting downtown, and using the elevator there.

The receptionist told him Pontes was out for the day and sent him away after hastily scrawling his name and number on a pad. As Kelly stepped out of the elevator in the parking structure, he came face to face with Pontes.

"Lieutenant Pontes, just the man I'm here to see. I've been looking for you."

"I know," Pontes said, trying to step around Kelly toward the closing elevator doors. "Make an appointment."

Kelly stepped into his path again.

"No new information on the fire is available, Mister Papas."

"Actually, I wanted to ask you about a fire in that same building in eighty-three."

"I can't talk to you about that."

"You'd save us both a lot of time and effort. I put in a request for the records."

"You won't get them."

"Why not?"

"They're sealed."

"How can you remember that? It was a long time ago?"

"You're not going to trick me into talking about this with you."

"I'm going to find out what you're hiding, Lieutenant. Are you protecting the identity of the firebug? Is it a guy skulking around that place in a blue hoodie? Average height, slender build?"

"Are you describing yourself? Any blue hoodies in your closet? You are a person of interest in this case now, Mister Papas. I could hold you for questioning on what I have."

"You don't like me for that fire, Lieutenant. We both know that. Please stop jerking me around."

Pontes sighed and glanced longingly at the bag he clutched with the sandwich shop logo on it. "I sealed the records to protect the other kids involved in the eighty-three fire. Sure, they were troublemakers, but they didn't start that fire, and they didn't do anything to the Gottschalk kid. They deserved a chance at life without that mess following them around, not that it doesn't, anyway. Now, I'm looking at those records. I'm comparing similarities in the cases. It's my job, and I'm damn good at it. And I'm warning you, for your own safety, stay away from that mill."

"Are you threatening me, Lieutenant Pontes?"

The old man's face softened. "No, I'm trying to protect you, Mister Papas."

"Protect me from what? What aren't you telling me?"

"The awesome weight of what I'm not telling you would collapse the Bridge Street Bridge and send it to the bottom of the Nipwìmâw. Now drop this before you get hurt and let me go eat my lunch."

"Sounds like a threat to me."

Pontes glared at him.

"Not the lunch thing, the other thing about me getting hurt."

"I think if you ask around, you'll find I'm the last person in the world who would threaten anyone. Good day." Pontes eschewed the elevator and went up the stairs.

Kelly sat in his car, going over the strange encounter. The harder he pushed, the weirder Pontes got. The only thing Kelly could think of was that either Tyre Holdings or MillCom Real Estate had Pontes on some kind of leash, or maybe Pontes himself had skin in the game. What skin?

Chapter 13

Casey

Casey's awareness, dim and coppery, pumped from the artery of his consciousness into the body of another. The body in question wore a rough workman's shirt on his shoulders, and a stiff, heavy jacket on top of that. Wind from the north made him, or rather the body he inhabited, pull the coat closed. One meaty, calloused hand held an old-fashioned metal lunchbox that banged against his chest as he struggled with the buttons.

Ahead, the sidewalk of the Bridge Street Bridge stretched out before him. The girders were a shiny new green, free of rust. The man, for man it was, hummed a bee-bop tune to the rhythm of his footfalls on the sidewalk.

Casey didn't recognize the tune, but found it soothing. He did his best to gather himself, slowly, carefully, so as not to freak out. Not an easy thing to do after you'd died a second time and come back as a third person. Nope. Think about something else. Start with the essentials. The where was obvious: Bridge Street, headed... well, he knew where... Don't think about that. Who? A man, construction of some kind, or maintenance worker. When? Casey observed the cars on the bridge without trying to take control and turn the man's head. Judging by the great rolling behemoths going by belching smoke unashamedly from their tailpipes, Casey guessed it was the late '60s, but he was no expert on cars of this vintage.

The thoughts fluttered across his mind like someone spinning an old roll-a-dex. The one that landed on top was this: *I'm Casey again.* Leaving his own body, with its alcohol and nicotine dependence, borderline malnutrition, and premature decrepitude, freed him from the low self-esteem that went with it. He was just Casey again, or the consciousness of Casey. The hard-luck Casey of old was dead, drawn into the boiler by forces he didn't understand, and summarily executed for it. Burned alive. A fitting and inevitable end, he decided.

This line of thinking led him back to the situation at hand. He was back, in yet another body, once again en route, he assumed, to the Boiler House. Why? Why was he stuffed into a third body headed for the same place but at another time? Who was doing this to him? Who, or whatever it was, wasn't giving him any recognizable signs or instructions.

He thought about the purple glowing shard he'd picked up before he died. Shit didn't just glow purple like that. Not by itself. Were the purple things and the Skeleton Man connected? He didn't want to believe that. He didn't want to believe in magical purple shards, but there were no other explanations, just new life, and new death. Casey assumed that this new body would go into the Boiler House and burn like he did— like Freddie did. Why? Was this hell? Was he doomed to die a thousand deaths, burned alive in body after body? If true, what was his sin? What had he done to deserve this? He didn't go to church, but did believe in Jesus. He was baptized, had his first communion, all that. He decided it was probably the drink, and wondered where that fell among the seven deadly sins—gluttony, probably.

Casey's host cast his gaze toward the Boiler House. Glass stood in the windows facing the river, though many panes were broken. No trees grew from the roof. Yet, there was still a sense of malevolence and decay about the place, like some hidden evil within rolling out in invisible waves that struck at the heart and filled it with mud. He didn't want to go back.

Maybe this wasn't a punishment from God or torment from Satan, but a chance for resurrection, redemption. What if he was here to stop the incineration? He'd had some measure of control over the boy, Freddie. Maybe if he could figure out how to perfect that control, he could save this man's life. And maybe, just maybe, if he did, he'd get to heaven or even a second chance at his old life.

The man turned not onto State Street, but instead took a left at the end of the bridge and entered the Power House building attached to the Boiler House. Inside, giant steam engines were half dismantled, their parts stacked in giant metal bins. Men in work clothes talked loudly as they stored their lunchboxes along the wall and picked up their tools. Casey's host walked straight through the Power House and entered the Boiler House through a door at the end of the building. The old mill was almost unrecognizable to Casey. The roof and the floors above were intact. Pipes ran from what was left of three giant boilers, some into the floor, some across it and into the wall of the Power House. Above, there were catwalks, more pipes, gauges, coal chutes, and all the trappings of an old coal-fired plant. Most of the place was in some stage or other of being torn apart. The boilers on either side of the evil furnace in the center were half-shells; jagged torch cuts marked the edges of where their iron hides had been cut away, revealing their empty black hearts.

The thing that got to Casey, the thing that put its hooks into his brain and tore at the cold logic he'd been working so hard to build and hold on to, was: the boiler in the center of the room, the boiler he knew inside and out, the boiler he'd died in—twice, stood whole and complete in the center of the forced entropy that surrounded it.

An icy dread seized him. Logic slipped away. That giant slab of iron looked back at him hungrily, longingly. The words he'd heard as he died screaming, engulfed in flames, came to him then, seared into his psyche. "You're gonna burn!" He heard them now as if the boiler said them aloud for everyone to hear. "You're gonna burn!" It shrieked and screamed in the gurgling voice of a man with his throat cut with a dull, rusty knife, "YOU'RE GONNA BURN! YOU'RE GONNA BURN! BURN AMONG THE FIREY STONES!"

He must be going mad. Of course he was. How could you burn alive—twice—and not go insane? How could you live in someone else's body and not be a lunatic? Alone. Casey was alone and at the same time, as close to another human being as anyone had ever been. He couldn't speak, couldn't cry out for help, for God's mercy. He couldn't beg for a quick, pointless, FINAL death. Casey was a prisoner, locked away in a strange body, a strange head. It was the perfect prison, the ultimate solitary confinement. Best to roll with it. Let the madness take him, pull him down into a world of raving nonsensical thoughts, too insane for more pain.

"Hey Pontes!" a voice shouted from the side of the mill, "you gonna stand there all morning, or are you gonna earn a day's pay and get that number two boiler cut up?"

His body turned toward the voice. A red-faced man with a close-cropped black beard pointed a crooked finger at him. The pointer was dressed in work clothes that were a noticeable degree cleaner and nicer than anyone else's.

"I'm not paying you to stand there, gawking. If you want to get that brother of yours through school, you'd better get your ass in gear."

"Yes, Mister MacIntyre." Casey's host replied.

So, I'm Pontes this time. Must be a last name.

Pontes put his lunch box along the wall and walked over to the boiler. Along its side was a stepladder, and beside the ladder sat two torpedo-shaped bottles of gas on a green metal cart. Atop the gas bottles were gauges and a hose coming from each. The hoses ran side by side in a great coil around the whole contraption. A pair of dark-tinted goggles hung from the brass knob next to the gauges. Pontes strapped these on. The lenses rested against his bare forehead. Next, he grabbed the cutting head of the torch, a brass contraption as long as his forearm, with three knobs and a squeeze lever. After turning the knobs and checking the gauges, Pontes stuck a sparker in his pocket and climbed the ladder.

Six feet up the side of the boiler, Pontes pulled the dark goggles over his eyes, fiddled with the knobs, held the sparker in front of the tip, and squeezed. The torch barked to life with a "WHUMP!" and a gout of orange flame.

Oh, sweet Jesus! Casey cried inside Pontes's head. The flame and the noise brought images of burning flesh and memories of indescribable pain. "You're gonna burn!"

No. No, I can't. Not again.

Pontes adjusted the torch so that the long orange flame turned into a short sharp instrument of destruction with five glowing blue tips. Satisfied, he squeezed the lever, and the torch screamed like a rocket engine. Long flames shot out.

No. I can't. I can't. Please. Logic abandoned Casey. He couldn't concentrate on stopping his host. His universe shrank to the size of the flame jetting from the torch.

Pontes released the lever and trained the flame on the thick iron hide of the boiler. Orange flames shot out in all directions like a star exploding in the black of night. In the center, the boiler's skin glowed red. The red spot wavered and melted, just a little. Black spots formed and resolved into a skull. Its mouth opened, revealing rows of jagged teeth. "YOU'RE GONNA BURN!"

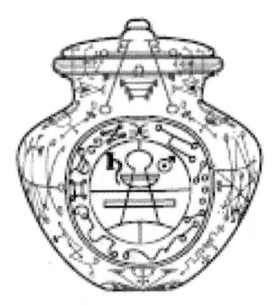

Chapter 14

Hili

Water cascading out of the black carried Hili into a new host as a hand touched the pot. As soon as she realized what was happening, she put the pot down, and once again, darkness returned, but only for an instant. Then she was back in the man, again, trying to pick up the pot. Once again, she put it down and went into the black. It happened a third time. And a fourth, but this time a different man tried to lift the pot. Hili, using the stranger's hands, put the pot down again. Blackness.

Again the sensation of flowing water. A new man grasped the pot. Four others flanked him. Three wore red togas and held shields and spears. One at his right hand was adorned in colorful fabric and hand-tooled leather armor. The man holding the urn looked like a king, draped in the finest cloth. Hili wavered in the flickering torchlight, and she knew what that meant. Death approached.

"I can pick it up as easily, Lieutenant Papas," the King said. "If this is a jest—" He stared as the glyphs started glowing purple. Then, cradling the pot under his arm, he grasped the lid.

Thunder shook the temple walls so hard that dust fell from between the ceiling stones.

"Alexander!" Papas reached out a hand, then drew it back.

The pot lid came free, and smoke poured into Alexander's nose.

"Sire?" Papas took a step back.

When the last smoke entered Alexander, he turned his eyes, now so full of blood that no pupil showed, to his companions and said, "On me!" He drew his sword and dashed from the room.

Hili floated alongside Alexander, inhabiting his shadow as he ran through the ruined temple. When they emerged into the cloudy daylight, a city stood in ruins, and from the looks of it, long abandoned. All around, soldiers worked with hammer, chisel, rope, and pulley, tearing down the once-proud buildings and hauling them, block by block, to the sea.

"On me! On me!" the beast within Alexander shouted.

The workmen put down their tools and followed.

"Bring the fleet to the causeway," Alexander said to the man who'd been beside him in the temple basement. "Load up the men, bring them to the breach in the south wall."

"Sire," the man, struggling to keep up with his king, gasped, "there is no breach."

"Not yet," Alexander sneered.

The sound of footfalls on stone rang out like the applause of a great crowd. The knowledge of the bloodshed to come filled Hili with dread. How could the gods deign to keep a beast such as this? How could they let it out and condone such bloodshed and destruction? There was nothing she could do but put the beast away promptly after doing their dirty work.

Rain started falling as Alexander leaped onto a pair of ships linked by a wooden platform that held a battering ram. "To the south wall!" he shouted. "Form up the troopships behind us!"

Within minutes, the twin ships dropped anchors on heavy ropes, and the sailors rocked the giant timber battering ram back and forth.

As the iron-tipped ram reached the zenith of its backward stroke, Alexander lept atop it and pointed his sword at the one-hundred-and-fifty-foot wall. He was bothered neither by the swinging motion, nor by the jarring impact when it bashed into the massive stone blocks. He spoke in a language older even than Hili's, though she understood the words.

Mixed awe and terror filled Hili as this king with blood-red eyes chanted. "I am the storm. I bring the rain of death. Let it pour."

The clouds thickened, black and full of thunder. The battering ram crashed against the wall again and again, shaking the earth and giving the water around the ships a tremulous motion. Fat drops of rain landed on Hili as the ram swung back.

Alexander's voice rose until it matched the sound of the thunder itself. Then, when the ram met the wall, thunder blasted across the sky. The great rampart made a thunderous sound of its own as massive blocks of stone buckled and fell inward. Alexander launched himself from atop the battering ram as the stones fell around him.

"EEEYAAAHH!" the King screamed, slicing through the first Tyrian defender before his feet hit the ground. Alexander ran into the city as his soldiers poured into the gap behind him. He soon found himself surrounded by enemy soldiers running from other parts of the wall to repel the invaders.

Alexander swung his short sword repeatedly, cleaving pike, spear, flesh, and bone. A cloud of gore flew about the King, turning the rain red. Bodies and entrails piled up around the possessed Alexander, who had to climb atop them to make more.

As it had in Umer, the blood strengthened Hili. With the sun gone, and the demon casting no shadow, Hili diffused, as if she were inhabiting the bloody air around Alexander. She wished she had a better understanding of the magic that bound her to the demon and its prison.

The King worked his way toward the temple at the city's center with unnatural speed, killing all who crossed his path. He wielded his sword as a chef wields a knife, cleaving his enemies at the shoulder, loin, thigh, belly, heart, and head. The ground at his feet became slick with the unmade sausage of human remains. He beheaded a soldier. Then he killed another with his backswing, sending an arm pinwheeling through the air. The dead piled up in the streets like hearth logs ready for the blaze.

At the temple steps, Hili formed into Alexander's shadow again in the flickering light of torches hung between the great pillars, one of gold, the other of emerald. He halted suddenly at the red-painted threshold, unable to enter.

The King turned from the temple and looked down as his army gathered the defeated Tyrians in the square. The captured army stood shivering with fear and cold as the gods doused the fire in their hearts with gray sheets of rain. They marched in by the thousands, under heavy guard from Alexander's men.

Hili flickered as the torchlight between the temple's massive pillars waxed and waned. She wondered why she had not yet been called to return the demon to the pot. She shuddered as she looked at the sodden pathetic figures trembling in the square. And then she knew, storming the city was only the beginning.

When the flow of prisoners into the city center slowed to a trickle, Alexander stepped to the edge of the temple steps. The rain stopped. The only sound in the square was water dripping from roofs and dashing itself onto the bloody paving stones. "You have defied me, Tyrians. You denied my request to sacrifice to your own god; you killed my emissaries and threw them over the wall. Now... Meet their fate!" Alexander shouted. He turned to his lieutenant. "Punch a hole in the east wall. Kill all of them and dump their bodies in the sea to complete the causeway."

"Sire, we have never treated a defeated foe with such disrespect." Lieutenant Papas said.

Alexander grabbed the man by the throat. "Never have you treated me with such disrespect. Still. Perhaps you're right. Make a ring of crosses outside the wall. Encircle the island. All these bodies at the bottom of the sea won't show the world what it means to defy me. Crucify two thousand. Dump the rest in the water. Do it now." Alexander let go of the Lieutenant's throat. He charged down the steps and hacked away at the defenseless crowd in the square.

Blood spewed, bowels burst, and bones cracked under the demon's assault. The lamb-like objects of the demon's wrath involuntarily voided their bladders in terror. So much so that the stink of excrement and urine overpowered the coppery smell of blood. Alexander moved his sword to the terrible beat of battering rams on the east city wall. When the great cracking of the stone echoed through the city like the drum of doom, Alexander and his men herded those captured soldiers still on their feet toward the new breech. There, they cut them down and pushed them into the red, foamy surf. Body after body tumbled through the wall after meeting Alexander's blade.

Hili found herself behind the eyes of another. Familiar words came to her mind, and as she spoke, the pot appeared at her side. "Harken, Demon. He who is known as Milcom!" she shouted. "Return to your prison. Diminish, and await destruction at the hands of the least. By pride, shalt thou be undone, by shame, vanquished. Enter the vessel." At these words, Hili expected Milcom to slit his throat as her brother had done, as the barbarian had done, so the blood would turn to smoke and return to the pot. But Alexander just smiled and spread his arms.

The blood covering the King steamed and smoked. It roiled around his body like a gossamer cloak. It drained from Alexander's eyes, and smoke exited his mouth, joining the foggy garment around him. "I see you, Papas," the demon sneered. "I will remember."

Hili lifted the pot, open end toward the King, and the smoke poured in. When the last wisps of smoke entered the pot, blood dripped sideways from Alexander's armor and coated the lip of the pot lid. Hili pushed the lid into place, sealing the vessel.

Alexander looked around, surprised and trying not to show it. He stepped to the breach in the wall and regarded the pile of bodies that stretched from the rocks below out into the water. Then he turned and looked at Hili. "I'm tired. You're lucky." He turned to a nearby soldier.

"Take him to the temple with the others." Alexander turned back to the bodies poking above the waves like a volcanic island. "Who did this, Hephaestion?"

"You did," the soldier holding Hili's arm said. Then, sensing the looks from the other soldiers around him, he added, "Sire. Shall we bring those in the temple to join their kin in death?"

"No. Gods no. Spare them."

Hili wanted to run. She wanted to get the pot away from Alexander in case he decided to open it again, but the pot had not told her where to go.

Alexander glared at her, then at the urn, and shivered. "Get that out of my sight. Take it to the temple."

The soldier guided Hili toward the square. The temple seemed the safest place, and the pot hadn't given her instructions to the contrary. At the temple, the soldier tossed her in. She smacked into a priest in the darkened doorway.

The urn grew warm in her hands. The glyphs glowed.

The priest reached out a hand and ran a finger along the surface of a glowing symbol, then drew back, shaken. His eyes changed, not to the blood-red of the demon, but to those of one who *knows*. "You have brought that for safe-keeping, but it is not safe here. We must take it to the most secure temple vaults in the world. Someplace where it will be safe until the end of time. Someplace that will never fall. The pot must go to Rome."

Chapter 15

Kelly

As Kelly steered the old Toyota across Trull, he kept an eye out for Casey. He arrived at the offices of The Ware Patriot, flustered from the search and the ravages of noonday traffic. The paper's offices were in a large Colonial house with a historic placard on the front: Clark House 1773. After several calming breaths, he ascended the wooden steps, crossed the wide porch, and turned the brass knob set in the green-painted door. Inside, a receptionist sat behind a desk in what must have been, at one time, the parlor. The rest of the room served as a waiting area appointed with antique chairs, tables, and photos. Above a formidable mantle, a framed portrait of the paper's founder and a copy of the first edition shared the place of honor.

Kelly stepped over to the receptionist's desk.

She was an attractive young woman, dressed rather casually in jeans and a T-shirt, but her tone was all business. "Can I help you?"

Kelly told her he wanted to access the archives regarding the Boiler House and added that the Chronicle had torpedoed the story with as little bitterness as he could.

"Well, normally we'd just say no, but I have a feeling Mister Petbe will find this interesting. Just a moment."

Kelly expected her to use the phone at her desk to call Petbe on the intercom. Instead, she rose and exited down the hall on wide creaking floorboards.

She returned less than a minute later, wearing a mischievous smile. "I was right. Mister Petbe will see you." She turned, and as Kelly followed her down the hall, she added, "he likes to stick a thumb in the Chronicle's eye when he can."

"Both thumbs. Both eyes." a voice called from an office on the left.

As they entered, a portly, balding man rose from behind a desk so buried in piles of paper that Kelly doubted the man would be visible from a sitting position. "Seth Petbe," the man said, extending a pudgy brown hand. His slight accent and physicality indicated the Middle East.

Kelly took the offered hand in a firm shake, leaning precariously over the piles of paper to do it. "Kelly Papas."

"Ah, Mister Papas, I've read your work. Solid writing."

"Really? You're very kind."

"Of course. I read the Chronicle. One must keep an eye on the competition. I think you're wasting your time there. Anyway, let's talk in the kitchen. We'll be more..." he looked around the cluttered office, "... comfortable."

The kitchen was what Kelly expected from an old farmhouse except that instead of microwaves and blenders, there were old Teletype machines, copiers, and all manner of office accouterments.

"Have a seat, please." Petbe motioned to the large slab of polished oak surrounded by modern office chairs occupying the place where a kitchen table would be. "Coffee?" Petbe asked, grabbing a mug from the counter.

"No, thanks, had some before I made the drive."

Petbe poured himself a cup and sat down opposite Kelly. "Sedative then?"

Kelly raised an eyebrow.

"Kidding," Petbe grinned. "Now, Mister Papas, what's this all about?"

Kelly hesitated. He realized that he'd expected to be rejected out of hand and hadn't thought of how he'd tell the story and keep the crazy parts to himself.

"If the Chronicle won't publish it, there's no harm in telling me. Besides, if you want access to our archives, we will have to come to an arrangement."

Kelly nodded, then dug in. Mostly he stuck to the text of the story he'd submitted to the Chronicle. He told Petbe about his brother's disappearance, the mysterious fire, the fire in '83, the Gottschalk boy's disappearance, and Pontes's reluctance to look in the boiler for his brother. Then, finally, about Pontes's strange warning.

"Sounds like you've got something interesting here. And the Chronicle won't publish because of its connection to Tyre holdings? Is that right?"

"Yes, MillCom, the realty company that owns the Boiler House, is a wholly owned subsidiary of Tyre Holdings."

"So, if I help you, I can stick it to both The Chronicle and Tyre?"

"Potentially. It isn't a story yet, really. My editor was right about that part. There's a lot of supposition. Lots to confirm."

Petbe grinned. "Oh, it's a story. What we've got to do is turn it from another conspiracy theory into news. If we do, I want to print it."

"We?" Kelly asked. He expected Petbe to turn him loose in the basement to paw through the microfiche files. But, instead, the man talked like a collaborator, someone who wanted to share the byline.

"Yes, I'm willing to devote some of the paper's resources to this. It's for a good cause," Petbe grinned again. "Can we work together?"

"Sure," Kelly smiled.

"Won't cause trouble with your editor at The Chronicle?"

"Fuck The Chronicle." Kelly spat.

"I like you, Papas. Any sign of your brother yet?"

Kelly clasped his hands together tightly on the table's dark surface. "Not yet."

"Son...."

Kelly looked up.

"Why don't you spend some time on that this afternoon? It's family. I'll have Sheila dig through the archives. Send me your notes. If there are big potatoes in the muddy ground, we'll dig 'em out. I'll call you if we find anything." Petbe rose.

"Thank you, Mister Petbe," Kelly said, reaching for the man's hand. "This is much more than I expected."

"I like that. Could be a new slogan for the paper: The Patriot, more than you expect."

Kelly drove back to downtown Trull, awash in guilt. He'd gotten so wrapped up in the strange details of this Boiler House business that he'd put the search for Casey in the back of his mind. Some brother. He kept flashing back to the night he'd kicked Casey out of his loft, out of his life. Over what? A bank account not worth nearly as much as a twin brother.

Guilt drove the Toyota. Kelly was merely the copilot. He went to two homeless shelters, a separate soup kitchen, and drove the streets where the homeless congregated. He pulled over a few times, showing his brother's picture to anyone who would look. A few people knew Casey. One or two even expressed mild concern, but no one had seen him in days.

Casey's face peered out from every dismal doorway that collected the evening shadows and wove them into a tapestry of despair and obscurity. His brother's unruly mop of brown curls peeked out from abandoned cars to watch Kelly pass, then vanished in a puff of good old-fashioned Catholic guilt. Finally, the streetlights, the ones that still worked, bathed Farbank in their ghoulish purple glow and changed the look of the mean streets from dim despair to dark desperation. Kelly wrenched the wheel of the old Toyota and headed home.

He did his best to wash off the cold, stark day in a shower so hot that when he got out and looked in the mirror, he saw a beast that would be more at home in lemon juice and melted butter than a soft towel. Robed and slippered, he sat down at the computer to check his email. There was a message from Petbe. It read:

Kelly,

I found this article from '70.

Petbe

There was an image file attached. Kelly opened it.

Chapter 16

Casey

The grinning skull at the center of the blowtorch's flame sneered at Casey. "You're gonna burn!"

Casey was half-mad with fright. His thoughts fought to organize themselves along the thin thread of sanity he had left. Terror, fierce and tenacious, gripped him as the skull wavered, danced, and tormented him among the flames. Its teeth working up and down. "Burn! Burn! Burn!"

Fuck you! Casey raged. The torments of the flaming head galvanized his mind. Anger supplanted terror. He wrestled for control of Pontes's hand. When he had it, he squeezed the handle of the blowtorch. The skull exploded in a shower of orange sparks. He released the lever. Only ordinary orange and blue flame remained. *I did it!* He cheered, though Pontes made no outward sound. *I fucking did it. I'm getting it! I'm getting control! I'm going to do it! I'm going to fucking win this time!*

Pontes moved the torch aside and examined the pockmark in the boiler's iron skin through his goggles, then sighed and once again trained his torch on the spot. Again, the red puddle of melting metal formed.

Casey smelled smoke and... brimstone, wet sand, and blood. The hairs on his neck stood up. Sweat ran down from Pontes's head to the small of his back and glued those fine hairs to his rough, creased skin. In the glowing red puddle, a shape formed. Casey quailed; his terror kindled anew. *No, please, not again...* He tried to control Pontes's hand again. Squeeze the trigger. Blast the horrid thing away, but terror clamped around his mind. His will died. The head shape wasn't the flaming skull this time. The face that stared back through the flames was his own.

Something squeezed his neck. It extended up from the visage of his head in the flames — a rope. His fiery effigy swung back and forth under the torch tip. It was hard to make out, but those weren't the clothes of a bum. This *wasn't* him. He was looking at his brother. It was Kelly, hanging from a flaming rope.

Oh, Kelly.

"Casey!"

Did the flaming Kelly actually speak? Or was this all happening in his mind? Casey wasn't sure.

"I'm coming for you, Casey! I'm coming for you!"

No! Casey moaned. *Not you too, Kelly.* He didn't know why the cursed boiler was showing him these things. Was Kelly already dead? Was he going to die in the boiler, too? Or was it just showing him these gruesome things to scare him?

A core of rage smoldered in his consciousness. This ghastly fucking boiler may have taken him, imprisoned him, and sentenced him to die a thousand burning deaths, but it wasn't going to get his brother. Somehow, he would find a way to stop it. He seized control of Pontes's hand and squeezed. The flaming effigy of Kelly in the molten metal disintegrated in a shower of fiery sparks.

"Casey, NOOOO!" it screamed.

It's not real. Fuck you, boiler. Casey tightened Pontes's hand on the torch. Sparks showered all around him.

"Pontes, what the fuck are you doing?" a voice screamed behind him.

"I'm scrapping this boiler, Mister MacIntyre," Pontes said, releasing the oxygen lever.

"The fuck you are! You've been up there for half an hour. I don't see a single cut. Not even a fucking hole. Do you even know how to use that torch?"

"Yes," Pontes said through clenched teeth.

"Do you see any other boilers in here, Pontes?"

"No."

"NO. Because they're already scrap. Yet you can't seem to put so much as a hole in this one. What the fuck is the matter with you?"

"It just won't cut."

"It had better cut, or I'll make some cuts of my own. I'll cut you from this job."

Thunder boomed outside the mill.

"Terrific," MacIntyre yelled, "and a storm." His finger shot out at Pontes. "You're gonna cut this boiler up, and you're gonna load up the scrap in the rain. I don't care if you're here all night. You hear me?"

"Yes," Pontes growled.

Casey felt pain in the man's mouth where his teeth ground together. Pontes and MacIntyre stared at each other. The only light in the old mill came through the massive windows that faced the river. Dark clouds rolled in. Thunder exploded overhead loud enough to make Pontes wince. His dark-tinted goggles magnified the gloom.

MacIntyre became a shadow outlined in gray, silhouetted against the window. His eyes glowed yellow-orange for an instant. "What the fuck are you staring at? You're gonna burn up all your daylight. Get back to it."

Pontes turned.

MacIntyre's words echoed and rearranged themselves in Casey's mind: *you're gonna burn up. You're gonna burn. You're gonna burn.*

Pontes adjusted the knobs on the torch to run wide open. The blue gouts of flame at the tip, once short and sharp, became long fuzzy spears. The torch roared as its flame split the air. "Effing son of a Bee," Pontes muttered. Once again, he trained the torch tip on the boiler's mottled black surface. Long tendrils of flame licked the side of the boiler with forked orange tongues.

Even through the ripping of the torch, Casey could hear rain pelting the windows of the old Boiler House. *Does it have to rain every time?* He wondered. The night he died, there was a storm. When Freddie died, there was a storm. Now he was inside another man's head, and there was a storm. Was it God, then? Sending him this torment time after time? And what about Pontes? Hadn't he seen the flaming skull in the melting hide of the boiler? Hadn't he seen Kelly swinging from the rope? Or MacIntyre's flaming eyes? He must not have. He had no reaction at all to any of those things. They must not be real, or real to Pontes at any rate. They must only be there for Casey. A special horror show just for him. Just to fuck with him. Everyone loves to fuck with Casey. Just keep fucking with Casey, and then kill him again. Fuck. Come on, Casey. Figure it out. Figure it out and beat this evil fucking boiler.

What did he and Freddie have in common? They'd both climbed into the boiler in a storm. Now a storm raged around Pontes too. Not good. So, all he had to do was keep Pontes from climbing into the boiler for some reason. Except, why would Pontes climb into the boiler? Casey didn't know. He could only wait and try to stop Pontes when the time came.

Another crack of thunder ripped the sky apart, this one close enough for Casey to feel it in Pontes's chest. It rolled away with the sound of a thousand cannonballs on a cobblestone street. Lightning lit up the world around Casey, illuminating scratch marks on the boiler's skin. Hash marks, like the marks made on a prison cell wall by an innocent man, or the marks made on a gunstock by a guilty one. There were hundreds. One, two, three, four, slash... One, two, three, four, slash... all the way down the side of the boiler. When the next flash of lightning lit the mill, they were gone.

Just fucking with old Casey. No way you climb into this boiler Pontes, no way.

The metal pooled and began to flow. A face appeared in the molten puddle. The glowing points of its eyes leered out with malevolence. "Pesadelo Vivo..." Pontes whispered.

He's seen it! It's happening! What is Pesadelo Vivo? Is that its name? Freddie called it something else, Der Ungeisthasse. Casey had no time to ponder further. He had to get Pontes out of there.

Pontes hit the lever. The torch broke through, sending a shower of red sparks through the hole into the boiler.

"Gotcha..." Pontes trailed off. A rush of foul air poured through the hole with a moan. Pontes's torch went out. The moan became a scream. A stream of darkness, like smoke sucked into a vacuum cleaner, rushed out of the hole and into Ponte's torch.

The torch's handle grew hot through Pontes's thick glove.

The wail grew louder, coming both from inside the boiler and from the torch, as if the furnace expelled some putrid spirit and imparted it *to* the torch. They shrieked together.

"Pontes! Backflow!" someone shouted.

Pontes turned. The torch cables were on fire. It raced up the hoses toward the tanks of flammable gas. Pontes jumped from the ladder, landing on his knees. He struggled to his feet and lurched for the tanks.

Run, you fuck! Casey screamed, trying to gain control of Pontes's feet, but all he managed to do was slow the man down.

Pontes scrambled for the tanks, reaching a hand out for the valves that would shut the gas down. The fire raced up the hoses like a thing alive. It looked at Casey, just for a moment, as Pontes began to turn the valve. Then the fire dove into the tanks.

The flash turned the world the color of fresh blood. A wall of fire propelled him through the air, except... not *all* of him. Hardly any of him, in fact. His head, Pontes's head, struck the boiler and bounced away like a soccer ball. That's when Casey realized that's all there was left: just Pontes's charred head. He didn't know how many thoughts per second a person had, but he knew it was a lot. He wondered how long. Shouts. Footsteps.

Everything turned cloudy red.

MacIntyre's muddy feet blocked his gaze.

Must have been out in the rain.

Pontes never climbed into the boiler.

The world darkened.

Chapter 17

Hili

Hili traveled out of the blackness on a cascade of water, pouring into a body that regarded a cave lined with shelves. The shelves held wooden boxes turned on their sides, displaying many thousands of rolled-up scrolls and clay tablets. The pot sat on a marble table. Next to the pot, a pile of clay tablets and two oil lamps lay on the table.

A man stepped out from behind the shelves, hands spread in front of him. "Hello." He wore a toga so white it hurt Hili's eyes. "Forgive my caution; I didn't know what would happen, exactly."

Hili nodded, unsure what was happening. She could just let go of the pot and go into the black. But instead, she decided to see what was going on, to make sure the vessel was safe.

The man stepped closer, hands still spread in front of him, open-palmed. "I'm Vitus Domitius, Keeper of Scrolls. What is your name?"

Hili looked down at her toga and the weak, slightly flabby body of the old man in it. She'd come to accept always seeing the world through a man's eyes, in a man's body, but she didn't like it. And there was no danger here. Still, there was something strange about this encounter, about the man. He was frightened, and at the same time excited. No, that wasn't right. Awed. The man was in awe of her. "Surely you know me?" she asked, betting on the fact that random people wouldn't be allowed in a room like this.

"Are you not *his Cossus praefuit daemonium*?" The man drew his eyebrows together and froze mid-step.

"Yes." She was so surprised at the words 'demon warden' that she forgot all pretense.

Vitus drew in a breath. "Incredible. May I know your name?"

Hili shuddered, overcome with emotion. With longing—on the brink of satisfaction. How long had it been since she'd talked with someone who knew it was her, Hili, and not the body she was in? She'd spoken with people, of course, but they weren't speaking to her. They were speaking to the body she was in, the eyes she was imprisoned behind. No one spoke to her. She'd tried with Kishar. Come close. But Kishar had never believed. Not really. This man was different. She could make him see her, or as close to it as she'd ever get until the pot released her. "I am Hili," her voice wavered. She straightened. "Daughter of Uten."

"You're a woman?" Vitus touched a hand to his chest.

She should have known. To have someone to talk to, just for a little while, ruined because she was a woman. She let go of the pot and faded away.

No sooner had she gone than Hili was back again, staring out of different eyes. A woman's eyes. She felt the body around her. It soothed her like soft, cool, linin sheets after sleeping naked on hot sand. The body was young, no more than twenty, well proportioned, but soft.

Vitus stood in front of her, smiling, hands at his sides. "Please, Hili, daughter of Uten, stay. Talk with me. I have many questions."

"I have many questions also."

"Will you..." Vitus shifted his weight from foot to foot. "Would you like to sit and drink wine?" He gestured to a doorway behind her.

Hili could see the flickering light of a candle in the next room, but little else. "Yes, thank you."

Vitus led the way to a table laid with a jug and two cups. He took the chair nearest the door. Hili sat and put the pot between her legs so that her calves squeezed it, maintaining contact. She'd never thought about it, but she supposed a person didn't need to touch it with their hands necessarily. When she took her hand away, she found she was correct. She took the wine and sipped.

"I'll start," Vitus said. "How old are you?"

This was a question Hili pondered on the journey from Tyre. She hadn't gotten much rest on the ship, constantly brushed against and jostled. "I don't know."

"It is the year six ninety-five—"

"Since what?"

"Since the founding of Rome."

"That doesn't mean anything to me."

Vitus's eye grew wide, his brows raised. "Where were you born?"

Hili took another sip of the wine. It wasn't the rich, hearty beer of Sumer, but for wine, it was decent. "Umashk."

Vitus shook his head. "I don't know that name."

"In Sumer?"

"I'm sorry," Vitus said.

"The land between the rivers?"

"Babylonia?" Vitus offered.

Now it was Hili's turn to shake her head. "What about Tyre?"

"Ah, yes, of course. Was Umashk near Tyre?"

"Three weeks east by caravan."

"So, Babylonia then. Strange, I've not heard of Sumer. You must be very old indeed."

"How old?" She knew she shouldn't dread the answer, but she did. Her home was gone. Her city, gone. The whole realm of Sumer was dust and out of memory, for everyone but her—living only in her mind.

"At least a thousand years."

Hili reeled. She finished her cup of wine in one gulp. "Do you have any beer?"

"Quintus," Vitus called toward the doorway at Hili's back, "fetch some beer."

Receding footsteps echoed off the stone.

"My turn," Hili said. "How did you know about me?"

"There are some of us who still know the old ways, the old gods. Scholars, scribes, priests all study the old texts. The glyphs on your pot appear on tablets found in Babylonia, along with texts that explain them and warn against their use. I have tried to duplicate them, but they remain scratches on paper and clay. Whatever gave these symbols their power is lost in time.

"My turn for a question. Have you seen what resides in the vessel?" Vitus tapped his finger on the edge of the table.

"It is a demon of great power whose name I will not mention. I have seen it twice. I wish I hadn't. I wish I could never see it again."

"So, you are not the warden by choice?"

"No." Hili waited as Quintus entered, set a jug of beer on the table, and departed. She poured a beer and sipped it. The fluid was thin, yeasty, and tasted of spices. "This is beer?"

Vitus smiled. "Is it not to your liking?"

Hili shrugged. It felt good to shrug, drink, and talk like a living person, even if the beer was terrible.

"The changes in the world since your time must be...difficult. Tell me, how did you become warden then?"

Hili told Vitus the story of her brother and of her journey through the desert.

Vitus nodded. "Tell me, the records indicate this pot came to Rome in four twenty-one, after the destruction of Tyre. Were you there? Did you see it?"

Hili did the math in her head, set her cup down, and stared. "The pot has been here for two hundred and seventy-four years?"

"You are quick with numbers. I would have to use my fingers, but that sounds right. Do you not feel the passage of time?"

"It's like going to sleep, then waking up in a strange place. This is the first time I've woken and found no danger."

"Remarkable. Tell me about Tyre."

"My turn." Hili wagged a finger. "Why then are there not good deities with pots of their own? Spreading, I don't know, joy, peace, happiness?"

"What makes you say they're not?"

"I've never seen or heard of such. Not in the way Milcom is, with a sword and a body."

"When the gods think it's necessary, you have a body to do good. More than that, goodness is the gentle hand. Evil is the sword. You cannot compare the way evil works to the way good works. They are opposite and work in opposite ways."

Hili knew it was the priest's turn for a question, but she pressed on, not wanting to talk, or even think about the carnage at Tyre. "But why let the evil out in the first place? How does killing eight thousand souls serve the gods?"

"Who knows? Maybe they worshipped the wrong god. Maybe, since you say the only survivors were in the temple, the gods took vengeance through the demon. Remember, these bodies," he grabbed Hili's arm, "are just chariots that carry the soul. Maybe the gods wanted those souls somewhere else. Only they can say. Think of it this way: imagine a river flowing along perfectly. A rock tumbles in, causing the current to change. That change causes the current to erode the sides so that eventually, a whole village washes away. Maybe a whole city. All because of one little rock."

Hili's brows drew together. "So, what are you saying?"

"The demon is not good or evil. It is the hand that moves the rock. It is a tool of the gods. Come, no more delay. Tell me about Tyre, and I will show you what nearly all of the glyphs on your pot mean. You should know, because the time for the demon to rise again is nearly upon us."

Hili stared at the priest, shocked. "How could you possibly know when Milcom will wake when I do not?"

"I will tell you after you tell me about Tyre."

Hili took a sip of beer, and then another. She sighed and told the priest about Alexander opening the pot and standing, incredibly, on the battering ram. She told him about the slaughter of the six thousand and the crucifixion of two thousand more.

"What about the survivors in the temple?" Vitus asked.

"Milcom was back in the pot by the time the news reached Alexander."

"It is as I thought," Vitis nodded. "Come, let me help you understand your situation a little better." He cleared the wine and beer to the side of the table. "Quintus, more light."

The servant entered with the oil lamps from the scroll room, set them on the table, and departed.

"Let's see the demon's prison, then."

Hili took the pot from between her calves and placed it on the table, keeping her hand on it.

With no preamble, Vitus started pointing at glyphs, careful not to touch their glowing purple lines. "This one, I think," he pointed to a series of squiggly lines in a box with rounded corners near the pot's lip, "is what calls you forth when the pot is touched. And this one next to it is what allows you to slip forward in time when you're not needed." He put a finger to his chin, then pointed again. "Here, an ancient symbol for speech. This one allows you to speak and understand the language around you. Otherwise, well, I don't even know what language they spoke in Sumer."

Hili had never stopped to think about how she'd understood what the people in Tyre said, or even this priest who'd never even heard of Sumer.

"This glyph," he pointed to one that looked like a dog's head in a spiral, "ties the pot to you. No matter where you go, the pot follows, yes?"

Hili nodded.

"It is exquisite, one of a kind." Vitus's voice dropped to a reverent whisper.

Hili did her best to fix each glyph in her mind, along with their meaning as Vitus pointed them out. But there were so many, and some with obscure meanings even Hili didn't understand.

"Do you know about the inside of the pot?"

"No?" Hili hadn't thought there might be glyphs on the inside.

"All this knowledge comes from tablets I reconstructed from Babylonia. Some, broken into pieces as small as a marble. I tell you this because some of my knowledge is simply guesswork."

"What about the inside of the pot?"

"I'm getting to that, but I want you to understand that what I'm about to say, I don't fully understand myself. You see, the magic that can hold a demon such as this one is as strong as it is strange and dangerous. Death is held there, on the inside skin of the pot, and twisted magic made to serve the gods' will. Never touch the inside. Ever. If you touched the inside and a glyph on the outside at the same time, the magic would become twisted, perverted, and unpredictable. There is no telling what would happen."

Hili absorbed this for a moment, then asked. "Why would I do that?"

"I don't know. I'm just telling you, don't do it."

Hili could bear it no more. "Tell me how you know the demon will rise soon?"

"Have you heard of Germania?"

"No."

Vitus raised an eyebrow. "I'm surprised the demon hasn't made an appearance there yet, but he soon will. You see, giants live there. Men head and shoulders above any centurion. They shave the sides of their heads and dye their yellow hair white so that it looks like the mane of a warhorse. They fight naked, or nearly so, these barbarians. The Legions are frightened, unwilling to fight. Imagine, the Roman Legions, afraid. It's almost unthinkable. Caesar needs something to help him defeat the barbarians, some powerful magic. This is that magic."

Hili couldn't believe this knowledgeable man could be so stupid. "But you can't just release the demon and have him fight your battles. It isn't a pet dog. You can't teach it tricks. The pot can only be opened if the gods will it."

"Caesar will open the pot."

"How can you be sure?"

"Don't you know, my dear? The gods always favor Caesar."

Chapter 18

Kelly

Kelly clicked on the attachment Seth Petbe sent over from the Ware Patriot. When the window opened on his laptop screen, he read the following:

The Ware Patriot, May 2, 1970

Explosion Kills 1, Wounds 2 in Trull Mill

A twenty-five-year-old man was killed yesterday when the torch he was using ignited coal dust in a boiler he was cutting for scrap, fire officials said. Thomas Pontes of Farbank, a scrap metal worker, was cutting through the side of an old boiler in the Boiler House building, abandoned since 1953, with an acetylene torch when the accident occurred, police said.

Pontes was using the torch to cut the boiler, about the size of a school bus, into scrap for salvage. The boiler, long empty, should not have contained enough coal dust to make it ignite, fire investigators said. Two other boilers in the mill had been dismantled and scrapped successfully earlier in the week. The exact cause of the blast is still under investigation.

Police said that the explosion in the boiler ignited Pontes's torch and caused a second explosion, decapitating him and blowing him thirty feet in the air.

Two nearby workers were treated for burns and later released from Trull General Hospital. Pontes is survived by his brothers

Floyd Pontes, a student at St. John's Seminary in Boston, and Jacob Pontes, 14.

Kelly leaned back in his chair and rubbed his eyes. So, Pontes's brother was killed in the Boiler House, killed by the boiler that still sat there. Had to be the same one. The Gottschalk boy in '83 was killed in that boiler, and Floyd Pontes investigated. No wonder he was acting funny about the whole thing. Pontes's words came back to Kelly: "The sheer weight of what I know that you don't would send the Bridge Street Bridge to the bottom of the Nipwìmâw." The sheer weight. Kelly was beginning to understand that weight. Pontes's brother, Freddie Gottschalk, now Casey, all killed or missing in that mill, and Pontes was wrapped up in all of it somehow. Kelly wondered how Pontes had gone from being a seminary student when his brother was killed, to a fire investigator working cases that involved the same mill that killed his brother in 1970.

Pontes had told him he was the last man to threaten anyone. Now that Kelly knew Pontes had been a seminary student, a man of the cloth, he thought he understood why. If that were so, then Pontes's warning to stay away from the Boiler House had to be taken at face value. The Boiler House killed people, and Pontes knew it better than anyone. Any old fire-damaged building was dangerous, but the weight of Pontes's words, the weight of what Pontes knew but wasn't saying, pointed toward some darker unspoken danger. Kelly couldn't deny that the building gave him the fucking creeps. He also couldn't deny

The Pull

He wondered if Casey felt it, too. Why else would he hole up in such a place if not for... that? It was as if the boiler inside that old mill was an iron Venus fly trap that made his reptile brain want to climb into its hungry steel maw.

All right, this is ridiculous. It's late, you're tired, and you're creeping yourself out. Boilers and old buildings didn't pull anything. They weren't hungry. And defrocked priests turned firefighters didn't run around warning people away from haunted furnaces.

It was the first time the word 'haunted' had reared its ugly head in his thinking. That led to another thought about Pontes. Maybe that's exactly what Pontes was doing. If Pontes were 17 in 1970, he would be past retirement age now. Did Pontes quit seminary school to learn about fires and understand the circumstances surrounding his brother's death? Unable to do so, was he also unwilling to retire?

"Jesus, Kelly," he said aloud, "you've gone around the bend. Go to bed." As he brushed his teeth and got undressed, Kelly kept thinking about Pontes. He said he had a wayward brother, too. Did the wayward brother fit into this somehow? Wayward... wayward how? A drunk like Casey? Driven to drink by the death of his brother? Kelly realized he'd gone pretty far afield in his thinking. He climbed into bed and turned out the light.

The darkness closed in around him, enveloping him, pushing him down like a leaden blanket. His throat squeezed the air in and out of him. The old brick wall at the head of his bed was rough and unforgiving under his fingers. He was in another old mill, not so different from the Boiler House. He wondered if there'd been deaths in this mill before they turned it into lofts with hefty price tags. When sleep wouldn't come, Kelly sighed, slid into his slippers, and headed for the cello. The bow lay ready.

Kelly always rosined it after he practiced, so if inspiration struck, he wouldn't have to break his creative stride.

He slid the horsehair across the wound metal. The instrument groaned out an experimental low G. The deep rich tones crept from the sound hole and slunk for the darkened corners of the loft. Kelly followed the imaginary trajectory of the notes and found there the trace outline of a mill girl. The image, there and gone in an instant, must be the product of his musings and imaginings moments before, in the bedroom. Had he not invoked the ghosts of mill girls, this apparition wouldn't have materialized. Kelly shook it off as imagination, but he put the cello down out of superstition.

He couldn't ever remember feeling so alone. There was no one to talk to about this, about anything. The ache of his empty arms traveled to his heart. He wanted, needed, the closeness of another human being. The half-hearted thought of going to the bar crossed his mind. He dismissed it. There was no comfort in the gay bars at this hour. No companionship. In the middle of the night, just before closing, the bars were full of 'icky guys,' just looking for a free drink and a bathroom blowjob. Kelly could take care of his sexual needs on his own without all the self-esteem-killing grossness. He just wanted to feel close to someone.

In the morning, he was up and out early, prowling the streets, looking for Casey. He showed Casey's picture to a panhandler on the corner of Bramble Street, but the man only shook his head. The weight of despair pushed down on Kelly. He pointed the car toward Dunkin' Donuts, but stopped along the curb outside Saint Mary's.

A homeless man descended the church's granite steps carrying a black garbage bag.

How could he be so stupid? Why hadn't he checked with Father Murray two days ago? Father Murray was a soft touch and could be counted on at any hour to provide clothes or food for the homeless who agreed to spend a little time talking and praying with him.

Kelly shut the car off and ascended the steps to the towering stone and stained glass cathedral. He opened the large arched door in time to see Father Murray's stooped form shuffling down the sanctuary aisle toward the door to the rectory. Kelly crossed himself (old habits die hard) and entered. "Father?" Muted echoes of his thin voice drifted through the vaulted rafters.

The old priest turned. "Hello, yes?"

"Could I have a word?"

"Of course," Father Murray said, coming back down the aisle. "Is that Kelly Papas?" he asked, squinting through thick horn-rimmed spectacles.

"Yes, Father."

"It's been a long time, Kelly, too long."

"Yes, Father," Kelly said, looking down. This was why he hadn't come right away. The guilt. For Kelly, it was like a visit to the dentist. In order to get his toothache taken care of, he'd have to endure a lecture on his poor dental hygiene habits. At Saint Mary's, in order to get his heartache taken care of, he'd have to endure a lecture on his lack of spiritual hygiene.

"What can I help you with?"

"I'm looking for Casey. I was wondering if you'd seen him?"

Father Murray studied the ceiling for a moment. "Why?"

"Because he's my brother. Because I'm worried about him."

"Have you forgiven him?"

"I—what?"

"Have you forgiven him, Kelly?"

"I guess. I mean, for what?"

"You know what."

"Has he been here?"

"Before I answer your question, I'll hear your confession."

"No. I don't have time, I have to find—"

"Don't lie to a priest. Come." Father Murray turned and walked to the confessional without a backward glance at Kelly. He entered his appointed side and closed the door, leaving Kelly alone in the sanctuary.

This wasn't going the way he'd expected at all. Kelly sighed. He entered the penitent door and sat on the bench in the close little booth. The smell of incense and dust brought back memories of his early teens. He felt very much like a thirteen-year-old boy as he faced the priest on the other side of the window. "Father Murray, please—"

"*Bless me, Father, for I have sinned,*" the priest prodded.

Kelly sighed. "Bless me, Father, for I have sinned. It's been..." he had no idea how long it had been since he'd sat on this bench, "... a long time since my last confession."

They did the verbal dance dictated by Catholic canon, and then Kelly told Father Murray about the fight with Casey and subsequent eviction of his brother from the loft. He spoke about his feeling that Casey was in the old mill on the night of the fire.

When the ritual was complete, Father Murray was silent for a time.

Kelly squirmed.

"Have you forgiven him?"

"Yes, I think so."

"Good. God has forgiven him, and God has forgiven you, too. Now you must forgive yourself. If Casey was in that fire, it wasn't your fault. He was there because that was God's plan for him, just as it was God's plan for you to come see me."

Kelly opened his mouth to say that he didn't believe God scripted his life, thought better of it, and shut it again.

"For your penance, you will come to mass tomorrow morning at ten o'clock."

Kelly started to protest.

"Are you going to argue with me? Here? In the confessional?" Murray raised a thick eyebrow, a trace of a smile on his lips.

"No, Father."

"Good. Now come, let's have a cup of coffee together. I'll tell you what I know about Casey."

Kelly nodded. The two men stepped back into the sanctuary through their respective doors. Kelly followed the stooped priest into the rectory.

Chapter 19

Casey

Blood, pouring, spurting, dripping down into a new body, carrying Casey with it. Not again! He was running, or rather, the body he inhabited was running. He was following others who were running, too. They were in a long wooden tube. Rain hammered on the planks above and dripped down between the cracks. The boy swiped an arm across his face to wipe away the rivulets of water. Wet clothes chaffed his thighs like a woolen cheese grater. He was short this time, eye level with the bottoms of the occasional windows to his left. Each one showed the deluge outside, and through the gray curtain of rain, the Boiler House.

The Nipwìmâw thundered at the old wooden bridge, which shuddered and trembled as chunks of river ice bashed against the upstream side. Casey's feet splashed through the rising water inside the walkway. The floor underneath was slick on the worn leather soles of his shoes.

"Hurry, boy!" A man dressed in work pants, suspenders, and a flat cap ran past.

Nineteen thirties. Before the steel bridge.

The wet slap of dozens of running feet echoed through the covered walkway.

"Faster! The water's coming up!" someone shouted behind him.

Water rose halfway up his shoes. The roar of the flood grew louder. The bridge groaned. The timbers swayed under Casey's feet.

"Go! Go! Faster, damn it!" someone shouted.

The gray light of the storm at the end of the walkway grew larger. Closer. Closer. He emerged from the walkway and didn't slow until he passed through the door to the Power House. The giant steam engines on either side of him were silent and still. Ahead of him, the workman he'd followed through the bridge walkway slowed to a trot. A line of men stood at the windows, looking out at the river. The boy shouldered his way through the forest of soggy backs and peered over the sill. The Nipwìmâw was higher than Casey had ever seen it. Chunks of ice floated down the river and hammered at the side of the bridge. Just for a moment, so fast that Casey couldn't be sure he saw it at all, a man floated by, clutching a clay pot with glowing purple markings. Not good.

"Folks must be crazy trying to cross that thing today," someone above him remarked.

"They don't want to go hungry," another voice said. "I came to try to save this place. Don't want to be on the breadline tomorrow. There ain't enough jobs in the WPA for all of us."

The boy watched from the safety of the Power House's thick brick wall as the bridge bucked and swayed. The black torrent of the Nipwìmâw lashed its wooden sides. The slate gray sky heaped an insulting deluge on the injuries caused by the river.

"All right, enough gawking!" a voice boomed behind him. "If we want to save this place and have jobs tomorrow, then we'd better get to it."

The crowd turned away from the window and faced a portly man with an enormous mustache.

"Two teams," mustache man bellowed, "First team, carry everything that isn't bolted down and bring it upstairs." He pointed to the stairs with a wrench. "Second team, make sure the boilers and engines are as sealed up as we can make them, then cover everything the water can hurt with grease. Every valve, every shaft, every door handle, all of it. Now I know there aren't this many people who work in the Power House, so if you don't work in this building, get to the building you *do* work in and... um, get to work!"

The boy slipped through the murmuring crowd and entered the Boiler House. Casey quailed as he caught sight of boiler #2, lined up with the others like a long black nightmare. The room was cool, like the air outside. No one shoveled coal into hungry boilers. Instead, workers bustled around the room, gathering tools and equipment and lugging them up a set of iron stairs by the window.

"Daniel!" a voice rang out near the boilers.

Casey's host turned and hurried toward a tall, thin man in a shabby suit. "Yes, Mister Jones?"

So, Daniel this time. This time. Jesus.

Why the fuck was he in another body? Again?

"When I say it's time to go to higher ground, you go. No arguments. Deal?" Jones held out a bony hand to the boy.

"Deal." Danny shook Jones's hand.

"All right. Get what you can carry and take it upstairs."

Danny did as he was told, gathering tools and clanking up the rattling iron stairs. With each trip, he stared out at the dark, raging waters. Ice piled up against the wood-clad side of the bridge.

Casey searched for a plan, some way to stop this kid from dying, and in the process, hopefully, free himself. Before Pontes, he'd thought all he had to do was stop his host from entering the boiler, but now, well, apparently, just being in the vicinity of that evil hunk of iron put the boy in danger, put *him* in danger. As with Pontes, Casey didn't interfere with the kid's actions. He saved his efforts for a time, which would surely come, when the boy connected with boiler #2 in some way. The trouble, he discovered with Pontes, was recognizing the moment, and acting.

Each time the boy's gaze fell across the old boiler, bottomless black terror welled up inside Casey's consciousness. Images of flaming skulls with jagged teeth sneered at him. "You're gonna burn!" echoed through his mind. Other times, a ghostly effigy of his twin dangled from a flaming rope. He could still feel the soles of Freddie's shoes boiling into the flesh of his feet.

A deep rumbling sound came from outside the mill's rain-spattered windows. A monstrous rending of wood followed.

"It's the bridge!" a voice rang out among the pandemonium.

Danny ran over in time to see the blocks of ice piled up on the side of the bridge push straight through. The wood planks closed around the ice like broken wooden teeth swallowing a dirty marshmallow. Then the entire structure fell into the dark waters and floated downstream in tangled chunks. Shouts and cries erupted from the workers lined up against the window.

"That's it!" Jones shouted. "Everyone out! Make for the bridge at Nipwìmâw Street, then up the hill."

"That'll be underwater, too," someone called.

"They should have shut and closed the locks," Jones answered. "Go! Now!"

People ran toward the door opposite the Pickering House. Wind howled in, pushing back on the door and the panicking crowd. Danny tried to keep up, but he tripped over a pile of loose coal. Someone stepped on his hand. He tucked himself into a ball to avoid being trampled.

"Calm down, you bastards!" Jones yelled.

Hands gripped Danny's coat and hauled him to his feet. He turned to see that they belonged to Jones. "Go on with you, boy," Jones smiled sadly. "You did good today. I won't forget."

Yes, for the love of God, get out! Casey yelled in the boy's head. Go!

"Aren't you coming, Mister Jones?"

"I'll be along in a bit; I just have a few things to button up."

"I want to stay and help."

NO! You fucking fool, kid! Go! Casey screamed.

"We had a deal, remember? No arguments. Go! Hurry! Catch up with the others."

"Okay. You'll come soon?"

"I'll be right behind you in a minute or two. Go on!"

Casey knew this was his moment. He focused on getting the boy's feet moving. It worked. Danny ran as if the hounds of hell were at his back, and, Casey supposed, that wasn't far from the truth. On State Street, Casey could see the group of workers from the Boiler House turn onto Bridge Street, heading away from the river. They disappeared around the corner. Casey pushed the boy to run faster. Every step away from the Boiler House brought an increasing sense of triumph.

Seconds later, a wall of water roiled down Bridge Street. The water pushed white chunks of ice, splintered planks, and bodies to the top of the seething wave and dashed them against the cobblestones as it hurled its fury forward. The wave spilled some of its wrath onto State Street, gnashing its black waters toward Danny.

Casey let go of the boy's running legs as if he'd had the wind knocked out of him. An evil face sneered in the churning water. The Skeleton Man's face. Despair gripped him.

Danny turned around and ran back toward the Boiler House. No escape. Whatever lurked there, whatever was killing the bodies Casey inhabited, had no intention of letting him escape.

Danny dashed back into the mill and slammed the door behind him.

"What are you do—" Jones began.

"Water's coming," Danny panted, racing for the stairs.

Jones dropped the box he was carrying and followed.

Danny's feet pounded the iron treads. Jones's footfalls clanged behind him, audible even over the cacophony of the river and the rain.

Glass exploded below them as the angry river burst through the windows. A chunk of ice the size of a car smashed into the side of the stairs. The bolts that held the stairs to the brick ripped free. Metal groaned. The stairs listed toward the center of the mill.

Danny screamed.

The stairs tilted further. The vibration from the bending metal traveled up the handrail into Danny's fingers. River water swirled through the mill. The stairs fell. The top step landed on top of boiler #1 with a clang that rattled Danny's teeth. Jones flew into the raging waters. Danny scrambled up the stairs, now on their side, using the balustrades of the steps like a ladder. He climbed onto the rounded top of the boiler, dropping to his hands and knees on its slick metal surface. He called out for Jones above the din of the rushing waters and debris banging against unseen obstacles underwater.

A voice, faint and weak, called from somewhere in front of the boiler. Danny advanced toward the sound, slipping and sliding on the wet-slick metal. Casey intervened and dropped the boy's body onto his belly, making him crawl across its black surface like a drowned lizard. Danny peered over the edge.

Jones thrashed furiously in the water about twenty feet away.

"Mister Jones!" the boy called.

"Danny!"

"I'll come help!"

No, you fucking won't! Casey focused on holding Danny's feet to the spot.

"Stay there, boy. I'm stuck on something underwater. Don't come in. You'll get stuck too, and the water is so cold. You'll never get warm again."

"But I can—"

"Stay there!"

"O-okay." He looked at the water swirling over the sills of the great arched windows, then back at Jones.

"I have to go under for a few seconds to pull with both hands, okay? I'll be right back up." Jones stared at the water swirling around his chest as he drew in a deep breath. Then he plunged into the black water and was gone.

Each second hung in the air like a drop clinging to the top of a watery hourglass. No bubbles in the black spot where Jones disappeared. No ripples.

Casey started to give up hope.

"Hail Mary full of grace," Danny whispered, "the Lord is with thee. Blessed art thou among women and blessed is the fruit of thy womb Jesus. Holy Mary, mother of God, pray for us sinners now, and at the hour of our death—"

Jones's head and shoulders shot out of the water. He gasped and sucked in air.

Amen, Casey finished.

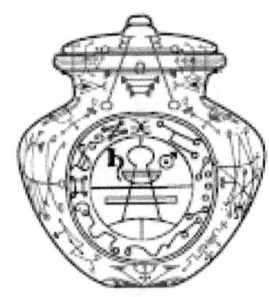

Chapter 20

Hili

Hili came out of the black into a man's body. His breath steamed into the chill gray dawn. He sat on a horse in a small clearing amid a vast dark forest that stretched away and disappeared into the distance on either side. A short way ahead, the woods cleared onto a plain of gentle hills that ended on the banks of a distant river. On the plain, two camps just a mile apart faced each other in the tall grass; two hills of ants, one black, the other red and gold. A small knot of men gathered around Hili's host, who held the pot in arms bedecked in hand-tooled gold bracers.

"But Caesar," one of the soldiers said, "the Germans are twice our number, and each one a head taller with longer reach."

"The tribes of Germania," the body she inhabited started, "may be gathered, but they are far from united under this Suevi King, Ariovistus. Moreover, they are men, and often naked men at that. Are you telling me you can't go forth with armor, shield, and spear to kill a few naked men?" Hili tried to turn the man's body, but she did not have control. Rather, she inhabited him only as a passenger.

"But Sire," another among the circle began, "even the dauntless Gauls fear the Germans."

"So the Gauls, whom we have decimated to near extinction, are afraid of these unclothed savages? I assure you, the Gauls are now more afraid of the Roman Legions than they ever were of the Germans, and the Germans will soon know why. Now, priest, how does this magic work?"

"All you have to do, Sire, is open the pot. The magic will enter you. Vitus's scrolls say that you must only open it as the battle is joined, for the magic inside is difficult to control."

"You will accompany me to the front, priest. It is time. Manius, form up the Legions."

The group of Romans rode out of the forest clearing and onto the plain under a pot-ash sky. They diverged as they passed a large fortified Roman camp, with Caesar, his guards, and the priest riding on toward the front line.

At the bottom of a gentle slope, a second Roman fort stood overlooking the German camp some quarter-mile distant. In contrast to the Roman's, the German camp was merely a collection of wagons circled around what Hili estimated to be at least seventy thousand barbarians and their wives and children. Turning back, she watched as Roman Centurions, Legionaries, and Cavalry formed up in three long lines, each a dozen soldiers deep. Then, as the last of the Romans fell into formation, Caesar opened the pot.

Thunder exploded, then rolled across the battlefield. Rain fell in ponderous drops.

Hili became Caesar's shadow as the smoke escaped the pot and entered the General's nose. His eyes blazed crimson as he dropped the urn onto the trampled grass and surveyed the Germans lining up against him in the distance. Hili, weak and spindly in the cloud obscured light, stared up as the great

General turned to his lieutenant and said simply, "Charge!" On this command, the Roman trumpets sounded.

"Sire, the javelins, the missile attacks!" The lieutenant called after Caesar, but it was too late. Milcom had Caesar now.

The Legions roared as they advanced. The hoofbeats of the cavalry thundered across the plain and shook the earth. A gray curtain of rain fell on the soldiers and plinked on their armor.

The Germans answered, screaming with such intensity and volume as to block out the noise from the advancing Romans.

Caesar grimaced wickedly as he ran, outpacing the horses.

Then the Germans dashed forward, and before Hili could fully grasp what was happening, she was entangled in a sea of hairy, wet, naked bodies.

At first, Hili wasn't sure these were men at all, but maybe some kind of beast. They were as pale as spirits in the moonlight, with skin so translucent, Hili could see their blood pumping in blue streaks underneath. It wasn't until they screamed, flailing axes and swords, that Hili recognized them for what they were.

Caesar slashed into the Germans. They reared back under his vicious blade. Moments later, Caesar's troops were at his side, swords flashing and slicing into naked German flesh. As the Suevi warriors fell amid the stink of sweat, urine, and the lime water they used to bleach their horse-mane hair, the survivors formed up into squares. Each square had sixteen men to a side and formed both walls and a ceiling with their rough wooden shields. Caesar leaped on top of the formation, lying on their wet-slick shields and thrusting down into the press of men. The center of the German phalanx collapsed. Caesar, screaming unintelligibly, fought his way from the inside out. He emerged moments later, spattered in gore with an ear between his teeth.

The Romans cheered at the sight of their great General emerging from among the barbarians. The sounds of battle around the General intensified.

Caesar spat the ear into the shadow Hili inhabited, and as before, with each drop of blood, Hili became more and more corporeal. Equal parts disgusted at the spraying blood and heartsick at the loss of life, Hili vowed she would find a way to stop the demon. She would no longer wait for the demon to emerge, kill countless men, women, and children, then dutifully return it to the pot. The time she'd spent as a hapless pawn of the ancient nameless gods of creation was over. She was Hili, the oldest woman in history, and now, a demon fighter. It might be too late this time, but she swore a mental oath that she'd find a way to end all this death the next time the lid came off the pot.

Caesar never let up. He leaped atop the shields of the next square formation of German barbarians and hacked away with his sword until he made a hole. In the center, he faced a German twice his height clad in bearskins. Caesar's sword hacked the giant's shield nearly in two before becoming hopelessly stuck. The barbarian howled, showing a patchwork of blackened teeth, and cast the shield aside. He bore a club that more resembled a small tree. The great wooden bludgeon whistled past Caesar's ear. Caesar jumped up, wrapped his arms around the giant's neck, and bit deep into the startled barbarian's jugular. Blood spurted from the massive neck and fell like rain on his companions. Caesar let go as the big man fell, and taking up the giant's club, rained blunt violence down on the barbarians surrounding him.

Though the German tribesmen were superior in numbers and size, the exploits of their General buoyed the Romans. This, along with superior discipline and tactics, pushed the mixed tribes of Germania back toward their camp of circled wagons.

As Caesar rained down an arc of death with the giant's club, the remaining barbarians in the phalanx broke ranks and ran. Cheers rose again from the Legions as more and more barbarians gave up the fight. Some ran for the camp, some for the river. Caesar dropped the club, pulled his sword free of the fallen barbarian's shield, and gave chase. The fleeing Germans were no match for the demon-induced speed of Caesar's legs. He cut down the fleeing tribesmen as they limped, bloodied, for the scant safety of their circled wagons.

The camp offered little protection for the fleeing combatants and proved more of a hindrance than a help. Caesar, filled with unbridled demonic violence, sliced through the defeated soldiers and the women who tried to help them past the wheeled barrier. As the Legions caught up with their general and entered the camp, the inhabitants fled toward the river with just the clothes on their backs.

Hili's usual feelings of despair and disgust at such a spectacle turned to resolve and burning anger. She concentrated her will on leaving Caesar's shadow and entering the general's body to battle the demon directly. Caesar's victims' blood that fell into her shadow strengthened her, even as the rain diluted it. Her shadow-self crept up the General's legs, but she lacked the power to move higher. Blocking out all sensation, Hili pushed her will upward and inward, yet even so, she couldn't penetrate the possessed body of the Roman General.

"Hili, stop. Do not interfere," the whisper of Nigmah's voice came on the wind.

Hili struggled on, paying her brother's otherworldly warning no heed.

Caesar pressed forward, slicing through the fleeing barbarians. Bodies littered the grassy plain, turning it from lush green to crimson. The screams of men, women, and children alike pierced the bitter twilight as the Romans pushed the fleeing barbarian hoard toward the black waters of the river. Most never made it that far.

Hili continued to struggle, desperately trying to gain access to Caesar's body so she could stop the bloodshed. She cursed the gods, the demon, and the blood-slick grass as she inched her shadow up Caesar's body, aiming for his mouth. She hoped that perhaps if she could get the demon to swallow his own shadow, she could fight the evil creature for dominance of the Roman General's body. The blood she'd absorbed thus far in the battle didn't afford her the strength to make the climb. The killing continued.

As Caesar approached a pair of women, better dressed than the rest of the barbarians, a voice called out from behind.

"Sire, those are King Ariovistus's wives! Surely they would better serve as hostages or sla—" Whoever the speaker was, he had no time to finish.

Caesar sliced through the two women in one stroke, severing their spines and leaving their bodies in a mismatched jumble of parts.

A scream rose above the din of battle. A kingly barbarian in a small boat stood and shouted words in a tongue Hili didn't understand.

Caesar reached the river ahead of his Legions. He turned and slashed at the few remaining Germans still able to crawl into the water and either swim across or drown trying. Hairy, half-dressed tribes-people piled up at the General's feet, eviscerated, disemboweled, and dissected. Ropes of intestines looped from one corpse to another, and the stink of bile and shit overpowered the bitter scent of blood around the General.

One of the last barbarians to limp to the river readied his sword as he approached Caesar.

Naked save for a badly splintered shield and bloodied sword, the barbarian towered over Caesar. And when the great General turned his blood-filled eyes toward the German, the barbarian uttered these words, "Der Ungeisthasse!"

Instantly, Hili was inside him. "Harken, Demon. He who is known as Der Ungeisthasse!" she shouted. "Return to your prison. Diminish, and await destruction at the hands of the least. By pride, shalt thou be undone, by shame, vanquished. Enter the vessel."

The gore covering Caesar popped, sizzled, and turned to smoke. The demon spoke through his mouth, his words hissing like the blood evaporating from the General's armor. "Gottschalk, I see you. I will remember."

Without pausing to consider what the demon's words meant, Hili picked up the pot and lid at her side and held it out. Once again, the blood-turned-smoke funneled into the pot, and, when it was done, blood coated the lid. Hili sealed the vessel.

The General stood, dumbfounded for a moment.

Hili ran for the river. She dared not look back until her feet splashed into the black water.

Caesar stood watching her, still dazed.

The cold, rushing water swirled around her. Using the urn as a buoy, Hili let the current push her downstream, out of range of the Roman archers that peppered the waters with red-feathered arrows.

When at last she reached the far bank, bedraggled and half-drown, she got up and ran, fearing the Romans would soon mount a pursuit. Hili concentrated only on running, only on the ground disappearing under her feet.

Strong arms reached out and stopped her. Ariovistus. The kingly barbarian yelled from the boat.

"Gottschalk, what is this?" The King reached for the vessel in Hili's arms.

In that moment, the vicious slaughter of the King's wives as they ran away came to mind. Maybe she wouldn't try to stop the demon next time. If it had come to the hands of this king of murdered wives and children, maybe this time she'd let it avenge them.

"Gottschalk? What is this pot?" Ariovistus asked again, stopping short of grabbing the urn.

"Salvation," Hili answered, then faded into the black.

Chapter 21

Kelly

Kelly sat on a scratchy red couch in Father Murray's apartment in the church rectory while the priest put the coffee on. He leaned back against the afghan that adorned the back of the couch. Its concentric rings of green, orange, and black, so ugly that Kelly wondered if the old priest was color blind. The rest of the apartment was outfitted in once respectable furnishings worn down to the nub by one cleric after another.

"So," Father Murray handed Kelly an 'I heart God' mug filled with unexpectedly aromatic brew, "Casey *was* here."

Kelly stopped with his mug almost to his lips. "He was?"

"Yes."

"When?" Kelly could hardly control his excitement. Maybe his brother came here after the fire.

"Let's see... it's Saturday, so I'd make it Tuesday."

"Oh," Kelly said. He sipped his coffee to hide his disappointment. The coffee, at least, was delicious.

"He told me about the falling out you two had. That's how I knew."

"You tricked me into confession."

"Tricked?" Murray put a hand to his heart. "Never. I helped you to help yourself. Anyway, I encouraged him to get treatment.

I told him I'd drive him myself. I told him I'd find an AA meeting." The priest sighed. "In the end, I gave him an old herringbone coat and eight dollars."

"He probably just drank that money up," Kelly said, sullenly studying the threadbare area rug under his feet.

"Don't you think I know that, Kelly? Do you think I'm so naïve? The way I see it, this way, he didn't have to do something wrong to get the money. Steal or who knows what. It cost me eight dollars to save him, and maybe someone else, a lot of trouble. Pretty small price for that."

"Are you trying to make me feel guilty about the thing with him looking at my bank accounts, Father? He was going to steal a *lot* of money."

"Oh, hang the bank accounts. What I'm getting at, is that his drinking isn't your fault, and it isn't my fault. If you hadn't kicked him out that night, he might not have come home the next night, or the night after that. Only God or Casey can help him now. And right now, Casey doesn't want help. Not a single thing would be different if you let him stay that night."

"But the fire—"

"—would have happened anyway. If he had something to do with that fire at the old mill, there's no one to blame but Casey. You didn't send him there, and you didn't light the match. And this is important, Kelly, if he was there, it's all part of God's plan for him, just as coming here was part of God's plan for you."

Kelly sipped his coffee to avoid scoffing at the priest.

Father Murray smiled sadly. "It's true whether you believe it or not."

"What do you know about that old mill, Father?"

Murray sighed, got up, and opened the curtains. Pale clouds obscured the sun. Gray light fell on the worn carpet. He stood looking out the window, hands clasped behind his black button-down shirt. "I know it's an eyesore, has been since before Thomas Pontes died."

"Do you know about Freddie Gottschalk?"

"I do."

"Don't you think it's strange? All these deaths?"

"People die. It's part of the cycle God set before us, but we rise again through Christ."

"You didn't answer my question."

"No."

"Well?"

"Just between us, Kelly, that place gives me the willies. The way Thomas Pontes died, and then what happened to his brother...."

"The Lieutenant," Kelly offered, searching for the fireman's first name, "Floyd?"

"No. Forget it."

"Father, what about Lieutenant Pontes's younger brother?"

"No, I'll not gossip. It's a family matter. I shouldn't have said anything."

"It's for Casey."

"Don't lie to a priest, Kelly; it's for a newspaper story."

"No, it's—"

Father Murray turned and shot Kelly a stern look.

"It's *also* about Casey, about finding out what happened to him. I won't use Lieutenant Pontes's brother in my story. I swear on the Bible."

"That can be arranged, and you'd better mean it."

"I do."

"All right, Kelly, I'll give you the tiniest sliver of information, something you could find out over coffee in the rec hall after mass—if you ever came to mass. After Thomas Pontes died, his younger brother Jacob snuck into the old place. He was never right after that. Both parents were dead, and Thomas was young Jacob's guardian. Floyd quit seminary to take care of Jacob. Then became a fire investigator to find out who was to blame for his brother's death."

"Did he?"

"Not that I know of."

"I think he's still working on it," Kelly said. "What's wrong with the brother?"

"I can't say more. I've pushed my ethics to the limit already."

"Come on, Father."

"No. If you want to know more, come to mass, stay for coffee, and get it from one of our white-gloved old ladies with the flowers on their hats."

"Sneaky way of making sure I come to mass," Kelly smiled.

"I've been in the God business a long time, Kelly. Turns out I'm good at it."

At mass the following morning, Father Murray delivered a spirited sermon on forgiveness. Kelly felt the priest's eyes seeking him out among the parishioners. He shrank down in his pew. During the hymn, Kelly caught sight of Lieutenant Pontes standing with a man at his elbow. Kelly surmised it was the wayward brother, who, as Father Murray put it, 'wasn't right.' Kelly flicked his eyes toward them now and then during the rest of the mass. He couldn't tell from this distance, in a crowd, without talking to the man, how he wasn't right. All he *could* tell was that the brother had hunched shoulders and looked down most of the time.

After the service, Kelly adjourned to the rec hall in the basement for coffee and donuts. He strode across the worn tiles to the counter, got a cup of java and a plain donut, then stood awkwardly to the side, sipping and nibbling. He searched for a knot of parishioners he'd feel confident joining. There were no faces he recognized.

After a few minutes, Pontes and his brother drew coffee from the large stainless steel urn and moved toward the back of the hall.

Kelly stepped out to ambush them. "Good morning, Lieutenant."

Pontes frowned and fiddled absently with a paisley tie that Kelly was sure had been in Floyd's closet through the fashionable, unfashionable, and now vintage phases of style.

"Just Floyd today, Mister Papas."

"Kelly, please." During the awkward silence that followed, Kelly's eyes shifted from Floyd to his brother, hoping the Lieutenant would take the hint and make the introduction.

Floyd's brother, lips parted, eyes wide, mouthed a single word: how.

"My brother Jacob," Pontes said finally.

"Kelly Papas," he said, extending a hand.

Jacob took it in a dry, limp shake but said nothing. The shock never left his face.

"If you'll excuse us," Floyd said, trying to squeeze between Kelly and the back of a man engaged in conversation to his right.

Kelly had no intention of stepping out of the way, but a hand on his shoulder made him turn and allowed Floyd and Jacob to slip past. The hand belonged to Father Murray. Kelly shot him a look, but the priest only smiled.

Kelly frowned.

"What is it?" Father Murray asked.

"I was trying to—"

"I know what you were trying to do. Come with me; there's someone I want you to meet."

Kelly followed Father Murray to the far wall where a man who looked old enough to have sold Noah flood insurance sat sipping coffee. Kelly glanced over his shoulder to see Floyd and Jacob disappear among the coffee crowd.

"This is Mister VanOwen," Father Murray said loudly. "He worked at the box factory next to the Boiler House. He's also something of a local historian. Mister VanOwen, this is Kelly Papas. He's a newspaper reporter. He's interested in the old Boiler House."

"Oh," VanOwen said in a thin unsteady voice, "seems I recall some Papases that lived up Riverside Ave. Father was an uh...."

"Pedorthist," Kelly supplied.

"... foot doctor of some kind."

"That was my father," Kelly said a bit louder.

"Oh, well then...."

Kelly pulled up a gray steel folding chair.

"Excuse me," Father Murray gave Kelly a knowing smile, then slipped into the crowd.

"So, you're interested in the Boiler House?"

"Yes, Mister VanOwen."

"It's Lars. My father was Mister VanOwen. He was a stoker up't the Boiler House until they shut down after the flood in oh, thirty-six, I believe it was."

"Why did they shut down?"

VanOwen went on as if he hadn't heard the question. "I used to work in the Pickering House next door, 'course that was in nineteen-fifty. It was a box factory by then."

"Why did they shut down the Boiler House?" Kelly asked again, louder this time.

"Well, seems to me it was too expensive to fix after the flood. So the textile businesses all moved down south, where the labor was cheaper. Anyway, that place was a dinosaur; everything else was electric by thirty-six, no need for boilers and steam to run the mills. It was dangerous too. Boilers blew up; people got caught in the machines."

"Were there a lot of injuries in the mills? I've been looking through old newspapers, but I can't find much."

VanOwen considered this for a moment, then said: "There were plenty of injuries to go around, deaths too, but you won't find it in the papers."

"Why not? Did the papers get paid off or something?"

"Well, I s'pose that could be, but more 'n likely they never got wind of it. See, the mills got most of their labor from young girls right off the farm. Looked after them, put them up in nice boarding houses. Made them go to church even. If folks in the countryside got word that it was dangerous, that girls were getting hurt, maimed, killed even, why, they'd never let their daughters go to the mills in the first place. Then the mills would run out of cheap labor. So, soon as someone got hurt, the overseer would whisk them right the hell out of there and into the street, give them a few dollars and tell them to say a carriage or streetcar did it. Anything but a mill accident." VanOwen leaned forward conspiratorially. "The way some tell it, in the worst cases, they'd say a girl lit out for home, and no one would hear from her again. If the parents kicked up a fuss, the mill owners would shrug and suggest that she ran away with a fella."

"That's very interesting, Mister VanOwen, thank you."

"Sure. Not many folks interested in that kind of history anymore, even though those old mills stare them in the face every day."

"Can you tell me anything specific about the old Boiler House?"

"That was haad work. You shovel coal all day, come home, back and arms aching somethin' awful. Not many stayed long. My father said that sometimes guys would just stop comin' to work, or disappear in the middle of a shift. Just throw down their shovels and not come back."

"Any deaths? Anything weird?"

"Well, there was the Pontes brother in... what was that, seventy? Seventy-one?" He leaned in toward Kelly again. "Blew his head clean off the way I heard it. And the Gottschalk boy, of course, disappeared in there."

"I heard about that. What about Pontes's brother Jacob?"

"Well, I don't know how unusual that is. The boy missed his brother. Overcome with grief; he goes down t' the Boiler House. Floyd comes in on the train from Boston after gettin' a telegram and can't find his only living brother. Found him in the Boiler House and dragged him out. Like I said, the boy was overcome. Says he saw his brother's ghost and went on about fire, demons, and the like. 'Course that's all just gossip. What's for sure is that he was in the mental hospital for a long time. Even now, I think he's in a halfway house. Damn sad story. Some people just can't seem to move past that sort of tragedy. Haad to blame the boy.

He'd already lost both parents, then the older brother that was looking after him. Damn shame."

"How did the parents die?"

"Well, I don't rightly remembah. Cah crash, maybe? Nothing t' do with that old mill, anyway. Just a run of bad luck for that family."

"Anything else about the Boiler House?"

"Nothing I can think of right now."

"If you think of anything else, will you call me?" Kelly produced a business card from his pocket and handed it to the old man.

"Why sure."

"It was nice to meet you, Lars."

"Nice to meet you too, Mister uh...."

"Kelly Papas."

"Right, the foot doctor's son."

"That's right," Kelly smiled.

The crowd in the church basement had dwindled down to less than a dozen. Pontes and his brother were nowhere in evidence. Father Murray, seeing Kelly was done talking to VanOwen, came up and smiled. "See, aren't you glad you came today?"

"Yes, Father, thank you for introducing me to Mister VanOwen."

"Was it a good talk?"

"Yes, thank you."

"Good. Three things before you go."

Kelly sighed. He knew that at least one of the items would involve coming back next Sunday. "Okay."

"One," Father Murray held up a finger, "please stay away from Jacob Pontes. Questioning him won't do you much good, and it will upset him a great deal. Understand?"

"Yes, but—" Kelly began. The rationalization machine in his head was already cranking along in high gear. Everything from 'it's for Casey,' to 'preventing others from suffering the same fate as Pontes.'

Father Murray was having none of it. "Your word." The priest's eyes bored into Kelly's.

Kelly sighed. "You have my word."

"Good. Two, come back next Sunday."

"I can't plan that far in—"

"Come back next Sunday, and I'll introduce you to someone else."

"Who?"

"Come back next Sunday."

"You should write for the TV soap operas."

Father Murray grinned. "Who says I don't? Three," he held up a third finger. "Stay away from the Boiler House."

"Why?"

"Kelly," the priest's face was deadly earnest, "if this is a house of God... well, the Boiler House is the house of... something else."

Chapter 22

Casey

Casey stared at Mister Jones through Daniel's eyes. The fading gray light turned the stuck man's skin pale and ghostly. Water rippled around him as his shivers became violent convulsions. Rain, driven by vicious storm winds, pelted the side of Daniel's face. He lay on his belly atop the cold, wet boiler. Water continued to rush through the broken windows. It swirled throughout the mill. Bits of splintered wood, trash, and ice floated on the black torrent. A hat floated by, a fedora with a white feather. It moved as if an unseen man walked under it just below the surface of the flood. The hat stopped in front of boiler #2. It sat perfectly still. Faint lines of current trailed from it, but the hat stood fast in defiance of the moving water. It turned left, right, and sank straight down without a ripple.

Jones watched it too, then said, "Okay, Daniel, I'm going to try to get myself loose again. I'll be right back up, okay?"

"O-okkay," the boy sobbed. But it wasn't okay, not with Casey, and surely not with the boy.

The water rose further still. Only Jones's head and shoulders were still above the rising waters. He took a deep breath and plunged beneath the dark surface.

Casey counted in his head.

Daniel recited the Hail Mary again.

22, 23, 24. The water churned above Jones. Casey lost count. He imagined something monstrous and unseen, fighting with Jones. Maybe the body that belonged to the floating hat, its bloated, drowned arms coiling around him.

Jones's head broke the surface. He expelled black river water in great wracking coughs.

"It's no good," Jones said when he'd got his breath. "It's a coal bin; it's full and tipped the other way. I can't reach it."

"I-I can swim over and get it."

"No, boy, you'll end up stuck too, or freeze to death once you get in the water."

Listen to him, Casey groaned.

"So, what do we do?" Daniel asked.

"We pray they come for us, Daniel."

They prayed together. The water rose. The daylight faded.

When the water reached his chin, Jones said: "Daniel, will you pray with me one more time?"

"Of course, Mister Jones."

"The Our Father, then," he began the prayer. Daniel joined in. When it was done, Jones squinted at the water swirling in through the shattered windows. "All right then. I'm going to try one more time. I..." Jones faltered. When he spoke again, Casey could hear finality and despair in his voice. "I want you to look away, Daniel. You must promise that you won't look until the water reaches that window." Jones pointed to a pane of glass, still intact, about a foot above the water's surface.

"But Mister Jones—"

"Promise me, boy."

"Please don't leave me alone, Mister Jones."

Please, God, don't leave us alone, Casey wailed inside the boy's head. He didn't know what that evil fucking boiler had in store for them. He didn't know if it was the rising waters, the deepening dark, or his awareness that the number of heartbeats Jones had left was counting down. All he knew was he felt it coming. Something evil and malevolent drew closer and squeezed at Casey's heart.

"You won't be alone, Daniel," Jones had to tip his head back and stare at the ceiling so he could keep his mouth above the rising water. "God is here with you."

No, he fucking isn't! Casey screamed.

"Now, promise you won't look."

"I," sob, "promise."

"Good boy," Jones said, drew a breath, and disappeared.

True to his word, Daniel looked away. His gaze fell on boiler #2, and in his fear, Casey was powerless to make the boy turn his head. The boy's vision clouded with tears. The world jerked up and down with the power of his sobs.

Sweet Jesus, it's almost here.

The boy's gaze was stuck on the evil boiler.

Do your worst, you evil fucker, Casey thought, then instantly regretted it. *I take it back. Oh holy fuck, I take it back.* Maybe the cursed thing hadn't been doing its worst. Maybe burning alive twice and having his head blown off was nowhere near the worst that evil thing could do. Maybe up 'til now, it was just toying with him, warming up for the main event the likes of which Casey couldn't imagine, and didn't want to.

The wind slackened so that the rain which had pelted the boy through the window stopped and fell straight down outside. Thunder boomed and rolled away in the distance. The boy flinched and stared at the spot where Jones had been, even though the water hadn't reached the appointed window yet. Blue-white lightning lit the mill.

Jones's blond hair waved on top of the water like long-dead fingers, beckoning.

Daniel turned his face away and stared into the gloom toward boiler #2. Its black rounded form stuck out of the water like a waiting leviathan. Waiting for what?

Another clap of thunder, this one so close the mill shuddered, bashed into the stormy air. A hand, imbued with its own ghastly light, rose from the water between the boilers.

Oh, fuck! Here it comes!

Daniel screamed and looked away. It was full dark now. The lights of Farbank glittered in the distance through the broken windows.

Casey traced the lines of light on Bridge Street and Riverside Ave as a way of comforting himself, desperately trying not to think about what that ghostly hand was doing behind his back.

Lightning turned the vast expanse of floodwater in front of Casey electric blue for a moment. When it was over, the lights of Farbank were gone.

It's here.

The darkness was so complete that Casey thought the boy had gone blind. Time measured out in drops of water falling from shards of broken glass and plinking onto the ruined metal staircase. Gradually, shapes formed in the night: the mill's arched window frames, the swirling waters, the toppled staircase.

The boy turned his head slowly. The hand was gone. The only visible shape, the hunchback of boiler #2, sticking out of the darkness. Casey wondered if the hand had ever been there at all, or if it was some bit of debris forming a ghastly illusion. He trusted nothing, not his senses, and not the boy's. Certainly, not his sanity, that he knew, was gone.

Daniel shivered violently. He lay, still sprawled atop boiler #1. The cold of the metal and his waterlogged clothes ran in his blood to every muscle, sinew, and bone. Outside, the storm quieted. The sounds of the maelstrom were replaced, incrementally, with the sounds of dripping water and a faint hiss. The hiss came from somewhere in the center of the mill. Both Casey and Daniel strained to make out the source, but the darkness was impenetrable.

"Daniel," Jones's voice whispered from the darkness.

Daniel looked at the spot where Jones had drowned. There was nothing to see in the darkness.

"Daaaaneillllllll." Jones's voice whispered.

"M-mister Jones?" The boy's teeth chattered so badly with fear and cold, the words were barely coherent.

No kid, whatever that is, isn't Jones.

Sloshing sounds came from the other side of boiler #2.

"Mister Jones?" Daniel called a bit louder.

No Kid! Casey was beside himself. He knew that evil fucking hunk of iron breaching the black water not ten feet away was trying to swallow him again.

"Daaaannnnielll, it's warm over here," Jones's voice gurgled.

"M-mister Jones?" the boy asked again, squinting into the gloom.

"Yesss, Daniel, I got loose. Now I'm over here where it's nice and warm."

"I-I can't see you. Come out so I can s-s-s-ee." Daniel's teeth knocked together so hard that the noise echoed off the bricks.

"But it's cold over there, Daniel, and it's sooooo warm over here."

"I-I'm afraid."

That's it, kid. Don't listen. Don't believe it. Casey put his energy into holding the kid in place. He concentrated on the wet-wrinkled tips of the boy's fingers against the cold metal.

"Don't be afraid to get warm, Daniel," the ominous gurgling voice switched to a sing-song lilt. "I only want to help. I'm just trying to take care of you, Daniel. Just a quick swim and a climb onto the next boiler, then you'll be warm."

"No. You told me not to. You said I'd get stuck."

"It's such a short swim," Jones's twisted voice cooed, "just a few feet, then a quick climb, and you'll be warm. Very, very warm."

Thunder rattled the mill, shaking loose shards of glass that still clung to the window frames. Lightning followed, illuminating wisps of steam where boiler #2 met the water.

"Daaaaannniel...."

"No! You're a liar. I saw the steam in the water. If I go over there, I'll burn."

Yes, kid! Casey cheered. *Fuck yes! Don't listen. Stay here!*

"Oh yes, Daniel, you'll burn. You'll BURN!" The pale blue tips of ghostly fingers appeared at the top of boiler #2 as whatever had stolen Jones's voice climbed up the other side.

"No," Daniel whispered. Then he shouted. "No! Help!"

"Hello?" a man's voice with a thick Irish brogue called from the night. It was a sane, normal-sounding human voice.

"HELP!" Daniel called again.

A lantern floated in the air outside the windows on the far side of the mill. It illuminated a man in a rowboat floating in the space between the mill buildings. "Who's there?"

"Daniel."

"Hold on, Daniel," the man said.

The boat thumped against the bricks outside. Its prow bashed through the window by the door leading to State Street. The ghostly fingers were gone.

"Who's in there? How many are you?" the man called.

"Just m-me, Daniel Costa."

"All right, Daniel, I'm going to try to get to you. Can you hang on until I get there?"

"Y-y-yes," Daniel called.

Casey was elated. *Take that, you fucking boiler son-of-a-bitch! We're getting saved! SAVED! It took a few tries, but I beat you, you fuck!* He knew his thoughts were premature. They weren't out of the woods yet, but he also knew how the boiler meant to get him this time: it meant to boil him alive in the fetid water or fry him like an egg on its surface, flaying the skin from his body. But help was here now, and Casey wouldn't let Daniel get anywhere near that boiler, no way.

The man knocked the remaining glass from the window with an oar from his boat. The noise made Daniel flinch so violently that Casey had to strain to keep the boy glued to the top of the boiler. "W-what's your name, mister?" Daniel called.

"Seamus Sullivan," the man replied. He scooted to the bow of his boat and held the lantern above his head. "Seems I can't get the boat all the way inside. Can y' swim?"

Casey seized control of the boy's mouth and did his best to make the foreign feeling lips and tongue say the word 'no.' What came out was "ywno." *Good enough.*

Daniel, startled by the sensation of his mouth refusing his commands, slid a little down the side of the boiler.

Casey again launched his will into the boy's arms and fingers and curled them into a death grip on the cold metal.

"Er, well, I suppose I'll just have to come get you then, Danny boy."

"Mister S-s-s-ullivan, I'm scared. I-I've seen things...."

"I imagine you have. A flood is a terrible thing, Danny. All sorts of things can wash away and then wash up again. It'll be all right now; I've come for ya." With that, Seamus Sullivan climbed slowly over the bow of his little boat and into the water. "Oh Jesus, Mary, and Joseph, that's cold!" He held the lantern out before him, moving forward with agonizing slowness.

"Be c-careful, M-mister Sullivan."

"Don't worry, I've been through a lot worse than this, Danny boy." Then, as he sloshed forward, the water nearly up to his neck, he sang. "Danny boy, Danny boy, the pipes, the pipes are calling..." he picked his way around unseen debris on the submerged floor. The path brought him within half a dozen feet of Jones's corpse. During the hours since Jones's death, the water had receded about a foot so that now the man's head bobbed in the murky water, face down, hair dancing like floating worms. His arms stuck straight out as if he'd been crucified.

Seamus Sullivan faltered just for an instant in his song. His blue eyes flicked to Daniel in the lantern's light, and the smile never left them. "From glen to glen and down the mountainside...."

Steady now, Sullivan, nice and easy...

Seamus sloshed his way up beside boiler #1 and stood, lantern held aloft. "Okay, Danny boy, just ease yourself down to me. Get right on my back, and I'll walk you back to the boat."

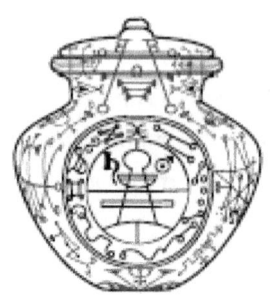

Chapter 23

Hili

Hili floated in the darkness. Not on the water. She *was* the water. Then the sensation of falling, pouring, filling the body of another. Hili found herself standing on an outcrop of rock, looking down at the armies assembled on the plain below. To either side of her, mountain peaks stretched away in the distance. Judging by her height, the look of her hands, and her position to the right of two larger men, she assumed the body was a boy. This boy had moved many layers of wrappings aside to surreptitiously run his finger along the glyphs etched on the pot he carried.

With the armies massed below, Hili knew the demon would come. She could cause the boy to move his finger off of the pot so that she could go back to her dreamless slumber, but curiosity stayed her, or rather his, hand. It was the same curiosity that killed Nigmah and trapped her in this eternal pairing with the pot. She needed to know who the demon would wreak havoc upon next, because, if it were Caesar again, she'd let the beast do its worst.

The man on the far side of Hili, a king, judging by his clothes, addressed the man next to her. "You are sure of this, Gottschalk?"

"King Hermeric, my family has kept this pot safe, hidden from prying eyes, for more than four hundred years, waiting for this day."

"But are you *sure*, Gottschalk? Attacking an entrenched Roman army after crossing the Pyrenees, without siege engines, rested cavalry, reinforcements—if you're wrong, it's suicide."

"Sire, my sons ride with you. The sons of all the Suevi, the Vandals... My lord Hermeric, the sons of all Germania ride with you. I would not risk the lives of all our people if I weren't sure."

"Why did your forefathers not turn this power against Marcus Aurelius?"

"It was not time, or that is what they wrote. The glyphs did not glow purple as they do now. In the time of Marcus Aurelius, we could have won the battle yet not defeated Rome. Now, we can wipe the Roman scourge from Hispania utterly and claim it for our own."

"I do not understand this magic or the thinking of your forefathers. But I do believe in it. Show me the glowing glyphs again; then, we will put the fate of our entire people in the hands of the gods."

Gottschalk turned to Hili, and seeing the boy's hand on the glyphs, he slapped it away. "Don't touch that."

Hili went into the black.

She came back as Hermeric's shadow. He grasped the pot above her. She could hear the shifting of feet and the creaking of leather, a soft whisper on the wind, stretching out in both directions. The sky darkened. Black clouds formed overhead.

The pot lid popped free with a malevolent hiss.

Thunder echoed off the mountains and rolled across the plain.

Smoke left the pot, and every swirling gray particle entered the King's nose.

Hili steeled herself for what was to come. That steel, tempered in her disgust for what the demon had done through Caesar, to King Hermeric's people, would soon be quenched in Roman blood. And for the first time in her thousands of years, Hili was glad of it.

Bloated drops of rain patted into the dirt, but the sound was soon lost in the battle cry of the Germans as they followed the bellowing King across the plain to the waiting pikes of the Roman infantry. Hermeric dashed himself into the shield wall. The strength of the Roman soldiers, who'd grown soft in their pastoral Hispania garrisons, was no match for the possessed Suevi King. Shields splintered into a thousand pieces as the blood magic that coursed through Hermeric slammed into the ranks. The King's sword flashed blue as lightning struck its tip, cutting arcs of hot metal and azure fire through the bodies of the opposing Romans. Their forward ranks shrank back under his otherworldly onslaught. The ranks behind, unable to see through the deluge and the chaos, pushed the forward ranks back into the path of Hermeric's fury.

The demon-powered king broke through the first line of Romans into the no-man's-land between the first and second lines. He doubled back and attacked the back of the first line, pushing the ranks up against the rest of his clan, which battered the Romans from the front. Hermeric sliced through the tightly packed human meat sacks of centurions three at a time, sending blood and gore into the rain, turning the world crimson around him. When he met his clansman, he turned again, weaving back and forth across the line of Romans, creating a quilt of carnage.

The bloody water washed over Hili, trapped in the gossamer shadow of the Demon King. She grew more substantial as limbs and organs rained down on her and made wet plops on the muddy ground. Inside her, the righteous rage against the Romans flowed away in bloody rivulets. The cries of the dying soldiers were so pitiful, so mournful. These men called out for their mothers, their wives, their children, and their gods. These weren't Romans anymore. The first slice of the demon's blade made them no different from the Suevi, the Tyrians, or the Sumerians; these were just men. Sons, husbands, and fathers, spilling their blood for a few coins. These men no more deserved to die at the hands of Milcom than did the Suevi at Caesar's hands, or the Tyrians at Alexander's. The pointlessness of their deaths defending this patch of muddy ground overwhelmed Hili. She saw how wrong she'd been. And as she had on the banks of the river in Germania, she willed her shadow to climb Hermeric and enter him.

The blood splashing Hili as she began her shadowy ascent up the wet-slick armor of the German King brought her a measure of strength. Shadow incarnate, Hili concentrated her will on reaching Hermeric's mouth, entering, then doing battle with Milcom. She no longer cared about the will of the silent and absent gods who'd imprisoned the demon. All her thoughts centered on stopping the senseless bloodshed. She struggled to impose her will on Hermeric's shadow. It wanted to lie flat on the ground or rest on the struggling forms of the Romans dying in a circle around the berserk King.

The forward line of the Roman army collapsed. The survivors ran back to the second line, throwing themselves on the shield wall. The lucky ones slipped in between gaps their comrades made for them. The Suevi, led by the possessed King, rushed onward, driving against the second line of centurions. They crushed the ranks against one another at the point of impact. Again Milcom, working through Hermeric, swung his sword like a paintbrush, coloring everything in his path with blood. The second line collapsed into the third and final line of the Roman armies of Hispania.

Hili toiled. Her dark incorporeal form clung to the demon-infested King like a thin obsidian curtain, creeping up him bit by bit. His body, or the will of the gods, Hili wasn't sure which, pushed against her like an opposed lodestone, repellant and defiant. Still, she climbed, grasping and clawing with insubstantial fingers.

At last, the Roman defenders broke ranks and fled en masse, running flat out across the open plain. Hermeric deftly dodged the cast-off swords, armor, and equipment the Romans jettisoned to make their flight lighter and faster. Few of the fleeing soldiers survived the blood lust of the demon and the hoard at his heels.

Hili reached Hermeric's neck, wrapping her shadowy hands around it and pulling herself toward his chin. Hair by hair, pore by dust-choked pore, she inched her way toward his mouth.

She smelled the underworld in the demon's exhaled breath; it tasted of violence and hatred.

The Suevi chased the remnants of the Roman army to the edge of the field of battle and down the road that led toward a village in the distance. A rustling in the bushes on the roadside caught the King's attention. He veered off and parted the shrubs with the tip of his sword.

Hili reached Hermeric's face, obscuring the monarch's features, making him a hole in the daylight. The gate of his mouth was closed to Hili. She pushed and punched at the wet opening in the King's flesh, but her shadow could not displace the thing that dwelt there. New energy entered her awareness. Two farmers and a boy crouched in the bushes at the tip of Hermeric's sword. As he rammed his sword through the first man, the other gasped, "Pesadelo Vivo!"

"Harken, demon!" It took Hili a moment to realize she was in a body, once again corporeal. The voice, her voice, came from the body she was in. Her mouth moved with the words, and she lent her will to them. "He who is known as Pesadelo Vivo!" she shouted. "Return to your prison. Diminish, and await destruction at the hands of the least. By pride, shalt thou be undone, by shame vanquished. Enter the vessel." She reached out without looking away from Hermeric, and the pot came to her hand.

"I see you, Pontes," the demon spat, "I will remember."

The blood covering Hermeric hissed like fat in a hot pan, then turned to smoke and entered the pot, its slimy gray tendrils licking at the rim reluctantly as the darkness inside consumed it. As before, the blood remaining on Hermeric dripped sideways onto the rim of the lid. Hili slammed it closed.

Hermeric looked bewildered for a moment, then raised his sword.

Without thinking, Hili kicked the King in his stones so hard her other foot left the ground, then she grabbed the boy's hand, and ran.

Behind them, Hermeric bellowed with pain and rage.

They crossed a narrow field, then entered another copse of trees.

"Who are you?" the boy asked as they struggled through the dense brush.

Hili guessed he'd seen ten summers at most, so she tried to fool the boy. But if the boy was already asking, he must know. "I don't understand?"

"Well," the boy said, grabbing Hili's hand and pulling her onto a trail through the brush, "You are not my uncle."

Hili didn't want to lie; she might need to form a friendly relationship with the boy to get the pot to safety. "How can you tell?" she asked. She wanted to know where the boy was leading her, but asking would be admitting that she was not his uncle.

"My uncle is... simple. He only says a few words."

"Where are we going?"

"Back to the farm, to hide."

Hili didn't understand this boy at all. Why was he leading her to safety if he didn't think she was his uncle? So she put this question to the boy.

"You saved us from that soldier. You must be a friend."

"You are not afraid?"

"Not anymore."

"What happened?"

"You saw. They just killed my father."

"He drinks with the gods," Hili said, trying to make the boy feel better.

"I'm not sad. He was cruel. The Romans raided our farm yesterday. They took everything to feed their army. They gave us some coins. When my brother tried to tell them that we'd go hungry... he tried to grab our horse away from them. They killed him."

"That seems to be all they understand." Hili flashed back to Germany in her mind. She almost ran into the back of the boy. He'd ducked into a crouch in some bushes where the path met a road. "But that doesn't explain why you are not afraid."

"I have nothing. No way to feed myself or my uncle. There is nothing left that they can take from me, except my life, which isn't worth much."

Hili dropped into a crouch beside him. She wanted to wrap her arms around the boy. She wanted to tell him that things would get better, that all was well, but she couldn't lie to him like that. "Do you still have the coins the Romans gave you?"

"At the farm," the boy said. "You never told me who you are."

"I'm Hili."

"That's a strange name." He said. "Are you a god?"

"No." Hili almost laughed. "It's hard to explain. I have to get this pot someplace safe, then your uncle will return, just as he was."

"Oh," the boy looked down. "Let's get back to the farm."

"It's not safe," Hili said. "The Suevi will raid the farms."

"There's nothing there to raid." The boy darted across the road and into the brush on the other side.

Hili hid the pot in the bushes there, not wanting to be weighed down while on the run, and followed him. She knew the pot would return to her as it always had. After a few minutes of walking, they came to a small stone house. The boy didn't go inside. Instead, he went to the stick shelter that, from the smell of it, the pigs used to sleep in.

"What is your name?" Hili asked, realizing she was about to shout "Boy!" to get his attention. She didn't know what he was looking for, but she felt vulnerable standing in the open dusty farmyard.

"Xavier."

"We need to go, Xavier. Someplace safe."

"Where?"

"Someplace far away from the Romans and the Suevi."

"Across the sea?" Xavier came away from the sty with a small jingling sack. "The coins the Romans left."

"Tuck that away," Hili hissed. "How far is the sea?"

"Three days walk. That's what I heard. I've never been."

The wind carried distant screams.

"Do you need anything from the house?"

Xavier shook his head.

"Then lead us toward the sea, and it would be better if we could stay off the road."

"I don't know the paths further than the next village."

"Show me." Hili motioned for Xavier to lead, and they set out through the woods.

Hili need not have worried about finding paths away from the road. By the time they reached the next village to the west, they were just two of a stream of villagers heading west on hidden footpaths away from the invaders. Hili grew frustrated at the pace of the other villagers, weighted down with bags and possessions of every description. Xavier began to slow toward the evening. Hili noticed with some wonder that she was fit, ready, and rested, even after a day of walking. "This is too slow," she whispered. "The Suevi have probably already passed us on the road."

"Carry me," Xavier said. "Alfonso is strong. He often carries me home when we are far afield."

"Who?" Hili didn't make the connection until the boy waved a hand at her.

"My uncle," the boy said, "Alfonso Pontes."

Chapter 24

Kelly

On Monday morning, Kelly called Petbe at the Ware Patriot to see how the search for suspicious deaths in the old Boiler House was going, and to pass on the information old man VanOwen gave him about injured workers being dragged from the mill.

"Well shit," Petbe said, "that muddies the waters considerably. Searching for anything that happened in that area is much more difficult, not to mention that it will severely limit what we can print. If the deaths can't be directly attributed to the mill, we'll need an eyewitness."

"Any witnesses will be long dead," Kelly cut in.

"Exactly," Petbe said. "Still, I think this story is worth pursuing. Maybe if we find the right angle, we can dig up relatives or diaries or something."

"I gave my word to Father Murray I'd stay away from Pontes's brother, but you...."

"Let's be very careful with that one," Petbe said. "If we make an enemy of Fire Investigator Pontes by bothering his brother, we might lose a good source. See if you can track down the kids involved in the Gottschalk boy's death. I'll keep digging through the archives. We'll save Pontes's brother as a court of last resort. Maybe we can get this story to print without him."

"Will do." A thought struck Kelly. "Why are you sticking with this?"

"What do you mean?"

"I mean, the angle of the story is thin, it's research and staffing intensive, and it's got a faint conspiracy theory tang to it. Your rivalry with the Trull Chronicle aside, why do this?"

"You're right, Kelly, you know what? Let's forget the whole thing. It doesn't hang together, and it's not worth my time. Good luck, son—"

"Wait—"

Petbe burst out laughing. "Got you!"

"You son-of-a—" Kelly laughed. He wasn't sure he'd laughed at all since Casey went missing, but he laughed now, good and long and loud.

"Seriously, though," Petbe said, "I've got ulterior motives too. See, when I was just starting out, MillCom bought a bunch of houses around my mom's place out by the Ware line. They were putting up that god-awful shopping center over on route thirty-two. Anyway, my mom wouldn't sell. My dad passed away in that house, and mom wouldn't part with it. Finally, some bastard at MillCom greased the right palms at City Hall, and they just took it. Eminent domain. Gave her pennies on the dollar. A lot less than the neighbors who sold to them willingly. Punishment. We tried to sue, but MillCom has deep pockets and a clown car full of slick lawyers. Never went anywhere. So anytime I have a chance to stick it to MillCom and Tyre holdings, I don't pull my punches."

"I'm sorry," Kelly said, unsure of what else to say.

"Not your fault; just a story about an old house and an old woman, both long gone. Let's hope there's still a chance for your brother."

A lump formed in Kelly's throat—Casey. It took him a minute to find the wind to talk around it. "Thanks. Keep me posted."

"Will do, Kelly."

After the call, Kelly paced the loft, trying to think of a way to get the names of the kids involved in the Gottschalk case out of the sealed files. Everything returned to Pontes: the sealed files, the strange brother who'd seen something in the mill, Pontes's investigations of the fires, and the deaths there. There must be a way to get Pontes to talk. He needed an in, and all he could think of was Pontes's brother Jacob and his promise to Father Murray to leave Jacob alone. The problem was that there were giant fucking neon signs pointing to Jacob with the words 'he knows' blinking on and off in Kelly's brain. And though even Petbe was loathe to go after Jacob Pontes, Kelly couldn't get the picture of the man's thin lips mouthing the word 'how' out of his head. He had to stop. This line of thinking was useless.

What he had to do was track down the Gottschalk family. There were fifty or so listings for Gottschalk in the Trull phonebook. He could start at the top, cold calling each one, but put that off in favor of looking for old McCormack Middle School yearbooks online. He jotted a few promising leads down on the scratchpad beside his laptop and was about to start in on the Gottschalk cold calls when his phone rang.

"Have you been in contact with my brother?" Pontes's voice bellowed through the phone when Kelly hit the green button.

"What? No!"

"You better not be messing me around, Papas."

"I'm not. I swear."

"All right. Dunkies, Riverside and Bridge, half an hour."
Pontes hung up.

"What the fuck?" Kelly stared at the phone. "What is this?
A hostage exchange or something?"

Kelly put himself together in clothes that wouldn't look out
of place in Farbank; jeans (designer though), a crisp blue T-shirt
under a leather blazer, and, though he hated it, duck boots for
the slush that plagued New England this time of year. He steered
the old Toyota across the bridge, only craning his neck to look at
the Boiler House's crumbling bricks and broken windows twice
on the journey. He went into the Dunkin' Donuts and spied
Pontes sitting in the corner. Kelly ordered a 'large regular'
(pronounced laaaage regula) and sat across from the stout ruddy
Pontes.

The old man glared at him.

"What?" Kelly blew across the top of his coffee.

"You swear you haven't contacted him in any way?" Pontes's
words were in the form of a question all right, but in the tone of
a statement.

"I swear." Kelly said, "I promised Father Murray."

"Murray?" Pontes growled, "what did he say about it?"

"Nothing. Said it was family business and none of mine."

"Humph. Must have said something, or he wouldn't have
made you promise."

"No," Kelly lied. He decided God wouldn't mind him telling
a half-truth to protect a priest. "I heard a few things from Lars
VanOwen."

"That old blabbermouth. The Devil's going to kick him right back upstairs just to get him to shut up. I saw you talking with him in the church basement yesterday." Pontes sipped his coffee, mulling something over. "All right, then let's go."

"Go where?"

"To see Jacob."

"Lieutenant, what's this all about?"

Pontes sighed. "Okay, look, Jacob is a little off. Has been since...." Pontes stared at some point over Kelly's shoulder. "... our brother died. After seeing you yesterday, he was very upset and insistent that he has to talk to you. He's called me seven times, and the man that runs the home where he lives has called twice, telling me Jacob is... that he has...."

Kelly waited. He took a sip of coffee, burning his tongue.

"... that he's very upset. Now, I think it's a terrible idea, but I love my brother, and if there's a chance that talking to you will make him feel better, I'm willing to take it. But if you aggravate him more, or if I find out you're lying about contacting him...."

"I thought you were the last person to make threats," Kelly said, recalling their conversation in the parking garage outside Pontes's office.

"I didn't make one." Pontes sagged. "I couldn't think of anything. Come on."

Outside, Kelly headed for his Toyota.

"That your car?" Pontes asked, looking disdainfully at the battered, rusted machine.

"I live downtown," Kelly said.

Pontes nodded. "We'll take mine."

Kelly climbed into the red fire department sedan and buckled himself in. The air in the car had the consistency of a lead brick, and as they drove down Riverside Ave toward Bramble Street, it grew heavier. As they rolled past Kelly's childhood home, memories of Casey piled up on top of one another in Kelly's mind, adding to the angst of the moment.

"Can we turn on the siren?" Kelly asked.

Pontes glared at him.

"Just trying to lighten the mood."

"Well, don't."

They turned onto Bramble Street and pulled up in front of a nondescript three-decker house with lime green vinyl siding. No sign or placard marked the building as any different from the other three-decker homes that lined both sides of the street.

"Get in the back and wait here," Pontes said, getting out.

"What? Why?" Kelly thought he was going in to meet Pontes's brother. He'd pictured them sitting and talking in a shabby common room under the watchful eye of some glorified turnkey.

"Just please get in back. I'll be out in a minute."

"Okay." Kelly got out, slid onto the long bench seat in the back, and closed the door on the November chill. The 'ssssshhh' of tires on wet pavement punctuated the ticking of the cooling engine.

The air inside the car grew cold.

A few minutes later, the Pontes's descended the sagging wooden steps and trudged across the slushy sidewalk toward the sedan. Outside the car, Floyd said: "Why don't you sit in back with Mister Papas so you can talk? I'll drive us somewhere quiet."

"Somewhere you don't have to be seen with me," Jacob said.

"It's not like that."

"It *is* like that! It's always been like that. I'm the dirty little family secret."

"Jake, stop. I can't have us seen sitting around talking to a reporter."

"He's a reporter?"

"Yes, so watch what you say."

"I heard that," Kelly called.

"Good," Floyd said, opening the back door for Jacob.

"I always have to watch what I say," Jacob muttered, getting in. His heavy woolen pea coat hissed as it slid across the vinyl. He scraped the slush from his sneakers on the doorjamb, then set them gingerly on the red rubber floor mat as if he were afraid of it.

Kelly and Jacob studied one another. Kelly put the man at maybe fifty-five. Silver stubble stood out on his face and peeked out around the bottom of the watchman's cap atop his head. Dark shadows ringed the bottoms of his wild gray eyes.

After regarding Kelly for a minute, Jacob said: "How are you alive?"

"Jacob," Floyd said from the front seat, "that's no way to start a conversation."

"Shut up, Floyd. I'm a grown man. When are you going to stop correcting me?" As he spoke, Jacob's voice rose in pitch and volume.

"Calm down, Jake. Did you take your pill this morning?"

"See! See! This is exactly what I'm talking about!"

"Okay, Jake, I'm sorry," Pontes said as he pulled out into traffic.

"I didn't take it." Jacob mouthed, then winked at Kelly.

Inwardly, Kelly groaned. He was beginning to doubt this interview would be useful at all. "Let's start again, Jacob. I'm Kelly Papas. Why did you want to talk to me today?"

Jacob's mischievous smile faded. He turned away and stared out the window. When he spoke, his words were slow and hesitant. "I see things sometimes, Kelly. Terrible things." He fidgeted in his seat, but still didn't meet Kelly's eye.

"I'm listening, Jacob," Kelly said, then waited. He didn't feel that grilling the man would do any good, and if it didn't rattle the already unhinged Jacob, a reporter-style interview would almost certainly piss off Floyd in the front seat. Probably lead to him swinging the car around and taking Jacob right back home. It seemed to Kelly that Jacob was in desperate need of validation. He needed to be listened to, and more importantly, believed.

Jacob kept looking out the window away from Kelly as he continued. "When I was a boy, I... um, Kelly, I know this is the long way around, but I need you to understand, so I have to start at the beginning, okay?"

"It's okay, Jacob. I'm here to listen," Kelly said.

Jacob turned then. He searched Kelly's eyes for the intent behind that statement, then smiled weakly and turned back to the window. "I don't remember my father. When I was a boy, my older brother Tom was like a dad to me. We did everything together. We went sledding in King Park in the winter. Fishing by the dam in the summer. We went for ice cream, read lots of books. My brother loved to read." Jacob fell silent, wiped his eyes with the back of his hand, took a deep breath, and went on. "When Floyd went off to seminary, we were even closer. I was kind of a bookish kid and didn't go out much. I guess Tom was bookish too, so it was just the two of us. I'm telling you all this, Kelly, because unless you understand how close I was to my brother, the next part won't make much sense."

"I understand, Jacob, go on," Kelly said, then sipped the cold forgotten coffee in his hand.

"I was at home after school one day. Tom was late. There was a knock at the door; it was a policeman and Father Driscoll. They sat me down and told me Tom was dead. You can't imagine what a shock that was. I..." Jacob swallowed audibly. "Do you know about the five stages of grief, Kelly?"

"A little. I don't remember them all, or the order."

"I know them intimately, Kelly. The first is denial. As I cried into Father Driscoll's shirt, in my ten-year-old mind, I became convinced that they had it wrong. He couldn't be dead. Not my brother. Not Tom. No way. He would never leave me like that. They must have missed him in the confusion after the explosion. Don't forget, I was just a boy."

"I understand," Kelly said. The houses outside the window grew further apart as the car climbed the hill by McCormack Middle School. Floyd parked in the Hillerman Park lot.

"As I lay in the dark that night, staring up at the ceiling, I became more and more convinced that they'd overlooked my brother. I was sure he was up at that mill, hurt, calling out for help, but no one was there to hear him. He had to be. You understand? For a ten-year-old, that's how it *had* to be.

"I got dressed over my PJs and snuck past Father Driscoll, who was sleeping on the couch until Floyd came home from Boston. The whole time I walked to the mill, I could hear my brother calling out for me. When I got to the bridge, I ran. At the mill, there was police tape. I busted through it like a marathon runner. The mill was dark and quiet. I stood in the doorway, panting and listening for my brother's voice. I knew he was there. I knew he'd be calling out to me. I heard him in my head all the way there, but there was no sound. Just silence. So I called out: Tom? Still nothing. He had to be there. He *had* to be. I called out again: Tommy? Then I thought maybe the explosion messed with his ears. Maybe he didn't hear me or recognize my voice or something, so I yelled: Thomas Pontes?

"Then, faintly from the center of the mill: *here!* It sounded weak and raspy. I started to walk toward the voice. A gust of wind behind me blew the door shut, taking the only sliver of light with it. I called his name again. Silence. My footsteps echoed in there like it was the fucking Grand Canyon. 'Thomas Pontes!' I yelled.

"'Here,' the voice groaned. I felt my way forward. As my eyes adjusted to the darkness, I could make out the shape of a big boiler. I called out again. 'Tommy?' This time, the voice answered: 'over here,' it said in a gurgling whisper. I got close to the boiler. I put my hand on the boiler. It was hot. I didn't realize at the time—it should have been cold. I jerked my hand back.

"'Jakey,' the whispering, gurgling voice said. Jakey is what Tom used to call me sometimes. The voice came from the floor, so I looked down and...." Jacob burst into tears. He put his face in his hands.

"Hey," Kelly said, putting a hand on the man's shoulder, "it's all right now."

Jacob flinched as if Kelly had punched him instead. "It's not all right now. It's never been all right. It just keeps fucking happening." Jacob spoke a little more, but Kelly couldn't make it out.

"All right," Floyd said from the front seat, "this is over." He put the car in gear, laid an arm across the passenger seat, and turned his head to back up.

"Nooo!" Jacob yelled. He grabbed his brother's hand. "Let me finish, Floyd. I have to tell him. I have to." Tears ran from his eyes and dripped from the silver fuzz on his jawline. Mucus ran from his nose and across his mouth in clear, thin strings.

"Then get ahold of yourself, Jake."

"Oh fuck you, Floyd. My whole life, people have been telling me to get ahold of myself, take it easy, or try to forget. But it's because you don't believe. It's because you haven't seen what I've seen. Well, now it's my turn. Now. This conversation. The most important conversation I've had since I was ten years old. You are going to shut up for once, Floyd, and let me have this, because this man," Jake pointed to Kelly, "has the answer."

"Oh, I don't think—" Kelly began.

"Just wait 'til I'm done before you say that, Kelly. You have the answer. You might not know it, but you do."

Floyd put the car in park again.

Jacob took several deep breaths, wiped his face on his coat, then returned his gaze to the ball field outside the window. "Next to the boiler," Jacob continued in shuddering breaths, "was a patch of dried blood, black in the moonlight. 'Jakey,' a different voice, then Tom's voice said, 'run!' It was Tom. I know his voice like I know my own name. Once I heard it, I knew the voice that called me over wasn't his voice at all, just a bad imitation. It was the mill's voice." Jacob paused. His hands twitched in his lap, dancing back and forth as if he were pantomiming tying knots in thick rope. "A mouth formed in the bloodstain. It had huge pointed teeth. It screamed: 'Pontesssss!' in a voice like... I don't know...." Jacob's hands moved faster in his lap, tying the invisible rope tighter and tighter. "... like a chorus of children whose feet are being held in boiling water.

"I turned, started to run. Then I tripped and fell on my ass, but somehow I was facing the blood again. The bloodstain rose up from the floor in a black cloud of droplets. I couldn't move. It... it formed the mouth again, not just a mouth, but a whole face. The eyes were like... like cat's eyes. It came at me through the air so fast I couldn't get up. 'You're gonna burn!' it screamed, then it sank its teeth into my leg."

Kelly didn't really believe this part, of course, but he was absolutely sure Jacob believed it, and it was about the creepiest thing he'd ever heard.

As if sensing Kelly's incredulity, Jacob reached down and pulled up the leg of his jeans, and pushed the sock down. "It made that," he said, looking at Kelly as if daring him to refute it.

A jagged scar marked the edges of where a hunk of calf muscle the size of a cowboy's belt buckle was missing from Jacob's calf. In the front seat, Floyd stared straight ahead, facing forward. All Kelly could see were Floyd's gray eyes in the rear-view mirror.

Jacob dropped the pant leg and continued. "I kicked at the thing again and again until it tore away with a piece of my leg in its horrible teeth. 'Give me a kiss, Jakey,' it hissed, gore running down its chin.

"Anyway, the thing I'd tripped on was an old pile of coal. I picked up a piece and threw it. Then I threw another. I started pelting it with coal. "I hate you!" I screamed. Flames shot from the thing's mouth. The air filled with the smell of burning meat. The whole face burst into flames. 'You're gonna burn!'" Jacob's hands danced a staccato rhythm as they tied the invisible rope faster and faster. Then he snapped back into the moment. His hands came to rest in his lap. He looked at Kelly. "I know," then softer, "I know how it sounds. And I know a lot of things in a mill in the process of being scrapped could have cut my leg, but just hear me out." Jacob seemed more composed now that this part of the tale was over.

"Okay," Kelly said. He tried to make his face a mask of compassion. On the inside, he was sorely disappointed that Jacob had turned out to be just a garden variety schizophrenic, not someone who could shed any light on what was really happening at the mill.

"I heard a groan of metal. The door of the boiler swinging open. I stopped with a lump of coal in my hand, ready to throw. Something inside there glowed purple. I swear it was purple. The burning face screamed and disappeared.

"I got to my feet, somehow, but it was almost like it wasn't me. There was no pain in my leg. It was like... like something was pulling me into that boiler.

"I was so scared. I couldn't make a sound. I couldn't stop my feet from moving toward the dark opening of the boiler door. I felt a presence inside. It felt like sewer water, maggots, and dead birds. I can't explain how I felt it... just... inside." Jacob paused. His breath came in jerks, like someone who'd just stopped crying.

"Come on, Jake. Stop doing this to yourself—" Floyd began.

But Jake held up a finger, took a deep breath, and said. "No, Floyd, he needs to know. I need him to know. You both need to know the rest. I kept it from you all these years. Now, you'll see why I can't anymore. Something's changed.

"So... so as I got closer, hands grabbed my shoulders and yanked me back... Floyd's hands."

Kelly looked at Floyd. He just stared straight ahead.

"Oh yes," Jacob said, "j'accuse! See, he'd taken the train from Boston, got to the house, and talked to Father Driscoll and found me gone. He came to the Boiler House. He knew I was there. Claims it was the logical place to look, but was it really? Or was he pulled there the way the boiler was pulling me in? He claims he didn't hear anything, didn't see any glow in the boiler. He says he doesn't believe any of this, but I still wonder.

"See Kelly," Jacob almost smiled, "you had to hear all that, so you'd understand this next part. When I got home, and they finally got me to sleep—"

"Valium was involved," Floyd added dryly.

"I've always felt like that boiler is still trying to pull me in. I can feel it when I see the old mill or get close to it. When I think about it on rainy nights, I feel...

The Pull

"I have dreams. People climb into the boiler, one after the other — a man in old-fashioned clothes, a boy, others. Sometimes, the boiler belched fire between them. Sometimes big torrents of black water poured out of it. I had that dream a dozen times a year, always the same... until nineteen eighty-three. Thirteen years after my brother died, I saw a new boy climb in. He was wearing modern clothes. The next day I find out there was a fire, and a boy supposedly climbed into the boiler, and he was missing."

Kelly stared.

"Coincidence," Floyd said. "False memory, medication. You remembered after you read it in the paper."

"Maybe," admitted Jacob, "but the dreams continued after that, same as before, a dozen or so times a year, except now the last one in was Gottschalk. I'd seen the others, my brother, the Gottschalk boy, all climbing into the boiler... and dying. Then, the other night, I saw someone new climb into the boiler. Then, the next day in the paper, they said there was a fire at the Boiler House."

Kelly sat bolt upright. Gooseflesh stood out on his arms and neck. "Who did you see?"

"Mister Papas, in my dream, I saw you die."

Chapter 25

Casey

It could be a trick. Maybe the Irishman standing below him in the icy black floodwater was an apparition, another tool of the evil fucking boiler. Casey would not, could not, relinquish control of Daniel's fingers, which held the cold metal of boiler #1 in a death grip.

"What's the matter with ye, boy? Slide down t' me now. Be quick, this water's cold, and it's a dangerous bit o' business I'm doing now in a building by a flooded river. Sakes, *in* a flooded river. Come on with ye, lad!"

Casey risked shifting his focus away from the boy's fingers to take over the foreign workings of the boy's mouth. "The other side. I can climb down the broken stairs on the other side."

"Every step is a risk in here, boy. I'll not risk that many more. Now, slide down onto my back, and let's be gone from this place."

Daniel looked down into the light of the lantern the Irishman held aloft. Casey could see through his eyes the freckles that stood out on Seamus's ruddy skin. Red curls spilled out from under a flat woolen cap.

Seamus nodded encouragingly at Daniel, held out a strong meaty hand, and sang again. "Danny boy, the pipes—"

Casey detected no sign that this man had anything to do with the evil that lived in this mill. In Casey's estimation, the kindness in Seamus's voice and eyes couldn't be faked or reproduced by something as malevolent as the cursed old boiler. Together, Casey and Daniel reached out for Seamus's hand.

"That's it, lad, slow and easy." Their hands clasped, Seamus's almost as cold as the boy's own.

Man and boy each had their arms extended to the limit, Seamus's up, the boy's down. It was the full height of the lad from atop the boiler to the shoulders of the man. Daniel started easing his leg toward Seamus, grasping at the smooth black skin of the boiler with both hands, fingers spread, looking for purchase.

A gust of storm wind moaned through the shattered windows. A burst of thunder followed, attacking their ears, drawing back, and attacking again in a staccato one-two rhythm, like the heartbeat of some unspeakable monstrosity.

Daniel flinched at the noise. Casey, unable to counter the boy's sudden movement, ended up a helpless passenger sliding uncontrollably down the side of the boiler toward the black depths of the flooded mill. An inarticulate cry escaped Daniel's mouth as he splashed into the inky water behind Seamus. Seamus hollered as Daniel's death grip on his hand wrenched his arm behind his back. The cold water stabbed at Daniel, and Casey endured every sharp spike of agony in the boy's legs, stomach, and groin. Fingers of cold pain grasped his lower body and pulled him down.

"There—" Seamus grunted, looping the boy's arm around his neck, "—y' are. There y' are. Easy as fallin' off a log."

Daniel clung to the Irishman's back, wrapping his arms around the man's neck so tightly that Seamus gripped the boy's wrist and pried it away from his throat to breathe.

"Easy lad. Easy now. Yer chokin' me... there now. Almost done. Just a quick cool stroll back to the boat."

Casey stared at boiler #2 as Seamus made slow, careful steps through the chest-deep water between the boilers. There was no sign of the ghostly fingers at its crest, clawing their way up. No sound of macabre voices. Only the echoes of dripping water and the sloshing progress of Seamus as he worked his way between the furnaces.

Casey *felt* the boiler. He *felt* the heat of its hate radiating through the water. And he *felt* its malevolence penetrating the boy's bones like the sting of the icy water surrounding them. He searched the surface of the black water inside the lantern's pool of weak light for some sign. Something to tell him if the feeling was real or imagined. There was nothing. Not a wisp of steam or a stream of bubbles to indicate that the boiler was turning up the heat. He'd heard that if you put a frog in a pot of water and turned up the heat slowly, you could boil it alive without the frog jumping away. It would just sit in the pot and die. Casey couldn't help but wonder if he, or rather Daniel and Seamus, were the frogs.

Seamus lurched forward. His face plunged into the water. The arm that held the lantern shot out reflexively to catch his balance, and it too disappeared beneath the surface. For a moment, amid the splashing chaos, Daniel was alone again above the water. In the dark.

The door to boiler #2 swung open with a groan. Daniel screamed. Seamus's head exploded out of the water. A shower of fetid droplets sprayed the boy.

"Oh, Jeysus! Stop yer bloody screamin' boy. Yer puttin' the heart cross-wise in me! I just took a bad step, is all." Seamus held up the lantern, now only a shadow. Water drained out of it. "Fuckin' great," he moaned. "Come on, boyo, let's get the fuck out o' here before we catch our death."

Or our death catches us.

The boiler door stood open to his right, at once beckoning and defiant.

Thunder exploded in the night, rattling what little glass remained in the windows the same way a solid punch rattles the broken teeth of a fighter on his way to the canvas. A double flash of lightning lit the shattered building in electric blue. The first flash showed a wicked grinning Jones standing, arm outstretched, pointing at the open boiler door. The second flash, an instant later, showed him again as he was supposed to be, floating face down with his hair splayed out like rotten spaghetti.

Seamus started singing again.

Casey couldn't tell if the Irishman had seen the gruesome spectacle, but he could tell something had gotten to Seamus. Be it cold, or the sight of a dead man standing in a lightning flash, or the boiler. Seamus's voice was flat this time, with none of the reassuring joviality it had earlier. His notes warbled through a thin, reedy, hesitant voice. He picked up the tune where he'd left off minutes before. "The summer's gone and all the roses dying," when he sang the word dying, something hitched in his throat, and the word came out as a croak.

Come on, come on. Get us out of here! Casey was nearly out of his mind. The confidence he'd felt on top of the boiler was long gone. The sure feeling that the boiler was going to swallow him up again like a snake swallowing a rat settled into the pit of his stomach. *Let's go! Let's go!*

Seamus cleared his throat and continued his song as they rounded the front of boiler #2 and crossed toward the boat, wedged in the window frame. "... tis you who must go...."

Tap... tap... tap... the sound of metal on metal. The door to the boiler door creaked as it inched open wider. The sounds grew closer together as the door opened a little faster, tap tap tap.

The vibrations traveled up through the floor as if the whole mill were wired into the door to the boiler. *FUCK YOU! I'M NOT... WE'RE NOT GOING IN THIS TIME!*

"Bless me; I don't like the sound o' that boyo. I think maybe the weight of the water is too much for this floor or somethin'. We might have to swim for it, after all." Seamus quickened his steps.

There was a tremendous cracking, like a long string of firecrackers set off next to your ear. The building shook with each explosion of sound.

Seamus lunged for the boat but was pulled back by the force of the water rushing into a hole in the floor behind him.

Casey looked at the boiler for some sign, a face of flame, an odious voice, but there was nothing.

Seamus cursed and grunted, straining to keep to his feet against the force of the rushing water. He moved a foot forward, then the other. One more step, two...

Fuck yes! Fuck you, boiler! I'm going to live!

Icy hands grabbed Daniel's legs. Sharp claws pierced his flesh through his pants. Their touch burned with cold; their grip was iron.

Despair washed through Casey. *NO! FUCKING NO! NOT AGAIN! I CAN'T!*

Daniel struggled, kicked, and yelled, "something's got me!"

Seamus toppled over backward in the water. Casey could feel him struggling to the surface, struggling to free himself from the boy's burden. He succeeded and was gone.

Daniel scrabbled at the place where Seamus had been. Icy claws traveled up his body as if the unseen beast were using him as a ladder. The top of a skull broke the water's surface, lumpy, mottled, and black. Glowing red eyes appeared, like those of a cat. The black, slitted pupils radiated hate. The nose followed, but it wasn't a nose, just two slitted holes in the leathery skin. The stink of death and brimstone poured forth from the openings. The mouth appeared; shrunken lips revealed gums populated with oozing sores. The teeth were long curved needles interlaced and dripping with stinking black slime. The lips pulled back into a grin.

"Daemonium in Medio Umbral," Daniel gasped.

Skeleton Man!

"Daniel Costa, last of his bloodline!" the thing shrieked. Its jaws opened wide enough to swallow a bowling ball. It lunged. Its teeth sank into Daniel's neck.

Daniel screamed. Casey screamed. Hot blood spurted across their shared face. The thing dragged them down into the black water. Broken floorboards raked across Daniel's chest as the thing dragged him deeper into the water under the floor. Casey took control of the boy's body as his lungs filled with water. He choked and gasped for air. He kicked and fought at the thing that held his neck. Bright spots of sickening color danced across his vision. Dried blood fireworks, vomit green, piss yellow, puss white.

A voice sounded in the water, its vocal cords decayed, its throat choked with a hundred years of foul mud. "I remember, Costa. I *remember*. You'll die a violent death, Daniel. A violent death in the heart of the seas!"

Down, down, down, into the mud, filth, and a thousand years of decayed leaves and dead fish. Down... down...

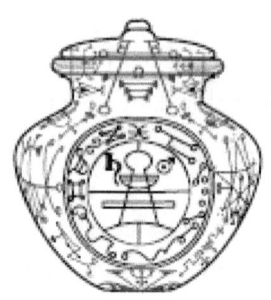

Chapter 26

Hili

Hili and Xavier reached the coast, sharing what little food the other pilgrims had, sleeping little, and walking through the night. The port was nearly empty of ships when they arrived, but they were able to purchase passage on the last ship bound for Britania. There in the dark swaying hold, Hili went into the black.

She came back into Alphonso Pontes to find Xavier pressing his uncle's hand to the side of the pot.

"Hili, are you there?" Xavier asked.

"Yes," she said.

"We were boarded after you... left." Xavier pointed to a group of Roman soldiers conspiring in the shadows of the hold. "They demanded that the boat go to Rome. Now we are at the port, but it is full of men who are called Visigoths. I have seen them. They look just like the Suevi you rescued us from. The soldiers are now demanding the captain re-provision and sail for Constantinople. What should we do?"

"You should go with them. It is not safe here."

"What about you?"

Hili felt

The Pull

toward the shore. "I have business here. Go with the gods, Xavier." She kissed the boy on the top of the head, took up the pot, and approached the Romans. "I will share my food with you if you can open this pot. The lid is stuck."

As soon as the closest soldier grabbed the pot, Hili was behind his eyes, looking up at Alfonso. She jumped to her feet and ran, clutching the pot to her. She was up the ladder and off the ship before anyone could protest. Her sandals slapped hard on the wooden docks as she ran, casting off the trappings of soldiery as she went. It wasn't hard to find clothing; the bodies of Romans littered the streets.

As she pulled on the filthy robe of a dead peasant, the smell of death overpowered her. She cried as she ran. Each footfall that echoed off of the paving stones was a staccato beat of despair. This life she'd been forced into by the gods tore at her soul. All the death, all the loss of life dragged her down. The hardest to cope with, still, was the loss of her own. Would she be with Nigmah now, in the afterlife, if there were no pot? It didn't matter. It happened, gods or no gods. Nigmah was gone, and she was still here, chained to a demon.

Her bitter tears mixed with the sweat dripping from her brow as she ran. Hili could almost feel Nigmah's fingers wiping them away. "I will come for you," she huffed. "Nigmah, I will come for you." It was more than a vow, more than a promise made to the heavy, uncaring air. For Hili, it was a certainty. She would find Nigmah in the afterlife. But first, she must stop the demon, stop the loss of life, and reclaim her own life, or death.

Along the road to Rome, Hili ran into Visigoths, pulling carts of supplies from the coast to the besieged city. She felt the pot *pulling* her toward them. When night fell, she hid among the supplies in the cart, arranging the sacks of grain over her body.

When the carts stopped, she got out and addressed one of the fierce-looking Visigoth soldiers. "I am supposed to bring this to the King," the pot put the words into her mind as she spoke them. "I know not where to find him."

The barbarian looked at her, then at the pot. "Is this some Roman trap? A trick?"

Hili caressed the glyphs. They glowed purple under her fingers. "It is a gift."

The astounded soldier, never taking his eyes from the pot, whispered, "The Salaria gate," and pointed away down a crossroads.

Hili hurried down the street as the soldier indicated, ignoring his shouted questions. She found the King's guard at dawn and, after showing them the glowing purple glyphs, entered King Alaric's tents. When at last she stood before the King with the glowing pot, she said, "This is the pot of Sumer. It is said that only the man destined to conquer Rome can open it." She did not understand why the pot had put these particular words in her mind until Alaric reached for it. A mighty crack of thunder split the morning air.

Hili gazed up from Alaric's shadow, knowing what was to come, and dreading it. Alaric popped the lid free, and the demon entered him. The King drew his sword and left the tent, shouting for his army to form up behind him. The sky, clear when Hili entered the tent moments before, now loomed over the proceedings and began dousing Rome. Arrows rained down from atop the wall, but they parted around Alaric like a many feathered curtain. The Demon King gave the heavy wooden gate a mighty kick, and it fell inward. Screams erupted from the city as Alaric and his Visigoths rampaged through the streets, cutting down the half-starved defenders. Women, children, and soldiers alike fell to Alaric's sword as he hacked and slashed his way toward the city's center, paving the streets in blood.

Hili no longer cared about the will of the gods. As soon as she turned to shadow, she climbed Alaric. The blood spattering the King from his many victims gave a small measure of substance to Hili. She worked her way up, slipping on his bloody, rain-soaked armor. Her shadowy form slid across his chest plate. She grasped the collar of his tunic and pulled, all the while feeling herself grow stronger. Images flashed across her mind, lending a growing mental fortitude to her physical power: Gutian barbarians disemboweling peasants even as they ran away from the hacking swords. The carnage in Germania and the bodies of Tyre piled up one atop the other in her mind.

She climbed.

Alaric ran into a building with great white pillars and stone steps as wide as a Phoenician ship. He bellowed with rage at finding no fleshy home for his sword. His footsteps echoed loud on the marble floors, but he found no one to kill.

There was no time for Hili to marvel at the incredible scale of the buildings or the opulence of their furnishings. She had only one purpose: get inside the King and stop the demon. If the beast could be stopped, the invisible chains that bound Hili to the demon broken, she could find her brother.

The King ran from one building to another, killing anyone who crossed his path, slicing them with wide wicked arcs, spraying blood into the rain. He entered a temple. Inside, at the far end of the building, two men kneeled in front of a grand statue of a man in a crown of brambles hanging from a cross of stone. Alaric screamed and charged at them.

Hili, determined to save the lives of these priests, shoved her shadow into the demon's mouth.

Hate radiated out of him like the heat of a smith's fire. The nauseating violence inside the King, inside the demon, gnawed at Hili. She ignored the pain as the evil chewed on her consciousness. She spread her arms into the arms of the King, her legs into his legs, and now they were three: Demon, King, and Keeper. She concentrated all of her being, everything that she was, into stopping the Demon King Alaric's feet.

The priests turned, still on their knees. One held up a cross of wood that hung from his neck.

Alaric slowed and came to a stop. He slashed his sword in the air in front of the terrified men, but could not reach them.

Hili, surprised that the demon had stopped, didn't let her resolve waiver. She held tight to the sensation of the King's limbs outside her own.

"Lord God," the priest spoke with a trembling voice, "I lay down my life for you. I dedicate my death to you as I have dedicated my life to you. Please Lord, do not let this creature of hell defile your temple." He lifted the cross so that it was between his face and the demon's sword. "You are Daemonium in Medio Umbra!"

Her thoughts like water into a new mind. "Harken demon!" Hili shouted triumphantly as soon as her perception shifted to that of the priest holding the cross. "He who is known as Daemonium in Medio Umbra! Return to your prison. Diminish, and await destruction at the hands of the least. By pride, shalt thou be undone, by shame, vanquished. Enter the vessel."

As it had every time before, the blood covering the demon sizzled and turned to smoke. "I see you, Aemilius Costa. I will remember," and so saying, the demon entered the pot. Hili slammed the lid into place. An inarticulate cry of triumph issued from her lips and echoed through the cavernous marble temple. She allowed herself one long moment of elation. She had the fourth name, only two left to learn. Then she could join Nigmah and free them both of the pot's curse. But there was no time to revel; she had to get the urn out of Rome.

"Brother Costa," the astounded priest next to Hili lowered his cross. "What just happened?"

"There is no time to explain. We must flee the city quickly. The barbarians will kill or enslave anyone they find."

"But how did you know the demon's name?"

"I don't know," Hili said, rising to her feet.

The priest glanced around gape-mouthed, as if someone would come out of the shadows and explain.

"We must go," Hili said. "Come!"

"There is something I must get from the archives."

"There is no time for possessions!" Hili could run off and leave the priest, but she *felt* she needed him. This city, the buildings, the people, the clothes, and the gods were all so strange to her. She needed a guide to get her to safety.

"When you see what I want to fetch, you will think differently."

"Quickly then."

The priest rose and made a strange sign across his body, up and down, side to side, then he ran. Hili followed after, clutching the cursed vessel to her chest. They wound their way through passages, then down a set of stairs. Hili followed the pool of light cast by a torch the priest grabbed from the wall. The passages twisted and turned until she found herself in a familiar room. The same room where she had spoken with Vitus... how long ago?

The priest pulled scrolls from their niches, opened them, closed them, and returned them.

"We have no time for scrolls. We must go now!" Hili insisted.

"We have time for this one. After what just happened, I would sooner die than leave Rome without it."

"What is so important?"

"It is a scroll written by a pagan priest named Vitus Domitius. It tells about the demon, the pot, and its keeper spirit."

"We do not need the scroll. I am the keeper spirit, and I tell you we must go."

The priest looked up at her in surprise. A knowing look came into his eyes. "I would not believe you if I had not just seen... it. Still, The Lord has spoken to me and told me to take the scroll and go home." He opened another scroll. "I have it!" Clutching the scroll under his arm, the priest took the torch from its holder and stepped quickly into the passage from which they came.

"We must wait for nightfall. Alaric's men will kill us."

"No," the priest said over his shoulder, "they will not kill priests. They are Christians."

Hili didn't know what a Christian was, but she put her faith in the priest. "What is your name?"

"I am Orde. By what name shall I call you, spirit?"

"Hili."

"When we reach the daylight, put the urn under your cloak and waddle like a fat man. They may not kill priests, but they will certainly rob them."

"Any fool will see through the ruse."

"The Lord will blind their eyes to the truth," Orde said. "He stopped the demon from killing us. It is God's will that we should live."

Hili thought it best not to disabuse the priest of the notion that his god had saved him. She tried not to let his belief throw her victory into question, but the priest's assertion cast doubt in her mind.

With the demon in the pot, the unnatural rainstorm abated. The sun hit the wet paving stones and caused them to send steam up Hili's robe as she ran. Sweat poured down her face as she followed Orde through the twisting, winding alleys. As Orde predicted, the Visigoth warriors paid no attention to them; instead, they ran from house to house looking for gold or walked away carrying it.

Orde led Hili through a lesser gate in the city wall. Refugees packed the surrounding streets. Hili despised the press of bodies with their sweat, tears, and the stink of fear. When at last they were through, Orde, spry for a man of advanced years, ran ahead of Hili and didn't stop until they reached the docks.

Orde went from ship to ship, boat to boat, looking for one that suited them.

"Why are we not taking this one?" Hili asked as Orde returned, shaking his head after talking with the crewman of the ship.

"This one and many of the others are going to Egypt or Africa to get away from the Goths. They now have the whole Empire in their hands."

"Are we not trying to escape the Goths as well?" Hili didn't understand why they were not already at sea.

"As I have told you, Brother Costa... I mean, Hili, The Lord spoke to me. I am to take you home."

"To Sumer?"

Orde looked at her, confused for a moment, then said, "No, to *my* home. Eire."

The sun had almost reached its zenith by the time Orde found them a ship. Though he was a priest, and most of the refugees worshipped his same god (Hili could tell by the crosses that hung about their necks), it took Orde a long time to find a ship. In the end, he found them a ship bound for Eire, which was already untying from the dock. The captain, from Eire himself, agreed to take the two priests to safety. Once aboard, Hili went into the black.

Chapter 27

Kelly

Kelly's jaw slackened. "What?"

"In my dream, I saw you die. I saw you climb into that boiler, and when you'd gone, I saw fire shoot out of it," Jacob whispered.

"Jake—" Floyd began.

"No, Floyd, stay out of it. I saw the Gottschalk kid die like that the night it happened. I saw Tom die in my dream, then it happened. But here he is, still alive. If... maybe... maybe Tom is still alive... somewhere."

"No, Jake—" Floyd started.

"Fuck you for saying no!" Jacob shouted.

"How," Kelly sobbed, "how was I dressed? Did you see?" Kelly tried to hold back his tears. He tried to fight for control of his emotions. During this last part of the story, he'd come to believe Jacob. He'd come to believe that somehow this man's dreams were correct. If they were, then Casey... His mind recoiled.

"Oh, I see the dream perfectly. You were dressed like a bum, except you had a coat with a herringbone pattern."

Kelly burst into tears. Unable to control the overwhelming emotions, he buried his face in his hands.

"Stop it!" Jake said. "Stop crying and tell me how you did it. Did you see my brother? How did you escape that mill? How are you alive!?"

"Jake—" Floyd began again.

"Floyd, shut up. Tell me, Kelly!"

"Jake!" Floyd shouted.

"What?!"

"Kelly believes his identical twin was in the Boiler House the night of the fire."

"Id... twin... what?"

Kelly took a handkerchief from his pocket and wiped his face. "It was my brother, Casey." He sobbed involuntarily. "He, he just got a herringbone coat from Father Murray...." A fresh jag of crying overtook him. "He just got it." He buried his face in his hands again. "He just got it."

"I..." Jake stammered, "twin...."

"Twin," Floyd said somberly. "I could have told you that if you'd just told me about the dream. I could have saved us all this."

"So... so Tom can't be alive?"

"No, Jake, he can't."

"And my brother is dead," Kelly sobbed.

"They're just dreams," Floyd said, but his voice lacked the conviction of his words.

"Do you still believe that, Floyd?" Jacob asked, hands clenched into fists.

"I don't know what I believe anymore," Floyd said, turning and staring out the windshield at the empty ball field.

The car was silent on the way back to Jacob's house. At the curb, Jacob got out and ascended the steps without a word. Kelly remained in the backseat on the ride back to his car. He did his best to get himself under control. He stifled his sobs. Castles of logic formed in his mind, trying to discredit Jacob, to make his words and his dreams unreal. When they reached the parking lot, Kelly got out. He didn't know what to say, so he said nothing. He simply walked away.

"Kelly," Pontes called after him.

Kelly turned. Hot tears froze on his cheeks in the frosty November night.

Pontes closed his mouth.

"I need some time to sort through all this. Figure it out," Kelly said.

"Good luck. I've been at it since nineteen seventy."

"Okay," Kelly said, started turning again, then turned back. "Pontes?"

"Yeah?"

"Knowing what you know, do you think my brother is dead?"

"I don't know. I think he's in the same place my brother and the Gottschalk boy are, and I don't think they're coming back."

"Yeah," he looked down, then said more softly, "yeah."

Kelly slipped off his duck boots on the mat just inside the door of his loft, hung his coat on the peg, then stood in the middle of the room, staring blankly at nothing; pulled in so many directions at once—paralyzed. Part of him wanted to just crawl into bed and cry over Casey. Another part of him wanted to jump in the car and go searching for his brother, find him alive, prove Pontes wrong. Still another part, the part that won the tug-of-war, wanted to find out what was really going on at the old mill—and stop it.

He sat down at his desk and opened his laptop. The desktop picture was of him and Casey in their little league uniforms, arms around each other. The tears welled up inside him again. "No," he said to the empty loft, "I'm not giving up. He's not dead. I'm not taking the word of an unbalanced adult child. I'm not relying on the flimsy residue of a dream. Casey is a fighter. Casey is a Papas, and we are sons-of-bitches." He ran a hand through his short, thinning hair. "Casey is out there, and I'm going to find him."

There was an email from Petbe with a PDF attachment. It read:

Kelly,

This one looks interesting. It could be part of what we're looking for. Could show a history of negligence on the part of Tyre Holdings. They owned the building before MillCom split off from the parent company. In fact, and this *is* interesting, Tyre had *always* owned the Boiler House. They helped the Connecticut Mill Company finance the construction. They had a hefty lien on it since before it broke ground in 1891. Anyway, check out this article.

Petbe

Kelly opened the attachment. It read:

The Trull Chronicle April 3, 1931

Two dead, one missing, bridge gone in Trull flood

The heavy rain of the past few days combined with an early thaw sent the Nipwìmâw River some twenty feet above flood stage yesterday. The river crested around 5 PM when it washed away the Bridge Street Bridge, officials said.

"As early as 3 PM, chunks of river ice washed down from New Hampshire and began to stack up on the upstream side of the bridge," said Lawrence Hemming, spokesman for the Trull

Department of Public Works. "As that happened, the ice channeled water onto Bridge Street on both sides of the river. By 5 PM, the combined force of the ice and floodwater was just too much for the old wooden structure, and it gave way, sending a surge of water and debris downstream. Less than an hour later, a wall of water twenty feet high rolled downstream from the burst Miller Dam in Ayre. The surge inundated Bridge Street and entered buildings as far as five blocks from the river.

The flood had claimed the lives of Seamus Sullivan and Daemon Jones. Listed as missing is Daniel Costa. The death toll is expected to rise as communications to all parts of the city are restored.

Damage from the flood is estimated at half a million dollars, and Public Works officials say it may be weeks before some Farbank residents are allowed to return to their homes.

There was more to the article. Kelly skimmed it. The bodies were found by the Boiler House. Kelly read it again. He wondered if the Costa boy was ever found. He also wondered at the verbiage 'the flood was believed to have caused the deaths.' Did that mean there was evidence that something else had caused the deaths?

Kelly paced back and forth across the pale, wide pine boards of the loft. Each new piece of information raised more questions than it answered. Kelly wracked his brain, looking for commonalities in all these deaths.

1. The Boiler House, obviously. That might not be statistically significant. People died all the time in the city. A few deaths in one spot could barely be considered a coincidence.

2. None of the bodies were ever found. That one was the most troubling. They should have been found. Even if the kids in '83 built a coal fire, there should have been something, a bone fragment, a melted filling, something. Floyd Pontes had sealed the files. Why? Because there was something in there he didn't want the public to see? That brought him to the third thing these cases (excluding the flood in '31) had in common: Floyd Pontes.

3. Floyd Pontes investigated his brother's death, the Gottschalk boy's death, and the fire that Casey... was involved in. Could Floyd Pontes be involved in the deaths somehow? It was awfully convenient how Floyd arrived by train all the way from Boston in time to save his brother. Moreover, guessing correctly where Jacob was. What if Floyd was already there? What if he saved his younger brother from getting caught in the same trap he'd set for his older brother? Was he lying in wait for the kids in '83? For Casey last week? Was there a motive?

Kelly didn't like it. Pontes was a secretive and prickly bastard to be sure, but Kelly didn't figure him for a killer. Pontes's words from the parking garage echoed in his mind: "the sheer weight of what I know that you don't would send the Bridge Street Bridge to the bottom of the Nipwìmâw." It had to be a coverup. Maybe Pontes was covering up for his disturbed brother who'd committed these acts. After today's performance in Floyd's car, Kelly didn't believe that either. He knew he had to get Floyd Pontes to talk, he just didn't know how.

All right, put a pin in the Pontes issue. What else did the deaths have in common? A storm. Kelly stopped pacing in the middle of the loft and almost giggled. *It was a dark and stormy night...* But seriously, both the night Casey... and the flood in '31 were stormy. He went to the desk and looked up the weather on the dates of Gottschalk's and Tom Pontes's deaths. Both had forecasts for heavy rain. Something bothered him, something besides coincidence.

It was New England, after all. You could look up seventy days' worth of forecasts and come up with rain, maybe even heavy rain, on half of them. Kelly looked up the forecasts for the night Casey... and the '31 floods. They all featured the same two words: heavy rain. Not an amazing coincidence, but it bothered him.

He remembered that night, standing in the sickly yellow pools of the Toyota's headlights, pounding on the door of the mill. Rain pelting him, running off his hat onto his trench coat. He remembered the feeling that Casey was inside, in trouble. He remembered the weight of that feeling. The weight of the powerlessness and guilt. Again, Pontes's words echoed in his mind: "The weight of what I know that you don't...." The weight. Heavy rain. Heavy. In fact, the weight of rainwater and ice *had* sent the Bridge Street Bridge to the bottom of the Nipwìmâw in 1931.

There was simply no way around it. Pontes had the key to this puzzle, or at least a pocketful of enormous puzzle pieces. It all came back to Pontes. Kelly resolved to call him in the morning. Too late to call now. The clock on his laptop read 11:46.

Kelly showered and considered going to a bar. As always, he climbed into bed instead. Going to a bar to meet someone compatible verged on ridiculous for someone who didn't drink much. Oh sure, a glass of wine now and then, but at midnight on a Monday, the only men he'd be likely to meet were heavy drinkers. Certainly, that factored into his decision, and that was the reason he liked to give himself for staying home, but the real reason was much deeper.

Kelly knew how he would feel sitting at the bar. The cold isolation clinging to him like the cigarette smoke clung to his clothes when he got home, alone. He was sure the others at the bar would smell it, like the smoke. When he tossed them in the laundry basket, they nauseated him from across the room, reminding him of one more night's quest for a meaningful connection to another human being—failed. The stench of failure becoming so strong that eventually he had to get up out of bed and drown those clothes in the steel kill jar of the washing machine.

What was worse, though, what was oh so much worse, was sitting at the bar and having a cute guy come up and touch his arm to get his attention. The shock of that momentary connection, innocent, at least initially, buzzed deep into him. He could feel the shape of the void, the yawning chasm inside where love should be. When that stranger's fingertips brushed his arm, and the blue-white nerve impulses shivered through him, circling the void of his soul, that's when he knew how long it had been since anyone touched him, for any reason. He knew just how lonely he was, how absolutely desperate for a hug. Not just a hug from anyone, oh no, the energy from such a hug would circle the drain, a beam of bright light falling down the black hole of that desperate hidden place inside him. No, the only contact that could fill a hole like that was contact from someone who loved him. Someone who knew him, knew who he was, and wanted to hug him anyway. Such contact came only from love. Love that couldn't be found in a gay bar in Trull at midnight on Monday.

So there he'd be as the stranger's hand moved from his arm to the bar as the stranger slid onto the stool next to him, grinning wolfishly, wondering what his cock looked like, or how well he could use his mouth. Kelly would want to scream, shout out that it wasn't fucking love, and all the Jack Daniels and cum in the world would fall right through that hole inside him, and no matter how hard Kelly got fucked, the stranger's cockhead could never touch that place, much less fill it.

As Kelly's eyes slid to half-mast, he saw, or thought he saw, the trace form of the mill girl who'd begun showing up occasionally in his peripheral vision ever since Casey went missing. He tried ignoring the ghostly impression, then whipping his head around to catch the intruding poltergeist unawares. But the effort proved fruitless. After a few minutes, Kelly concluded, again, that all the strangeness surrounding the Boiler House had permeated his subconscious, producing speculative images in his mind's eye. The only sensory evidence Kelly had that there was something to his mental impressions was a chill his comforter seemed powerless to dispel.

Chapter 28

Casey

Again the sensation came, coppery and tingly, like someone pouring cold blood across Casey's mind and imparting in its wake the body of another. A man, this time, smelling faintly of old sweat and cigarettes under a layer of soap, strode across the wooden covered bridge. Cigarettes, even the stink of old cigarettes on the man's clothes, made Casey tremble. *God, what I wouldn't do for a cigarette? Maybe I can get this guy to light up.* He didn't, though; the sight of the Boiler House through the window stopped him cold. *Oh, fuck you! You fucking piece of shit building!*

That building just kept beating him, killing him, and Casey knew, sure as fuck, it was happening again. He had two choices: fight again, or give up. Casey gave up. He sat back and rode like a passenger across the bridge. There was a new sound on the bridge this time, hooves. The clanking of Model T-era cars came interspersed with the clopping of horses and carriages. 1900-1920, Casey figured. It didn't matter. He was a lamb for the slaughter, and he was going to do his best to treat the whole thing like a movie. Except, God damn, did he really have to feel the pain of their deaths every time?

He had to wonder, couldn't help but wonder, since he was going steadily back in time, what would happen when he reached the time of the boiler's creation? Did that hateful thing kill someone at the factory where it was made? At the smelters? The mine where the ore for the boiler was extracted?

Whatever the game was, or whomever the game maker turned out to be, Casey was no longer playing. Burned alive twice, blown up, and drowned. Game over.

Casey, much as he hated to, and as much as he said he wasn't playing, went back through the events leading up to the deaths. He realized that everyone, besides himself, had said something strange when the Skeleton Man killed them. Freddie Gottschalk said, "Der Ungeisthasse," when Skeleton Man appeared. Pontes said, "Pesadelo Vivo," when he saw the face in the puddle of molten metal. And Daniel Costa said, "Daemonium in Medio Umbra," when it came out of the water.

No more. He couldn't take it. Not again. He could grab control of this new host and make the man jump into the river or run out in front of a car on the bridge. What would that accomplish? Would he come back as that man again and again until the boiler got what it wanted? Would he die forever, finally? Until he understood the game, how could he win? His thoughts came full circle. Not playing.

The man stepped off the bridge into a squall of wind carrying the first drops of rain. Casey's host gazed up at the black, anvil-shaped clouds gathering over the mill. The dark recesses roiled with pent-up violence. Swirling mists of suspended water loomed over the Boiler House, and just as he looked away, descended toward it. Thunder blasted through the air as the man opened the door to the Power House. Casey almost forgot his sense of impending doom as he walked between giant steam engines that chugged, clanked, and belched steam. Connecting rods as long as a car and thick as his arm pistoned back and forth. Men in coveralls scurried about with oil cans dabbing here and there at the massive machines. A few feet away, a man stood tapping an errant gauge that extended from a pipe like a clockwork lollipop.

"Excuse me," Casey's host said.

The man turned.

"I'm looking for John Tyree."

"Who's looking?" The man's black eyes peered suspiciously from under bushy brows like a couple of beetles.

"Connor Walsh, engineering."

"You new?"

"Yes."

"Through there," beetle eyes grunted and pointed to the door at the end of a room with the wrench he was holding.

"Thanks," Walsh said and headed for the door.

It was a door Casey knew well and dreaded. It was the door to hell — the door to the Boiler House. *Oh, of fucking course,* Casey wailed, but he made no move to stop the man from entering. *Let's just get this shit show over with.*

Like the Power House, the Boiler House was alive with activity. Men shoveled coal into the fiery maws of the boilers. Other men added more coal to the piles. Still, other men checked gauges and turned huge iron valves. Walsh walked up to a meaty man standing in the center of the cavernous space, arms folded over a belly that stretched his coveralls to their limit. He wore a dour expression, and when Walsh spoke, it took a few seconds for the man's dull eyes to track over and look. "Mister Tyree?"

Casey wondered if the guy was slow to acknowledge Walsh deliberately, asserting his power. Even if he wasn't, Casey pegged the guy as one flavor of asshole or another.

"What?" the man asked. After his mouth stopped moving, his jowls shook an instant longer, giving the impression they were wagging fingers of flesh saying 'no, no.'

"Are you Mister Tyree?" Walsh asked again, more firmly.

"Yes. What?"

"I'm Walsh. Engineering."

"Took you long enough," Tyree said, shouldering his way past Walsh, though there was plenty of room to go around. He walked back the way Walsh had come and stopped at the corner of boiler #2, closest to the Power House door. "Masonry's cracked." Tyree pointed a gnarled finger toward the brickwork that encased the bottom of the boiler. "It's going to start leaking exhaust from the flue soon. Might be already."

The crack ran from knee level to the floor, almost wide enough to stick a finger in. Walsh stepped around Tyree close enough for his coat to touch Tyree's coverall and make a momentary 'scree' sound.

Good for you, brush this asshole back off the plate.

Along the backside of the boiler, another crack weaved from the top of the brickwork along the zigzagging mortar line to the floor. "This whole corner is sinking," Walsh said.

Tyree 'humphed' in answer.

"Where's the crawlspace hatch?"

"You tell me," Tyree sneered, "you're the engineer."

Walsh stared him down. Seconds stretched out between them. Finally, Tyree pointed to a square crack in the floor about ten feet away, with a recessed metal ring on one side.

"Tanks," Walsh said, but his tone had no thanks in it. He made his way over to the hatch, got on his knees, and flipped the trapdoor open. "de fo shealbh?"

Based on the sea of trash floating in putrid black water and the tone of the remark, he guessed it was Gaelic for 'what the fuck?'

"Have y' been shitting in here?" Walsh asked.

"No, we're not Mics. We use the toilet." Tyree pointed to a little pine room in the corner of the mill.

Walsh clenched his fists.

The two men stared at each other for a few moments, then Tyree walked away. When he was out of earshot in the noisy mill, Walsh let out a long string of angry Gaelic.

I don't know what you said, but I'm with you. Fuck that guy.

Walsh searched around the mill for a few minutes, finally finding a broom and going back to the hatch. The broom handle sank into the water about two inches before touching the earth underneath, then it sank further into the mud and kept sinking. Walsh pulled it out when the broom's bristles were at the top of his fist. Gooey black mud clung to the smooth wooden handle like the loose excrement of a thousand incontinent alcoholics. Another string of bitter-sounding Gaelic escaped Walsh.

Fuck, Casey echoed, *I'm with you. How much are they paying you for this shit?*

Walsh dropped the broom, closed the hatch, and walked out.

Fuck yeah! Take this job and shove it! No boiler for me this time! As Walsh walked down the street, Casey half expected to leave the man's body. If he wasn't going to die in the Boiler House this time, there was no point in him being here, right? Except nothing happened. *What is the fucking game here?*

Walsh entered another mill building about a block away, one that in Casey's time had been converted to shops under apartments. At this time, though, it was a carpentry shop. Saws, drill presses, and other contraptions Casey didn't recognize ran from wide leather belts hooked to driveshafts running along the ceiling. The noise of the saws, belts, and spinning shafts was deafening.

A man in a blue apron came over. He stood head and shoulders above Walsh and sported an impressive mustache. The two men conversed, rather heatedly, in rapid-fire Gaelic, each flailing their arms and gesturing with their hands for emphasis. At the end of the conversation, Walsh slumped his shoulders and said simply: "tha."

Walsh took a wheelbarrow from along the wall and filled it with all manner of tools, parts, nails, and wood planks. That done, he pushed the wheelbarrow out the door and back toward the Boiler House. It was raining in earnest now. Walsh quickened his pace.

I should have known it was too good to be true. Here we go again. I wonder how this fucking boiler is going to kill me this time?

There was a great deal of awkward effort in getting the wheelbarrow through the Power House door, through the Power House, through the Boiler House door, and over to the hatch. No one helped the dripping little Irishman.

Bastards.

Walsh took the wood at the trapdoor and began sawing and hammering at it with amazing speed and skill. Within a few short minutes, Walsh opened the trap door and tossed his wooden creation in.

Well, I'll be a son of a bitch; he built a raft.

Walsh laid out tools and parts around the hole and climbed down into the bowels of the Boiler House. It smelled like bowels too, the bowels of a great beast of the industrial age that devoured the young, chewed them up, and spit them out old and crippled.

The mud squelched under the makeshift wooden platform. On hands and knees, Walsh held up a lantern and peered into its feeble glow. Squat pillars of brick rose out of the mud about four feet to support the rough-hewn floor joists of the mill. They ran at ten-foot intervals, stretching away into the darkness beyond the lantern's light. The puddle in which Walsh's wooden platform sat wasn't much bigger than a man. At its edges, tiny dark shapes wiggled in the mire and refuse. Walsh held the lantern a little further out in that direction, and the mottled brown carapaces of cockroaches showed for an instant before diving into the trash away from the light. They'd been feasting on the rotting corpse of a rat, and they weren't alone. Maggots crawled across its mangy fur and into the hole its intestines spilled out of.

Walsh let out a grunt and turned the lantern toward the persistent hissing close at hand. The sound made Casey think of a warped record playing the sound of an angry cat, the needle skipping rhythmically. Hisss. Hisss. Hisss. Hisss. The lamp light shifted to reveal a water pipe coming out of the darkness along the underside of the floor supports, making a right angle and turning up into the mill. A spray of water jetted from the pipe in a thin spurting stream, splashing onto a floor joist that sat atop the nearest brick pillar. Bits of rotten wood lay in the mud at the pillar's base. The floor joist already sagged about an inch, causing the bricks around the boiler above to crack.

Walsh muttered and gathered tools and materials from around the trapdoor and placed them on the platform below. As Walsh worked, Casey wondered if that fucking boiler intended to crush them under the collapsing floor, or boil them alive in a jet of steam. Despite swearing he wasn't playing the boiler's game this time, dying crushed into the fetid mud seemed particularly awful. Moreover, he'd come to like this little Irish man. Though he didn't understand a lot of what the man said, he gathered by Walsh's voice that they were the same things he'd say. And this job Walsh was doing was the kind of job he'd had at the box factory next door when he'd still had a job... and a body.

Casey's thoughts were interrupted by a change in pitch of the hissing water. Walsh fitted a collar around the pipe, but the pressure was so strong that he struggled to tighten it into place over the leak. As he did, the sound changed from a hiss, hiss, hiss to a pesst, pesst, pessst.

Thunder shook the mill above, sending thin puffs of coal dust down on Walsh from between the floorboards. Just outside the dim circle of lamplight, several pairs of red eyes appeared.

Chapter 29

Hili

Tingling. Then, flowing. Hili's thoughts, sensations, and consciousness poured into the body of another like water passed between bowls. Wooden surroundings creaked and swayed in the light of a lantern held aloft by the body. The roll of the sea rocked the shadows back and forth, casting the way ahead in alternate swathes of light and dark. The pot thrummed with power under the stranger's arm.

This time, as with the time before, Hili had no control over the body holding the urn.

"What's taking so long down there, Maewyn," a voice called from a distant patch of moonlight. "If you don't bring gold up from that hold right now, there'll be no breakfast!"

The bounding stride up the ladder to the deck suggested youth. Topside, ragged men from a second ship tied alongside held the crew, bound at sword point.

Orde, eyes wide, hands tied, stared at the body that even now bent to work on the accursed lid. "No!" he called out. "You must not!"

The same foul pop that sent the lid tumbling in the air turned Hili to shadow. Thunder blasted into the night, shaking the deck timbers and announcing the demon's arrival. This time, Hili welcomed it. Her mind was loose, agile, ready to climb inside this pirate boy and wrest control of him before the demon could take too many lives.

If Nigmah could possess the pot and not have a name, if the barbarian in Sumer could, then the designs of the gods were fallible. The fates of people could be changed. Lives could be spared. If all these things were true, then Hili could countermand the will of the gods.

Smoke twisted from the black orifice of the vessel into the nose of the scruffy teen. Blood filled the whites of his eyes. His lips drew into a thin sneer made crazy in the light of the sallow moon.

Unseen in the darkness, Hili felt the worn-smooth decking slide under her shadow self as the demon youth rose and advanced on the closest sword-wielding pirate.

"You came to my shores and enslaved me!" he shouted. He grasped the surprised ruffian's sword and filleted the man with it.

Both sickened by the gore and quickened by the blood, Hili climbed. Thread by thread, she clawed her way up the trousers of the demon-filled pirate.

Bloated drops of rain spattered the ship, mixing with the crimson essence of the demon's second victim. Though it continued to storm, the moon showed through a hole in the clouds, lighting the macabre spectacle. The gold hoop earring of a beheaded pirate glittered on the slick planks.

Hili, little more corporeal than a thought, a whisper, pulled at the pirate's clothes. Shadowy fingers intertwined with homespun tunic. Hili grasped, reached, and grasped again. Now near the collar. Now the beard, and up. The young man stank of old sweat, blood, and despair.

The moon disappeared as the gale intensified. Wind drove cold spray in the demon's face, quickening Hili.

Milcom kept his feet, but Hili was peripherally aware that others fell and slid as the ship sawed back and forth through the building seas.

The rain came hard, washing blood from the planks in scarlet rivulets. Pirates dove into the sea rather than face the vengeful blade. Maewyn swept his sword across any man fool enough not to jump. Bodies thumped dull and lifeless to the deck, then twitched in rhythm with the waves.

Hili clung to the pirate's beard, straining to reach the demon's mouth.

A man crossed his fingers in front of him as he backed away. He stared wide-eyed and said, "Deamhan Claidheimh!"

Instantly, Hili was inside the man who'd spoken. "Harken demon!"

The pirate-demon stood frozen, looking at her.

"He who is known as Deamhan Claidheimh!" She grabbed a cleat to steady herself and ignored the spray in her face, saying, "Return to your prison. Diminish, and await destruction at the hands of the least. By pride, shalt thou be undone, by shame, vanquished. Enter the vessel."

The blood covering Maewyn bubbled, popped, and turned to smoke.

Surf dripped from Hili's chin.

"I see you, Walsh," Deamhan Claidheimh said, "I will remember." The smoking blood drew into the pot.

As soon as the blood-coated lid slid into place, Maewyn dropped the sword.

The rain stopped. Canvas flapped in the diminishing wind.

Maewyn stood for some seconds, gape-mouthed and horrified. He stared, stupefied, first at Hili, then the victims, then to the crew tied to the mast. "I did not start this thing. These men...these snakes, stole me from my home in Britania and forced me to pirate with them. I swear my life to the service of our merciful Lord God. And I vow, ere I die, I'll drive every one of these murderous snakes from the shores of Eire." So saying, he sliced the bonds of the captured crew. "And henceforth, I shall be known as Patrick, servant of the Lord."

Hili grabbed the pot and rushed to Orde. "Are you well? It's Hili. You must see this pot hidden safely."

"I will. There is a monastery high in the rocks off the coast."

"Thank you," Hili said, and went into the black.

Chapter 30

Kelly

Kelly leaned back in his desk chair and rubbed his eyes. He would never find out what happened to Casey. He would never get the story for *The Patriot*. And *The Chronicle*, he was fairly certain, would never buy his work again. Petbe at the Ware Patriot had turned up nothing new, and Floyd Pontes dodged him like an eighteen-year-old with a draft notice. So Kelly spent days doing his own research, which turned out to be just as fruitless as Petbe's.

He decided to go for a walk to clear his head. An icy rain fell on the world outside, forcing Kelly to bundle up in a thick sweater under his ubiquitous trench coat. Hat, gloves, and duck boots in place, Kelly went down the stairs and out into the rain.

His mind worked on the problem as he walked. None of this amounted to a hill of beans in any rational, scientific light. Kelly wondered if he, the consummate reporter, could distance himself enough from the story to seriously consider the nonscientific perspective that lurked at the edges of his consciousness.

He was out here to clear his head, though, not muddy the waters further. He concentrated on the sound his rubber soles made on the wet sidewalk. He studied the pink splashes the raindrops made in the puddles that reflected the streetlights. Black water. Black roads. Low, rolling thunder bowled across the sky. Kelly's feet fell one in front of the other on the wet pavement until they hit dirt. There were tufts of winter deadened grass, gravel patches, trash, and bricks. Kelly found himself outside the Boiler House without any conscious thought given to getting there. Fresh green boards were bolted tightly over the smoke-blackened windows.

"It's worse when it rains."

Kelly jumped.

Pontes stood about five feet away, hands behind his back, rain tapping on his fire department slicker.

"Jesus wept! You scared me." Kelly touched a hand to his chest.

Pontes just stood there looking at Kelly, his expression patient, inscrutable.

"What's worse when it rains?"

"*The Pull*," Pontes whispered.

"*The Pull?*"

Pontes flashed a wan smile. "Never mind. What are you doing here? Come to break in and have a look at the boiler?"

"What? No. I-I don't know, really. I just went for a walk to clear my head, and..." he trailed off.

"You just went for a walk on a freezing November night. In the rain. To clear your head?"

"Yeah, when you say it like that...."

"Do that a lot, do you?"

"No. I..." Pontes was leading him somewhere, to some conclusion he knew intuitively, but couldn't see.

"Ever do it at all before your brother went missing? Walk in the cold rain to clear your head?"

"No."

Pontes nodded, a sad little smile on his lips.

"*The Pull?*"

Pontes nodded again. "Notice anything else strange about tonight?"

Thunder boomed so loud it made Kelly jump. He smiled weakly. "Startled me."

"Nothing else strange?"

Kelly thought for a moment. "No."

"Ever hear of a thunderstorm in November this far north?"

"I never really thought about it."

"Doesn't happen, not unless there's a heatwave, some kind of freak hot weather, which there isn't. You need a hot air mass to collide with a cold air mass to get a thunderstorm. Whatever's making the thunder here tonight, it isn't that."

Kelly opened his mouth, then closed it again.

"Come on," Pontes said, "Let's get out of the rain. I'll buy you a drink."

"Coffee," Kelly said. He didn't want to cloud his mind with alcohol right now. He needed to think.

"Suits me," Pontes said. The fire department sedan was parked right on the corner of State Street.

Kelly must have walked right past Pontes's car, close enough to touch, without noticing.

The Pull

As he got in, Kelly noticed a figure standing in a darkened doorway across the street. It was hard to tell, but maybe it was the same man he'd seen the night he visited the Boiler House after the fire. He mentioned it to Pontes, pointing at the doorway.

"Yeah, I saw him."

"That could be your arsonist."

"It isn't."

"How do you know?"

"The sheer weight of what I know that you don't—"

"You've used that line on me before," Kelly said.

"Damn. It's one of my favorites." The dashboard lights lit up his smile in shades of sickly green.

"Are you going to tell me who that is?"

"Not right now." Pontes turned right on Bridge Street and pointed the sedan toward Dunkin' Donuts.

"So when we met in the parking garage outside your office—"

"When you accosted me," Pontes cut in.

"Accosted? Don't you think that's a little strong?"

"Maybe."

"Anyway, that's when you used that line about the weight of what you know that I don't sending the bridge to the bottom of the Nipwìmâw."

"So?"

"So, are you willing to share some of that information?"

"I am now."

"Why not then?"

"I wasn't convinced your brother was really involved. That being the case, there was no way I was going to talk to you about this."

"But you're convinced now? Why not after Jacob said he saw my brother die?"

"Well, I was partly convinced then, but Jacob's dreams are unreliable evidence."

"Seemed pretty credible to me. The herringbone coat? How could he possibly know that? Anyway, what tipped you over the edge?"

"Seeing you at the Boiler House tonight. You walked right by like I wasn't there. That's when I knew."

"Knew what?"

"That you felt
The Pull.
That means your brother *was* there."

"What is
The Pull
anyway?"

"I'm not sure."

As they crossed the bridge, Kelly tried not to look over his shoulder at the Boiler House, but he couldn't help himself. There were no boards on the windows facing the river; they were too large and inaccessible. Their arched sockets stared out over the nighttime black waters of the Nipwìmâw.

A horn blared. The car jerked to the right. Kelly turned in time to see Pontes's head snap away from the sight of the Boiler House.

"Sorry. Like I said, it's worse on rainy nights. I always tried to tell myself that it was just me, that
The Pull
was all in my head. But another part of me knew better. Somewhere deep down, I know different. I've always known." Floyd turned the sedan into the drive-through line. The conversation stopped as they ordered and received their cups at the window. Pontes parked in a spot on the edge of the parking lot where the Boiler House wasn't blocked by the auto parts store

across the street. Both men flipped the plastic tabs on the top of their cups and blew into them in a vain attempt to cool the coffee inside from 'nuclear' to 'drinkable.'

"Does Jacob feel
The Pull
too?"

"I think it's different for him. I think it pulls him in his dreams."

"Does it affect anyone else?"

"The only one I know of is David Gottschalk."

"Freddie's brother?"

"Yeah, the guy you saw in the sweatshirt tonight." Pontes blew on his coffee again.

"Son of a bitch, I've been trying to figure out how to find him."

"I knew you would get around to that sooner or later. That's why I sealed the files."

"So I couldn't find him?"

"Because I didn't want you bothering him. Because I didn't want to have to explain all this weird stuff to a reporter, or have David or Jacob see it in the paper."

"Why didn't you seal them before?"

"Never needed to. No one's ever looked this closely, except me."

Kelly stared at the black sockets of the Boiler House windows in the distance. They stared back.

"Tell me about David Gottschalk."

"This is just between us. It doesn't go in the paper. Anything I tell you is because of your brother. Because you feel
The Pull

too, understand?"

"Completely off the record," Kelly said. "I think my story is pretty much dead. There's no way I could put any of this in the paper. My editor would tell me to submit it to the National Enquirer."

"Okay. When I interviewed David Gottschalk after the fire, he became hysterical. He said Freddie climbed in because he'd told him to. Part of a gang initiation, you see. Except Freddie never came out of the boiler. When David opened the door, he said he saw a skeleton in a suit surrounded by a purple glow in there with Freddie. Then, the door slammed shut and David couldn't open it."

"A glowing purple skeleton?"

"Swears it up and down, but they were all stoned on marijuana. There's something else about David Gottschalk. When I say, he *said*, what I mean is, he wrote. You see, David hasn't spoken anything but The Lord's Prayer since the day his brother climbed into that boiler—carries a notepad everywhere.

"A few days after the fire, I was at the Boiler House in my car on the pretense of staking out the place, looking for more kids coming and going, but really, if I'm honest, it was

The Pull.

"Then, here comes David Gottschalk walking down the street. He walked right by me like I wasn't even there, just like you did, just like I imagine Jacob did the night my brother...

"I got out of the car and followed him. He started climbing the fire escape on the building across the way. See, in those days, the boards on the windows were new and tight. The only way in was across a fire escape bridge with a locked gate. That's how the kids got in when Freddie Gottschalk was killed. Well, I couldn't have him going in there, so I climbed after him and grabbed him, put him in my car, and drove him home. All the way to his house, he's writing notes and trying to make me read them while I'm driving, telling me that his brother is still in there. He says he has to go back. He has to see. He was so much like Jacob had been the night my brother... was lost. The same way you were the night of the fire."

Kelly stared at him, in half-belief, unable to accept what he was hearing and equally unable to deny what had just happened.

"I know," Pontes said, "I know. I've tried to look at this scientifically, from a fire inspector's perspective. It just doesn't fit in a neat little box. Nothing fits in that box, actually. Not *The Pull*,

not the stories of the kids involved in the Gottschalk boy's disappearance, not the missing bodies, not the eyewitness accounts of my brother's... disappearance, none of it."

Pontes was going too fast for Kelly to keep up. Missing bodies plural? Did he mean Gottschalk and Casey, or were there more? Kelly had no idea what eyewitness accounts he was talking about. He wanted to tell the old man to slow down and explain each point, but Pontes kept going.

"—Fires with no point of origin that spread against the wind. It makes no sense. None of it."

"Why don't you—"

"Don't you think I've tried everything?" Pontes set his coffee on the dashboard so hard the brown liquid splashed up, then ran down the windshield in slow-moving brown rivulets. He turned to face Kelly full on. "I've had it condemned, filed public nuisance complaints," Pontes ticked off the points on his fingers, "started petitions to have it torn down. Heck, I even lobbied the city council to declare eminent domain and put in a nice riverfront park there." He sighed, and his shoulders dropped. "Nothing seems to stick to MillCom Real Estate or Tyre Holdings."

"Tell me about the missing bodies," Kelly asked softly.

"Well, you know about Casey. I'm sorry," Pontes said as Kelly's face fell, "but you asked. You already know we never found Freddie Gottschalk."

"Yes."

"They never found my brother, either."

"I thought there was an explosion...."

"Yes. The fire investigator at the time said he was vaporized." Pontes paused and touched the corners of his eyes with the thumb and forefinger of his hand. "I didn't believe it. Didn't seem right. I dropped out of seminary to become a fire inspector. I wanted to find out the truth about his death."

"And now that you *are* a fire inspector?"

"I know he wasn't vaporized. There should have been something, a...." Pontes paused and took a deep breath, "... a scrap of flesh, a body part, a tooth, something. They found nothing."

"You said there was an eyewitness account that didn't match."

"This is starting to feel like a newspaper interview."

"It's not," Kelly said, "I'm just trying to understand what happened to my brother, same as you."

Pontes nodded. "I talked to my brother's friend who was on the job too, years later. He said a gout of fire came from the hole my brother cut in the boiler and traveled up the hoses of the cutting torch. They call that 'backflow.' It only happens under extreme circumstances when someone is very new or careless.

There are check valves to prevent it. My brother was neither new nor careless. The friend said my brother rushed to the tanks to shut them off. He was working the valve when they exploded. Anyway, not a single scrap of flesh was ever found."

Chapter 31

Casey

Walsh, oblivious to the red eyes peering at him from just beyond the weak pool of lamplight, continued to struggle with fitting the collar on the spraying water pipe. Casey, however, focused his undivided attention on the eyes. He broke his vow to sit back and do nothing. He took over Walsh's eyes and made the man look.

Walsh dropped the wrench and picked up the lantern. Furry faces appeared in the lamplight. Rats. Rats of all sizes. Some as small as mice, some as big as cats. Their eyes glowed purple, their heads misshapen, almost human-looking. They all mimicked a face Casey couldn't forget, Skeleton Man. As if the thought summoned him, the rats parted, revealing the crawling figure, suit dragging in the mud. Behind it, that damnable purple glow again. The glow that signified the coming of pain.

Thunder shook the mill, sending a rain of dust through the floorboards above.

The crawlspace afforded no escape. Only a maze of mud and brick pillars stretching into the darkness.

Please, God, I can't. Not again. Please. Casey ceded control to Walsh, who just sat frozen in terror.

The Skeleton Man had more flesh than before; it hung in jiggling gray curtains from his ruined neck.

"No! No!" Walsh screamed.

Skeleton Man lunged.

The purple glow in the mud intensified.

Skeleton Man shrieked. Violence and rage worked its jaw up and down in satanic vibrato. Cockroaches, worms, maggots, and a thousand filthy varieties of insects poured from its mouth.

Walsh reached for the trapdoor above and grasped the edge of the opening. The door slammed shut on his fingers, crushing them, pinning them in place. Walsh howled in pain. Blood ran down the wood and dripped onto the makeshift raft.

Insects crawled onto the raft and feasted on the blood. They piled out of Skeleton Man's mouth onto the raft, crawling all over Walsh. Up his pant leg. Down his collar. In his ears. The platform began to sink into the mud.

Casey's thoughts were a tangle of nonsense. He couldn't look away from Walsh's impending destruction. He screamed. Free of the need to draw breath, Casey's shriek never paused. Never diminished.

Skeleton Man crawled into the light. He gripped the raft. Flesh flapped away from the bones on his fingers, disgorging still more putrescent vermin.

"Deamhan Claidheimh!" Walsh cried.

Casey stopped yelling long enough to register the words in his mind.

The giant rat bit down on Walsh's crotch.

Walsh and Casey bellowed in unbearable agony. Walsh punched at the rat.

The host of insects, some inside Walsh's clothes, some on the sweat-slick surface of his face, bit down at once. The encircling rats leaped onto Walsh. Fleas and lice flew from their pelts and fell like rain. The rats bit and tore at his clothes.

The lamp fell from Walsh's hand and went out. A thousand needle teeth tore into his body. Mouths of every size bit and tore into his flesh. Blood sprayed everywhere. He kept screaming even as the insects crawled into his mouth. They poured and tumbled into his throat. His lungs filled with vermin, chewing and biting. His nose became host to a million lice. Cockroaches crawled across his open, sightless eyes and there, feasted. The rats tore his stomach open. A massive set of jaws clamped down on his skull. White-hot spikes of death sank into his brain.

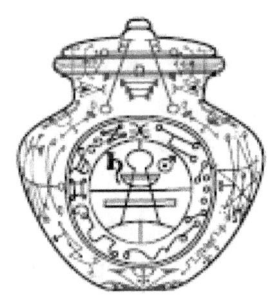

Chapter 32

Hili

Hili came out of the black with a pouring sensation. There was no sound but the creaking of wooden floorboards. Her consciousness streamed into the body of a woman. The lady wrapped a cloth around the pot. The thin veil of fabric was enough that Hili no longer felt herself inside the woman's body, but there was still enough of a connection that she didn't go back into the dark. Clasping the pot to her chest, she tiptoed through a door, down three sets of squeaking stairs, and into the street.

Hili found herself confined to the skin of the pot, looking out through the thin fabric at a strange world. The buildings on either side of the street rose high into the sky, but their wooden frames sagged. The trash, filth, and manure lining the sides of the street blurred into a single putrescent shadow in the twilight. The lamps that hung from poles at intervals along the road were dark. This must be a rich place indeed to have so much wood for buildings and poles.

The woman wound her way down the narrow alleys until she came to a section where the buildings grew nicer, and lights on poles cast a flickering glow on the clean street. She wrapped her knuckles on a door with green writing Hili couldn't read.

A man dressed in black, wearing a hat with a brim that went all the way around it opened the door and motioned her inside.

"Missus Walsh." The man touched the brim of his hat with the tips of his fingers.

"Mister Grove." Mrs. Walsh nodded and stepped past him into the building.

"You've brought it. Good." Another man dressed head to toe in black stepped out of the dark recesses of the richly appointed room and into the light of a single lamp on a table at its center.

"And who would you be?" Walsh asked.

"I'm Alexander Tyre."

"So, the famous Mister Tyre." She turned to Mr. Grove. "Why didn't you say so when you spoke to me in the street?"

"We had to be sure you have the correct item," Tyre answered. "We can't have it known that agents of Tyre Holdings accost women in the street seeking to buy old earthenware. There would be a line of immigrants," Tyre spat this last word, "outside my door by sunrise."

"Well, I've brought you the cursed old thing. Let's see the color of your money."

"Let's see the item first. Set it on the table there."

"Fine." Fiona set the pot down.

With the release of Fiona's touch, Hili expected to go into the black, but instead, she hovered over the proceedings. The pot sensed danger, and so did Hili, in the form of a prickling sensation in her consciousness. She didn't believe it was an accident that this man had taken the first name of the man who'd wielded the pot in Tyre and then taken Tyre as his last name. No. Something was wrong here.

Tyre walked around the pot, leaning over occasionally and peering closely at the markings. "And how did this come to be in your possession?"

"Me husband found it."

"Where did he *find* it?"

"He didn't steal it if that's what you're implyin.'"

"Make no mistake, Missus Walsh," Tyre donned a pair of white gloves. "I don't care whether he stole it or not. I'm interested only in tracing its origin."

"It's something Paddy's Great Grandfather found in the ruins of a monastery."

"County Kerry?"

"Yes," Missus Walsh said, "how did you—"

"It doesn't matter." Tyre picked up the urn.

The man's touch revolted Hili, even through his gloves. It reminded her of how she climbed into the demon's mouth in Rome. Violence, hate, and greed radiated from the man like a raging fire. He must not get this vessel. If Nigmah could take the pot and it wasn't destined for him, if the barbarian in Umer could, then Hili could affect the gods' plan too. And this Tyre must not be allowed to get it.

"It is genuine," Tyre said at last. "Come, Missus Walsh, my safe is in the back room. Let's get you the reward you so richly deserve."

"It'll be two hundred now," Fiona said.

"That is not the price you agreed upon with Mister Grove this morning."

"That was before I knew how much it meant to you."

"And before you knew the buyer was quite wealthy." Tyre let out a small laugh. "It's too bad you weren't born a man, Missus Walsh. You would have been quite good at business."

"I *am* quite good at business."

"Hardly," Tyre said evenly. "You live on Irish Hill. How good could you be?"

"Good enough not to let this out of my hand until your money is in the other. You've a reputation, Mister Tyre." Fiona stepped around Mr. Grove, who'd come quite close to her now, and snatched up the pot in one quick motion.

"Quite," Tyre said.

Hili didn't understand all that was going on, but she understood enough to know that Tyre was vexed.

"This way, please, Misses Walsh, let us conclude our business." He led her to a door and motioned her through, but instead of entering another room, she'd stepped into an alley beside the building.

Hili wanted to wrap a protective cloak around the woman. She felt so helpless. She willed herself into the skin of the pot, as close to the woman as possible, and to her surprise, it worked. As they stepped into the alley, Grove pointed some kind of hollow stick at the woman.

"Why?" Mrs. Walsh asked. "You've got the money."

There was no trace of a sob or a quaver in Mrs. Walsh's voice. She stood proudly facing the two fancy men. Hili felt sorry for her, and a kind of kinship. This woman was strong and proud.

"It's not about the money. You see, Missus Walsh, no one must know I have this pot. Your husband has been writing quite a few letters to the academic community. A community I am quite active in as a collector of antiquities. I have looked for this urn since I read about its power as a young man. Have you ever heard of the writings of Vitus Domitius?"

Fiona said nothing.

So, this Tyre had somehow found Vitus's work. One more sign that perhaps he wasn't meant to have it. But even if he was, Hili was determined that she would thwart him.

"No matter," Tyre continued. "Now, hand over the pot."

"So you can shoot me? Get fucked, Mister Tyre."

"Quite the mouth," Tyre said. "Grove, take it, but do not touch it."

"What?" Grove turned to Tyre. "How shall I do that?"

In response, Tyre grabbed for the pot.

Fiona yanked it away, then ran.

The sound of thunder filled the alley.

"Fool!" Tyre shouted. "You'll damage the vessel!"

Footsteps echoed off the buildings behind Mrs. Walsh. Hili meant to lend her strength to the woman and concentrated on running. To her surprise, she found herself in full control of Mrs. Walsh's body. She outran her pursuers, but only just. Her body, clothes, and heavy shoes were meant for work and were used to it. Both the clothes and bodies of Grove and Tyre, she suspected, weren't. After running down alleys and across empty streets, she heard rushing water and moved toward it. She passed an immense building, as big as any in Rome, made of tiny bricks. Ahead, a bridge stretched out into the darkness above the rushing water. Hili turned and ran across a muddy field. The pot glowed purple. The pursuing footsteps stopped abruptly. Then cursing.

Hili chanced a look behind her.

Tyre and Grove stood on the edge of the empty lot, knee-deep in the filth. Hili started sinking. She wanted to run on, but even the stout body of Mrs. Walsh had its limits.

"Come back," Tyre called. "We will make a new arrangement."

"No!" Hili and Walsh shouted together, "You shall not have it!"

"Mister Grove is a crack shot, and it seems perhaps you are quite stuck."

Hili did not know what a crack shot was, but she knew it was a threat. She tried to move her feet and found that Tyre was right.

Grove's hollow stick flashed.

A sharp thunder-crack.

Falling.

Then nothing.

Chapter 33

Kelly

Kelly had trouble sleeping after he spoke with Pontes. The most difficult thing to deal with was the now almost certain knowledge that Casey was gone. He didn't want to believe in

The Pull

and Jacob's dreams. He didn't want to believe in his feelings on the night of the fire that Casey was dead. It seemed now that the search had gone the way all searches go for people in dire circumstances: the objective changed from finding Casey to recovering the body and finding out what happened. Almost as difficult to accept, was the fact that Pontes had been working on the mystery of the Boiler House longer than Kelly had been alive, and was no closer to solving it.

Perhaps he could bring a fresh perspective that Pontes didn't possess. Maybe using the objectivity he brought as a journalist, he could turn evidence into the light in a new way and come up with the answer. Pontes had the science, the fire investigations; he even acknowledged

The Pull

but he discounted his brother's dreams almost entirely. Kelly found Jacob's dream, featuring his brother's herringbone coat, quite compelling.

Seen through the objective eye, what was happening at the Boiler House wasn't the work of a serial killer or an arsonist. The missing bodies,

The Pull

and Jacob's dreams negated that. So, if it wasn't a man, what was it?

While Kelly acknowledged there were forces at work in the world other than those his five senses could detect, a haunted boiler was a bridge too far. The problem was, if you ruled out a human antagonist, what you were left with was the supernatural. Kelly pondered the meaning of the term 'supernatural.' Super-natural. Super nature.

Darkness closed in on his mind. It wrapped itself around him, gripping, squeezing, strangling, and tightening. His breath came in jerks and spasms. He tore blindly at the sheets. He was vaguely aware that he was dreaming, but was powerless to wake. The ghostly mill girl stood in the doorway of his dream bedroom, beckoning him with a finger, drawing him up and out of bed toward some unknown end.

The Pull

permeated even his dreams.

He had to go. He needed to go, to see, to find Casey. He had to stop it from happening again. It must be stopped!

He woke with the dawn only a pale promise in the eastern sky, tangled in the sheets by the front door. With the coming of a new day and the rain gone,

The Pull

released him. He rubbed his eyes and tried to remember struggling for the door wrapped in his bedding. No such memory came. He stumbled back to bed, but sleep remained elusive.

Super-natural. "No," Kelly said aloud to the cold, empty room, "not supernatural." That implied a heightened nature. Whatever was happening, it wasn't that. Nature had little to do with it. Super *unnatural* was more like it. So... what was nature? Nature was either God's creation in the form of the environment, or the form of one's instinctual behavior, i.e., Mother nature or man's nature. So, logically, unnatural was against either the environment or one's natural behavior. Normally, the blame for all things unnatural, nuclear waste for example, rested squarely on humanity's shoulders. What did you get on the other side of the equation when you added God into the mix? The Devil?

Following that line of logic suggested that when Kelly and Pontes acted on

The Pull

and wound up at the Boiler House—the Devil made them do it. Kelly just wasn't ready to go down that rabbit hole. What next? 3 AM infomercial Evangelists reading carefully selected scriptures and asking for donations to fight Satan?

Kelly gave up on sleep. He tied on a fuzzy plaid robe and made coffee. Cup in hand, he sat down at his desk and opened his laptop. The first message waiting in his inbox was from Petbe:

Kelly,

This just keeps getting weirder. I exhausted the Patriot's archives without finding much more on the Boiler House, so I decided to call a friend at the UConn, Trull Library. He put me in touch with a student doing doctoral work on immigrant life during the industrial revolution. He's got diaries and all sorts of materials. Fascinating stuff.

After too much coffee and chit-chat, he showed me the diary of a Mrs. Walsh whose husband went missing on the job at (you guessed it) the Boiler House. In it, Mrs. Walsh claims that on March 3, 1905, Mr. Walsh went to work at the Connecticut Mill Company as a Mechanical Engineer and never returned home. She documents her attempts to get the police to investigate and her conversations with Walsh's supervisor. The police asserted that since there was no body, there was no evidence of a crime. His supervisor said that, since Walsh didn't want to perform the assigned task and argued about it, he ran off. Mrs. Walsh refutes this vehemently, insisting that the two were deeply in love and that Walsh was a man with a deep sense of responsibility; he would never run off on a job, or her.

According to Mrs. Walsh, her conversations with her husband's supervisor revealed that Mr. Walsh was tasked with fixing a leaky pipe and reinforcing a rotten floor joist under the floor in the center of the Boiler House.

Now, honestly, I feel we've strayed away from any kind of negligence story we could hang on Tyre or MillCom, but I'm intrigued and absolutely fascinated, in fact. Despite the lack of a newspaper story, I'm going back to Trull tomorrow to go through some more historical materials. Perhaps if there's nothing in this for the Patriot, we could collaborate on a book.

I'll let you know how it goes.

Petbe

A book! Kelly slammed his laptop shut. Didn't the insensitive bastard realize his brother was missing, probably dead? Kelly closed his eyes and concentrated on his breathing. Once he had himself under control, he sipped his coffee as he paced. He thought about

The Pull

It was worse, as Pontes had pointed out, on rainy nights. Sometimes he didn't feel it at all, and he'd never felt it before the night of the fire. What was

The Pull

and why did he (and Pontes, and David Gottschalk) feel it when Kelly felt it? He sat down and looked at the dates. Walsh 3/3/1905, Daniel Costa 4/2/1931, Thomas Pontes 5/1/1970, Freddie Gottschalk 10/5/83, and Casey 11/4/2009. Kelly found no pattern in the numbers, but admittedly, he was no numerologist. There were large gaps and short ones. He tried to make something of the sequential months of the first three deaths: March, April, and May. These dates also had decreasing days of the month, directly inverse of the months themselves: 3rd, 2nd, 1st, while the month numbers rose, 3, 4, 5. He didn't see what the pattern could possibly mean. The numbers jumped when it came to Freddie Gottschalk 10/5 and Casey 11/4, but again, the month number rose while the day numbers went down. Following that pattern, if there were some kind of magic (for lack of a better term) happening in the Boiler House, it might be strong again on 12/3, less than two weeks.

Ridiculous. Absolutely ridiculous. Still, what else did he have? Either there was something supernatural happening there, or there wasn't, and, as his accountant friends might say, the numbers don't lie.

Okay, so there was some order in the chaos. Question was, was there more order in the chaos that he just wasn't seeing yet? What about the victims? Walsh, adult, age unknown. Freddie Gottschalk, a boy. Daniel Costa, a boy. Tom Pontes, young man. Casey Papas, a man. No age similarity. All male, all of immigrant descent: Italian, Portuguese, German, Greek, and Irish. Why? Also, the most recent three victims had brothers who were all adversely affected, more than what was normal for the death of a brother. Jacob Pontes was borderline crazy. Kelly himself was obsessed and felt

The Pull

as did Floyd Pontes and David Gottschalk, and David couldn't even speak now. All brothers. No women victims, no sisters.

The number 12/3 rolled around in Kelly's head all day. 12/3... 123... 1, 2, 3, Go! The more Kelly thought about it, the more convinced he was that on 12/3

The Pull

would be strong. The beginnings of a plan formed in his mind.

Kelly didn't hear from Petbe the next day, so he spent it searching fruitlessly for Casey. Though his gut and the evidence he'd gathered about the Boiler House told him it was in vain, Kelly had to try. He checked the usual haunts, Marv's diner, the package stores, and the streets around Farbank—nothing.

He spent the rest of the week much the same way, searching for his brother by day and puzzling over the Boiler House by night.

After nights of puzzling, Kelly came to the conclusion that the only way he was ever going to know what happened to Casey, or any of the others that disappeared at the Boiler House, was to be there on December third, 12/3, and look inside the boiler. Maybe you had to look on that specific day. That idea begged the question: did anyone look into the boiler on the same day the victim disappeared? In his brother's case, he didn't think anyone looked until the fire was out and cold, if at all. The very earliest anyone, Pontes included, could have searched was well after midnight. Kelly doubted anyone checked when Walsh disappeared because Walsh never went into the boiler, and it was still in operation. No one was likely to look the same day Daniel Costa was killed either. The place was flooded. In fact, the only cases where someone had looked inside the boiler on the day someone disappeared were Pontes and Gottschalk. Jacob Pontes gazed into its black maw that same night, and he was never right after that, same with David Gottschalk.

That intelligence clinched it for Kelly. On December third, he was going to look inside that thing, even at the risk of his sanity. There were some problems with this plan, of course. If he remembered correctly, and in this case, his memory was suspect, the floor in front of the boiler was burned away, so there was no way to get to the front of the boiler. Less of a problem, but still a factor, was that the Boiler House was boarded up tight, and removing the boards was going to be time-consuming and noisy. Third, Lieutenant Pontes was likely to feel

The Pull

on that day too, and be on the lookout for him. If Pontes caught him or got wind of what he was up to, Pontes would surely try to stop him.

The only way to figure out how to do it was to do a little recon. He had to go back in to see, but this time he wouldn't go alone.

Chapter 34

Casey

Blood. The viscous liquid dribbled and poured out of the darkness, carrying Casey into the strange headscape of yet another body. The pain of being eaten alive still reverberated through his consciousness. He could still feel the cockroaches devouring him from the inside out. *Please, God, please, no more! I'll do anything. I'll do whatever you want. I'll go to church every Sunday, every day. I'll never drink again. Not a drop. Not ever. Just please, no more!* If God was listening, there was no sign of it.

As with every time before, he found himself crossing the Bridge Street Bridge on foot. He glanced out of the rectangular windows of the wooden walkway as he passed, and... without even thinking about it, Casey took control of the body and stopped at a window. The black waters of the Nipwìmâw rushed below the bridge as they should. And the bridge appeared much as it did the last time he was here in Costa's body, but the view out the window was wrong. The Boiler House and the Power House were gone. Casey stared. The riverbank where those buildings should be was just a muddy patch of ground outside the Pickering House and the other mills along State Street. It took Casey a minute to puzzle it out: the clopping of horses' hooves on the bridge, the fact that he was in an earlier era each time he was in a new body. The Boiler House and Power House weren't gone; they didn't exist yet. This threw out almost all of the theories he'd come up with. If the boiler or the Boiler House weren't responsible for the deaths, what was? Why was he here now?

"Hey, Mister Papas," someone passing behind him said in a thick Italian accent, "Better get across the bridge. I hear Gottschalk is a stickler about being on time."

It was like someone carpet-bombed Casey's consciousness. He couldn't even comprehend what was happening. First, the Boiler House wasn't even there. Now someone was calling him Papas, *and* he was supposed to report to a man named Gottschalk. He was inside someone with his own last name, about to report to someone with the same last name as another person he'd died inside. He relinquished control of the body as he grappled with the shock.

His host started moving forward again. "Thanks, Mr. uh, Costa, isn't it? Foreman of the masons, right?"

"Anthony. Yes. You are foreman of the carpenters?"

"That's right," Casey's host said, "Patrick Papas." He extended his hand. Costa gave it a quick shake as they walked side by side across the bridge. "Don't worry about Gottschalk, he barks like a German, but he's a pussycat."

"Lousy weather for the first day," Costa said, "not sure how much we will get done. The site looks very muddy."

Casey's host peered out a passing window at the rain. "Yeah, we'll just have to see what Gottschalk has in mind. Do you know any of the other foremen?"

"I've worked with Pontes. He runs the steam shovel crew. Good man. What about you?"

Papas, Costa, Gottschalk, now Pontes? It was like the grim reaper's greatest hits.

"The only other fella I know on this job is Walsh; he's working on the cofferdam. I worked with him on that shoe factory by the falls."

"Little guy, always clears his throat?" Costa asked.

"That's him," Papas replied.

Sweet Jesus, that's the last name. Every single guy I've died inside has a relative on this job. I mean, it can't be a coincidence, can it? Not like this, under these circumstances. It must mean something. Casey reflected on the strangeness of being inside his Great-Great-Grandfather or uncle or something. What if he changed the time stream and made it so that he never existed? Or what if he failed at whatever he was supposed to be doing here with the same result? No more Casey and Kelly. Poof. Nothing was out of the realm of possibilities. One thing was for sure, since he'd died in that boiler, the realm of possibilities had become a very, very big place.

Casey's host exited the bridge with Costa and turned left onto the muddy plain that was the future site of the mills. The rain made patting sounds on his flat fabric cap. Tiny puddles formed in the footprints of the men who'd crossed the mud before them, and as they walked, the mire splashed their pant legs. The two men strode toward the center of the field, past piles of wood and other bulky shapes hidden under canvas tarpaulins. A few men stood gathered under an umbrella talking in low tones.

"Ah," the big man with the umbrella said as they approached, "Mister Papas, Mister Costa." He pulled a pocket watch on a silver chain from his waistcoat pocket, looked at it, and replaced it. "Right on ze time."

"Mister Gottschalk," Papas said, extending a hand, "good morning."

Costa shook Gottschalk's hand and exchanged 'good mornings' as well.

"Now," Gottschalk said from under a thick walrus mustache, "Ve have all ze foremen here. I don't know who knows who, so I will go around ze circle. Mister Papas leads ze carpenters," he said, pointing at Casey's host, "Mister Costa leads ze masons, Mister Walsh ze engineers on ze cofferdam and river operations, Mister Pontes leads ze Teamsters on ze steam shovel, and supplies from ze barges unt ze wagons.

"Ze rain this week has put us quite behind. Ve will have to work together if ve want to keep all ze crews working. I will be under pressure from ze owner to cut ze men until ze weather clears. So, if you want your men paid, ve must keep them busy. Mister Papas, have your men make sure everything is covered, and the tarps are tied off tightly. I expect ze wind to rise, then work with Mister Pontes to secure ze supplies as they come in—"

"We've got to do something about the cofferdam," Walsh began. "The river is still rising."

"Take some of Papas's men," Gottschalk replied, glancing at Casey's host.

Gottschalk kept talking, but Casey wasn't listening. He was trying to remember the term for having your worldview shattered. He'd thought, after all the things he'd experienced... recently? How could he say recently? In the last hundred years? Time had no meaning. He wondered how much time had passed since he'd died in the boiler. He hadn't eaten, hadn't taken a shit, or brushed his teeth in a century, give or take. Cognitive dissonance, that was the term. Until now, he was sure bad old boiler #2 caused all the evil he'd been subjected to, but now there was no boiler, not unless it was hiding under one of these tarps—time to reevaluate.

Each time he'd died, it was in the same spot, boiler or no, and each time the host had said a strange word, like a name. In fact, Casey was sure they were names before they died. The names must be important. Put a pin in that. Each death was all but unavoidable. He no longer thought he was supposed to stop these people from dying. All these deaths were in the past of Casey's future (that thought made his head spin for a second), and you can't change the past. No, for good or ill, he was almost sure that he was experiencing these deaths because he was supposed to learn something, but what? The names? It was a lot of energy, a lot of suffering, just to learn a name. Be it God or the Devil that was sending him here, they were making him suffer more than anyone ever had, dying over and over. He wondered how that stacked up to crucifixion. It took Jesus a couple of days to die, and crucifixion was a horrible way to go, but even the Son of God only had to do it once.

So, what did he have to show for all his suffering? The names and precious little else. That was the part Casey got stuck on. If whatever supernatural force had put him here just wanted him to learn the names, surely there were much easier and less painful ways to do it. There had to be another reason for all this pain and death. Had to be, but Casey, for all his thinking, couldn't figure out what was. So, what did he have? Just the names. Costa had added another: Milcom. The name Milcom resonated somehow from his own time and place, but Casey couldn't make that connection either. Why hadn't this happened to Kelly instead? He was much better at this sort of thing.

The confab in the center of the muddy plain ended while Casey mused. Now he rode shotgun in his ancestor while Papas walked around and gave his men instructions, lending a hand where needed, and encouragement when not. The mud got deeper as the day drew on; maybe deeper wasn't right, it got looser, changing from the normal consistency of mud to something like porridge. Men bogged down, losing shoes and crawling on hands and knees to retrieve them.

As the sky darkened, shouts erupted near a pile of boards at the center of the field. Papas made his way over to investigate, his feet sinking in deeper with each step. The mud pulled and dragged at his shoes, nearly pulling them off. Each time he extracted a foot from the muck, it made a sucking sound like a stubborn cork popping from a bottle. When Papas rounded the woodpile, he found two men sinking in the mud, one to the knees, the other almost to the hips. The man sunk to the hips was nearly hysterical, begging his fellows to pull him free. The other mired man stood perfectly still, his eyes wide with fear. Several men lay across the stack of planks, reaching out for their sinking comrades.

"McMullen," Papas called. He'd stopped on the far side of the stack of wood, afraid to get trapped himself.

"Mister Papas," a man laying across the planks answered, "Paddy got stuck, and Michael tried to help and got stuck himself. This mud is too deep to work in."

Casey remembered Costa, and how he'd built a makeshift raft to sit on top of the mud under the mill. He moved forward, seizing control of the unfamiliar mouth and forming the words:

"Start throwing planks off the top of the stack. Make a walkway to the tools. Get hammers, nails, and saws. We'll put together a raft so we can free them."

"You mean duckboards?" McMullen asked.

Casey didn't know what duckboards were. He moved back from controlling Papas's mouth to see how the man would answer.

Papas shook himself and stared down at his hands as if his body had betrayed him.

"Mister Papas?" McMullen asked.

"Somethin' came over me for a second there. Whoa. Yes, duckboards. And get rope. Hurry now." Papas made his way to the woodpile and began the slippery, precarious business of sliding boards off the pile the men stood on and throwing them into the mud.

"Please, please, God, help me." The man stuck deepest in the mud cried.

"Easy now," Papas said. "It's just mud. We'll have you out in a few minutes. Yer caterwauling like the Devil himself has got you by the ankles."

He just might.

The men knew their craft. In a few short minutes, a walkway three planks wide took shape around the entrenched victims. Then, the walkways started to sink into the mud as the workers gathered around the stuck men and pulled. The mud and the coming night turned the world a monochromatic shade of obscurity.

"Careful now," Papas said. "We don't need anyone else caught in the mire. Get some ropes around them, string them back to harder ground. I want another team on the ropes." Papas pointed to a knot of men gathered around to watch some thirty feet away. "Be quick now."

The men followed Papas's orders. Soon, two teams pulled on ropes looped around the victim's chests. Those closest on the duckboards pulled on any limb they could grab. Inch by inch, the stuck bodies rose from the mud.

The man submerged deepest screamed, "Me ribs, oh God, you've broken me ribs!" His breath came in gasps, his face contorted in agony. The rope slackened a little.

"Keep pulling!" Papas called. "Better broken ribs than drowning slowly." The rope tightened again. The man screamed.

The scene on the duckboards was like something out of a nightmare. Tangles of muddy arms and legs pulled, slipped, and struggled amid the screams of the trapped men. Rescuers tried to wipe mud from their faces with even muddier hands. They managed only to smear the filth around until they were black from head to toe, save for their wild, terrified eyes. The light of lamps held aloft by rescuers gave the filth a sickly yellow pallor.

Casey had no concept of the passage of time. Things played out in infinite slowness. The seething mass of slimy bodies made up a single mud monster with dozens of wiggling arms and legs. By the time the men lay moaning on the sinking duckboards, Casey was convinced he knew how Papas would die, how he was going to die—this time.

Filthy men struggled to help the injured men away; arms slipped for purchase on muddy clothes, slime slopped out of their boots onto the duckboards, causing them to slip and teeter over the ooze as they made their way to safety.

"Everyone back," Papas called, "line up under the eves of the Pickering House." He pointed to the brick wall of the building that lined the east side of the construction site. When Papas was alone on the diminished pile of lumber, Gottschalk made his way across the duckboards.

"Zis is no good. Ze steam shovel is sinking as well."

Papas turned.

The ends of the steam shovel tracks disappeared into the mud. The machine itself belched great clouds of smoke as it backed up along the rails toward the edge of the field. "I hate to see the men lose wages, but it's better than losing *them* to the mud."

"Ya, I don't think your men vill be back to work for a long time," Gottschalk said, gazing at the injured men being loaded onto the back of a wagon. When he turned back in Papas's direction, his eyes grew wide. "Scheisse."

Papas followed Gottschalk's gaze. An ornate carriage, black, a hole in the night, drawn by six black horses, emerged from the bridge and stopped at the construction site. The carriage was visible only by the reflection of swaying lamps on raindrops dotting lustrous dark wood.

"Who?" Papas asked.

"Tyre himself," Gottschalk breathed, "ze owner."

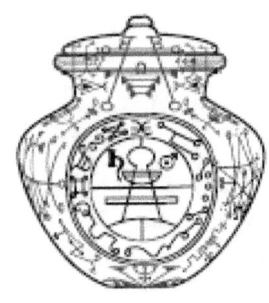

Chapter 35

Hili

Fiona Walsh hit the mud with a wet slapping sound. The rain came harder. The life drained and ebbed from Hili's body; she was alone. She felt the pot in the woman's hands and clung to it with dead fingers. Rain fell into Fiona's open eyes.

Mud oozed up around her. Somewhere in the distance, Tyre and Grove shouted at each other. Hili paid no attention. Whatever Tyre discovered about the pot made no difference now. There was no way anyone was getting out in the middle of this field of mud to get it. Yet, if the vessel was safe, why hadn't she gone into the black? This was something new. The person she inhabited had died, yet here she was.

The cold, slimy filth reached up, gripped her, and pulled her down. The rain tapered off, and just before the mud closed over her, the clouds opened, and a single shaft of moonlight shone down on her.

Deeper and deeper into the oozing recesses of the mire, Hili sank. The cold left her. No sensation at all but the smooth clay vessel in her arms. Then after a time, she went into the black.

She came back, time and again, rising out to the black to the sound of digging. Sometimes it was just the dull thudding of shovels that roused her. Other times, the digging was close enough for Hili to hear muffled cursing.

Chapter 36

Kelly

On Sunday, Kelly dressed in a crisp checked shirt and designer jeans, then headed off to church. It wasn't some newfound sense of piety, though his ruminations about nature, God, and the supernatural were still rolling around in his mind as he went through the sit, stand, kneel routine of a Catholic mass. Kelly went because Father Murray promised to introduce him to someone having to do with the Boiler House.

The sermon was about forgiving yourself as God forgives you, and embracing new beginnings. Kelly got the distinct feeling Father Murray had targeted the sermon at him. He sank low in his pew.

Afterward, in the basement, as Kelly sipped the bitter church coffee from a white foam cup, Father Murray approached with a scarecrow of a man at his elbow. The scarecrow, dressed in black work pants and shirt, kept his head bowed as Murray led him through the crowd. A tattoo in flowing blue script ringed the man's neck in words Kelly couldn't make out.

"Kelly," Father Murray said, "this is David Gottschalk."

"Hi David," Kelly said, extending a hand.

David's eyes snapped to Kelly as if he'd been somewhere else entirely until the priest spoke his name.

Rather than the firm alpha ex-con shake of someone with neck tattoos Kelly expected, David's was limp and tentative.

"I wanted you two to talk. I've spoken to David about what you're up to, and he's agreed to meet with you," Father Murray said. "I'll be back in a few minutes," and with that, the priest disappeared into the crowd gathered in the church basement.

Silence formed a gulf between the two men. David's eyes drifted away.

"David, I—" Kelly began.

David's eyes snapped back. He fished a pad from his pocket and wrote: Father Murray told me that your brother might be... David's pencil faltered. ...that he...

Kelly opened his mouth to help David, but the words turned to ash when David wrote: ...the boiler...

He looked up at Kelly suddenly, and with an intensity Kelly didn't think the man possessed a moment before. Then he wrote: You want to know about Freddie?

Kelly couldn't help feeling bad for David. Like he was exposing this man, picking at psychological scabs. "I want to know as much as you're willing to tell me."

Do you mind if we talk in the sanctuary? David wrote, casting his eyes around to the knots of people in the rec hall.

"Whatever makes you the most comfortable," Kelly said.

David led him up the back stairs and into the church proper. He crossed himself and sat down in the pew closest to the altar. Kelly did the same.

We weren't good kids, David wrote on a fresh sheet of paper. He pinned his eyes on the crucifix behind the altar as if somehow trying to catch the eye of the plaster Christ that hung there. He wrote on: We smashed mailboxes and driveway lights. We stole cigarettes and drugs from our parents. I guess our parents weren't good adults either, but that doesn't excuse anything. We all have choices, right? Even Freddie had a choice. At least that's what I've tried to make myself believe, but you know how kids are. He wanted to be a part of something. He wanted to belong. I was his big brother. I was supposed to be looking out for him. I—well, I realize now that Paddy and I were high, not just on dope, but on power. We had power, even if it was just over my little brother. Hazing, that's what they call it, or initiation. Turns out it was really murder.

The silence stretched. At first, Kelly thought David was just lost in memories. Then David's lips moved with faint whispers of breath. So, he *could* speak.

Sorry, David wrote at last, I... sometimes if the memories are strong, it helps to pray. He drew in a breath and let it out slowly, then flipped the page on his pad and started writing again. It happened fast. So fast, and yet I remember every detail diamond perfect. It doesn't play out in my head as much as it used to, but still, when I do see it, it's best to be here. I even got a job here, cleaning up, maintenance, doing the grounds. I sleep here most of the time. Father Murray lets me. So I guess you want to know what happened? What I saw?

Kelly nodded, but David was again staring at the crucifix, lips moving.

After another long pause, David picked up his pen and began again: Freddie went in, climbed into that boiler like a zombie. He was scared. I don't blame him. It was creepy. I was even a little scared, too. Part of me wanted to call it off, tell him to forget it, but I was the leader... so... so I closed the door on him. It couldn't have been more than a minute. Less probably. Then

I opened the door. I called him, and he didn't answer. I called again—same thing. I tried to get Paddy to check, but Paddy said it was my idea so—so—so I climbed into the hatchway. David crossed himself. Then he spoke in a whisper: "Our Father who art in heaven, hallowed be thy name. Thy kingdom come. Thy will be done on earth as it is in heaven. Give us this day—"

As David finished the prayer, his hands trembled. A tear formed in the corner of his eye and bled down his cheek.

Sorry about that, David wrote: I can't help it. Freddie jumped up and started laughing at me. Then something rose up behind him. It was silhouetted in a purple glow from deep inside the boiler. The light behind him kept getting brighter. The thing was like a skeleton, but in a suit... David stopped writing and whispered: "Hail Mary, full of grace, the Lord is with thee...." He started writing again: It looked at me. I saw into its eyes. Cat's eyes. "Blessed art thou among women and blessed is the fruit of thy womb Jesus."

The bits of prayer interspersed with David's narrative made the hairs on the back of Kelly's neck prickle. He found it disconcerting, but it also pointed to the sincerity of David's tale. Even if Kelly didn't fully accept what he was reading, he couldn't deny that David absolutely believed.

David flipped another page and wrote: I could see the glow of the boiler all around it. "Holy Mary, mother of God...." David's pencil moved faster, the writing becoming almost illegible: I saw in its eyes, and in my head at the same time, people dying. "Pray for us sinners..." He wrote: It opened its mouth wide, wider, impossibly wide, like a snake about to swallow a rabbit. "Now and at the hour of our death..." David's pencil resumed its shaky scratching: I started to back away. I tried to warn Freddie. He just laughed. I jumped out of the hatchway. "Pray for us sinners. Pray for us sinners. Pray for us sinners..." The thing bent down.... The boiler door slammed shut. "Now, and at the hour of our death...."

"Amen," Father Murray said. He stood next to David in the aisle and laid a hand on the man's shoulder. "Why don't you sign David? I'll interpret for you."

David nodded. His hands started moving.

"We heard Freddie screaming," Father Murray said, translating David's rapid-fire sign language, "Paddy and Tammy tried to open the boiler door, but it was stuck. Hannah laughed. She thought Freddie was playing a joke on us. I should have done something; he was my brother. I was so scared. I'm still scared. The thing inside the boiler, it's like it was inside my head. I could hear it. N-none of the others say they heard it...."

"Our Father who art in heaven," David whispered.

"It talked to me while it killed Freddie," Father Murray continued his translation, "While it burned him alive."

"Hallowed be thy name, thy kingdom come...."

"Its voice was like a thousand screaming babies in my head." Father Murray looked as if he were going to choke while interpreting David's words.

"Thy will be done, on earth as it is in heaven...."

"It's okay, David. You're safe. The Lord is with you." Father Murray said.

David wept. He brushed his tears away with a balled fist. When he lifted his hands to his face, the same script tattooed on David's neck peeked out from his shirtsleeve. Just a few words: 'a guardian cherub.'

David signed when his tears were under control.

Father Murray translated. "It said Freddie walks among the fiery stones. Then it laughed."

"Give us this day our daily bread...." David whispered, even as his hands formed different words.

Father Murray kept his hand on David's shoulder as he interpreted. "The laugh was so terrible, so evil. I heard Freddie scream louder. I heard him banging on the boiler."

"And forgive us our trespasses... oh Lord forgive me...." David broke into uncontrolled sobs and hid his face in his hands.

"It's okay, David. You were forgiven long ago," Father Murray said.

David's hands moved again.

"It screamed in my head." Father Murray moved his hand gently on David's shoulder. "FIERY STONES! It was so loud. It, that thing was inside me."

"As we forgive those who trespass against us...."

"I wanted to help Freddie. I wanted to open the boiler, but that thing was inside me. Oh, God."

David buried his face in his hands again.

"God is here with you, David. Finish the prayer." Father Murray placed his other hand on David's head.

"And lead us not into temptation...." David wailed and sobbed uncontrollably.

Kelly felt vaguely dirty observing this spectacle. David put himself through this at Kelly's behest, and Kelly didn't know what to do. Should he say something soothing or put a hand on the man's arm?

"But deliver us from evil," Father Murray said, finishing the prayer for David.

"Amen," David sobbed.

"Amen," Father Murray said in a tone of agreement.

"Amen," Kelly breathed in spite of himself.

"You are delivered, David. You are delivered from evil," the priest said.

Kelly remained silent. His sense of being an ugly, unbelieving voyeur was stronger than ever. "I'm sorry," Kelly said. The hollow pointless words tumbled from his throat automatically. "I..." further speech wouldn't come. If Kelly had any remaining doubts about the supernatural nature of what was happening in the Boiler House when he started this interview, they were gone now.

It took David several minutes to regain his composure. Kelly wanted to excuse himself. He couldn't just get up and go. He couldn't walk out on a man who'd just exposed that level of pain. David laid his soul bare in front of Kelly. There was another reason Kelly couldn't go. As much as he hated himself for it, he had to have answers. He needed to know about the words tattooed on David's skin, and he had to know about how David experienced

The Pull

After David settled down, Kelly said: "thank you for telling me—" he almost said, 'your story,' but realized how terribly belittling it would sound, so he said: "—the truth. I can see how painful it was. I think the same thing happened to my brother, and I'm grateful to know maybe how it was for him. If you don't mind, can I ask... can you tell me about your tattoos?"

David dropped his head and examined the words ringing his wrist, marching across the skin like little black ants. He signed.

"Scripture, old testament, for protection," Father Murray articulated. To David, he said, "Having God in your heart is all the protection you need, David."

"No. I have to feel the pain of the needle. I have to have these words on me. I don't expect either of you to understand. I just have to."

"Can I ask you one more thing, David?"

He nodded.

"I saw a man in a hooded sweatshirt outside the Boiler House, twice now. Was that you?"

"Yes. Sometimes... I know it's weird, but sometimes I just have to go. I have to be there. It's almost like Freddie is back. Just inside. Waiting for me to come get him, but... but I can't go in."

Chapter 37

Casey

"Z is is bad," Gottschalk said as the impossibly thin coachman climbed down and opened the carriage door with a flourish.

"Why?" Papas asked, "because of the work stoppage?"

"Yes," Gottschalk never took his eyes from the coach, "but zere is something else. Zat man..." Gottschalk whispered low, "... is evil."

"The hell you say." Papas shot back.

"You will see."

The men quit their various tasks one by one and took shelter from the wind and rain against the wall of the Pickering House. Papas turned his attention back to the carriage.

A man stepped out dressed in a fine wool suit and black hat. He surveyed the scene, stamped his cane into the ground, then picked his way along the darkened field o f m ud t hat h ad just tried to claim two of Papas's men. "Gottschalk!" he shouted as he neared the center of the construction site. The duckboards slowed his determined stride.

G ottschalk rose, whispered: "pray for me," then advanced along the planks toward Tyre. "Herr—I mean, Mister Tyre, it's good—"

"GOOD?" Tyre bellowed, "*Mister* Gottschalk, nothing is good. The job you are doing is not good, the weather is not good, and you know damn well it is not good to see *me*. Nothing that is happening here is good." Tyre softened his tone to something approaching conversational, but it held back oceans of venom. He put a fist on his hip, drawing back his coat flap to emphasize the pistol in his belt. "So tell me, Mister Gottschalk, what were you about to say was good?"

"I-I vas going to say it's good to see you."

Tyre laughed. It was not a kind laugh.

Gottschalk shrank back and snatched the cap off his head, holding it in both hands.

"That's a lie, isn't it? It isn't good to see me, is it?"

"Nein, I mean no, sir."

"You have trouble with English, don't you, Mister Gottschalk?"

"Yes, Mister Tyre," Gottschalk pronounced each word with great care.

"Yessss," Tyre hissed. "Tell me, *Mister* Gottschalk, since you're such an aficionado of that filthy language, what does Gottschalk mean in German?"

"I—"

"I'll tell you what it means. It means Servant Of The Lord, *Mister* Gottschalk. So, tell me this, are you a servant of the Lord?"

"Y-yes Mister—"

"NO!" Tyre raised his cane as if to strike the man.

Gottschalk took a step back along the wood plank.

"You are NOT a servant of the Lord."

"I serve the Lord our Go—"

"I AM THE LORD OF THIS PIECE OF GROUND MISTER GOTTSCHALK!" Tyre's voice thundered and rolled away across the black muddy plain. Then, in an almost casual tone, he said: "While you are here, while I'm paying you, you are supposed to serve me. And I can tell you—" Tyre swept his cane in a wide arc that forced Gottschalk to duck, "—that I am not being served here. Now tell me, Mister Gottschalk, why is no one working?"

"The weather—"

"The weather? Really, Mister Gottschalk? Have you hired a bunch of straw men that will wilt and bend in the rain?"

"No, the—"

"Paper then? Are they made of paper?" Tyre advanced a step.

"No, Mister—"

"Plaster, perhaps?" Tyre set the foot of his cane on the toe of Gottschalk's boot and pressed.

"No. Ouch!"

"Paper mâché then?"

"Please, Mister Tyre. Ve have been vorking hart—"

"I see no work. On what have you been working? I see only the same field of mud I saw when I rode by two days ago."

"Zhe cofferdam, Mister Tyre, and ze granite to shore up ze river bank. Ze river is rising with ze rain. Ve have to stop ze river from overtopping ze cofferdam."

"Surely, it doesn't take all the men to do that. Why is no one else working?"

"Ze rain has made the ground unstable. Ze granite just sinks in the mud."

"THEN ORDER MORE GRANITE!"

"I have Mister Tyre, but ze river is too vild, rough I mean, for ze barges to bring it down from New Hampshire."

"So you are telling me that the first hundred tonnes of granite I've had you dump down here haven't had any effect? You can't even lay a cornerstone?"

"Everything sinks, Mister Tyre. No matter how much we put, a pit always forms."

"It looks flat to me," Tyre was saying. "Show me. Step out into the field and show me."

Gottschalk didn't move. "Ve have already almost lost two men in ze mud. Ve broke their ribs trying to pull them out."

"Tut, tut, Mister Gottschalk." His voice mellowed for a moment, then Tyre shouted again. "Four hundred dollars a day, and your men are doing nothing!" Tyre clouted Gottschalk on the head with his cane. "YOU'RE FIRED! Get out of my sight."

Gottschalk clapped a hand to his head and hurried away, his lantern bobbing along the duckboards at half-mast.

"YOU!" Tyre pointed his cane at Papas. "What's your name?"

Papas stood erect. "Patrick Papas."

"These duckboards, they are your doing?"

"My carpenters, yes, sir."

"You are in charge now, Mister Papas."

Shouts from the river's edge interrupted him. "More sandbags!" and "The pumps can't keep up!"

Tyre frowned. "Those pumps are the latest, most modern, most expensive steam pumps money can buy. Papas, stoke them up and get this operation moving. Save my expensive steam shovel, and make sure those cofferdams hold. Everyone else is to start digging. Find me bedrock, Mister Papas. We have a building to erect."

"You want the men to dig, sir?"

"With their bare hands, if there are not enough shovels."

"Yes, Mister Tyre."

Here it comes. This is when we die. He wondered what was going through Papas's mind. Fear? Anger? Determination? He wished he could somehow communicate with the ancestor whose body he was hitchhiking in. Tell the man what was about to happen. Certainly, Papas was about to die in the mud. Would Casey hear another strange name at the end to add to his collection of enigmas? He didn't think he could stop Papas from dying. He was frightened of dying. Frightened of the terrible pain of it, but he was fairly certain, now, that he wasn't supposed to stop it. Casey still didn't know why this was happening. The only thing he could latch onto was the growing list of names his hosts uttered as they died.

Papas stomped off down the duckboards barking orders, sending men to the pumps, and forming sandbag crews to build up the cofferdam. He sent another team to try to shore up the tracks for the steam shovel. The rest of the men groaned when Papas told them about Tyre's order to dig.

"But Patrick—" Pontes started when Papas drew near.

Papas waved a hand for silence, walked right up close, and whispered: "Find Gottschalk, have him meet me behind the steam shovel."

Pontes nodded and hurried away.

"Mister Papas!" Tyre bellowed.

Casey's heart sank. Had Tyre overheard the beginnings of what Casey assumed was some kind of mutiny?

Papas turned and picked his way across the duckboards, holding a lantern in front of him. "Yes, Mister Tyre?"

"What did you say to that man?" The light from the lantern held at Casey's side cast ominous shadows up at Tyre's already sinister face.

Papas trembled. "I told him that he should start digging if he wanted bread on his table tonight."

"Excellent." Tyre smiled, and in the lamplight, the shadow of his mouth stretched into eternity.

The rain picked up in intensity. It pelted Papas's clothes as he hurried around the edge of the mud toward the steam shovel. On the other side, he found not only Gottschalk, but Pontes, Costa, and Walsh, huddled around a lantern, whispering.

"Papas, come." Gottschalk extended a beckoning hand. "Tyre is evil."

"Yes," Papas said, "yes, he is. He's going to get men killed today if this keeps up."

The voice belonged to a newcomer, just outside the circle of light.

"Unt who are you?" Gottschalk asked.

A black man of about forty years, in a fine suit, stepped into the light, holding an umbrella. "Dr. Douglas Freeman—"

"A negro doctor," Walsh scoffed.

"Zis is not ze time, Mister Walsh!" Gottschalk glared at Walsh.

"Yes," Freeman went on unphased, as if Walsh had merely asked about the weather. "I hold a doctorate in the study of antiquities from Howard University." He paused to look at each of the men, then focused on Walsh. "You wouldn't happen to be the son of Liam Walsh?"

"You leave me Da out of this," Walsh said, rising.

"I'm afraid your Da is very much a part of this. I've just been to see him, and he told me where to find you."

"What do you want with my family?" Walsh looked like he wanted to punch Freeman.

"I came across some letters written to my predecessor many years ago, letters that, sadly, went unanswered."

"No one would believe an Irish immigrant laborer about some old pot he claimed was valuable. Anyway, if you've been to see him, you know it's too late. Now, be gone with you. We've bigger things going on than my father's love of some old urn."

"There is nothing more important, I promise you. No one believed your father because of who he was, where he came from. Do not make the same mistake with me."

"Speak your piece, Mister Freeman," Papas said, "be quick about it."

"Very well. I've come all this way because three pieces of information point to what could be a disaster about to happen right here. The first are your father's letters and drawings, stating that the pot is here in Trull. The second is that Tyre had been looking for that pot for many years. You see, he also regularly corresponded with my predecessor at Howard University about the pot's probable location. He stopped about fifteen years ago as if he suddenly lost interest—"

"Or he learned where it was," Costa put in.

"Me sainted mother...." Walsh sagged, his fists loosened.

"Yes," Freeman said, "I'm very sorry, son. The timeline seems to match. Tyre stopped looking for it right about the time your mother disappeared with it."

"I'm gonna kill him," Walsh started forward.

Pontes and Costa held him back.

"Walsh, for God's sake," Gottschalk said. "Hear zhe man out."

"Please wait, Mister Walsh," Dr. Freeman said, "if I'm right, you're going to need my help, and we *are* going to have to kill him."

"Why? What's so special about zhis vase?" Gottschalk asked, "What does it have to do with our troubles today?"

"I'm getting to that, Mister Gottschalk. You see, I don't think Tyre had it. If he did, something terrible would already have happened."

"I've seen men digging here," Costa said. "And I've heard rumors that Tyre himself comes out on rainy nights to dig."

"Aye, you can see him when the moon is full. He turns into a vampire," Pontes laughed.

"Not a vampire, and not yet," Freeman said. "The third piece of information that brought me to you was found in the university archives. A scroll, written by a priest, Orde Olivarius, in 410 AD transcribes an earlier scroll written by one Vitus Domitius in 58 BC. This scroll contains drawings and information about a pot that holds great evil. The sketches your father sent us match the drawings on the scroll. After speaking with your father, Mister Walsh, I'm convinced that the pot that so fascinated him, the pot your mother disappeared with, is the same pot that's somewhere in that field of mud."

"What makes you think it's there?" Gottschalk asked.

Freeman fixed him with a knowing look. "Why else would Tyre have everyone digging in the mud?"

Casey, who'd been riding shotgun in Papas's head, listening, now sank into despair. Some of the story made sense to him now—terrible sense. The purple shit he'd picked up just before he died was a broken piece of a pot. He understood now. He could see it. And if it was there for him to pick up in 2020, it meant that these men would never find it.

"Does all of this have anything to do with Ezekiel's prophecy in Chapter 28?" Pontes asked.

"It may," Dr. Freeman replied. "Do you have a Bible handy?"

"I don't need one," Pontes said. "I know it."

"Be prepared to recite it," Freeman said.

"So you know how to stop Tyre, stop ze evil?" Gottschalk asked.

"I know from the ancient texts. I know the beast has six names. And I know that the one who will speak them... is coming."

Chapter 38

Hili

Flowing thoughts, moving through her stream of consciousness, then cascading a waterfall without form into the body of another.

Mud. Cold, wet, slimy mud oozed through fingers, frozen nearly stiff. This was a cold place, a gray place, an unhappy place. The body she inhabited now kneeled in the mire, digging by hand in a long row of others, doing the same. Her fingers rested on the rough, hard form of the pot, buried in the mud.

"Oh my God!" The man who'd been digging near her jumped to his feet and staggered back, mud slopping over the tops of his boots.

The wan yellow light of a lantern set in the filth revealed the rotten face of Mrs. Fiona Walsh.

Shouts of fear rose up all around her. Lanterns and men dashed from their holes in the mud and gathered to see the gruesome spectacle.

"What's going on here?" A man in black boots stared at Hili. There was something faint in his eyes, an almost imperceptible purple glow. Like the magic of the pot. His mouth hung open. He could *see* her, and even more incredible, she could see *him*
"You can *see* me?" she asked.

"Of course I can see you," magic eyes replied. His gaze fell from her face to the half-buried pot.

Hili followed his eyes. The glyphs on the pot glowed purple.

"You're the demon?" he asked.

"No." She held up a muddy hand. "No. But he's coming."

A man with a walking stick in a fine suit sped toward them, shouting. "What have you found? I demand to know right now!"

The man with the purple glow looked over his shoulder.

"I think *that's* the demon," Hili whispered.

"Hurry, we have to bury it before he gets here." He dropped to his knees and started slinging mud over the vessel.

Hili had to trust the man with the purple glow. There was no time for anything else. She clawed at the porridge-like dirt, raking it over the cursed urn.

"You're one of the good guys, right?" magic eyes asked.

"Good guys?" She didn't look up. She needed to hide the pot, bury it.

"What have you got there?" The man with the suit and cane was almost on them.

Chapter 39

Kelly

On Monday, Kelly received a message from Petbe:

Kelly,

Though I've begged off of the Boiler House story, I did get an email from a contact I had poking around at the UConn archives. There is a reference in the journal of a man called Helmut Gottschalk concerning an altercation between the workers building the Boiler House and a Mr. Tyre, founder of Tyre Holdings. There was a one-day general strike, or something very like it. Unusual given the attempts of the Mill girls to organize less than a generation earlier. He also details his study of the Bible and writes that Tyre, as in Tyre Holdings, was a city in ancient Lebanon, destroyed by God because the inhabitants worshipped a false idol called Milcom.

Connection to MillCom Real Estate, perhaps? Even more interesting is that the rest of that journal is illegible. The pages are stuck together with what appears to be dried mud.

Petbe

MillCom, Tyre, Gottschalk, all the names connected, but to what end? Petbe's email illuminated nothing. In fact, it deepened the darkness in which Kelly found himself enveloped.

And there were other fish to fry. He was knee-deep in planning what he'd come to think of as the December 3rd assault on the Boiler House. In light of the disappearances and the floor in front of the boiler being gone, he needed some help. A ladder would just sink into the mud, and besides, he just had a bad feeling about what was down there—a *very* bad feeling.

Problem was, Kelly lacked the contacts for what he had in mind. He'd been poking around on various websites for a week since the idea occurred to him, but he couldn't just come out and ask Joe hobbyist to risk his life in the commission of a crime. Kelly suspected that money would be a poor incentive for the average person. No, it needed to be the right kind of guy to pull this off—someone who'd do it for the thrill.

Eight days into his search, Kelly was beginning to despair. He was sitting at his desk sipping coffee, reading the paper when he came across this headline:

VANDALS SCALE CITY HALL

There they are. He read on.

Tuesday morning, a new flag fluttered in the breeze atop City Hall Tower with a simple message: Save South Common. The 8'x10' flag was hoisted some 180' above City Hall during the night by Frank 'FUBAR' Freeman and Stephen 'Steve' Walsh.

The southeast corner of the beloved public park is slated to be converted to low-cost housing. The two activists say they wanted to bring the city's plans into the public eye. Freeman and Walsh, neighborhood residents and mountaineers, said in a statement on City Hall steps that they believe it would be a great detriment,

Kelly skipped ahead.

Mayor Edward O'Malley said the city would not file charges if the two took down the flag...

Those are my guys, all right.

It didn't take him long to track down Fubar and Steve. A few phone calls later, Kelly had a meeting set up at Marv's Diner later in the afternoon. He'd given out as little information as possible on the phone because he needed the rest of the day to construct the conversation in his head. If he wanted this to come off, he couldn't just say, "will you rappel me into a haunted boiler?"

What *to* say, though? Kelly doubted this would be much of a technical challenge for two men who scaled a 180' tower in the dead of night. He'd have to appeal to their sense of adventure, and perhaps, perversity. Maybe such men would be in it for the thrill of breaking and entering, but just in case, he knew he needed to concoct a story to tempt them. It needed to contain just enough truth to be enticing, but not so much truth that they'd think he was a wacko, or full of shit, or both. Can't open the conversation with "Do you believe in ghosts?" either.

Kelly arrived at the diner early so he could wait and secure one of the seven coveted booths. All the booths were occupied when he arrived, so he sat at the counter and waited. Hazel poured him coffee, and they chit-chatted about this and that. He asked if she or Marv had seen Casey. She just shook her head sadly. Kelly expected that. He'd still been looking for his brother in the afternoons, but his heart told him that the Boiler House was the key.

When Hazel wandered off to help other customers, Kelly turned his mind to the meeting ahead. If he couldn't convince these men to help, he had no idea how he was going to get into that boiler on December third. Doubt chewed away at his mind. What if the dates didn't mean anything after all? What if the disappearances were just coincidences? It was entirely possible that one or two were the work of killers, the rest, accidents. As far as

The Pull

dreams and visions, and his own ill-defined sense that Casey was there, well, that could be chalked up to guilt-induced delusions.

A booth emptied. Hazel motioned him to sit while she cleared away the dishes. Kelly sat with his coffee, looking out at the busy street. He wished, as he often did, that he had a hand to hold, someone next to him, reassuring him, lending him strength. The cars that passed weren't new, most of them at least a dozen years old. The businesses along the street were a collection of mom-and-pop specialty shops, second-hand stores, insurance agencies, and the like, most doomed to fail. It was the hangover, Kelly supposed, from the end of the industrial revolution. When the people and resources of Trull were used up or became aware of their value and got expensive, the robber barons of the early twentieth century packed up and moved south to warmer and cheaper climbs. They left the mill towns from Maine to Connecticut to flounder in depression. Trull never fully recovered, there not being enough money and jobs left to nurse her crumbling brick infrastructure back to health. The bleakness of this city left a faint smudged fingerprint on the souls of everyone who called her home.

Kelly was roused from his contemplation when two men walked in and spoke to Hazel at the counter. She motioned them toward Kelly's booth with a word and a vague swish of the half-full coffeepot in her hand. The first of the two, a tall, lean, brown-skinned man of about thirty, introduced himself as Steve, gave Kelly a firm handshake, and slid in across from him.

Kelly had a hard time believing the second man could even scale a ladder to change a lightbulb. He was a little older than Steve, brown-skinned as well, pot-bellied, wearing a rumpled T-shirt, khakis, and funny-looking sneakers.

"Fubar," he said, enfolding Kelly's hand in a bone-crushing grip.

"So, what's this all about, Kelly?" Fubar asked as he slid in next to Steve.

"I'm a reporter," Kelly began.

"Yeah, for the Chronicle. We know you. Checked you out." Fubar said.

"Not anymore. I'm freelance now, doing a story for the Ware Patriot."

"What happened?"

The question annoyed Kelly, as did Fubar's blunt manner. Too rude and forward for a first meeting. Still, Kelly wanted to build trust, so he answered. "I wanted to report news they didn't want to print."

"Like what?"

Jesus, this guy has balls. "Doesn't matter."

"Does to us," Fubar said.

"I don't see how it matters." Kelly folded his arms across his chest. "I'm here to talk about a little climbing adventure."

"Don't bullshit us, Kelly. We're not a couple of dopes on ropes. If this were a trip to El Capitan, you would have told us over the phone. You didn't, but you did pique our interest enough to meet with you."

Kelly nodded. He was going to have to tell them more than he'd planned. He just hoped they'd still agree to help when he was done. "Okay, I wanted to publish a piece that painted MillCom Real Estate in a negative light."

"Same sons-of-bitches that are trying to put apartments in the park," Steve said.

Kelly almost smacked his forehead with the heel of his hand. All he'd had to do was check a little further, maybe read the whole newspaper story before diving into this. "The place we'd be going into is owned by MillCom, and figures into the story."

Fubar smiled. "Go on..."

"Well," Kelly continued, "My brother disappeared the same night as a recent fire there. In eighty-three, a thirteen-year-old boy disappeared there, seemingly right in front of his brother. In nineteen seventy, a scrap-iron worker was involved in an explosion there. His body was never found...."

"So, what are you saying? There's now a very geriatric killer living in there?"

"I don't know what I'm saying. That's the problem."

"Where do we come into it?" Steve asked.

"It all seems to center around an old boiler in the middle of the room. The fire inspector is evasive about whether the boiler was searched after my brother disappeared. The floor around the boiler is burned away."

"And..." Steve raised an eyebrow.

"And I was hoping you could rappel me in from the roof to get a look inside," Kelly said, crossing his fingers under the table.

"Belay," Fubar said.

"Huh?"

"When I do it myself, I'm rappelling. When I lower you, you're on belay."

"When?" Kelly smiled, "not *if*?"

"Slow down," Fubar said. "We'll need to get a look at the place first. Honestly, though, what do you think you'll find in there?"

"I really don't know."

Chapter 40

Casey

Papas, and so Casey also, went around the site, offering encouragement to the men. He checked on the pumps and the cofferdam and made sure the lamps had oil. Then he told his carpenters to expand the system of duckboards to aid with the digging. Casey noticed the men eyeing Tyre. There wasn't much to see, though. The dark-suited Tyre stood in the center of the pitch, tapping his obsidian cane into the black muddy night.

The rain turned to a deluge. Thunder bashed the sky into an avalanche of sound that rolled across the site and sent some men scurrying for cover.

"Get back to work, you immigrant scum!" Tyre shouted, "I'm paying a solid wage, and I want a solid day's work! There is still half an hour to go! PAPAS!"

Here we go. I'm ready for you, fucker. Freeman said there were six names, and this body I'm in, this ancestor, has the last one. The final piece of the puzzle to fucking kill you and stop all this!

Papas hurried across the duckboards. "Yes, Mister Tyre?"

"I put you in charge so that you could get a decent day's work out of these filthy animals! Get them moving again!"

Casey felt Papas shaking with rage. Papas's mouth opened to speak, but he was interrupted by a shout before the first words came out.

"Oh my God!" someone called from the line of men digging on their hands and knees.

Papas hurried over, squelching through the thick mud. A growing knot of men rose and backed away from a hole. Some crossed themselves in the lamplight, their lips moving in prayer.

A skeletal face peered out of the mud.

Casey took control of Papas and looked at the figure digging with him, gauging his reaction. Casey had to be sure the face in the mud was real, and not another trick of the boiler, or whatever the fuck had brought him here across time.

The man kneeling next to the hole had a strange purple glow about the eye. The same purple...

Casey stared.

"You can see me?" the man asked.

"Of course I can see you," Casey replied, not wanting to tip his hand until he knew what the hell was going on.

Something caught his eye. There in the mud, the purple glow. But not shards this time. An earthenware jar the size of a baby lay swaddled in filth, pulsing with purple power. Whole and complete, the thing that, in Casey's future past, started it all. Son of a bitch. The purple glowing pot—the faint purple eyes—this was it. This was the confrontation. Casey steeled himself. "You're the demon?" he asked.

"No." he raised a muddy hand. "No. But he's coming."

"What have you found? I demand to know right now!" Tyre shouted, advancing down the line of digging men.

"I think *that's* the demon," the man with the glowing eyes whispered. "Hurry, we have to bury it before he gets here."

Casey dropped to his knees, and they both dug madly, flinging mud onto the urn, trying to blot out the glow.

"You're one of the good guys, right?" Casey asked. There was no time to bury it. Tyre was on them.

"Good guys?" the man asked. "I'm goo—"

"Run!"

The man gazed at him quizzically.

"If you know what's good for you, you'll get the fuck out of here," Casey urged again, rising.

The urn glowed into the night, despite the mud on top of it.

"That," Tyre pointed as he stomped to a stop on the plank beside Casey, "is mine."

"Fuck off," Casey wound up to punch Tyre.

Tyre swept him aside, hurling him into the mud like a rag doll.

Thunder pounded the night.

Lightning forked down from heaven.

Tyre picked up the pot and worked the lid free. "AT LAST!"

"Saa ya sita kupita kilele cha jua, siku ambayo," Dr. Freeman stood on the edge of the mudflat shouting, "jumla yake ni sita, sema majina sita ya huyo pepo na ataangamizwa. On the sixth hour past the sun's meridian, on the day whose sum is six, speak the six names of the demon, and it will be destroyed."

"You don't know the names." Tyre drew his pistol.

"I know—"

Casey lept at Tyre.

Tyre fired.

All three fell in the mud, two together, one alone.

Chapter 41

Hili

As with every time before, the man who worked the lid open snuffed the urn's evil smoke up his nose.

The storm, shocked from its ebb, redoubled its effort to drown the night, and everyone in it.

Hili left the person who discovered the pot, pouring like blood into the demon's shadow. One with the glowing purple eyes who'd told her to run, picked himself up out of the mud, and stood facing the demon, fists clenched.

"You," the demon growled. "Ignorant fool. Die now!"

Purple Eyes stood his ground. He arched his arm back, preparing to strike.

The demon held the pot in front of him.

"You can break it, but only a Keeper can *destroy* it," the demon hissed.

Purple Eyes punched.

"NO!" Hili shouted.

The urn shattered.

Hili shifted, her perception liquid. She flowed back into the body of the man standing in the mud. "No. No, no, no!"

Chapter 42

Kelly

Kelly didn't sleep well. His dreams were filled with visions of the boiler door swinging open to reveal Casey burning alive inside. Then the vision changed: Kelly hung from a burning rope. Twice he woke as the rope burned through, and he fell into blackness. Deeper into the bitter darkness of the night, Kelly woke to the sensation that he wasn't alone. The mill girl stood in the doorway a heartbeat longer than she ever had before. She wore a white apron smeared in blood, and her dark hollow eyes looked right through Kelly. He opened his mouth to shout, "What?!" But by the time the word reached his lips, the spirit vanished. Kelly sat in the darkness pondering the strangeness of the ghost, and that he never seemed to remember his encounters with her after they'd occurred. Only when she visited again, would he recall she'd visited before. Once his heart stopped thundering in his chest and he realized there would be no further sleep, Kelly got up and made coffee.

Dawn's ghostly gray light crept into Kelly's window. It held a cold, pitiless quality that left Kelly feeling empty and alone. He did his best to shrug off his disquiet while he dressed and set off on his daily fruitless, and he was almost certain, pointless, search for Casey on the streets of Trull.

The search, as expected, revealed nothing. Casey hadn't been to the package stores or homeless shelters. Marv and Hazel at the diner hadn't seen him, and there was no sign of him among the bums sleeping in doorways or gathered under the bridge abutments along the Nipwìmâw. He ended sitting in his car parallel parked along State Street near the end of the old Pickering House, now turned condos. The feeble afternoon sun did little to warm the car, so Kelly left it running. Fubar and Steve were late.

As the minutes ticked by to the rat-a-tat-tat of the Toyota's laboring engine, Kelly thought about his brother. He had a sense, equally indefinable and unshakable, that his brother was close. He could feel a vague presence in his bones. Kelly knew it was impossible, or at least extremely unlikely, that if Casey were in the Boiler House, he was alive.

A rap on his car window brought him back to reality. Fubar stood hunched over outside with a large canvas pack on his back. Behind him, Steve stood with a similar bag.

"Wakey wakey Kelly," Fubar grinned, "we gonna do this?"

"Yeah." Kelly roused himself and opened the door, nearly knocking Fubar over. He checked the street to see if anyone was watching, but if he was honest with himself, he didn't think anyone would care. Hell, Fubar could almost pass for a hobo, not at all unusual on this end of State Street. He led Fubar and Steve down the road and around the corner to the V-shaped yard formed by the backside of the Pickering House and the Boiler House. The area was in its usual filthy, trash-strewn state. In the center, the great rounded brick smokestack rose into the pale winter sky, impervious. Kelly checked the boards on the lower windows, still bolted down tight.

"You didn't say anything about breaking in," Fubar said.

"Just checking to see if there was an easy way," Kelly replied. He pointed to the fire escape that climbed the Pickering House and then moved his finger, indicating the bridge spanning the two buildings with the locked gate at its center. "That's our way in."

"Terrific," Steve said with a wry smile.

"Lead on," Fubar grinned, "looks like fun."

"You're kind of fucked in the head, you know," Steve said, giving Fubar a playful punch on the shoulder.

"They don't call me Fubar for nothing."

The fire escape groaned and clanked as the three men ascended. At the top, Kelly stepped onto the bridge and swallowed hard. The rickety iron creaked and swayed with each step.

"Hmmm. Maybe one at a time on that thing," Fubar said. "You sure it's safe?"

Kelly turned slowly, doing his best not to look down through the grating at his feet. "No."

"I like you," Fubar grinned.

Kelly walked to the gate, grabbed it in a white-knuckle grip, and hoisted himself one foot at a time until he was standing on the handrail. He took a deep breath and swung his body out over the void. His sneaker slipped a little as he straddled the gate with his ass in the breeze. He swallowed his heart back down, hoping as he did, that it would push his stomach back down with it. Once on the other side, Kelly walked to the end of the little bridge, hoisted himself onto the handrail again, and made a desperate grab for the granite sill of the window above. He caught it in both hands and hoisted himself up.

Fubar crossed next, swinging himself around the locked gate like a fat, shabby Fred Astaire swinging around a lamppost. His nonchalance embarrassed Kelly; it made his fearful execution of the maneuver moments before look like a toddler getting in the pool for the first time.

"Grab this," Fubar said, hoisting his canvas bag up to Kelly.

The bag was so heavy Kelly almost dropped it.

"Careful," Fubar said, pushing the bag higher, "that's about two grand worth of climbing gear."

Once Kelly wrestled the bag through the window, he stepped down, making room for Fubar on the sill. Again, Fubar made things look easy, springing into the window like a cat on the prowl. Fubar took Steve's bag and jumped down next to Kelly. Steve came through the window so fast it seemed to Kelly that he'd just materialized there.

"So this is it, huh?" Fubar said, surveying the ruined mill. He wrinkled his nose at the astringent smell of pigeon shit and the bitter-sweet smell of moldy decay. He and Steve walked gingerly around the shattered remnants of the third floor, stepping around the piles of pigeon droppings and avoiding the larger piles of accumulated trash. The wind whistled through the gaping windows facing the river, filling the mill with its ominous sound.

Kelly joined Fubar and Steve as they stepped to the edge where the third floor disappeared in jagged, blackened floor joists that pointed to the abyss. All three peered over the edge at the mill below where boiler #2 protruded from the floor like a blackened thumb trying to hitch a ride out of there.

"That's the boiler you want to get into?" Steve asked.

"Yes," Kelly said, trying to keep his voice even in the presence of

The Pull

of the awful thing coursing through him. He was at once terrified and desperate to get a look.

Fubar studied it for a minute, then stepped back and inspected the ceiling. "Nothing directly above. The I-beams are exposed there and there," he pointed to two places on either side of the hole. "We'll have to rig up a bridle. Belay you from two points."

"The climb isn't bad," Steve said, "up the cross-member, then traverse over. Hell, Kelly, we could get it done right now. We've got all the gear."

"No," Kelly said, "it's got to be on the third."

"What's so important about the third again?" Fubar asked.

"It's complicated," Kelly said.

"Uncomplicate it for me."

Kelly sighed. "There are a series of dates where the disappearances happen. They form a pattern. 12/3 is the next date in the series."

"So, you think someone is going to do something in that boiler on December third?"

"I'm liking this less and less." Fubar frowned.

"I think Milcom is up to something," Kelly lied, "and I think they'll get up to it on twelve three."

"I wish you'd be more clear," Fubar said.

"I wish I *was* more clear."

"I think we should do a trial run," Steve said. "If you're expecting some kind of shenanigans, we should rehearse this part of it, at least."

Fubar rubbed his temples. "Okay, if we're going ahead with this, Steve's right. Training and practice are crucial for the success of any climb. Best to find any issues now, so that on the day, you're not shitting your pants when we send you over the edge."

"Okay," Kelly said. He hadn't expected this. He wasn't prepared to deal with more heights today. Negotiating the gate on the fire escape taxed his tolerance for vertigo to the limit.

"Go time," Fubar grinned.

Together, Fubar and Steve started taking gear from their bags, all the while speaking a language Kelly didn't understand. Occasionally, he'd hear words like 'carabiner' and 'harness' that resonated clearly, but most of it concerned things like 'fleet angles,' 'rappel masters,' and 'z-rigs.'

Within minutes, Kelly was fitted out in a harness with two ropes attached at the waist; one red, one blue. The other ends of the ropes went into coils strapped to the backs of the two climbers. Fubar and Steve, also outfitted in harnesses, scrambled up nearby vertical I-beams like hungry monkeys looking for bananas in the ruined ceiling. Kelly swiveled his head from side to side, watching first one climber, then the other, switch from vertical ascent to traversing the I-beams near the roof. Each of the two men had a web of ropes, slings, carabiners, and other devices that jangled into the silence of the mill as they climbed around.

"You're going to feel the ropes tighten now. When I tell you, step to the edge," Fubar called down.

First one rope, then the other, tightened, pulling Kelly toward the edge of the ruined floor and the boiler below. His stomach did a roll in his belly. He had to fight the urge to call up to Fubar and Steve and tell them to forget it; he didn't want to go.

"Okay," Fubar called, "step to the edge."

Kelly took a hesitant step. As he moved forward, the ropes tightened further until he was almost on tip-toes.

"Red belay on," Fubar called.

"Blue belay on," Steve called.

"One more thing before you go, Kelly," Fubar yelled down.

Oh, Jesus, what? Kelly didn't like the sound of that.

"This is pretty much a one-way operation. Down is easy; going back up is very slow and very difficult for us. So once you're close to the bottom, one of us will slack, and you'll swing to the side of the hole in the floor and unclip the ropes. Got it?"

Shit. So I have to wander around near that boiler and find the stairs back up. Terrific. "Got it!"

"Good. Now, when you step to the very edge, sit down into your harness. You're going to swing away from the edge a bit. Don't worry, that's supposed to happen."

The ropes formed a 'V' in front of Kelly. The red rope hung from Fubar's perch high above on his left, and the blue rope from Steve's on his right. He gripped each rope in a death clench. He sat into his harness and lifted his feet. His body swung out forty feet above boiler #2 like a child on a swing set. "OH SHIT!"

Chapter 43

Casey

"Saa ya sita kupita kilele cha jua, siku ambayo," Dr. Freeman stood on the edge of the mud flat shouting, "jumla yake ni sita, sema majina sita ya huyo pepo na ataangamizwa. On the sixth hour past the sun's meridian, on the day whose sum is six, speak the six names of the demon, and it will be destroyed."

"You don't know the names." Tyre drew his pistol.

"I know—"

Casey lept at Tyre.

Tyre fired.

Casey tackled him, too late.

Freeman collapsed at the edge of the muddy yard.

Casey grabbed the gun from the mud and pulled the trigger repeatedly as he struggled with Tyre, but the action was full of gunk. They got to their feet but continued to struggle. Tyre's hand, hot as a pot off the stove, pushed Casey's face away.

"Ezekiel 28:1, The word of the *Lord* came to me—" Pontes's voice thundered across the muddy plain.

Tyre froze mid-grapple as if unable to move while Pontes continued to speak.

"Son of man," Pontes continued shouting into the night, "say to the ruler, Tyre, This is what the Sovereign *Lord* says—"

"You see," Gottschalk said, holding his lantern aloft, "We know you. We know about the prophecy of Ezekiel in the Bible. You are caged now, demon, are you not?"

"NO!" Tyre's voice rang through their heads and rattled their bones in its volume and vehemence.

"... not a god, though you think you are as wise as a god," Pontes continued.

"You do not know my names. You cannot hope to destroy me!" Tyre bellowed.

Casey noticed that as Pontes spoke, Tyre began to sink into the mud. It oozed over the tops of his shoes.

"... Therefore, this is what the Sovereign *Lord* says..." Pontes continued.

Costa pointed at the sky. "The rain is a gift from God. It's sinking him."

"No!" There was a note, albeit faint, of fear in Tyre's voice. The mud reached his pant legs.

"... I am going to bring foreigners against you, the most ruthless of nations; they will draw their swords against your beauty and wisdom and pierce your shining splendor...." Pontes thundered like a Baptist minister.

"Zis is why you hate us. Zis is why you call us names unt despise us," Gottschalk shouted, "because God has ordained us to be your undoing!"

"FOOLS! You will not be my undoing! Do you think the pitiful words of your holy book can hold me?" The mud crept up his calves.

"—They will bring you down to the pit, and you will die a violent death in the heart of the deep," Pontes shouted. "Will you then say, 'I am a god,' in the presence of those who kill you?

You will be but a man, not a god, in the hands of those who slay you...."

"You see, demon, your pot is destroyed. You are as a man now." Gottschalk said.

"I am eternal! The pot is broken! I am free!" The demon shouted.

"Then why aren't you kicking ass?" Casey asked, sure he'd done right by breaking the cursed urn.

"You are not the Keeper," Tyre smiled. "You are just some imbecile." Tyre pointed to the man with glowing purple eyes. "*That* was the Keeper."

"You are a fool," purple eyes said to Casey. "You've doomed us all."

Casey had had it with possession, and demons, and dying, and guys like Tyre shitting on him. "You are Milcom!" Casey shouted.

"And he is Der Ungeisthasse!" Gottschalk added.

"The vessel is broken, not destroyed. You are *not* free." The man with the glowing purple eyes straightened. "When you are named demon, *you* are destroyed."

Casey didn't know what the fuck was going to happen now, but what they were doing was working.

"You are Pesadelo Vivo," Pontes shouted.

"You may be right, Keeper. But I can't be destroyed without *all* the names." He pointed to Freeman's crumpled form lying in the filth. "And now I can't be put away."

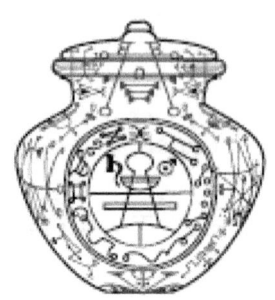

Chapter 44

Hili

She held a shard of the pot with no recollection of picking it up. Hili grasped it by the edges. She remembered what the priest in Sumer told her—never touch the inside of the pot. Picking up a shard by anything but the edge would mean she was touching the inside, twisting the magic.

"You *can* be put away, and you *can* be destroyed," she said. She scooped up the other shards of the urn, careful not to touch what was once the inside, and began placing the glowing pieces in a circle around the demon. The rain pelted her as she worked. She shivered, but not from the cold. The rain quickened her, lent her strength. It had never been the blood. Hili almost stopped what she was doing. The tingle she had felt as Alexander's shadow, that same tingle she had felt every time she became a shadow, it hadn't been from the blood hitting her. It was from the rain washing the blood away. Through her whole ordeal, the rain had been a constant companion. She hadn't realized that the water falling from the sky had also been an ally this whole time.

The man with the strange eyes, the one who could see her, had already started naming the beast, and though the demon wasn't moving, something didn't feel right. There was no blood or smoke. Nothing sizzled. The names had an effect on it, but it wasn't enough. It wasn't right. The incantations the men shouted from the boards on the edge of the mud held the beast. But for how long? This man acted as she did. He acted as the pot's warden, naming the beast, commanding it, but *she* was the warden. Hili could feel it, still. "Did you recite the incantation to put it away?"

The man with the purple glow in his eye gave her an empty look.

One of the three men on the wooden boards continued reciting his verse. "—from among the fiery stones. Your heart became proud—"

Hili hurried as best she could, holding the pot shards without touching the glyphs. One piece remained, and on instinct, she held it back. Keeping it in the bunched fabric of her shirt cuff. Hili began her own incantation.

"Harken, demon! He who is known as—"

"Milcom!" Purple Eyes added.

"And Der Ungeisthasse," added another man.

The man on the duckboards paused his incantations to shout, "and Pesadelo Vivo!"

"And Daemonium in Medio Umbra," said the man next to him.

"And Deamhan Claidheimh," cut in another.

Hili waited for the sixth name. There should be someone here from the sixth bloodline. This was the moment she'd waited thousands of years for. This was the time of the demon's destruction. She waited.

The man standing on the boards at the edge of the muddy field stopped speaking incantations. No one moved. There were no whispers. No sounds of clothes rustling. No coughs. None of the sounds Hili expected to hear from a crowd of a hundred people. There was only the soft patting of rain in the mud. No sixth name.

"Return to your prison," Hili continued, disheartened. "Diminish, and await destruction at the hands of the least. By pride shalt thou be undone, by shame vanquished. Enter the—" but, there was no vessel.

"Mud." Purple Eyes finished.

Would that do? Would a field of mud and a circle of pot shards hold the demon? But even as Hili wondered, the demon began to sink. The mud oozed around his knees.

"This filthy ground cannot hold me."

"Yes," Hili said. "It can. The very water the gods send from the sky condemns you. It saturates the soil and loosens it to swallow you, demon."

"Wet earth cannot hold me forever. The vessel is destroyed. Once the bloodlines are destroyed, I will roam the earth forever." The mud oozed around Tyre's chest now.

"No," Purple Eyes said, "you will walk among the fiery stones." At his words, the shards burst into violet flames and sank along with Tyre.

"No!" Tyre shouted. "You cannot imprison me here! I am meant to be free now! The vessel is broken!" The mud writhed like a living thing, licking Tyre's skin as it pulled him under. "Release me!"

Hili allowed herself to smile, just a little, as the mud closed over the demon's head and swallowed him entirely. There was no evidence that Tyre or the pot had ever been there. A wall of sound came rushing at Hili. She realized she'd been blocking out the world around her. She'd been in a bubble with the purple-eyed one, and now that the bubble was gone, there was chaos.

The men on the edges of the field, some standing on boards, some kneeling in the mud, were going wild. Some prayed, their hands extended in the sky, some shouted in triumph, others cowered in terror.

Now that the pot shards and the demon were interred, why she was still inside this body? With the pot broken, was the magic different now? Broken as well? But the priest, all those centuries ago, had said that she would inhabit someone when it suited the needs of the pot. It must not be done with her.

"Come," she said to Purple Eyes, "we have much to discuss." Hili started to make her way toward the men who'd named the demon. They stood frozen on the boards at the edge of the mud. She found the journey quite easy. The mud hardened, even while the rain continued to pour down on it.

"My name is Hili," she said as they walked toward the others, "daughter of Uten, guardian of the pot. What is your name?"

"Casey," he said. "My name's Casey, son of Michael, um... Keeper of Names? I guess?"

Hili stopped. "Do you have the sixth name?"

Casey examined his shoes. "No."

"You fucking imbecile! If you didn't have the sixth name, why did you destroy the urn?"

"I—"

"Silence!" Hili didn't know how to convey the agony of eternity. She wanted to shout that it was too long, that she'd served the pot, and now that it was broken, she wanted to go looking for Nigmah in the afterlife. There was no way to say these things so that Casey could understand, so she said. "I've been waiting a long time—for nothing."

"Not as long as I have, I bet," Casey mumbled.

"I have waited a thousand li—" she stopped. There was no time for this. "It's not important. Come."

"I'm not a dog," Casey said.

Why did it always have to be men that surrounded her?

She walked over to the man who'd been saying the incantations. He stood staring at the place where Tyre had been. "How did you know that incantation? How did you know it would work?"

"I didn't," the man said. "It was all I could think of. It's in the Bible. I didn't know what it would do."

"What is your name?" Hili asked.

"Pontes," the man said.

Hili's head swam. The man in Iberia was Pontes. And Walsh, could he be the ancestor of the man on Maewyn's ship and the woman who ran from Tyre? She wondered about the other men, the other names. They must be descendants of the six name bearers marked at the dawn of creation. "What are your names?" she asked the men standing next to him.

"I'm Helmut Gottschalk. What is your name?"

She told him.

"Are you a witch?" he asked.

"No. I am the Keeper of the demon."

"But he escaped," Gottschalk said.

"Yes." Hili glared at Casey. "What will you do with this place?"

"That's up to Mister Papas now," Gottschalk said, looking at Casey. "I don't work here anymore."

Papas, Hili remembered that name too. So, these were all descendants of the men she'd inhabited when she'd put the demon in the pot. She wondered if all six bloodlines had been represented each time the demon came out, or if it was just because this was supposed to be the last time. Had the broken pot doomed her to an eternity in this cold, dreary place? She was the Keeper. And she'd allowed the pot to be destroyed.

"Oh no," Casey said. "Tyre is gone. You have your job back."

It made sense to Hili now; just as she had inhabited the men who'd named the demon, so too was Casey, inside one of the six.

"I don't know if I want it." Gottschalk surveyed the chaos from under busy blonde brows. "Still, it's got to be done, so if you don't mind, Mister Papas..." he waved a hand at the men gathered in a large group around Dr. Freeman's crumpled form.

"Yes," Casey said. "Please, Mister Gottschalk, be my guest."

"Your guest?"

"Never mind. Please take charge."

"Zhat's it for today!" Gottschalk shouted. "Go home! And you men over there," he pointed to the men around Freeman. "Someone go for a priest, and a doctor, and zhe police." Gottschalk walked away.

"What now?" Casey asked.

"Now we make sure no one will dig here, then you and I will talk," Hili said. There were so many questions. How were there now two Keepers of the pot? And... well, so many.

"Do you know what they will do with this place?" she asked Casey.

"They will build a building on it," he said.

"Will they dig?"

"Not there," Casey pointed to the spot where Tyre sank.

Gottschalk plunked back across the duckboards. "Doctor Freeman is gravely wounded. I don't know if he vill recover. Will the demon stay captured, Hili?"

"I don't know. In your building, put the incantations you spoke. That magic may hold the demon, if mine does not."

"They are Bible verses, not incantations."

"Whatever they are, they worked. Put them in your building."

"I will," Gottschalk said.

Chapter 45

Kelly

"Oh shit, oh shit oh shit," Kelly grunted as he swung over the edge. His stomach swam. The Boiler House swung crazily beneath him.

"You okay?" Fubar called.

"Fuck, this is scary."

"You're good, Kelly; Everything is a-okay. We've got you. We're going to start lowering you in now. You might move a little side to side, but Steve and I will do our best to go at the same time and keep you stable. You ready?"

"Y-yeah, okay."

"Here we go."

First one rope, then the other gave a slight jerk. His insides did a somersault; then, he began to descend.

The sunlight coming in through the windows of the river side of the building lost its warmth as it passed the threshold, casting a pale, cheerless light on the trash-strewn floor of the Boiler House. Somehow the light didn't seem to touch boiler #2. The sun's thin rays touched other things further into the building, but the boiler was a hole in the world.

Kelly tried to look down into the jagged opening in the floor at the boiler's mouth, but the darkness was impenetrable, the obscurity complete. He realized he had no idea what was down there. The temperature grew noticeably colder as he descended. He tried to dismiss it as wind off the river through the great arched windows, but the air was dead still.

Think about something else, dipshit. Kelly heard his brother's voice in his head. Casey was always at his best in harsh moments like this. On the walls, Kelly found something else to think about. Two courses of brick were recessed from the others, running horizontally all around the room just above the arched window tops. What purpose this architectural detail served, Kelly couldn't guess. As he got a little lower, level with the recess, writing came into view. It wasn't visible from above or below. The words crouched, cast in white stone, like teeth between the red lips of brick. In the corners, a strange seal cast in the same white stone. "STOP!"

"What's the matter?" Fubar asked.

"There's something I need to look at for a minute," he called up. Kelly fumbled in his coat pocket for his phone. The harness didn't hold him upright, so he had to cling awkwardly to the ropes with one hand while he worked the flap of his pocket and rooted around for his phone with the other. At last, phone in hand, he started at the beginning and panned his phone until he'd taken a video of all the words and symbols. This is what he saw:

Because you think you are as wise as a god, I am going to bring foreigners against you. The most ruthless of nations. They will draw their swords against your beauty and wisdom and pierce your shining splendor. They will bring you down to the pit, and you will die a violent death in the heart of the deep. You will walk among the fiery stones.

"What the fuck is that doing in a mill boiler building?" Kelly said to himself. The words themselves had an ancient prophetic ring to them, almost biblical, but the seal at the beginning and the end was like nothing he'd ever seen before. Certainly not Christian, no crosses. The lines with circles reminded him of constellations inside the symbol for 'male' or 'mars' depending on the context. The god of war. What did it mean? Dangling forty feet above a malevolent boiler, he decided, was no time to contemplate these questions. While he examined the writing, his mind was calm, but as he fumbled to put the phone back in his pocket, the sensation of vertigo came rushing back in a tidal wave. "Okay," he called up to Fubar, "let's keep going."

Again, the ropes jolted as he descended. This time, the jolt was more like a bump down. "SHIT!" Kelly yelped as his phone missed his pocket and fell from his cold-numbed hand. He watched between his legs as the phone tumbled end over end, finally swallowed by the black hole in the floor below. "Fuck, fuck, fuck!"

Kelly's descent stopped.

"What?!" Fubar yelled.

"I dropped my phone."

"Well, that sucks, but could you please stop yelling like that? You're giving us a fucking heart attack up here."

"Sorry," Kelly yelled, "keep going."

The harness bit into his thighs and waist; all Kelly wanted to do was get out of the damn thing. Except now, he had to descend further into the hole to get his phone. Besides all the normal shit everyone kept on their phones, without which, one's life became a pain in the ass, Kelly needed that video. He had to find out where those words and symbols came from and why they were there. Anyone who would take the time and expense to build something like that into the architecture and cast it in stone must have had a damn good reason. Kelly was almost certain that reason would have something to do with the weird shit happening in the Boiler House.

The tips of his shoes were only inches from the top of the boiler now; Fubar and Steve had set the ropes perfectly. In a few more feet, he'd be able to reach the handle and open the boiler door. Of course, if he were right about the significance of the dates, he wouldn't see anything, but it was a good dry run. Rust spotted the surface of the boiler. He could just make out words stamped on the top of it. Pittsburg Boiler Works Model 6.

When he was finally level with the boiler door, he called out for a stop. There was another bump on each rope as the descent halted. Kelly reached out to open the boiler door. The metal was cold. He pulled. Dangling in midair with no leverage, all he succeeded in doing was pulling himself up against the boiler. He tried again, bracing his feet against the boiler. The door swung open with a groan. A frigid sigh of burned smelling air issued from the blackness of the boiler's mouth. A chill ran through Kelly, but not from the cold, from the feeling of a presence. He jammed a hand into the pocket of his coat, planning to use his phone as a light, but the pocket was empty. The darkness of the boiler was impenetrable. Below, in the mud about four feet below the shattered floor, he could make out the outline of his phone in the pale light coming in through the windows. The presence drew closer; Kelly could feel it. He slammed the boiler door. "Let's keep going," he called up. "I need to go down to get my phone."

"How are you going to get back out?" Fubar called.

"I should be able to climb out. It's only about four feet below the floor."

"Okay, but just so you understand, if we have to haul you up, it's a time-consuming pain in the ass."

"I remember. Let's go."

The ropes jerked. Kelly went down. He passed through a beam of weak sunlight coming in through the window. Its imprint on the ruined floor below formed a giant mouth with broken glass teeth. Continuing his descent, he passed into darkness again. The jagged ends of the floorboards crawled up his line of vision. His foot touched the mud. A high voltage beam of revulsion shot through him as if he and the mud were magnets of opposite polarity. He picked up his feet and leaned down, holding the ropes with one hand and reaching for his phone with the other. "STOP!" His heart hammered in his chest. His stomach muscles strained from holding himself horizontally. The tip of his index finger touched the mud-encrusted phone. His insides turned to ice. Bile rose in his throat. He grasped the phone. Thick fingers of mud held it in place. Kelly pulled harder. The mud tightened its grip.

"Oh God," he sobbed, "please!"

A gust of wind whipped through the window above, producing a low moaning sound.

Faint whispers echoed in the darkness.

He yanked the phone with all the strength he could bring to bear on its slimy surface. It pulled free. As he grasped it, something sharp bit into his hand, something stuck to the bottom of the phone. He didn't care, and he dared not stop to think about what it might be.

"Pull me up!"

"I thought you could climb?" Fubar called down.

"Sweet Jesus, pull me up!"

"Hang on; we have to set up the Z-rigs."

"Oh fuck," Kelly trembled in the darkness.

He wasn't alone.

Chapter 46

Casey

"Can I talk to you?" Casey asked, grabbing Hili's arm and leading her away from the duckboards and into the dark field, away from the others.

"Yes," Hili said as they walked. "We have much to discuss."

"Why do you always talk like Gandalf?" Casey asked, then regretted it. After all this, after dying over and over with no explanation, he'd finally found someone who knew something, and his first question was a sarcastic reference to a book that hadn't even been written yet.

"What is a Gand—" she began.

"Never mind that. I'm sorry. What I meant to ask is, what the fuck is going on? What is happening to me? Why am I trapped in other people's bodies? Why do I die their deaths?"

"That is a lot of questions," Hili said. "I may not have all the answers. Perhaps you should tell me what has happened to you."

Casey did. He told her about the Boiler House, and the boiler, and the pot shard. The deaths were hard to recount, but Casey managed it as quickly as possible, skipping the gory details.

"The shard you touched," Hili opened her hand. Bunched in the cuff of her shirt lay a pot shard. "Was it this one?"

It sure as shit was. The shard he would touch a hundred years from now lay in Hili's bunched-up shirt. How the fuck was this going to work? "Yes," he said. "Can we destroy it? Throw it far away so that I'll never touch it? Can I go back to my own time?"

"There is much I do not know, Casey. Where do you begin when you are in a new body? Are they touching the pot shard?"

"No," Casey said, "I'm always on the bridge. There." He pointed.

"Then that is your way home."

What the fuck was this person talking about? "I don't understand."

"Nor do I. Not fully. Not yet. Help me, Casey. You came from the future?"

"Yes, about a hundred years, give or take. What year is it now?"

"I don't know."

"Of course not," he muttered.

"And each time you were in a new body, the years were going backward?"

"Yes, they were many years apart, but for me, it was instant, almost."

"It has worked the same for me, but the years are further along each time I come out of the black. I don't recognize this world."

"So, we're both Keepers?"

"It seems so. With the pot broken, you picked up a shard of the pot that held both the glyph of the Keeper and the glyph that allows us to slip through time. And so we both became the Keeper, and both slipped through time."

"Backward?"

"I do not understand that yet."

There was a commotion near the edge of the field. Police caps, lanterns, and fingers pointing at them. "You said the bridge was my way back?"

"Yes, I think so," Hili said.

"Then we'd better run."

"Why?" Hili looked puzzled.

"Run!"

Police whistles sounded behind them.

"When last you told me to run, you destroyed the pot."

"Yeah, sorry about that." Casey grabbed her arm and ran, dragging Hili with him.

"Why are we running?" Hili asked.

"Well," Casey puffed, "we did just find a dead body, steal a historical artifact, and bury a very rich, important guy alive."

"I see," Hili said.

But from Hili's tone, Casey could tell she didn't. "So," puff, "how do I get home," puff "exactly?"

"We will have to hold the shard and jump together."

Casey was so surprised he almost stopped running. "What?"

"We will have," Hili gasped and continued, "to hold—"

"I heard you. Climb!" Fucking covered bridges.

Casey began to climb the aged timbers inside the bridge. There was no way to scale the wet-slick clapboards outside, so he aimed for the gap between the roof and the wall that allowed daylight inside.

"Stop! Stop! You there!" a policeman shouted.

Casey couldn't turn to look. The climb required all his attention.

Behind Casey came sounds of a scuffle.

"Stop! Stop!" It was a second cop's voice.

Casey grasped a beam and turned back. One cop had Hili by the wrist, and another was starting to climb after Casey. The look back was a mistake. He'd paused long enough to allow the cop climbing behind him to grasp his leg. Casey held on as the cop yanked him back. Below, the other cop was grappling with Hili. A second hand grabbed his leg, and the cop put all his weight on it.

Casey fell, landed on the policeman, and rolled away. His eyes turned to Hili, who managed to get the nightstick away from the cop she wrestled. She sent the billy-club into the policeman's groin like a battering ram, then turned and hit a home run off the second cop's skull. He dropped just two feet from Casey.

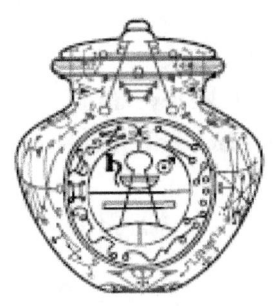

Chapter 47

Hili

Hili took no pleasure in causing these men pain, but she was glad she could.

Casey looked at her, shocked, from the plank floor of the bridge.

A sense of urgency seized her, the nature of which led her to believe that even broken, the pot still held sway. They needed to go, now. And the way Casey wanted to get to the correct spot wasn't going to work. She remembered that first day, right after touching the pot, when she ran faster than the winter wind and jumped ravines like a goat. That was the way. Trust the pot's power. Trust its plan. Yet, plan and pot both lay in ruins. Still, there was no other way. She ran. "Hurry!"

"Hey! You know you're running *towards* the cops, right?"

At the end of the bridge, Hili turned and stood on the rocks. More of the blue-uniformed men were coming across the mucky plain.

Hili turned and grabbed Casey as he emerged from the mouth of the bridge. "Here. We must jump."

"You're nuts. We'll hit the rocks below."

"You must trust me. Aim for the spot where you emerge from the darkness each time. You are a Keeper. It is within your power."

Casey cast a look back at the advancing blue men.

What was this fool waiting for? "Hurry! Take my hand." Hili had no choice. She palmed the shard of pot, placed his hand over it, and interlocked fingers with Casey.

"Jump!" she grunted with frustration as he stared at the rocks below.

Casey drew a deep breath. "On three. One... two..."

Hili leaped with all her strength, yanking Casey off the rock. He screamed in her ear as they flew in an arc out over the rushing black water. She felt his will shift, and sensing this was the spot, she allowed herself to fall, pulling Casey with her. They plunged into the water. The icy fingers of the river grabbed them and pulled them down into the black. Casey's hand was ripped from hers. The shard tumbled free, sending the last piece of the pot to the bottom.

She struggled, gasping and gulping at the water, flailing her arms. Hili tried to kick for the surface, but the black tumbling torrent made it impossible to know which way was up. She'd steeled herself for the death of this body, but in the moment, couldn't control its desperate struggle for life. Her lungs burned and heaved, trying to expel water only to take more in.

The sensation of cold slipped away. The waters entered her, filled her, and made her their own. Hili was the river. She became the darkness. Sensation ebbed. Now there was only the black.

"Hili?" It was Casey's voice. Yet it had no source, but instead, came from around her, and in her.

"I am here."

"Where are we?"

She understood the question, yet it made no sense. Where didn't exist. "We are everywhere and nowhere. We are in the black."

"The black?"

"The place you went to each time you died."

Silence for a moment, then, "God, I hate drowning."

Hili laughed. It was a ridiculous statement.

"Are... are you laughing at me?" Casey asked.

"Yes." She started laughing again.

The sound started small, just a chuckle, then grew all around her, and inside her. Casey filled the black with hysterical laughter.

Hili subsided first, then waited for Casey to settle down. When at last he had, she asked, "why did you laugh so hard?"

"I think I just drowned my great grandfather."

"Is that funny?"

"No. In fact, it's so *not* funny that it's hysterical."

"I don't understand you at all, Casey. This new world is a strange place."

"You came out of the ancient past because you're linked to a magic pot that held a demon, and you're telling me *my* world is a strange place?"

Hili laughed again. "Yes, I suppose I am."

"So, what happens now?" Casey asked.

"I don't know."

"What do you mean, you don't know? Doesn't this happen to you all the time?"

"When I go to the black, I'm not aware of it. I'm asleep, I suppose. What happens when the body you are in dies?"

"Same thing, I guess," Casey said. "I don't experience anything in between. When I come back inside someone new, it's just like waking up. Do you think we're stuck here?"

She reached out with her mind, feeling for the pot, the demon, anything. There, on the edge of her consciousness, she found the circle of shards glowing purple in her mind. In their center, she found the demon, twisting, writhing, trying to break free. If she could feel the pot shards and the demon, if the pot still held her life force in its service, that meant she'd be called on again. "No, Casey, we're not stuck here."

"So what happens now?"

"Now we wait for the pot to call us again, or for the demon to break free."

"Oh, God. I don't think the demon shows up again for another twenty years when Walsh is killed, and then again, for Freddie, Costa, and...."

"These are the deaths you experienced?"

"Yes."

"I don't think the pot will summon us for them."

"Why not?"

"Because you were the Keeper, and you were there."

"But I didn't know what the hell was going on."

Neither had Hili in Sumer when she touched the pot Nigmah left behind. The pot had always told her what to do. Yet, even what little she knew of the pot's magic wasn't making sense now. Why had Casey moved backward in time? Why had he experienced the deaths of the others and come to meet her in that cold, dark world? He'd picked up a shard, the shard with the glyph of time and the glyph of the wardenship... He'd picked it up. He didn't know not to touch the inside of the pot, and unless he'd picked it up by its edges, he would have done exactly that; touched what had once been the inside.

"Hili?"

"Yes, Casey?"

"I thought you left me; it's been a long time since you spoke."

"Has it?" Time. How could he be sure about time here in the black?

"It feels that way."

"I'm thinking."

"About what?"

"Shhh. Let me think. I'm trying to make sense of things." Curse this man-child. He talked more than a teenage girl.

"Maybe you could think out loud? I don't like this place, and not having a body, and the dark."

"Very well. I think you went backward in time because you touched the inside of the pot."

"When?"

"When you picked it up, the first time, in your time."

"I just picked up a shard, that's all."

"Yes, but you can't pick up a piece of broken pot without touching the inside unless you pick it up by the edges. Did you do that?"

"I don't know. I just picked up the magical purple glowing thing. Why does that matter?"

"The inside of the pot houses the demon. Its magic is different and permeated by the demon who dwelled inside. The magic on the outside gets twisted when you touch the inside. That's what the priest in Sumer said."

"Where's Sumer?"

"Shh! You wanted me to think out loud. Stop interrupting. So, you died inside all these men with the same names, as I did, the exact same names. These are the six. How many names do you have?"

She waited.

"Casey?"

"Five. I have five." He sounded pained. "I'm sorry. I don't like to remember."

"What are they?"

"Der Ungeisthasse, Pesadelo Vivo, Daemonium in Medio Umbra, Deamhan Claidheimh, and Milcom." Casey said.

"Curse the gods!" How long was she supposed to endure being chained to this cursed pot? This man from the future didn't have the sixth name either.

It came to her like a, well, like a pot floating down the river. "You weren't supposed to die with those people."

"I wasn't?"

"No. The shard you touched made you the Keeper, so each time you came out of the black, you were supposed to put the demon away."

"How the hell was I supposed to know how to do that?"

"The pot was *broken*, Casey. You only picked up the piece that made you the Keeper and moved you through time. The other magic, knowing the incantations, all the rest of it was lost to you."

"Then how did I know what to do on that mud field? How did I know what to say?"

"You just said a few names, and then said, 'mud.'"

"Yeah, but I *knew*, in my mind," Casey said.

"Perhaps when you touched the pot, whole, when you handed it to me, you got the rest of the magic." The picture of what had happened was becoming clear to her. She just needed a little more time to think.

"I don't understand. If you're the Keeper, where were you when I died inside those men?"

"That hasn't happened for me yet. But I don't think I will be there." Why would she? He was there. He was the Keeper, as well.

"You don't think we will go forward in time now to put the demon away in all the instances when I died?"

"No."

"Then what are we doing here?"

"I don't know yet. Usually, when the demon gets out, he just kills. You interrupted the plan. You destroyed the vessel. You saved the lives of all the men there, I think. But you also allowed the man with the sixth name to be killed. You released the demon from the vessel forever. You may have doomed humanity."

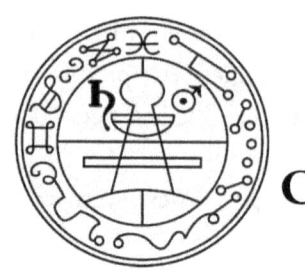

Chapter 48

Kelly

Red eyes appeared out of the darkness. First one pair, pinpricks of red floating in the void. Then there was another pair, larger, closer. Then there were a dozen. "Get me out of here!" Kelly screamed.

"Do you want to come up here and do this?" Fubar yelled back, "hang on!"

Kelly scrabbled at the splintered floorboards above his head. His fingers found purchase, and he yanked. The sharp ends of wood bit into his digits, and he felt the wetness of blood. Careful to keep his feet tucked so that he wouldn't come into contact with the unholy mud, Kelly pulled. The ropes inched upward.

Kelly risked a look down and wished he hadn't. A hundred pairs of red eyes advanced toward the dim light that shone through the hole in the floor. Kelly gave a great heave. His head and shoulders landed on the floor above. Broken floorboards stabbed through his clothes into his stomach. He heaved again and flopped like a fish onto the shattered planks of the Boiler House. The ropes continued upward, causing Kelly to slide toward the hole again. "Slack! For God's sake, slack!"

"Okay. Okay, calm down," Steve called.

The ropes slackened, and Kelly crawled away from the hole. "Oh God," he panted, "holy shit!"

"What the fuck was down there?" Fubar yelled.

"I don't know," Kelly answered. At least he'd gotten the phone. Except, where was it? He didn't remember putting it in his pocket. He jammed his bloody hands in his coat pockets and found them empty. Ignoring the pain in his stomach from the wounds the floorboards inflicted, Kelly sat up. His phone lay a few feet away, covered in mud. He must have slid it away when he grabbed for the floorboards.

He reached for the phone. Something stuck to it. The sharp thing he'd felt in the hole. When he turned the phone over in his hands, Kelly found something jagged and muddy, like a piece of a broken bottle. It gave off a pulsing purple glow. Kelly screamed and hurled the shard across the mill. He scooted himself away from the hole even further, sliding his ass along the splintered floor, the slack ropes trailing out in front of him.

"Now what?" Fubar's exasperated voice echoed off the walls of the old mill.

"We've got to get the fuck out of here," Kelly panted.

"Suits me. Unclip, so we can pull the ropes up."

Kelly got to his feet and fumbled with the carabiners with shaking, bloody hands. He couldn't get them undone.

"Push and twist," Fubar yelled.

When at last he got the ropes free, they jerked upwards. Kelly staggered for the stairs, shaking. At the top, he examined himself while he waited for Fubar and Steve to gather their gear and climb down. His hands were bloody, shredded, and peppered with splinters. His coat was torn badly at the chest and waist; fibrous filling spilled out like the intestines of a stuffed animal. Underneath, pinpricks of blood showed through his shirt, but the jacket had spared him the fate of his tortured hands.

"Well, that was fucked up," Fubar said as he reached the floor.

"One might say, fucked up beyond all recognition." Steve grinned.

Fubar shot him a look.

"What? They don't call you Fubar for nothing. Remember the time—"

"Hey, not in front of...." Fubar jerked his head toward Kelly. "So, Kelly, what the fuck happened down there?"

"I'll tell you later. Right now, I want to get the fuck out of here before dark."

"I'm with you on that one. This place is creeping me the fuck out," Fubar said.

"Me too," Steve agreed, "let's go."

Kelly was surprised to find that the drop from the window to the fire escape and even the precarious climb around the locked gate in the middle of the bridge didn't bother him, despite the cuts on his hands. After what he'd just been through, he was just glad to get the fuck out of there.

The three explorers agreed to meet up at Kelly's loft and go over things. The key in Kelly's trembling hand refused to find its home in the ignition on the first three tries. Kelly closed his eyes and took several deep breaths. Then stuck the key in and fired the old Toyota up.

Once they gathered in Kelly's loft, Steve helped Kelly clean and dress his hands, which, it turned out, weren't as bad as he'd imagined once the dried blood washed away.

"Got anything to drink around here?" Fubar asked.

"No, I—ouch!"

"Don't be such a baby," Steve said, pulling a particularly nasty splinter from Kelly's palm.

"As I was saying, I don't keep spirits around; my brother can't be trusted."

"My brother drinks all the good stuff, too. That's why I keep it in my car." Fubar grinned. "Be right back."

"You keep good booze in your car?" Steve asked.

"Don't judge me," Fubar said and stepped out the door.

"There," Steve said, wrapping Kelly's hand in gauze and taping it in place, "good to go."

Fubar returned and rooted around in the kitchen for glasses while Steve rooted for splinters in Kelly's other hand.

"Here," Fubar said, thrusting three fingers of whiskey into Kelly's freshly bandaged palm.

"Hey, easy," Kelly said, accepting the glass. He swallowed most of it in one go.

"Easy yourself. That's good single malt, not cheap bourbon. Now, let's hear about what you saw down there."

Kelly described the writing on the wall, the symbol, and the red eyes in the crawlspace under the mill.

"Probably just rats," Steve said. "They get pretty big that close to the canals. Big as cats, some of them."

"I'm with Steve on this one," Fubar agreed. "You were spooked from the descent and the writing. Are you sure you're going to be up to doing that again on a day when you *are* expecting trouble?"

Kelly told them about the glowing fragment.

"You sure?" Fubar asked.

"Yes." Kelly finished his drink.

"Well," Steve said, "why didn't you hang on to it? It might have told us something."

"Not after what happened down there. For all I know, that thing was attracting the red-eyed creatures," Kelly said. The scotch and the adrenaline from earlier left him queasy, but he was determined to look into that boiler on the third, red-eyed monsters or no.

While they spoke, Kelly wiped off his phone. It worked, except the time was stuck at 5 PM. He unlocked it with no trouble, found the video he'd recorded in the Boiler House, and hit play. The shaky image of the strange seal came into view.

"Look at this, guys," Kelly said, pausing the video. When they'd gathered around it, he hit play again.

"What the fuck kind of symbol is that?" Fubar asked.

"I don't know, Kelly replied.

The video panned across the words. In the background, they heard a mumbling voice.

"Are you reading aloud?" Steve asked.

"I don't remember saying anything," Kelly replied.

"Turn the volume up," Fubar said.

Kelly turned it up full. Pops, clicks, and a dull whine, like an AM radio that wasn't tuned in, came from the speaker. A voice that sounded as if it had razor blades stuck in it was speaking just on the edge of hearing: "... you'll burn, feet first among the fiery stones... down into the pit... violent death... alone in the mud...."

"What the—"

Fubar's words were cut short as the voice began screaming like a hundred burning children: "YOU'RE GONNA BURN! YOU'RE GONNA BURN AMONG THE FIERY STONES!"

"Jesus! Fuck!" Kelly scrambled to turn the volume down, but the button wouldn't work. He fumbled the phone and dropped it. It lay on the floor, still screaming.

"FIERY STONES! YOU'RE GONNA DIE!"

Steve raised a foot to smash it.

"NO!" Kelly yelled and dove for it.

"If this is a joke, it's not funny," Fubar said.

"It's not." Kelly stabbed the pause icon, and the screaming stopped.

"FI—"

"All right," Steve said, "I admit it. I'm seriously spooked."

"Me too," Fubar agreed. "How about you, Kelly?"

"I was spooked to begin with. Will you still help me?"

Fubar and Steve exchanged glances. "Balls enough for El Capitan, but chickenshit to belay someone in a haunted house? I'd never be able to look at myself in the mirror," Fubar said.

"Yeah, I'm in too," Steve said, "if only because I want to see where this goes."

They made plans to meet at the Boiler House at 4:30 PM on December third, in two days.

Kelly lay in the darkness. He checked his phone for the time; it still read 5 PM, but now he noticed something else. The date was wrong too. He guessed it was some time after midnight, so the date should read December 2nd, but instead, it read December 3rd. Had he slept through an entire day? Was it the third, or was it the same twisting of electrons that made the phone read 5 PM all the time? Kelly jumped out of bed, opened his laptop, and checked the date and time. It read 3:20 AM December 2, just as it should.

There was some small, cold comfort in the weird behavior of his phone. It meant that he really did need to be at the Boiler House on December 3, apparently at 5 PM. Kelly went back into the bedroom and closed his eyes, but sleep eluded him. The one person he could talk to openly and honestly about all this weird shit was gone. Kelly had pushed him out. Abandoned his twin brother to suffer alone in the street.

"I'm sorry, Casey," he sobbed into the darkness. "I wish I hadn't kicked you out. I wish—God, I wish so many things. I wish I knew where you were. I wish I knew what happened. I wish I could talk to you right now." As he stared into the darkness, the mill girl appeared in the doorway as before. He'd forgotten all about her. Again. The empty black pits of her incorporeal eyes stood in contrast to the crimson gore smeared on her apron. She stared at him, lingering longer even than her last visit.

"What?!"

She pointed at Kelly's phone on the nightstand.

Kelly's skin prickled as the hair on his body stood on end. A bitter chill filled the room. His heart raced as if to outrun the terror before him.

A weak "H-uh?" was all Kelly could manage.

The ethereal mill girl drew her arm back, and again, stabbed it toward Kelly's phone.

His gaze followed her finger, and when it returned to the spot where she'd stood, shadow took her place. Trembling, he picked up the phone. The screen changed without him touching anything. The 5:00 PM was replaced with the telephone app. This was followed by the words: Calling Casey... Kelly gaped at the screen. How could his phone call Casey? Casey hadn't had a phone since he became homeless. Kelly supposed maybe he hadn't deleted the old contact, but even so, the phone was calling his brother all by itself.

Kelly held the phone to his ear. He heard the same AM radio whine accompanied by the same pops and clicks as in the Boiler House video. His insides went cold. Whatever this was, it wasn't going to be Casey; he was sure of that much. He put the phone on the table and activated the speakerphone, not wanting the tainted, possibly evil phone touching his skin.

The voice of a hundred tortured souls came through the speaker. The same voice from the video he took at the Boiler House. "... you can't win..." it faded then came back. "...power, but you're too stupid to use it." More static. The digits in the center of the screen that usually rolled slowly by measuring how long Kelly was on a call, were frozen at 18:91. None of it made any sense to Kelly. Only pops and whines came through the speaker. "Casey?"

"Kelly?" his brother's voice came through in a barrage of clicks and whistles.

"Oh God, Casey!"

"Kelly, get out of here! He's..." Casey's voice faded out.

"Casey! Casey! Casey, I'm sorry!"

"I... rry too. I love you, brother." Now it sounded almost as if Casey were talking on a normal phone.

"Where are you, Casey? I've been looking for you everywhere."

"I don't know, Kelly. I don't know how to explain. I don't have any time. I need you to know I'm sorry for everything, the drinking, the stealing—"

"Forget all that shit, Casey, just come home. Stay with me. We'll work it out."

"I'm trying, Kelly. I'm trying."

As Kelly stared at the phone, talking to his brother, the numbers on the call time counter began to move. 18:92, 18:93, 18:94...

"Casey?"

Static.

"CASEY!"

The phone app closed. The lock screen returned. The usual photo of Kelly and Casey in their little league uniforms was gone. In its place was a picture of the Boiler House. One of the Bridge Street Bridge's green I-beams angled down across the corner of the frame. The time and date showed 5:00 PM December 3. Below that, the call timer was still running, except excruciatingly slowly. Not only was the phone not counting in a normal time span, but Kelly realized that the numbers weren't even measures of time at all, because of course, seconds only went up to 59. Kelly stared fixedly at the phone for some minutes calling his brother's name. There was no reply, no pops, no whistles, no sound. The numbers on the phone didn't seem to change at a set interval. Kelly took it to his desk so that he could look at the clock on his laptop and mark when the numbers on his phone changed. Six minutes... 18:96... eighteen minutes... 18:97... twelve minutes... 18:98... one hour and twelve minutes... 18:99.

Kelly paced, looking at his phone every minute or so, trying to log the time the numbers changed, looking for a pattern. The whole thing started with the... what? Call? With his brother. The numbers were stuck at 18:91 for about half the call before they started moving. What did it mean? What the fuck did any of it mean? 18:91, that number meant something. He'd seen it recently. Kelly started going through his notes on the Boiler House, but he didn't find what he was looking for before he thought of it himself. 1891 was the year the Boiler House was constructed. So, if his phone counted forward from 1891, where would it stop? Did it have something to do with Casey? The whole thing was fucking maddening. Kelly fought the urge to pick up his phone and throw it.

Could this whole thing be a trick? Had he really spoken to Casey at all? Was it the Boiler House fucking with him? Kelly opened his phone. The 'recents' tab in the phone app showed nothing. It was blank. He checked for Casey's contact number. Nothing. His other contacts were still there, at least, but no Casey. He went through every single contact, searching for some sign. Nothing. Of course, there was nothing. Kelly was as fastidious about his electronic hygiene as he was about everything else. When Casey had ceased to have a phone, Kelly deleted the number.

So how had the phone made the call? Kelly guessed that was just as inscrutable a mystery as the moving digits, the stuck date and time, and the lock screen picture. Still, his mind needed something to work on, some little piece of the puzzle he could figure out. He retraced his steps. He'd been lying in bed... Kelly laid down. He was thinking about Casey, talking aloud... he'd prayed, right before he picked up the phone, he'd prayed to talk to Casey. He wondered if he prayed again—"Dear Lord, please let me talk to Casey." Nope. His phone remained dark and silent. In his heart, Kelly knew it was a half-assed prayer, at best. It was sincere, but the urgency was gone. Casey was alive somehow, somewhere, and now Kelly knew it.

Wherever he was, Casey wasn't in good company. Casey needed him, and he'd needed Casey, and somehow the connection was made. Now the need was satisfied, and the connection gone. All but the ticking numbers, which must have a connection to his brother because they'd appeared when he talked to Casey.

Though he knew Casey was alive... or something, there was no less urgency. He would be at the Boiler House tomorrow at five. Something terrible was going on there, and his twin was mixed up in it. And at five tomorrow, he was going to look inside.

Since sleep was impossible now, Kelly decided to do some research on the writing and symbols in the video. He was loath to open the video again to look at it. Even the idea of pushing play and hearing that voice made his stomach drop like a rollercoaster. He decided if he saw it, he'd recognize it. The words accompanying the symbol were biblical in tone and syntax, so Kelly started a search for religious symbols. This yielded the usual slew of crucifixes, crosses, stars of David, pentagrams, and the like. He searched biblical symbols and old testament symbols with roughly the same result. But... it wasn't really a symbol, was it? More like a coat of arms or a glyph. It was only when he searched for religious seals that he found it. The seal of Solomon, given to Solomon by God in the form of a ring, used to trap demons and force them to do his bidding.

Trap demons? Seriously? Someone had trapped, or tried to trap, a demon in a mill building on the banks of the Nipwìmâw river? Kelly didn't go in for all this occult mysticism bullshit. The symbol, the words in white stone, the phone call,

The Pull

on rainy nights? The fucking voice on the video? Jesus Christ. This wasn't real. Couldn't be. This must be an elaborate hoax conducted by... who?

Who would go to all the trouble? Who had the tech-savvy to fuck with his phone? Someone at the Chronicle? Someone he'd scooped on a big story? Except Kelly didn't have any big stories in his folder, just dog shows and spelling bees. No one had the motive or resources to pull off a hoax of this magnitude, except...

What if old Victor Shields was in tighter with someone from Tyre holdings or MillCom Real Estate than he'd thought? What if Vic tipped them off that Kelly was pursuing his story despite Vic's insistence that he drop it? If Kelly got the story cold and found someone to print it, MillCom would stand to lose millions, maybe go out of business because of lawsuits and their inability to sell the Boiler House. That was a powerful motive. If it was true that the whole thing was a put-up job, that meant MillCom had the Pontes brothers, and David Gottschalk, maybe even Father Murray in their pocket. No. Kelly refused to believe that they had Father Murray; he was a dupe, too, same as Kelly.

So, MillCom had a bunch of guys on the payroll and some heavy-hitting tech nerds, all to scare him. It sounded like the most expensive episode of Scooby-Doo in recorded history. He could hear the MillCom exec in court: "And I'd have gotten away with it too if it hadn't been for that meddling gay reporter." Kelly snorted. Why, even in his silly fantasies, did people have to point out that he was gay? What did that have to do with it?

Okay, so the conspiracy theory didn't really hang together. It didn't explain

The Pull

or the words and symbols in the mill wall. Whatever the game was, whether a massive, expensive hoax to gaslight him or a real occult phenomenon, Casey was in trouble. Kelly had to keep going, had to stick with the program, and the program said the final act was going to be at the Boiler House tomorrow, December 3, at 5:00 PM. Get your souvenir program at the door and unwrap your hard candy before the performance starts. Kelly would go. He would find out what happened to Casey, and he'd go with open eyes and a skeptical mind.

Chapter 49

Casey

Darkness and black hate swirled around Casey. It bubbled around his consciousness like molten tar. Lost in the darkness, all he could feel was the presence of Tyre.

"Something has changed," Hili said. "The demon is breaking loose."

"I feel him," Casey said. "What happened?"

"Since we came to the black, I have been able to see the circle of pot shards holding the demon. One of them is gone, out of place. There is a hole, and the demon is trying to get through."

"You're a worthless drunk, incapable of even unzipping your pants to take a piss. How do you expect to defeat me?" it was Tyre's voice.

He remembered a sermon Father Murray had once given about the only force that could conquer hate being love. He did his best to conjure love to his mind. He thought of Kelly.

"You don't possess the capacity for the kind of love needed to drive me out," Tyre's voice hissed. "You're incapable of thinking of anyone else. If you're trying to think of love, why not think of your love for the bottle? Surely that is strong enough!" Tyre laughed.

"Hili, help!"

"What is it, Casey?"

"The demon is in my mind."

"Strange that he is not in mine. It must be more of the twisted magic from when you touched the inside of the pot."

"But your love of the bottle isn't real love either, is it?" Tyre continued. "No. You don't even know what love is. You've never put someone else first. You've never sacrificed at the altar of love. You can't beat me. You can't! Worthless! Selfish! Stupid!"

Casey wished he had fists to clench, to punch. His hate burned for Tyre. The molten darkness advanced on him, burning into his consciousness.

"Oh, yes, you hate me. But is it really me you hate? The messenger? I'm only telling the truth. I'm only saying what you already know. All that has befallen you, every bad thing that's happened to you in your entire life, you have brought down on your own head! And why? Why have you brought yourself to ruin? Because," Tyre's voice changed to that of a hissing snake, "you know the truth, Casey: you *deserve* it. You are a worthless example of humanity. You can't love, you can't hold a job, you can't do anything but drink. And the reason is that you don't love even *yourself*, because you're not worthy of love. I can end all this right now, Casey. I can put you back in that old mill with an enormous bottle of fine whiskey and a fresh pack of cigarettes. I can do it right now. All you have to do is say please."

"What is he saying to you, Casey?" Hili asked.

Casey ignored Hili. He was tempted, oh so tempted, to go back to the bottle. Everything would be back to normal. Hell, better than normal, good booze, real cigarettes... but he'd come so far. He'd died over and over for something. He was here for a reason; right now, in this moment, he was here for a good reason.

"It doesn't matter why you're here, Casey. All that matters is the pain. There are no *good* reasons, only reasons. And good? What kind of good would make a man die over and over? Would you call that good? There is no good. Just another entity out there using you for its own selfish purposes, making you suffer and die. Even the son of God only had to die once before he went to heaven. You've died six times. Do you think this is heaven? Do you still think God is coming to save you? No. You've been used up and left to rot here with me. You've been had. Betrayed by a vengeful God, the same way you betrayed your faggot brother when you turned your back on his help and tried to steal from him. Take my offer, Casey. You've done your best. Now have a drink."

Kelly, if I could just talk to him one more time, just to apologize. God, please, just one more time.

"Casey?" Hili called. "Casey?"

There was a strange sound, like static on an old television set. With it came the sound of someone tapping on a tight wire or a saw speeding up and slowing down. Through the static and the noise, he heard Kelly call his name.

"Casey?"

"Kelly?" he yelled. He wondered if this was some trick Tyre was playing.

"Oh God, Casey!"

Kelly shouldn't be here. He shouldn't — "Kelly, get out! He's going to hurt you!"

Static.

"Casey?" Static. "... I'm sorry." His brother's voice faded in and out.

"I'm sorry too. I love you, brother." He did. Casey realized at that moment that the beast, Tyre, was baiting him, trying to get him to give up, lying to him.

"Where are you, Casey? I've b... you... where?"

"I don't know, Kelly. I don't know how to explain." He felt Tyre's presence closing in on him. The malevolence grew closer. "I don't have any time. I need you to know that I'm sorry about everything, the drinking, the stealing—"

"Forget all... shit Casey," the connection grew weaker, "just... me home. We'll wor... out."

"I'm trying, Kelly, I'm trying." But Kelly was gone.

Whatever all this was for, the dying, seeing through other people's eyes, he wasn't meant to end here. To give up. He didn't know if it was leading up to this moment, this confrontation, or some other. What Casey did know was that he wasn't meant to be defeated. And whatever force was doing this to him, leading him through this, was good, not evil. Why else let him talk to Kelly, right when he needed Kelly most? He turned his consciousness toward the approaching evil.

"Wasn't that touching," Tyre purred, "a lovely piece of fiction. You don't think I'd actually allow you to talk to your bro—"

"No," Casey spat, "I don't. But you didn't allow me to talk to him. The pot did. That means you're not as powerful as you'd like me to believe. Go now Der Ungeisthasse, Pesadelo Vivo, Daemonium in Medio Umbra, and Deamhan Claidheimh, and whatever else you are called. Go, and let me pass. You have no power over me.

"Idiot. You have no idea what power I—"

"I hear weakness in your voice. Just because I don't have all six names doesn't mean the ones I know don't work, Der Ungeisthasse, Pesadelo Vivo—"

"STOP! MORON! It will take so much longer if you—"

"Be gone, Deamhan Claidheimh—"

"STOP!"

Suddenly, he no longer felt Tyre's evil. Then, without making any conscious action, he was moving. "Hili, do you feel that?"

"Yes, we are moving."

"Where?"

"Toward the place the pot needs us, to the person with the sixth name, to the end."

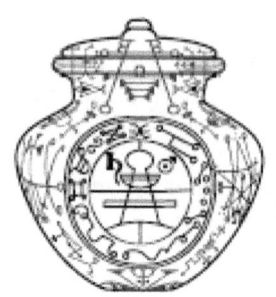

Chapter 50

Hili

Darkness. More impenetrable than ever. Hili waited, alone in the dark with her thoughts. Someone moved one shard in the circle, allowing the demon to escape. She felt sure it wouldn't be long now before she was called on to destroy the demon. There was no pot, so the next summoning would be the last. She was sure of it. It had to be. She'd waited long enough to be released into the afterlife. Waited long enough to find Nigmah.

"I just talked to the demon," Casey said, "and my brother."

"You spoke to your brother?" Hili's first reaction was jealousy. This annoying man-child had only served the pot for one hundred years. She'd been in its service for thousands, and she hadn't conversed with Nigmah since the cave where she died.

"Yes."

"How?"

"I don't know," Casey said.

No help, as usual. "Tell me what happened."

As she listened to Casey talk about his conversation with the demon, and the talk with his brother, she tried to deconstruct how it was possible. Not unless the brother had touched a shard. That could explain why an urn fragment was out of place. If Casey's brother had touched a piece of the vessel and the demon was out, could it be that the demon was already inside Casey's brother wreaking havoc?

"Do you think this is all a mistake?" Casey asked.

"Do I think what is a mistake?" Honestly, this man talked more than....

"Do you think the demon was supposed to be destroyed in 1891, and everything that's happened since is a mistake, the deaths in the mill, everything? All because I broke it?"

Hili had to admit that Casey had a point. Perhaps the demon was supposed to be destroyed in 1891, but this man's hot temper....

"Hili?"

"Yes, Casey."

"It got very quiet."

"Urg! I was just thinking that even if you destroyed it, that doesn't explain why there was no sixth name spoken."

"Freeman had it."

"Who?" She did not know what he was talking about.

"Before we met while digging the pot out of the mud, there was a man, Dr. Freeman. He claimed to have studied all about the pot. When Tyre opened it, Dr. Freeman said a bunch of gibberish, then he said, 'On the sixth hour past the sun's meridian, on the day whose sum is six, speak the six names of the demon, and it will be destroyed.'"

"Why didn't you tell me about this before?" This was a vital piece of information! How could this obtuse man hold something like that back? She remembered a strange man shouting, but Hili had been preoccupied with the destroyed vessel.

They had to figure this out, and the sensation of moving was speeding up. Wherever they were headed, they were heading there with increasing speed.

"I thought you heard him," Casey said.

"Ugh!"

"I'm sorry, geez. You are just all supernatural all the time. I thought you just knew stuff like that."

"No." Hili couldn't believe it. The conditions for the demon's destruction had been revealed. How many thousands of years had she been waiting to hear those words? And now, this village idiot had stolen that moment from her. But at least it was going to end now.

"Do you understand what it means?"

"It sounds simple. Everything except the numbered days and the hours past the meridian."

Casey shrugged. "Yeah, I don't get that part either, except I think PM is an abbreviation for Past the Meridian. So, six PM, but the day whose sum is six, I don't get that."

"I'm not sure it matters to us," Hili said. "The pot pulls us out of the dark when needed. Maybe that part only matters to the man with the sixth name."

"Hili?"

Curse the gods. Did he ever stop talking? "What?"

"If everything after 1891 is a mistake, if Freeman was supposed to have the last name of the demon, and so destroy it, we're in trouble."

"We're in trouble, even if it's not. The demon has broken through the circle of pot shards. If it breaks free further, it could hurt a lot of people."

"Hili, that's what I'm trying to tell you. This isn't ancient history, where people hacked at each other with swords. If that demon got inside the wrong person, or, well, the right person, it could destroy the entire world."

Chapter 51

Kelly

Kelly paced. It was December 3. He'd managed a decent nap after searching the internet for the symbol, but now, just a few hours before he was due to meet Fubar and Steve for his descent into the boiler, doubt gnawed at him. His phone kept lighting up, showing the picture of the Boiler House, and the time: 5:00 PM. The numbers on the call counter were still there, too, ticking by at random intervals. The counter stood at 19:70.

"I know, I know," Kelly said as he passed the place where the phone sat illuminated on the edge of the breakfast bar that separated the kitchen from the living room. The clock on the microwave showed 2:06, exactly seven minutes since he'd last checked. Two hours until it was time to go. He couldn't help feeling something was wrong with his plan. He didn't know what it was. As if reading his mind, his phone lit up again. The Boiler House was still there, the time was still there, and the numbers on the call counter had advanced slightly: 19:72.

"I know, I know, Boiler House, five o'clock, December third. I got it, okay? Fucking phone."

The phone blinked again.

"Look, if this is the forces of evil, could you please FUCK OFF? And if this is the forces of good, could you please send a talking burning bush or something a little more communicative?"

The phone went dark and stayed that way.

"Thanks for nothing." Kelly sat on the couch for exactly three minutes, according to the microwave clock. Then he got up and started pacing again. The minutes crawled by. The sky outside his window darkened. Clouds gathered. "Of course," Kelly sighed, "it's worse when it rains."

At four-thirty, the temperature was forty degrees. A light rain spattered Kelly's windows. He checked his pockets: phone, flashlight, bottle of water. It was a fifteen-minute walk to the Boiler House, and Kelly decided the exercise would do his nerves good. It did. By the time he neared State Street, he was much more relaxed. On the corner, that changed. Kelly felt the strong urge to just keep on walking, right across the bridge. His phone buzzed in his pocket. He took it out. It blinked at him like a nervous politician on debate night.

"Oh fuck you," Kelly said, "if you're not going to tell me...." The phone continued blinking. Kelly put it back in his pocket and continued down State Street toward the Boiler House. It buzzed incessantly in his pocket. He ignored it. As he approached the mill, a trunk popped open right next to him, making him stagger and grasp the chest of his coat. "Jesus wept!"

"Little jumpy?" Fubar grinned, getting out of the car. "Ready to go?"

"Yeah," Kelly said. He dropped his hand from his chest and stuck it over the buzzing phone in his pocket.

"You don't seem so sure," Steve said, closing his door and coming around to the trunk.

"It's just... you're going to think this is stupid."

"This whole thing is—ooph." Fubar started, then broke off as Steve elbowed him in the ribs.

"I'm all in," Steve said. "I've spent the last couple of days reading about the occult."

"Terrific," Fubar groaned, casting a reproachful look at Steve. "So, what's your problem, Kelly?"

"I have this nagging feeling that something is wrong with the plan and...."

"*And?*" Fubar asked, shouldering his pack and closing the trunk.

"And my phone is going nuts."

"Going nuts, how?" Steve asked.

"Well, you know how it's stuck at five PM?"

"Still?"

"Yeah. After you guys left, I noticed it was also stuck on December third. Anyway, it's been blinking on and off all day, the lock screen, I mean."

"As long as you don't see a notification for impending death—" Fubar stopped when he caught Steve's icy stare. "Sorry."

"Just now, I had the strangest urge to just keep going, not turn onto State, just keep walking onto the bridge. My phone started blinking like crazy; now it has added buzzing to its repertoire."

"Let me see it," Steve said.

Kelly took the phone out and handed it over.

"You changed the lock screen to the Boiler House?"

"No, *it* did."

"What are these numbers: 20:15? Wait, now 20:16. Are you on a call? Did you pocket dial someone?"

"It's something else the phone started doing."

"Crazy," Steve breathed. "You say it went even more nuts when you turned onto State Street?"

"That's right."

"Look at the picture—"

"I've been looking at it for two days and—"

"Look again. See, this girder in the corner?"

"Yeah, I get it; the picture was taken from the bridge."

"Why not the fire escape? Or from the other side of the river?" Steve asked.

"Fuck, I don't know," Kelly said, pinching the bridge of his nose. "Why any of it? None of it makes any rational sense."

"That's the first thing either of you have said in the last five minutes that I can agree with," Fubar said.

"What if the picture isn't telling you where to go? What if it's telling you where to *stand* at five PM?"

"Huh?" Kelly was so fixated on the Boiler House that he had trouble switching his thinking to entertain Steve's new idea.

"This is ridiculous," Fubar said, shifting the pack's weight on his back.

"No," Steve said, "It's intuitive, not literal. You had the urge to walk onto the bridge; the phone went nuts when you didn't. Maybe it wants you to stand in the spot where the picture was taken."

"Um," Kelly considered. As they looked, the phone started blinking like the slow frames of an old-time movie. "Well, shit..."

"You got this from reading about the occult?" Fubar asked.

"Just another way of looking at it," Steve said.

"Well, my phone seems to agree," Kelly said.

"Take a stroll on the bridge," Steve said. "We'll go set up."

"Who died and made you Darth Vader?" Fubar asked.

"Shut up, Fubar. C'mon," Steve said, shouldering his pack and heading toward the Boiler House. "See you in a few," he said to Kelly over his shoulder.

Kelly stared at his phone. It stopped blinking. The time on the counter read 20:20. The year? Could it be the year? Starting at the Boiler House's construction and ending... Kelly broke into a run. He had the feeling he needed to be in the right spot when the counter reached the current year. He didn't know how long it would take for the last numbers to turn, but he suspected it would happen at 5:00 PM.

Kelly raced onto Bridge Street, gasping for breath. He made a mental note to start doing some cardio. He passed the dirt lot in front of the Power House building and the door he'd pounded on looking for Casey the night all this started. He felt better. The feeling that his plan was flawed ebbed. Steve was right. Somehow, this was what he was supposed to be doing. His duck boots made a muffled flopping sound on the gum-spotted concrete of the bridge's sidewalk. The rain came a little harder. Kelly wiped it off the screen of his phone. He slowed to a walk, looking back and forth from the phone to the Boiler House, trying to find the exact spot where the photo was taken. He stopped, went back, stopped again, and retraced his steps — one, two, about here.

"I hope we're not talking millimeter accuracy," he said to the phone.

Thunder rumbled low from the swollen clouds.

The numbers on the call timer changed one last time. An earsplitting peel of thunder split the sky apart.

Chapter 52

Casey

Blood. That damnable, sickening sensation of becoming oozing blood running into the body of another. Casey was back. The bridge was once again made of green girders. The cars were modern, and the body he was in... oh boy! The body was his! Except... no. The body was just like his, but not his. This body was in pretty good shape. It breathed clearly. No aches and pains brought on by hard living. There was only one possible conclusion: he was inside Kelly.

Shit! Fuck! Shit! Shit! Shit! Now Kelly was going to die? The cycle was unbroken. Tyre was coming for them. Even though Casey knew it would come to this, he wasn't prepared for the reality of facing down the demon again.

KELLY!

Nothing.

KELLY!

Nothing. Just as it had been with the others, Casey couldn't communicate with his host. He could take over Kelly's mouth, talk to him... and say what? *God damn it!* There was still time. There had to be. He'd transferred into the other bodies hours before they died. There would be a time for him to talk to his brother using his brother's own mouth. Maybe it was best to see what his brother was up to first.

Kelly took his phone out and hit the home button. The image on the screen showed a picture of boiler #2. The boiler looked as it did in Casey's own time, except the angle was weird. The view was looking straight down from above. That was a nasty shock.

"It changed!" Kelly said, astonished. "It changed!"

What changed?

Kelly slipped his phone back into his pocket and hurried toward the end of the bridge.

WHAT CHANGED?

Kelly hurried on.

Casey had some hard thinking to do, and from the looks of things, that thinking needed to be done very quickly. He could, he supposed, stop Kelly from entering the Boiler House. He was sure that was where Kelly was heading. Question was: would that really help? Would it stop anything? Casey didn't think that was what he was supposed to do. He was pretty sure he hadn't been through all this just to steer his brother away from the Boiler House. And what if he did? Then what? Hitchhike in his brother's body forever?

Kelly turned the corner and kept going down State Street, then turned again into the filthy yard outside the Boiler House and darted up the clanking fire escape. Casey was astonished, given his brother's fear of heights. Kelly trotted onto the rickety bridge between the buildings, hoisted himself onto the handrail, and swung around the locked gate as if he'd done it a hundred times.

"Fubar," Kelly hissed, standing below the window to the Boiler House.

A face appeared, then an arm reached down. Kelly grasped the hand and climbed up through the window.

Inside, there were two men; Fubar, the one who helped Kelly up, and a second younger, more slender man. Both men were mocha brown and dressed in some kind of workout clothes with funny shoes.

"So?" the thin one asked as Kelly caught his breath.

"You were right, Steve," Kelly gasped. "I found the spot and stood there, then...."

"Come on," Steve coaxed.

"Well, then I just felt different."

"Different how?"

"Like... like I wasn't alone, but in a good way. I don't know how to describe it."

"This is ridiculous," Fubar threw his hands up.

"Shut up, Fubar," Steve said. "It's weird, sure, but you saw the video, heard the voice on it. You saw his phone, the time, the date, the blinking. Do you have an explanation?"

Fubar just sighed.

"Thought so."

"Anyway," Kelly continued, "after that, I checked my phone. The picture changed—and the time. Look!" Kelly held it up.

"I'll be damned," Fubar said. He walked to the edge of the shattered floor and looked down. "Taken from here," he said.

"What time is it?" Kelly asked.

Your fucking phone says, six, idiot. What the fuck is going on?

"It's quarter after five," Steve said.

"Why we're here so early?" Fubar asked.

The noise of someone kicking a glass bottle across gravel brought the conversation up short. Steve peeked out the window, then moved his head aside quickly. "Some guy in a fire department jacket," he hissed.

Kelly joined him at the window, peeked, then moved back to the center of the space. "Pontes," he said, "that's why we're here early."

"Now what?" Fubar asked, "we've already set the ropes."

Kelly gazed up at the beams. The blue and red ropes trailed down on either side of him, as before. "Now, we wait, I guess."

"I'm not getting arrested again," Steve said.

"He won't come in," Kelly said. "He never does."

Pontes? Now it's a party. Casey wondered if Steve and Fubar had last names that fit the others he'd died with; Walsh? Gottschalk? Costa? Was this to be a reenactment? It made him think, though. He had nearly an hour to dig into the problem. So why was he here this time, inside his brother's body? Was Kelly earmarked for death as well? Another victim of the demon's revenge? Another bloodline to snuff out?

Casey didn't like how Kelly had been dragged into all this. He wondered, if he were sober on that night, sober enough to feel the demon's name come to his mind, if Kelly would be here now? Maybe the name would have come to his mind, and the demon would have killed him long before he could touch that shard. Game over. Kelly safe.

But it wasn't Casey's fault either. It wasn't his fault at all, just the dumb luck of being a descendant of that long ago Papas. Probably the Pontes outside was a brother to the Pontes Casey died inside; he seemed old enough. Why hadn't he died inside one more person? Why hadn't that name and that form been revealed to him? He should have been inside Freeman in 1891...

but since Freeman never spoke the name.... Was it always going to go like this? To end like this?

The world darkened into night. Water dripped from the hole in the roof and echoed off the brick walls. The smell of decay in the mill grew stronger with the rain. The scents of mildew, mold, damp earth, and death permeated the darkness. The wind moaned a low note through the shattered windows facing the river, drowning the sound of rushing water below.

Casey wanted to talk to Kelly, pick his brain about what was going on, about the missing names; maybe Kelly would have some idea, especially about the name Papas was supposed to have. Maybe it was in one of the stories their father had read to them as a kid. Maybe Kelly would remember. But Casey couldn't just grab his brother's mouth and start talking in front of these men. He had to talk to Kelly. Time was slipping by.

Chapter 53

Hili

"What do you mean, the demon could destroy the *entire* world if he got into the wrong person?"

Silence.

"Casey?"

Nothing.

"Casey!"

She continued calling out to him even as she searched for Casey in her consciousness, feeling around with her mind. She felt the demon, and she felt the shards of the vessel, but not Casey. Where could he have gone? Sure, he annoyed her, but it was nice having someone to talk to. Someone who knew what she was going through. That thought brought her back to Nigmah, as such thoughts always did. Usually, she'd descend into a swirling spiral of self-pity, but there was a spark of hope this time. The pot was destroyed. The time and date of the demon's destruction had been revealed. Even if some of it made no sense to her, she knew it was coming. She called out for Casey once more. She wanted to know how he destroyed the pot. According to the priest in Sumer, she was the only one with the power to destroy it. And why hadn't she gone back into the pot when Mrs. Walsh died?

This latter thing wasn't unprecedented. She'd stayed in the minds of several people after the demon was put away, presumably because the pot wanted her out, wanted her moving it to the next place, or to keep it safe. Except, if the pot was nearly indestructible, why did it need her to keep it safe? Why did it need her to say the incantations instead of just returning the demon to the vessel on its own?

The only thing she was sure of, and what she didn't tell Casey, was that she knew why he had experienced the deaths of those men. The demon was trying to wipe out the six bloodlines, and the pot wanted someone besides Hili to know the names and put the demon away. Except Casey didn't have the urn's full power, having picked up only a shard. So the vessel did the only thing it could do. It made him a Keeper and tried to send him to put the demon away, too.

She could still see the glowing shards out in the darkness, but no matter how hard she tried to reach them, she never got any closer. The demon lurked out there too, somewhere between the mud and the abyss, circling and plotting. It was loose but not unfettered. The incantations Gottschalk put on the building must be holding it still.

Chapter 54

Kelly

K elly, Fubar, and Steve sat on the trash-strewn floor of the old mill, on the reasonably solid part of the upper floor in a dry spot. They sat cross-legged, sipping coffee Steve poured from a thermos into plastic camping cups with little hooked handles.

"There's something else I should tell you. Something you should know," Kelly said.

"Great," Fubar frowned, "And what's this eleventh-hour revelation?"

"Well, I told you I was working on a newspaper story about this place...."

"Go on," Steve said.

"Well, my research uncovered something: a journal written by Helmut Gottschalk."

"Isn't that the last name of the kid who went missing here in the eighties?" Fubar asked.

"Yes," Kelly said, "Anyway, in the journal, Gottschalk writes he was building this place, but the names bothered him, so he looked them up. Tyre, he says, is the name of an ancient city in the Middle East, one that God destroyed because they worshipped an evil god there—Milcom."

"Son of a bitch," Fubar said, "Millcom?"

"Spelled with one L, but yes."

"Ok, I feel like Alice, falling down the rabbit hole," Fubar said.

Kelly was about to say that the rest of the journal was illegible—but when he opened his mouth, different words came out. It was as if he were possessed, suddenly a passenger in his own body. His mouth said: "No matter how much they dug, no matter how many tons of granite boulders they dropped into the mud here, the ground just swallowed them up and covered them with more mud. When Mister Tyre himself came to the site to complain about the progress, Gottschalk knew he was a demon."

"Oh, come on," Fubar said, "I didn't think this was ghost story hour. Give me a break. Next, you're going to tell me he's buried under here."

"On that day in 1891, six men confronted Tyre and tried to destroy him, but they failed, and the demon, Tyre, sank into the mud below this building, buried alive."

"I knew it. This is all—"

"Listen," Kelly's mouth cut in, "the names of the men who tried to destroy Tyre were Gottschalk, Pontes, Walsh, Costa, Freeman ...and Papas."

"Wait..." Steve said, then trailed off.

Fubar and Steve looked at each other, then at Kelly. No one spoke for a long moment.

Steve broke the silence. "Did you say, Freeman and Walsh?"

"Yeah, why?"

Fubar shook his head. "So let me get this straight," Fubar began, "you're saying a demon is killing the descendants of the people who tried to kill him in 1891?"

"I'm just presenting the facts as I understand them." Kelly was so astounded at the information coming out of his mouth that he didn't struggle to resist the force taking over his body. It didn't seem to be a malevolent force, and it knew things, things *he* desperately needed to know.

"And how did these men in 1891 try to destroy the demon?" Steve asked.

"They were supposed to speak the demon's six names at the sixth hour past the meridian on a day whose sum is six. But one man died before they could finish."

"What kind of gibberish is that?" Fubar asked.

"Let me try," Steve said, "the sixth hour past the meridian is six PM. That's what PM stands for; Post Meridian and a day whose sum is six is today, 12/3."

"The date in Gottschalk's... journal was December 3, 1891." Kelly's body said.

"And the six names?" Fubar asked.

"I have the first five. They were in the uh, journal too," Kelly's mouth said.

"But you know the other one, *right*?" Fubar's cheeks flushed, his nostrils flared.

Kelly wanted to scream. Something has me! But he couldn't. The only thing keeping him from having a total psychotic break was that whatever had control of his body seemed to be trying to help them.

"But you know it, *right*?" Fubar repeated.

"I'm working on it." The thing inside Kelly answered.

"Well, Jesus Christ, that's fabulous. If I believe all this bullshit, which I'm not sure I do, you've got...." Fubar checked his watch, "about fifteen minutes to figure it out. It's almost time to gear up."

"No, wait," Steve said. "How do you know the other names?"

"The men spoke them in 1891—I mean, that's what I read."

Whoever this guy in my head is, he's a terrible liar, Kelly thought.

"All but one. Do I have it right?" Steve asked.

"Yes," the thing using Kelly's mouth answered.

"What was the name of the man who didn't speak the demon's name, the man who died?"

"What difference does it make? I don't have the sixth name."

"We've humored you a lot over the past few days," Steve said. "Your turn."

"Freeman. Why?"

Steve and Fubar looked at each other.

"His name is Freeman," Steve said, nodding toward Fubar.

"And his name is Walsh," Fubar said. "This is some bullshit."

"Yeah," Steve agreed, "freaky bullshit."

"Are you saying I'm supposed to stare down a demon and say a name I don't know? And if I don't, what?"

"A lot of people are going to die," Kelly's possessor said, "maybe all of them."

"God damn it, I didn't sign up for this shit. What the hell do I know about demon's names?"

"Does that mean you're suddenly a believer?" Steve grinned.

"Are you?" Fubar shot back.

"About fifty-fifty."

"Less than that," Fubar said. "This guy's trying to tell me I have to save the world."

Kelly was dumbstruck. This was all so weird, like a Twilight Zone episode. He tried to digest what had just happened, was still happening. Someone had taken over his body and, with his own mouth, laid out chunks of the puzzle he was trying to solve: six names, six o'clock, the sum of 6–666. He knew Casey was still alive, somewhere; he'd spoken to him. Kelly tried to recall the exact words on the phone call. What stuck out in his mind was that when Kelly told him to come home, Casey had said, "I'm trying."

The presence receded. Kelly shot to his feet and stared around dumbly.

"What is it, Kelly? Did you think of the name?" Steve asked.

"No, I uh...." Kelly was at a loss, a total loss. Should he tell them what just happened to him? No. Bad idea. They'd just think he was crazier than they already did, maybe back out altogether. "I...."

"That's it," Fubar said, "enough of this crystal ball bullshit. I'm pulling the plug. Kelly's gone to the zoo. I'm not putting him on a rope."

"C'mon, Fubar," Steve said.

"Don't you fucking Fubar me, this is nuts. And now I'm supposed to save the world or something. What the fuck? This is some kind of hoax. I'm not—"

"Shh," Steve said.

Fubar shut up.

Voices echoed outside.

All three crept to the window and looked down into the courtyard. In the faint glow of the streetlights from across the canal, they could just make out Pontes in his fire department jacket, talking to a figure in a hooded sweatshirt. The hood drooped over the figure's forehead, casting the face in shadow.

"Go home, David," Pontes was saying, "I'm keeping an eye on it. I've got a feeling about tonight."

The man wrote something on a little white pad and showed it to Pontes.

"Me too," Pontes said.

Kelly crept away from the window. Fubar and Steve followed.

"Who the fuck is David?" Fubar asked.

"David Gottschalk, Freddie's brother, the kid who went missing," Kelly said.

"Why is he writing on a pad?" Steve asked.

"He hasn't really spoken since his brother went into the boiler."

"Je-sus," Fubar shook his head. "Anyone else you're expecting?"

"No."

"Anything else you'd like to tell us?" Steve asked. "Now's the time."

"No," Kelly said aloud. Inside he said: *YES! SOMEONE TOOK OVER MY BODY!!!*

"Well, we can't leave without getting busted by Fire Marshall Bill," Steve said, "so we might as well do what we came here to do."

"I don't like it," Fubar said, "not one fucking bit."

"What's to like?" Kelly said. "I've got to take a leak before I put my harness on."

"Good idea," Steve said.

They each retreated to their own corners, and when he was alone, Kelly whispered, "is that you, Casey?"

"Yes," his mouth said.

"Prove it."

"You wet the bed until you were twelve."

"Jesus, Casey, of all the things... why do you keep lording that over me?"

"Because I'm your older brother."

"By 17 minutes. Why are you in my fucking head?"

"Shh, keep our voice down! It's too complicated to explain now. There's no time. Kelly, the name is Milcom. That's the name we're supposed to say."

"Of course, from the old stories—"

"What about Fubar?" Casey asked. "He never even asked for the name he's supposed to say?"

"He's the kind to try to figure it out on his own, see if it comes to him. That's his M.O. Besides; you know it, right? You can just yell it to him."

"I guess. It's just you haven't seen what this thing can do. I don't think we should be playing fast and loose, Kelly."

"It's a little late for that epiphany," Fubar said as he walked by, zipping his fly.

"Casey, this is pretty fucking flimsy!" Kelly hissed.

"There are other forces at work here. That's all I can say for the moment, except stay away from any glowing purple shit lying around."

"What? This is fucking nuts!" Kelly said.

Casey receded and didn't say anything more.

The men were quiet as they put on their harnesses. There was only the sound of dripping water and the moaning wind.

"Same deal as before," Fubar said, then shimmied up the I-beam.

Kelly stood a few steps from the edge of the ruined floor. Two ropes clipped to the front of his harness, a red one running up to the left where Fubar was getting into place, and a blue one on the other side where Steve was. The ropes formed a V ending at Kelly's waist.

"Red belay on," Fubar called.

"Blue belay on," Steve called.

"Okay, Kelly, step to the edge and sit into your harness."

Kelly didn't cry out when he sat into his harness and swung over the edge this time. He was glad of the obscurity, for once. The darkened mill yawned beneath him, distant and indistinct.

"Switch on your headlamp, Kelly; I can't see shit," Fubar called down.

Kelly did, and a pool of pale blue light illuminated his thighs and his shoes before becoming lost in the darkness below.

"Here we go," Fubar called.

Both ropes jerked. Kelly's stomach rolled up into his throat and back down. He began to descend. The wind whipped up and made a low 'ooooohhh' through the black window sockets on the riverward side of the mill. Thunder rolled through the night like a freight train.

The secret stone inscription and the seal of Solomon came into view, glowing with their own eerie supernatural light. Kelly tore his eyes away from that spectacle and stared down between his legs. He caught the first glimpse of the boiler below as the weak light of his headlamp made the rainwater on its surface glisten. As he descended closer, he could make out wisps of steam. They danced across its surface like a thin summer fog.

He descended closer still, and he could feel the heat. In that moment, he knew he'd been right: about the date, about the time, about the boiler. Now he needed, *desperately* needed, his brother to be right that Fubar would know the beast's name when the time came. And that time was very close indeed now.

He passed down below the top edge of the boiler, its inscrutable black surface now only an arm's length from his face. His feet came level with the door on the front, then his shoulders. "Stop!" he called.

Intense heat radiated out from the iron beast. Kelly reached out a hand and stopped himself. If he could already feel the heat, the metal was too hot to touch. He retracted his hand into the sleeve of his coat and wrapped the material into his fist, then reached out again. Hot, even through the sleeve of his parka. The stink of melting nylon infested his nose. He pulled. Stuck. Bracing his feet on the face of the boiler, Kelly tried again. The heat on his hand was almost unbearable. He yanked. Burning shot up through his shoes into the soles of his feet. Sharp tendrils of pain ran up his arm and legs.

He pushed himself back.

The door swung open.

The air filled with the smell of burning soles and the thick acrid smell of rancid meat cooked on an unclean fire. Graffiti on the back wall of the boiler 'Seek Zeek,' blood red at the top, blackened and bubbled at the bottom, was visible from the light of some smoldering thing on the floor of the boiler out of Kelly's sight. A shadow flitted across the opening too fast for Kelly to see. A humanoid shape appeared inside the boiler door, backlit by the red glow.

"Kelly, what's going on?" Fubar called.

Kelly opened his mouth, but no sound came. He felt Casey's presence inside him, but Casey wasn't doing anything, wasn't taking control. Abject terror gripped Kelly's insides and twisted, twisted, twisted until he was wound so tight he couldn't move.

"Kelly," the figure hissed with the voices of a hundred tortured souls, "don't you recognize me? Here, I'll give you a better look." It was a boy, used to be a boy. It flopped one leg, then the other into the crawlway inside the boiler door. The boy's movements were those of a rag doll flopped into a chair for a terrible tea party. Its pants smoldered, then caught fire, casting flickering light on its gruesome image. It was Freddie Gottschalk, just as he appeared in the newspaper picture. In this new light, Kelly could see that the boy was badly decomposed. Maggots crawled from Freddie's mouth, then dropped onto his flaming pants, where they popped and sizzled. Freddie's eye sockets were empty. Flaps of burned skin clung to his half-exposed skull.

"Recognize me now? I'm famous." The jaw worked up and down but lacked the lips to articulate the words. The voice came from somewhere inside its stomach. "I had my picture in all the papers." It was the same voice from the video on Kelly's phone. It was the voice of screaming children, desperate women, terrified men, all slightly out of synch. "Are you scared of little old me? BEDWETTER!" Its jaw dropped too low when it articulated this last. Something long, thin, black, and pointed showed in its mouth.

"Kelly, talk to me!" Fubar called.

Casey took control of Kelly's mouth and yelled: "Hold!"

"Is that the beggar I hear?" it hissed. "Well, won't this be fun? I suppose we can drop the puppet show then." Thin black things in the dead boy's mouth crawled out and revealed themselves to be fingers, illuminated by the light of the deceased child's burning pants. Four on one side, four on the other. The fingers started pulling the boy's mouth apart, wider and wider. Flesh tore, bones cracked, and at last, the head split. The top of the boy's skull fell into his lap. The two halves of the lower jaw hit either side of the crawlway, sizzling on the hot brickwork like a flipped burger. The torso fell forward onto its thighs, extinguishing the flames. Behind it, a dark shape rose in the unholy purple glow of the boiler.

Kelly knew its name, but his bowels had turned to water, and his tongue lay like a brick in the desert of his mouth.

The skeleton thing moved forward. Molten red showed through a jigsaw pattern of cracks in its mottled black skin. "Kelly," it hissed, "I've been waiting for you."

The heat of the thing intensified. Kelly coaxed the thick slab of his tongue into action. "Milcom, I know your name."

"NOOO!" It launched forward into the crawlway.

"FUBAR, GET ME OUT OF HERE!" Kelly screamed.

The body of the Skeleton Man burst into flames, but it wasn't consumed. It crawled over the boy's corpse, setting it alight again. A fireball issued from the tilted boiler behind the thing. The heat blasted Kelly's face.

"Mine's jammed!" Fubar yelled. "Steve, lower yours, swing him away!"

"Mine's jammed too!"

"Kelly," Fubar yelled down. "Rock from side to side, unclip one rope!"

Kelly reached up, grabbed the red rope, and pulled.

"Here," Milcom laughed, "let me help."

Something heavy slammed into wood on the far side of the mill, sending deep echoes off the bricks like a pounding drum.

The unclean wind of Milcom's breath washed over Kelly, bringing the reek of putrefied flesh. Milcom slashed the red rope above Kelly's head with a bony finger. The rope parted. Kelly swung violently to the right.

The pounding to Kelly's left ended in a smashing, splintering sound. A gleaming ax tip ripped through the plywood covering one of the windows.

"Fuck," Fubar yelled. "Steve, lower him!"

Milcom climbed to the edge of the boiler and bellowed in a voice full of broken glass and rage. Fire shot from the boiler behind him as he perched like a flaming gargoyle.

A bright beam of light from the window cut across the mill.

Kelly reached the end of his crazy swing and started to pendulum back toward the boiler, toward the demon. He pinwheeled his arms and legs in a desperate effort to slow his momentum, but it was no good.

As he swung back, Casey took control of Kelly's body. "Harken, demon," he screamed.

The beast held out a clawed hand and sliced the final rope as Kelly swung by. His momentum carried him sideways. He smashed into the splintered floorboards below the boiler, then fell into the mud beneath. He turned his head to the side and vomited yellow bile onto the shoulder of his parka. His head was a ball of pain. He tried to rise. The world went black.

Chapter 55

Casey

This time the blood spurted. From where Casey knew not. He only knew that it carried him home. When he opened his eyes, rotten wood greeted them, illuminated in wan blue light. He lifted a hand, his hand, at last, his *own* hand, but putrefied and decayed. It took a monumental effort. The stench of death overwhelmed his desiccated nose. Moldy slabs of gray, rotten skin fell away as he raised his head.

Kelly's body lay several feet away; headlamp pointed at the underside of the floor above him. Water dripped from the cracks between the boards, and each drop brought rejuvenation. He rolled over and belly crawled toward his twin, but stopped when Milcom came into view through the gaping hole in the floor, crouched at the edge of the boiler.

"GO BACK TO HELL!" someone shouted.

A torrent of water blasted the beast. Milcom fell back into the opening, clinging to the sides of the boiler door with thin clawed fingers. It tried to scream, but water filled its mouth and what came out was a choked whimper.

The water rebounding off of the demon doused Casey's body, bringing new life.

The demon lost its grip on the lip of the boiler and disappeared. Steam billowed from the opening around the rushing torrent of water — deep puddles formed around Casey, making him stronger still.

Casey crawled forward again. He put a muddy hand to his brother's throat and found a pulse there. The water pouring into the boiler stopped. Casey tried to drag his brother away from the hole in the floor above but found he lacked the strength.

"AGAIN!" came a shout from above.

Casey looked up in time to see the beast's fingers on the edge of the boiler. And again, a torrent blasted into the opening. The water around Casey and Kelly rose from the overflow. "No! we'll drown!" Casey tried to yell, but his voice left his lips only in a faint whisper. He pulled Kelly's limp arms back and tucked them under his brother's head to keep it above the rising water.

The wooden beams under the raised end of the boiler groaned under the weight of the water rising inside it. Casey struggled to sit up. Red eyes advanced in the darkness around him. "Oh fuck you," he breathed.

The unholy decayed faces of everyone he'd died inside crept into the light of Kelly's headlamp behind bony scuttling fingers. They bared their teeth and screamed in tortured voices. Rotten fingers clamped onto Casey's shin. A dead man's teeth sank into his thigh. The pain brought Casey into focus. "Harken D—"

The corpses scuttled back into the shadows.

Blood gushed from Casey's leg. He clapped a muddy hand over the spot to staunch the blood, even as the water rose to cover it. The filthy water lapped at Kelly's cheeks. Casey let go of his leg and tried to pull his brother into his lap, lifting him by the shoulders. As the water rose and Kelly began to float, Casey found he could.

The fire hose, for that's what it must be, continued to blast into the boiler above. What didn't go in poured down the face of the boiler, through the hole in the floor, and pooled around the twins.

Kelly's eyes cracked open. "Casey?"

"I'm here."

Kelly's eyes closed, his lips stretched into a thin smile.

"No time to nap bro, you've got to sit up before you drown." Casey glanced up at the boiler. Water still gushed into it, but almost as much poured out again. The timbers that held it groaned. The report of cracking beams echoed through the mill like a shotgun blast. "Can you stand, Kelly? We have to go!"

The final timber holding the boiler gave way with a thunderous crack. The boiler, along with the tons of water inside it, fell into the mud in front of Casey. The ensuing tsunami of water and filth buoyed him up, then launched him out of the hole.

Weak, drenched, and disoriented, Casey raised himself to his elbows, coughing putrid muddy water.

"Who's there?" a voice shouted from the window.

"It's Casey," he croaked.

"Who?"

"Casey! Who's that?"

"Pontes. Where's Kelly?"

Casey coughed and spat out more filth. "I don't know." He got to his hands and knees in time to see three men climb in through the window. The first was the speaker, old and a bit fat. A flashlight on the window sill lit up the fire department logo on his jacket.

Pontes turned to the other two men. "I told you two to stay outside."

"No way, Floyd. It's time you stopped bossing me around." The first of the two said. "This has to end. Tonight. Come on, David."

"Then help me look for Kelly," Pontes said. "Kelly!" He shouted.

Casey scrabbled around in the mud, jamming his fingers painfully on all kinds of hidden refuse. "Kelly!" he called.

"What about the... monster?" someone called from the ceiling.

"Who's that?" Pontes aimed his flashlight at the rafters.

"Abraham Lincoln," Fubar replied.

"Whatever," Pontes returned the beam of his light to the sea of mud on the mill floor.

The hooded man motioned wildly.

"David has him," Pontes called.

Casey tapped his last reserves of strength and crawled over to where the hooded figure bent over the mud.

David held Kelly by the armpits and hauled him out of the filth onto his lap. Casey crawled over and wiped the slime from Kelly's nose and mouth. Pontes leaned down and put his fingers to Kelly's neck.

"Good pulse," Pontes said. "Is he breathing?"

Closed mouth. Bloody nose. Kelly wasn't breathing.

Casey didn't waste time directing David to do the choking maneuver. He punched Kelly in the stomach, right below the sternum.

Kelly spewed black bile all over Casey's face. It ran from his eyes and dripped down his nose.

"That's not—" Pontes began.

"Ow," Kelly said.

"Will someone please tell me what the fuck—" the sound of tearing metal drowned out the rest of Abraham Lincoln's words.

The thick sound of bubbling, boiling mud filled the mill.

"It's coming back!" Another voice from the rafters called.

"No shit," Casey mumbled.

"Now what?" Pontes asked.

Casey remembered the way Costa quoted the Bible and held the beast in place back in 1891. "We have to read Ezekiel 28."

"Anyone got a Bible?" Jacob asked.

David pulled up his sleeve. "Our Father who art in heaven." He indicated the words tattooed on his arm.

Pontes squinted at it. "I can't read that; it's too small."

"If you're going to do something," Abraham Lincoln called from the rafters, "I'd hurry!"

The building trembled. A geyser of mud erupted out of the hole in the floor.

David passed the drooping Kelly over to Jacob, who rested Kelly's shoulders on his lap. Then David began taking off his coat.

"What are you doing?" Casey asked. "There's no time to—"

"KEEPER! FACE ME!" the demon roared, its voices discordant and disjointed.

Casey turned. The geyser of mud formed a column. *If this is where I end, at least I can buy Kelly some time.* He crawled away into the sea of mire that covered the floor of the mill.

"Harken, demon!" Casey shouted.

The demon, now formed in a ten-foot-tall effigy of an ancient warrior, lifted a muddy foot out of the hole in the floor and advanced toward Casey. "Thou art Milcom!" he shouted.

The demon lifted a second giant foot out of the hole.

"That should have worked," Casey said. "That should have stopped it long enough for us to say the names." He needed to think.

The demon swiveled its malevolent gaze around the mill, bending and peering into the sea of mud.

"I know you're here, Keeper. The incantation won't work. The pot is broken!"

"Hurry!" Casey hissed at David and Pontes.

"Time to die, Keeper." Mud fell away from its face, revealing red almond-shaped eyes, like those of a snake. Its mouth held a thousand broken needle teeth as long as a man's hand.

All Casey could think to do was start the incantation again. "Harken, demon. He who is known as Mil—"

The demon hurled a handful of mud, and the filth choked Casey. It took a step toward him.

"The word of the LORD came to me: Son of man, say to the ruler of Tyre, 'This is what the Sovereign LORD says:'" Pontes voice rang out through the mill.

Casey glanced over as he spat out the foul-tasting mud. Pontes hunched over David's back, reading the words tattooed there.

"Do you think the words of Ezekiel can stop me now?" the demon said, turning away from Casey toward Pontes.

"I know they can, Milcom!" Casey spat.

"You cannot win, Keeper!" the demon shrieked.

Pontes stopped reading from David's back and looked up.

"Don't stop!" Casey yelled. "It's not over! Everyone get under cover!" He moved weak-armed toward the demon. His stomach heaved. Only adrenaline kept him going now.

The others did as he said. Pontes and David took cover behind a pile of trash near the window. Jacob ducked behind a vertical I-beam some thirty feet from the hole in the floor.

"In the pride of your heart, you say, "I am a god; I sit on the throne of a god in the heart of the seas." But you are a man and not a god, though you think you are as wise as a god," Pontes continued.

Casey spat and searched for a clean spot on his clothing to wipe his mouth on. There was none. Milcom stood rooted to the spot by the Bible verses. Casey's hands shook with terror. Not all of it directed at the demon. More than anything, he was afraid he would fail, now, at the end of it all.

"Your heart has grown proud," Pontes shouted. "Therefore, this is what the Sovereign LORD says: Because you think you are wise, as wise as a god...."

"Shut up, fools!" the beast's tortured voices came from the heart of the darkness. It hurled something at Pontes.

Pontes dodged whatever it was and kept going. "I am going to bring foreigners against you, the most ruthless of nations; they will draw their swords against your beauty and wisdom and pierce your shining splendor. They will bring you down to the pit, and you will die a violent death in the heart of the deep."

Suddenly Casey understood. This was why the men in 1891 were all of different nationalities. Though, in his estimation, Portugal and Greece weren't exactly the most ruthless of nations. Germany, sure, Italy, okay, but Greece? The Spartans, maybe? Focus, Casey. He'd said Milcom. What was the next name in the sequence? Gottschalk. "Is there someone here named Gottschalk?"

"He is," Jacob said, pointing to the man whose back Pontes hunched over, reading the tattooed Bible verses.

Casey crawled to Gottschalk. His wide, frightened eyes stared back at Kelly from inside the pool of Pontes's flashlight. "Say the name!" Casey hissed.

The man shook his head.

"You will die a violent death right here, idiots! You cannot destroy me. You cannot stop me. This is my time!" the mud warrior screamed.

"Oh, fuck you!" Casey yelled. "I've come to destroy you."

"Keeper, you cannot, or you would have already." It hurled something at Casey.

Casey was too slow and too weak to dodge. A brick smashed his leg. He screamed. Then, gritting his teeth, he returned his gaze to Gottschalk. "Say it!"

"He can't speak," Pontes said, then continued reading from David's back. "You will die the death of the uncircumcised at the hands of foreigners. I have spoken, declares the Sovereign Lord."

"Say it!" Casey shouted.

"Der Ungeisthasse," David said.

"Louder," Casey urged.

"You are Der Ungeisthasse!" David shouted.

The mud barbarian bellowed with rage and fell back through the hole in the floor in an indistinct tsunami of filth.

Cheers went up from the men high in the rafters, but Casey knew the fight wasn't over. Two names down, four to go.

Something rose up, black as the night. Darker than mud. Darker than death. Its edges amorphous roiling smoke. It formed the shape of a man in similar armor to the first. Roman armor, maybe.

Casey caught movement out of the corner of his eye. Jacob stepped out from cover. He wanted to shout, "what the fuck are you doing, Jacob?" but he didn't want to call attention to Jacob's idiocy.

"I know you," Jacob said, still advancing on the man-shaped cloud of darkness.

"Oh, crazy Jacob—" the thing began.

"You are Pesadelo Vivo, the walking nightmare. That's where I know you, from my dreams."

"No! You cannot win! The third bloodline is destroyed!" the beast shrieked. Its smoky countenance receded through the hole in the floor.

"All this time," Jacob said, still moving forward, "all this time they said I was crazy—"

"Jacob," Casey yelled, "you got it, now get back. Aarrgh." His leg was a ball of agony. His stomach made its slow way to his mouth.

"—but it was you, in my head," Jacob continued, "moving around up there in my sleep, infecting my dreams." Jacob raised his fists at the receding darkness and extended his middle fingers. "Fuck you, Pesadelo Vivo!"

"Son of man," Pontes read on, "take up a lament concerning Tyre and say to him: This is what the Sovereign LORD says...."

Casey tried desperately to parse the demon's words, 'the third bloodline is destroyed.' Costa. Costa was the next name. Except, when the demon killed Daniel Costa, it said, 'Last of his line.' He didn't understand how they were supposed to destroy it without all six bloodlines. "Anyone here from the Costa bloodline?" he asked. But he knew the answer, or thought he did.

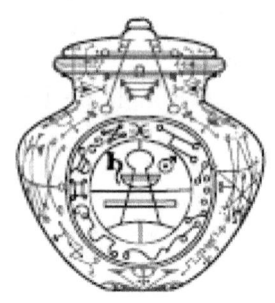

Chapter 56

Hili

Pouring, flowing, pure, clean water returned Hili to her body. Thunder rattled the boards above. She was nothing but a skeleton and some bits of desiccated flesh. What there was of her glowed violet where she lay in the mud. And not far away, a ring of purple shards lay in a heap. As she crawled toward the urn fragments, dripping water from the boards above lent her strength. New skin grew out of the decay. Blood began pumping, blood from the bones in this terrible place, and at the same time, her blood. It belonged to her. It was hers, and yet these bones were not. Hili crawled toward the shards. The water did its work, and by the time she reached the first, she was whole. In the light of the glowing fragment, she realized the brown skin of her hand was just that, *her* hand.

She wept as she gathered the pieces of the urn. Her robe, *her* robe, the one she'd worn for the last time in the mountain cave, reflected the ghostly purple light, unaffected by the mud, pristine. She lamented the missing piece, the two symbol shard she and Casey had lost in the river. She felt something in her hand. When she opened her fist, it lay in her palm.

The pile of fragments flashed purple when Hili dropped the last shard on top. They began to smoke, and the purple smoke entered Hili the way the smoke from the pot entered the bodies of those destined to host the demon. And when the last of the smoke was inside her, Hili knew she *was* the pot, the vessel, the agent of the demon's destruction.

"... You walked among the fiery stones..." a voice hollered somewhere above her. She recognized the incantation from the field of mud.

Somewhere under the floor, metal groaned.

"It's coming back!" another voice shouted.

A humanoid shape rose up and through a hole in the boards above. Thick mud oozed down its flanks.

"Someone look at it and say a fucking name!" Hili recognized Casey's voice.

"You were blameless in your ways," the incantation continued, "from the day you were created till wickedness was found in you. Through your widespread trade, you were filled with violence, and you sinned. So I drove you in disgrace from the mount of God, and I expelled you, O guardian cherub, from among the fiery stones. Your heart became proud on account of your beauty, and you corrupted your wisdom because of your splendor. So I threw you to the earth; I made a spectacle of you before kings."

"Do you think you are kings?" the demon spat. Its form writhing, unclear, like a tower of worms. "The sixth hour is nearly gone. You have failed. You do not know all my names! Time for all of you to die. The words of Ezekiel are almost spent!"

Hili rushed for the beast, climbing out of the hole and standing before the muddy thing in her true form, her robe pure white tinged with purple.

"So," the beast spat, "the second Keeper has arrived. You have failed. A thousand Keepers can't defeat me without the last names! The bloodline of Costa is destroyed!"

."No," Hili said, "it isn't."

"NO!" it screamed. "Impossible! The bloodline is destroyed!"

"The line of Costa is *my* bloodline. You may have killed all of my other descendants, but I remained tied to the pot, waiting." She stood before the giant muddy form of the Visigoth King, Alaric, hands on her hips. "You are Daemonium in Medio Umbra!"

The beast screamed and fell into the hole once more, back into the stew of filth and decay below.

Hili was inside a great brick building covered with a layer of thick mud. Not far away, a form in the mire glowed a faint purple. "Casey?"

"Hili?" it replied.

"Yes. How many names have been spoken?"

"Four."

The building trembled. A mound of slime bulged through the floor and coalesced into another towering humanoid shape. It rose higher and higher until the rapidly forming head of a pirate took shape in the rafters. It stomped a foot, and floorboards shattered, sending wooden shrapnel across the room. The fragments went around her like a rock in a stream, but behind her, someone cried out in pain.

"You are Deamhan Claidheimh!" a man perched high in the rafters shouted.

"NO!" the beast shouted. It poured back into the hole like tainted molasses.

Hili could hardly bear it. Five names spoken, one name left. One name away from the end. From release! She prayed to her long-forgotten gods that the sixth name would be spoken, here, now.

"Is that it?" the words came from one of the men in the rafters.

"No," Casey said. "One more."

Thunder peeled the sky open. The world flashed blue. The echoes rolled like boulders back and forth across the building, causing it to tremble. The ground shook so violently that Hili took an involuntary step away from the hole. Below, lightning arced across the swirling mud, sending traces of blue fire back and forth on the surface of the filth.

The mire frothed below Hili, and a bulbous form rose from the slime. At first, the form that rose from the floor looked like an effigy of Casey himself, dressed in a long coat, swaying and drinking from an upturned bottle.

"You son of a bitch," Casey spat.

Then it started changing again. Hili couldn't make out the features of the thing. The head faced away from her. "You filthy vermin," it spat, its voice full of derision, "cowards and beggars descended from the rejects of better nations. You cannot win. You cannot destroy me. I live in the hearts of the people. Those small, wounded little hearts."

And then the mud became the figures of two men—fucking. One looked like Casey.

"The... hell... with you," a voice said in the darkness. Again, it sounded like Casey. Except Casey stood beside her, eyes slitted in hate but decidedly mute.

The thing changed again in front of Hili.

"What do we do?" Casey asked.

"By your many sins and dishonest trade, you have desecrated your sanctuaries...." Pontes read.

"Pontes is going to run out of Bible verses pretty soon," Casey said.

"Someone here must have the name," Hili replied. If someone didn't speak the name soon, Hili didn't know what she could do to get the demon under control again. She didn't think this damaged building could hold it anymore.

"What the..." one of the men on the beams gasped.

The thing now again formed two men, except a clothed one whipped a naked one in chains.

"What?" Casey called.

The ceiling man's light shook back and forth. "Motherfucker..." was all he said.

He uttered a single word. A word Hili couldn't hear.

Then the flash, just a pinpoint of fire, came from the man, accompanied by a crack of thunder.

Flames burst out from the center of the mud giants.

"So I made a fire come out from you!" Pontes shouted.

The giant began to melt. Flames licked along its entire surface.

Thunder and lightning came from the man on the beam many times over. "Die you son-of-a-bitch!"

The monster burned and crumpled.

"Did he speak the name?" Casey shouted over the din.

"Yes," Hili said. She knew what she had to do, what Casey had to do.

"It is almost done," she said. "Can you feel it? Can you feel what you need to do?"

"Yes," he replied. "But I need to say goodbye to my brother first."

"You overgrown man-child. There is no time!" She couldn't believe this idiot was willing to risk the demon escaping.

"Yes, there is. I can feel it!"

"Casey!" she called, but he was already running to where his brother's broken form lay cradled in the arms of another man.

Flakes of ash fell into the mud.

The beast turned to her, its face melting to reveal its bottom teeth, pushed together and forming a white hill in the middle. "Your paltry weapons can't kill me. The six names can't kill me. Look, Keeper, the names are spoken, and I'm still here. Now it's time for me to be rid of you forever!"

Chapter 57

Kelly

Kelly opened his eyes to see Casey's face above him. "Casey," he croaked. The room spun around him. His head pounded, and the pain in his leg and side were almost unbearable.

"Kelly," Casey said and threw his arms around him. "I'm sorry for everything. I have to go. I love you." He rose to leave.

"Wait! Casey!" He tried to sit up but felt so nauseous that he leaned back into, well, someone was holding him.

Casey turned to look back.

"I'm sorry too, Casey. I love you!"

Casey smiled, nodded, then walked away.

Near the hole in the center of the room, a woman in a robe so white it hurt Kelly's eyes held a hand out to Casey. When his brother took the woman's hand, they both glowed purple. Together, and still clasping hands, they walked into the middle of the towering mud monster.

There was a crack of thunder and a flash of purple light. The mud exploded and splattered everything inside the mill. It choked him. He couldn't cough. Each time the urge wracked him, his chest lit up in white-hot agony. Splotches of color danced before his eyes.

KELLY WATCHED FROM the gurney as the paramedics loaded the unconscious form of his brother into an ambulance. It roared off, sirens blaring. He laid his head back against the sheet and felt a bump as his stretcher rolled into another waiting ambulance. The bright lights inside swam in ascending circles and became lost in the dark.

His world came and went like waves crashing on a rocky shore. There were sirens, a plastic mask over his nose and mouth, a jab in his arm. Voices asked questions. Darkness. Hospital walls rolled by, concerned faces leaned over. More questions. Bright lights. Darkness came again and stayed.

Kelly woke with the sun in his eyes. Pain greeted him all along the left side of his body, head to toe. He stared up at the ubiquitous white ceiling tiles of his hospital room, trying to clear the fog in his head. When he tried to turn to face the window, pain shot through him like a bolt from a crossbow. He found if he shifted his good eye, for there was gauze on the other, he could just make out the delicious buttery sun in the pale blue winter sky. Machines beeped with a regularity that was both cloying and comforting. He was alive, but what about... "Casey?" his voice came out in a dry croak.

"Hey there," a soft masculine voice said, "it's okay." A soft hand touched his wrist. Jacob Pontes leaned into his line of vision.

"Casey?" Kelly asked again.

Jacob shook his head.

Kelly frowned painfully. He couldn't seem to gather his thoughts. Every time he put a sentence together in his head, the words slipped away before they got to his mouth. "Casey's gone?"

"Guys, Kelly's awake," Jacob said, ignoring the question.

Faint groans. The rustling of clothes. Footsteps. The faces of Floyd Pontes, Fubar, Steve, and David Gottschalk swam into view. "What are you all doing here?"

"Been here all night," Fubar said, "it's not like I could just go home and go to bed after that. What else were we going to do?"

"Is everyone else..." words failed Kelly.

"We're fine," Floyd Pontes said. "It's you we're worried about. How do you feel?"

"My left side hurts a lot."

"Yeah," Fubar said, "you took a beating. Two broken ribs, broken shin–both bones, concussion, twelve stitches on your temple, and sixteen on your thigh. Rather impressive, actually."

"Thanks," Kelly said dryly. "What about Casey?"

"I'm sorry, Kelly," Pontes said. "He didn't survive the explosion."

Jacob squeezed Kelly's hand.

Casey...

"How... Why did you have a firehose?"

"I've got some juice in the fire department," Floyd said. "I told one of the captains my investigation pointed toward an agent of Milcom attempting insurance fraud via arson, and I wanted some gear on standby, just in case."

Casey...

"How did you *know* about last night?" Kelly asked. "How did you, or Jacob, or David?"

The Pull

Kelly recalled his research, the weird behavior of his phone, puzzling out the dates. "It's... complicated," he said.

"Same." Pontes smiled.

"How... the demon... the sixth name?" Kelly groped for the words.

"We've been talking about that all night," Fubar said, "comparing notes. The final form was... shame."

"Shame?" Kelly didn't understand; everything else was old world, ancient.

"Why not? The Ezekiel verse said, 'the most violent of nations.' No list of violent nations is complete without America, and nothing is more American than shame. Shame for being a black man—"

"Or being queer," Kelly mused.

"Or crazy," Jacob added.

Or a drunk...

Kelly tried to fit the last piece into the puzzle in his fuzzy, throbbing head. "The verse said God would bring foreigners against Tyre. It wouldn't say that unless that punished Tyre somehow. It talked about Tyre having a God complex, in so many words. All the other forms were rulers, or gods, or kings, or demons. How does shame fit in?"

"But shame rules America." Father Murray stepped through the doorway. He leaned over Kelly and clasped his hand. "It is a ruler who hates foreigners and queers and anything out of the narrow norm. It is a ruler who condones and incites racism, violence, and ignorance. Authenticity is its enemy."

Kelly tried to think about it, but all that came to his mind were images of his brother. "Casey...."

"He's a hero, Kelly," Pontes said. "He died to save us."

"We were there to save him, though." Kelly tried to sit up and fell back in pain. This wasn't the way it was supposed to happen. He was there to save Casey, to make up for kicking him out. This was all wrong. "I have to go. I have to—"

"Lie back," Jacob said. "I'm sorry he's gone, but we did save him, Kelly. The man I saw climb into the boiler in my dream was not the man I saw jump into the heart of a demon to save his brother. Somehow, he changed. He saved himself, Kelly. He was not ashamed."

Chapter 58

Kelly

Pain flared in Kelly's side as he slid his arm into the sleeve of his sport coat.

"Let me help you with that," Justin said, hurrying across the hospital room to Kelly's side. "Why do you have to try to be so macho all the time?" He lifted the collar and held the sleeve out so that Kelly could slide his other arm in easily. "Now, let me get these shoes for you."

"Justin, stop, I can—"

"What, Kelly? Bend down with broken ribs to put your shoes on? Am I just supposed to stand back and watch you re-injure yourself?"

"Well, you don't have to mother me."

"What if that's what I want to do?" Justin stood, leaned in, and kissed Kelly's forehead.

"It's at times like this when all I can think about is W.C. Fields."

"What about him?"

"He said: 'I was in the hospital, and I took a turn for the nurse, uh, worst.'"

"Well, I'm glad it's the former and not the latter." Justin smiled at him.

Kelly smiled back. Falling in love with his nurse took some of the sting out of Casey's death. At least he wasn't going through it alone.

"I still don't think you should be leaving the hospital, and neither does Doctor Marks."

"Like I told both of you, you can either let me go to my brother's funeral and come back, or I'll sign myself out."

"You're bluffing," Justin said. "You'd miss me too much."

"And you're hovering," Kelly said. He made shooing motions with his hand, then reached up and gingerly adjusted his tie.

"Hello?" Pontes called from the doorway. "Ready to go?"

"Floyd," Kelly called. "Yes, if you can get Nurse Ratched here to back off."

"Don't be an asshole, honey," Justin said.

Kelly jerked his head up, but relaxed when he saw the trace of a smile play across Justin's lips.

"Okay." Pontes glanced from Kelly to Justin and back, shrugged, and continued. "I wanted to be the first to tell you that following the events at the Boiler House, there was sufficient evidence to indict the executives of MillCom Real Estate with conspiracy to commit arson. The D.A. wanted to get them on insurance fraud too, but no one filed a claim. In fact, the executives listed in public records can't be found. The offices are empty. I don't think it will take long now to have the place torn down. The way I hear it, Fubar is already gearing up to have it turned into a nice riverfront park."

"That's fantastic news," Kelly said. "How's Jacob?"

"He's doing well. He's coming to stay with me for a while. Then maybe he'll get his own place."

"That's great! How about David Gottschalk?"

"Father Murray helped him get into his own apartment. He's even talking a little, but he's got a long road ahead. Speaking of that, how are you doing?"

Kelly squeezed Justin's hand. "I think I understand the sixth name now."

Justin squeezed back.

"And I've conquered it too."

CASEY EXPECTED VIOLENCE and destruction as he entered the mud-body of the demon. Instead, white light flashed. The world disappeared, and Hili's hand in his was the only solid thing anchoring him to reality.

"Where are we?" he asked.

"Not the black," Hili replied in a voice full of wonder and hope.

"Hili?" A man's voice, somewhere ahead in the blinding whiteness.

"Nigmah?"

"Yes. Come. It's wonderful."

Hili led Casey toward the voice, never letting go of his hand.

Epilogue

Kelly lay in his own bed for the first time in days, but sleep just wouldn't come. Even the comfort of finally having someone who cared for him sharing his bed couldn't assuage the feeling that something important still lingered. Even with the news of the imminent destruction of the Boiler House and the service finally putting his troubled twin's soul to rest, something still just didn't sit right.

The mercury vapor streetlight filtered through the window sheers, casting a macabre, dirty glow on Justin's sleeping form. Beyond that, a hazy white shimmer coalesced into a humanoid form, wavering in the shadowy void of the bedroom doorway. The mill girl, adorned in her bloody apron, beckoned him with a finger.

Kelly's breath steamed in the sudden chill. His heart pounded against his ribs. And though his skin crawled and shrank in fear and revulsion, Kelly rose, hypnotized, barely noticing the pain from his half-healed wounds as he followed the terrifying visage into the living room. There, the dead young woman stood, empty eye sockets drilling into his, pointing at Kelly's cello.

Don't miss out!

Visit the website below and you can sign up to receive emails whenever Len M. Ruth publishes a new book. There's no charge and no obligation.

https://lenmruth.com

Did you love *The Pull*? Then you should read *The Unrecovered*[1] by Len M. Ruth!

[2]

The virus doesn't kill you. The smile does...

Forty-eight-year-old recluse Sarah Sampson knows father died in The Vietnam War. But when a TV broadcast turns her world upside down, she has to find out for sure. Can she and her K-9 companions survive the horror of the pandemic long enough to learn the truth?

Reporter Erica Goldman knows the 'old boy network' at the newspaper will never give her a chance... Will she discover the

1. https://books2read.com/u/bopP6v

2. https://books2read.com/u/bopP6v

apocalyptic secret behind the smiling flu, avert Armageddon, and save her career?

Young Dr. Carl Parks knows his patient is a kindly old man...Until that patient reveals a doomsday secret...

But will anyone listen?

You'll love experiencing this genre-busting apocalypse thriller through the eyes of its complex, characters.

Read more at https://lenmruth.com/.

Also by Len M. Ruth

Smiling Flu
Rachael's Apocalypse Diary
Rachael's Apocalypse Diary Vol. 2
The Unrecovered

The Demons Within
The Pull

Watch for more at https://lenmruth.com/.

About the Author

Len M. Ruth is the author of horror novels *The Pull, Rachael's Apocalypse Dairy I & II, The Unrecovered,* and *Tales of the Doomed.* His stories were published in the anthology *Satan Rides your Daughter,* and featured in the Flash Fiction Forum. You can find his novels wherever fine eBooks are sold.

Len is part of the LGBTQ community and lives with his partner, Em, and dog Cooper in fabulous Las Vegas, Nevada.

Read more at https://lenmruth.com/.